NIGHT LIGHTS

An Anthology of Short Fiction

First Contact, Conspiracy, and Space Opera

Presented by Geminid Press, LLC

ISBN-13: 978-0997329216 / ISBN-10: 0997329211
Library of Congress Control Number: 2016903323
Geminid Press, LLC, Albuquerque, New Mexico

Contents

As the founders and owners of Geminid Press, LLC, we are very pleased to present this anthology of new short fiction. In preparing this anthology and selecting the works for publication, both of us realized how bright literature's future truly is. The writing talent that exists today around the world is probably greater than at any time in recent human history. As an independent press, we are pleased to shine a light on this talent, even if it only illuminates a small part of the modern writers' universe.

Founded in 2014, Geminid Press, LLC, is dedicated to publishing quality works of new writers. We have had the privilege of publishing three novelists and a children's book writer. And now, we have the privilege of publishing 21 writers in this anthology.

They include: Kurt Bachard, Robert Bagnall, Richard W. Black, David Boop, Tracy Canfield, Rebecca A. Demarest, James Dorr, Chris Doty, Daniel P. Douglas, Julian Drury, Milo James Fowler, Brian Leopold, Michael McGlade, Dennis Mombauer, Nick Nafpliotis, Russell Nichols, Frances Pauli, J.B. Rockwell, Suanne Schafer, Jamie D. Wahls, and Dean H. Wild.

Congratulations to all of them! We hope you enjoy their stories as much as we do. Please learn more about each by visiting the *Night Lights* anthology page at http://geminidpress.com/.

Paul and Phillip Garver
Geminid Press, LLC
February 2016

Imagination will often carry us to worlds that never were.

But without it, we go nowhere.

– Carl Sagan

BOOK 1

FIRST CONTACT

The alien came to play ball. Or so I thought.

It didn't say so outright. Not exactly. Couldn't speak English far as we could tell. But every day that summer, it would meet us there at the sandlot. The thing would come and stand behind the dugout, which was a rusty old hope chest Willie stole from his big sister. It would stand out there, the alien, not moving or nothing. Just observing, if that's even the right word. Then one hot afternoon, for whatever reason, the alien stopped observing.

We swore we'd never tell a soul about this encounter. Figured keeping our traps shut would keep our mothers safe. So we didn't tell our parents, not our teachers, nobody knew except the nine of us there at the sandlot.

For us, back then, the sandlot wasn't just a whole lot of weeds and stones and dust. It was older than dirt and since God made dirt, that slice of land was our scoop of heaven. Thought we'd be there forever. Every day playing ball as the sun kept its eye on us. Playing ball till our shadows got stretched, taffy-like. It was our space, our safe haven, rocks and all. And like my boy Roy the Righteous One used to say: "It ain't a real diamond without the rough."

In our world, we made our own rules: If you hit a homer on your first ups, you got a penny from everybody (you were lucky); if you knocked the empty Coke bottle off the cement wall in deep right field, you got an extra run and a dime from everybody (nobody got that lucky); if you struck out three times in one day, you had to ask out Nurse Paige (we usually let that one slide). But the most important rule was about timing.

The torn squares of cardboard we used for bases were hard to make out in the dust. So when it came to making crucial calls, they all turned to me with the same quizzical look: Safe or out? I was second baseman, but also umpire because I had the best eyesight of the bunch. Whatever's better than 20/20, that's what I had. Nothing got past me. I could tell in that split second whether the runner tapped the base before or after the baseman caught the ball. It was always one or the other. I didn't believe in ties. But at the same time, I didn't believe in aliens either.

Only one of us could say we saw this thing coming.

That would be Gort. His real name was Buddy Fowler III, but we called him Gort after the robot in that movie. Gort was a year older than the rest of us. Moved here from D.C. when his old man got transferred for some "top secret job" Gort couldn't talk about. What he did talk about was how we were all in danger. He was 110-percent convinced that aliens were real and that humans going out in space was against the rules. He said the aliens had plans to stop President Kennedy from putting a man on the moon.

None of us believed Gort. Especially after learning he lied about making out with Angela, that sophomore chick with the hazel eyes and good hair. But we played along for kicks.

"What kind of plans, Gort?" we'd ask him.

"I can't say," he would whisper, "but they're out to get us, man."

"Get us how?"

He said: "Just trust me on this. We ain't safe here."

That first time the alien showed up at the sandlot, Gort went nuts. Not because he was scared, but we had bet him 25 cents a pop aliens didn't exist. Two bucks gave him the right to scream like a girl. The rest of us had no voices to speak of.

We didn't call off the game because we had a streak going. But the "delay" lasted a good chunk of the day. We stood there watching it watching us. Not sure what move to make. If any. Gort was shaking his head, muttering to himself:

"There's no way out, there's no way out."

I tried to keep cool as an ice cream truck. It didn't seem like the thing was a threat, but I can't lie: Everything Gort had been saying over the years came rushing in. I remembered him talking about how only a chosen few would be spared--those who knew the secret hand signal.

"Of course I know it," Gort said one night during a camp out while swatting at mosquitoes. "But if I told you, they'd scratch my name off the safe list."

The alien didn't look like an alien was supposed to look. It wasn't green or red or blue. It was a weird color we didn't have a word for. No taller than we were. No shiny suit either. Just its bare, grotesque body layered with sheets of gills or eyes or something else entirely.

By the end of the week, we'd gotten used to the alien observing us.

The anxiety wasn't gone all the way. But it went down enough for us to go a whole game without somebody dropping a ball or screwing up a play due to the distraction. We had no idea what it was doing or thinking or learning, but we all knew one thing: We had us a fan.

And we put on airs, even though none of us would ever admit it. When the alien was watching, we'd swing that bat a little harder, dig our sneaks a little deeper, lob our snaps a little louder. We acted like the thing was an intergalactic scout, looking to recruit homosapiens for the biggest game in the universe. If the other guys weren't thinking that, I sure was. Who wouldn't want to be out there? That's what I asked myself every night staring out my window at the stars. Every night when Pops would come staggering home, banging on the door hollering: "Let me in, let me in."

Covers couldn't keep out the noise just like the lock couldn't keep out my Pops. I kept wishing the alien would take me back to wherever it came from. Somewhere else, somewhere safe. That was my dream, my vision. And I had real good vision. But I couldn't see far enough to stop what was about to happen.

It all went down on a late afternoon in July. Must've been mid-July because I remember it was about a week after the church cookout we had on the Fourth. I think it was Tuesday, but who knows. What I do know is it was hot out there. Hot as the devil's mama's sauna. Hot as Nurse Paige in a white bikini, holding a thermometer, telling me to stick out my tongue. We almost ditched our daily game to go bust open a hydrant. But Bearded Larry's old man got him a brand new bat. He wanted to break that baby in. We all knew good and well that a Louisville Slugger couldn't save that cat's batting average, but we went to the sandlot to keep the streak going.

Sweat turned our shirts different shades by the time we got there. Grime coated our faces like war paint. The wind had the day off, so we thought about swimming pools and lemonade to keep our blood from boiling over. The alien was there. Behind the hope chest as usual.

"Hope you all brought your pennies," said Bearded Larry, taking a few practice swings. He stepped up to home plate, which was a dusty stack of placemats Willie stole from his mom. "I could use eight cents right about now. What do you guys think? Should I get a Firecracker Popsicle or--"

"Think fast!" said Don from the pitcher's mound.

And he hurled the first pitch before Larry even got his feet set. The white ball whizzed by him and hit Roy the Righteous One's catcher's mitt with a smack. The rest of us were cracking up as Bearded Larry tried to protest:

"No, hold on. That's a do-over. I wasn't even ready, man."

Turns out none of us were ready for what would happen next.

Gort noticed it first. He didn't yell or nothing, but his words were loud enough for us all to hear and freeze up.

"It's coming out."

The alien was moving. Emerging from behind the dugout and coming toward us. It was one thing for the thing to observe from the sides, but coming out onto the field, see, that was a whole nother story. But we prepped for this. "Operation: Breakup," we called it: If the alien ever stepped on the field, we were supposed to split up, each one of us running in a different direction. Then regroup at Gort's house for Phase 2, which involved fake passports. But that plan fell apart. None of us moved a muscle. All we could do was watch.

As the alien moved, an outer layer--some kind of glass shell--began melting off. Like shedding skin or some shit. The thing got closer to home plate. Roy the Righteous One lifted his catcher's mask, took a big step back. Bearded Larry gripped his new bat like the alien was a piñata full of popsicles.

"Uh guys, there's an alien on the field," said Fat Frank a.k.a. PBP (Play-By-Play), the perceptive shortstop who smelled like bologna. "I'm not the only one who sees this, right?"

The alien stood there at home plate. Same as it had been doing over by the dugout, but now it was blocking the strike zone, holding up the game.

"Larry, tell your moms she's holding up the game," Willie called out from first base.

Bearded Larry didn't answer. Probably didn't even hear him, what with the alien being two feet from his bearded face. Then the alien let out a noise--like what it sounds like trying to talk underwater. I turned to Gort, but that cat was looking scared as all get out. I knew that "safe list" was a load of crap.

On the mound, Don said: "You think it's trying to tell us something? Like--I don't know--a signal or something."

The gurgle came again, and Bearded Larry stepped back. "Did he just say 'doo-doo eater.'"

"Doo-doo eater?" I asked.

"That's what it sounded..." Bearded Larry stopped when the alien uttered another sound, a similar wobble, but a different pitch.

"Oh, I heard that one," said Roy the Righteous One. "He definitely said 'date me.'"

"Doo-doo eater date me!" PBP hollered and laughed so hard he cried.

"That's not what it said," said Gort and everybody looked at him.

"Oh yeah?" said Willie. "What's he saying, then, since you're so smart?"

"To your leader, take me."

And we all cracked up at that. What a load of crap. Gort had definitely read too many pulps. Who knows what the alien was saying. All I knew was what I could see. I saw him standing there on home plate and figured that was as clear a signal as any.

And I said: "I think he wants to play."

Everybody makes bad calls.

My Pops made one when he got hooked on the bottle. Ernie made one when he beat his boyfriend senseless to prove he really liked girls. I made a big one when I told Mary I didn't need protection because I would pull out. At the time, in the heat of the moment, bad calls might seem like good ones, the right ones. But hindsight is diamond-like.

Of course, we had to learn that the hard way, in the real world, striking out consistently as husbands and fathers and rulers at large. Swinging, missing, swinging, hitting, running, going, going, gone. Strangers longing for acceptance away from home.

I saw what I saw that day. I said what I said. If I could go back and get a do-over, maybe I would, maybe I wouldn't, who knows. But I can't help but wonder how our lives would've played out had I made a different call. Maybe that day wouldn't have been our last day at the sandlot. And we wouldn't have split up, without regrouping. Gort never would've lost his arms in 'Nam. Willie never would've gotten himself locked up. Roy the Righteous One never would've got on that smack. Everything changed in that split second. It was all good, then suddenly it wasn't. But that's how the game goes. The Righteous One said it best: "Life ain't fair, so it must be foul, which means we're all fucked." Everybody runs. Nobody wins.

I say all this now at a safe distance from that last day. A good 50 years and 2,000 some-odd miles away. Damn if it don't feel like yesterday, though. When I close my eyes, I still feel the heat. I smell the cowhide of my oiled-down, blackened-up 11-inch glove. I taste the salt from my peach fuzzy upper lip. And I hear the guys, throwing their voices around the sandlot, wanting so bad to be heard.

"I wouldn't give up that bat if I was you," called Gort from right field.

"Yeah, you sure you wanna do that?" Willie chimed in from first.

Bearded Larry extended the bat. "If the alien really wanted to wipe out humanity, I don't think he'd use a Louisville Slugger."

"Guys, Larry's giving him the bat," said PBP.

"How you know it's a him, PB?" shouted Ernie from left field. "It might be a girl."

Leaning forward, Bearded Larry held the knob of the bat with his fingers. The wooden bat dangled from his wobbly hand in the heavy windless air.

Willie laughed. "You trying to hypnotize the thing, man?"

The alien didn't budge.

PBP stopped fanning himself with his cap. "Guys, he or she ain't taking the bat."

On the mound, Don shrugged. "Forget it then. If it don't wanna play, it ain't got to play."

Right then, a tentacle grew out of the alien and wrapped around the bat. Larry jumped back with a yelp as the thing held the bat up in the sun, studying it or something.

"This is a bad idea, man," mumbled Gort. "You got to trust me on this."

The alien scooted off the plate. It held the bat high in the air, straight up, at a 90-degree angle.

"Damn, Larry. At least show the thing how to do it right," said Ernie, flexing his biceps, pretending to swing a bat.

Bearded Larry said: "He's holding it his way."

I can't lie. It didn't look natural, not by a long shot. But who were we to judge a batter's batting stance?

"All right you guys, the rookie's ready to rock," said Bearded Larry, stepping out the way and clapping. "And if he hits a homerun, this still counts as my ups."

Off second base, I crouched low and punched the shallow pocket of my glove a few times. Gort hawked up a loogie. Roy the Righteous One pulled down his mask, squatted behind the plate. Don wiped the sweat off his forehead with his forearm. Then shrugged and brought the ball to his chest to pitch. Off first, Willie started chanting, "Hey batterbatterbatterbatter..."

That first pitch was low. Crazy low. Skidding off the dirt, past Roy the Righteous One and into the tangle of overgrowth behind the field.

The Righteous One pulled up his mask. "What was that, man?"

Don lifted his right hand. "I'm feeling the thing out, that's all."

The Righteous One went to retrieve the ball from the bushes. Tossed it back.

The next pitch was high, just inside.

The alien swung, but the timing was off. It hit a whole lot of air, but nothing else.

"Whoa!" said Willie, backing off from first. "He's trying to knock it out the park."

I stepped back too. We all did actually. None of us would ever admit it, but we all wanted to be the one to catch the pop fly. We all wanted that stat. Among us guys, those bragging rights would be priceless. How many in this country can say they got an alien out?

On the mound, Don pulled the ball up to his chest. Adjusted his cap. Shook his head twice, then nodded like the Righteous One was giving him a signal, but the Righteous One wasn't giving him no kind of signal, except: "Just throw the damn ball. My social security check's coming soon."

The alien did his wind up like the bat was a helicopter propeller.

Don fired a pitch that started inside, then curved out. The alien swung, a hair late, but nicked the bottom of the ball. We watched the white sphere fly up and come crashing back down, its fall broken up by outstretched gloveless branches. Foul.

Roy the Righteous One shook his head. He went to get the ball again. While he was back there sifting through thorny shrubs, the alien started acting real peculiar.

It stepped back from home plate. It held the bat in the dirt, then put its head--or what we guessed was a head--on the knob and started sliding its body, spinning around the bat. Spinning and spinning and spinning and spinning and spinning.

We stared, slack-jawed. We never did this around the alien, so where'd it pick this up? And why? Roy the Righteous One came back and he was like: "What on earth?"

I looked at Gort, who didn't say nothing, but kept looking around like he was expecting an invasion to commence. The alien was still spinning, kicking up a dustcloud. This must've went on for at least five minutes. Finally, when it stopped, it moved back to the plate and did its overhead wind-up again. Didn't seem dizzy or nothing.

Roy the Righteous One tossed the ball to Don.

Don looked back at PBP. "What's count?"

"One and two," said PBP.

Don nodded. He kept a straight face, but I could tell on the inside that cat was smiling, Cheshire-like. He already knew the count. He always knew the count. He asked for our benefit. The rest of us hoped to be legends for catching the fly ball, but Don had his own plan for immortality: to be the boy who struck out the alien.

Right then, the alien stopped winding up and pointed toward the falling sun.

"What the hell's he doing now?" said Willie, turning to Gort. "Is that the signal? He signaling the mothership?"

"I wouldn't doubt it," said Gort.

"I think he's calling his shot," I said.

"Man, get out of town," said Ernie. "Like the Babe?"

PBP said: "Yeah, he's pointing to the Coke."

We all looked back to the wall in deep right field, a good 230-feet away from home plate. The empty Coke bottle was sitting up there like always, snatching splinters of fading sunlight.

"No way he's hitting that," said Willie, eyes wide with hope and doubt. "No way, man."

Bearded Larry said: "But if he does, this still counts as my--"

"Think fast!"

Don launched that ball so fast, so hard, comet-like. None of us were ready. But, somehow, someway, the alien was.

In one quick motion, the thing brought the bat down and swung. There was a loud thwack that echoed across the whole field. The bat connected with the ball. The ball came blasting out of that batter's box like a goddamn missile. A vicious line drive straight to right field. Fair.

The alien grew more tentacles. They all reached out at the same time. Slapped down into the dust like octopus arms. The thing dragged itself across the dirt toward first base.

Gort darted forward, full speed. Scooped the ball off the ground with his bare hand.

"Throw it! Throw it!" Willie hollered, stretching his lanky frame as far out as possible while keeping his toe on first.

At that moment, everything else around me blurred up. There was nothing else in the world. No heat. No sweat. No time. No threats of nuclear war. No drunk fathers. No bruised mothers. No lost boys searching for home outside of home. All that was gone. Nothing existed except Willie's tawny mitt with the torn web and the tattered cardboard base.

Everything changed in that split second.

Seconds after my decision, Gort was scolding me. "What? Are you blind, man?"

He was rushing over to first base, where we all were gathering, except Roy the Righteous One who ran off to take a wiz. The rest of us were taking off our gloves, debating what just happened. Even though there was no debate. I made the call.

"I ain't blind," I said. "I saw what I saw."

"No way," said Willie. "You were looking dead at me. I got him out."

Bearded Larry said: "You can't argue with the ump."

"Like hell we can't if it's a bad call," said Ernie, puffing up.

The alien was standing on first base in the middle of us. Not moving at all. Still holding the bat with one of its tentacles. I doubted he knew what was going on. Gort snatched the bat from the alien and started pacing, pissed off. I could damn near see the smoke coming out his ears.

Willie said: "Look, either the ball beat the runner or it didn't. I was there and I say it did."

"Too bad nobody cares what you say, booger breath," said Bearded Larry.

"Nobody cares about you, pubic face," Willie fired back.

"Ask your big sis how I got this beard," said Bearded Larry, rubbing his chin.

"She already told me you like to eat out your moms," said Willie, pretending like he was munching an invisible cob of corn. "It's snackey time."

Before Bearded Larry could snap back, Roy the Righteous One came over, zipping up his fly and asking: "What'd I miss?"

PBP said: "Some people don't care too much for the call."

"What was the call?" asked the Righteous One.

"The wrong one," said Willie.

"Safe or out?"

"The call was safe," said Monte, the third baseman with a skin disorder.

"Shut up and go put on some steroid cream, Monte," said Ernie. "You're not even supposed to be out here."

"If anything," said Don, wiping his forehead, "and I'm not saying this is true, but from where I was standing, it looked like the ball and runner got there at the same time, which means he can't be out because you're only called out if you get beat."

"You lost me," said the Righteous One.

I said: "Tie goes to the runner."

Gort pointed the bat at me. "That's a bullshit rule and you know it."

I slapped the bat away. "Get that fucking bat out my face, man."

PBP said: "So is he safe or out?"

Gort glared at me. I glared back. His age didn't scare me. His conspiracy theories didn't scare me. Nothing scared me at that point, on the brink of our adolescent apocalypse.

I can't remember who swung first. I want to say it wasn't me, but who knows. I do know Gort threw his fist so hard into my jaw, I nearly fell over. It was pretty much all hell from there. Didn't know who was on whose side. We were all out for ourselves. Nothing fair. We'd fought before, but never like this. Ain't no coming back from this. And I remember wrestling in that sandlot, trying to rip that bat from Gort. But he had the better grip and he jabbed me in my gut. Then he got up, spit out a glob of blood and went to the alien, who'd been on first base the whole time, observing. Gort wound up, then swung the bat with all his might into the alien's body.

The hit didn't make a single sound, but small cracks spread out from the point of impact. They were there for only a second before a filmy substance oozed out from everywhere, hardening over everything. With all the chaos, nobody else caught that. Gort was above me, kicking me over and over, breaking one of my ribs. And in that split second before I got knocked out, I saw the alien running--running from the sandlot, his shadow stretched by the setting sun, going, going, gone.

THE SINGULAR MARTIAN INVASION
BY KURT BACHARD

To this very day, I still have vivid recall of that terrifying moment.

A short, haggard, pot-bellied, gentleman wearing rimless spectacles was reflected in the dark glass window of a tailor's shop in Central London. He was standing in a riot-torn street, wearing blue striped pajamas, his comb-over fluttering above the liver-spotted dome of his head like a dirty grey flag of surrender.

That sorry neuroscientist was me.

I turned away from my reflection in the polarized glass and surveyed the battle-ruined street around me. Most of the shop windows had been smashed by looters. Glass and rubble littered the pavements. Dark oily smoke billowed up from burning cars at the junction. Harrowing shouts and screams rang out, amid the alarms and police sirens and the sporadic rat-tat-tat of military gunfire.

Covering my mouth against the choking stench of burning rubber, I looked to see a police helicopter thundering above the smoky rooftops. The chopper's down draught swept away the thick curtains of smoke, revealing the red and blue Tube Station logo about a quarter of a mile away up the high street. It was my only hope of salvation. I knew if I could reach the station before the nuclear bombs dropped then I might find my way into the underground laboratory and safety.

Despite feeling bitter about Linda deserting me, I still wished we were together at this time, the world's darkest hour.

It was another explosion in the near distance that finally propelled me out of my shocked stupor. I set off on a course for the station, staying close to shop doorways for cover, and wondering how it had all come to this, how it was that the discovery of a seemingly innocuous Martian life form had brought the world to the brink of destruction.

It was a year before, on a clear and sunny morning, when billions around the globe watched the Segomo 1 successfully launch from its base in the English countryside. The rocket made its maiden voyage to the red planet in one hundred and fifty days without a hitch. Once the command module was in orbit around Mars, the two-man crew, Blake and Moore, crawled into their Lander module to prepare for the descent through a hazy pink atmosphere. Less than an hour later, the Lander touched down on Mars. Recording the historic event on a field camera, Blake climbed down the module's ladder. As he repeated Armstrong's immortal words, his right boot touched the Martian desert soil with a puff of rust-colored dust, and less than a minute later Moore followed him down. All around the world, people watched in fascination as the astronauts set out on their Mars walk.

All was going well, until Moore, setting up the seismic equipment, felt the ground shift. Before he could exclaim in surprise, the ground opened up like a giant maw and the two astronauts disappeared in a cloud of red dust before the shocked eyes of the world.

Satellite transmission abruptly ended, television screens turning black, the broadcast replaced by a newsflash. The watching world was assured that the astronauts were unharmed, but what the viewers back on Earth did not know was that the astronauts had fallen down a sinkhole into the crumbling ruins of an underground city honeycombed beneath the Martian desert. Further tentative exploration by the crew revealed the labyrinthine remains of an advanced civilization older than mankind. Shining their torches on the worn steps of an Aztec-like pyramid, they found a stone jar about two feet in diameter and covered in the hieroglyphs of a long-dead alien language. They used the movable stone blocks inside the pyramid to climb out of the pit, and carried the heavy jar between them back to the Lander module.

Puffing, Moore made a face behind his gold-tinted visor. "Some kind of urn?" he suggested.

"Storage for victuals?" said Blake.

"I'll stick to our diced goo, thanks," joked Moore, and cautiously lifted the lid to give them both a peek inside. What they saw resembled an outsized human brain, disembodied and suspended in a transparent solution. It was the Martian Brain. Immediately, ground control ordered the crew back to Earth with their extraterrestrial onboard.

As soon as they splashed down, the Ministry of Defence seized The Brain, and the crew was taken into quarantine and held under house arrest.

The Brain was secured in a secret location, a former Cold War bunker beneath Piccadilly Circus in London. Carefully removing The Brain from its stone container, they sank it into an oxygenated saline solution in an open topped glass jar easily large enough to accommodate it. Electrodes were attached and wired to an ECG, at which point, judging by the neural activity, it became shockingly obvious to the group of young technicians present that The Brain was alive.

Within days, somebody (a wet-eared technician was suspected) blew the whistle on the Ministry's secret by selling their story to the papers.

The furor spread rapidly. The next morning, mocked-up images of a large custard-yellow brain with big bulging eyeballs floating in a bell-shaped jar were splashed all over the front pages of the tabloids. The front-page of The Sun newspaper ran the caption "Sentient Martian held captive in top secret location" beneath a satirical cartoon of Dan Dare's encephalic archenemy The Mekon lashed to an autopsy table whilst men in comic strip British military regalia looked on.

The whole thing was thought a hoax, until an ill-advised statement by the Prime Minister changed that. Live outside number ten on the evening news, in the flicker of flash photography, he announced to a stunned Press scrum that The Martian was transmitting a message and that the Ministry was working hard to decipher the meaning of its frenetic brain pulses.

Overnight, world leaders became suspicious, accusing The British government of having something to hide. On a special edition of Question Time, a former Defence Secretary turned novelist/conspiratorialist speculated that The Brain's message was not a harmless one but a formula for super nuclear weapons, weapons that had once destroyed the Martian civilization, causing the aliens to retreat underground.

In an effort to quell public unease, the Ministry took the drastic action of granting a BBC camera crew access to the underground lab. But they were getting nowhere in attempts to read The Brain's signals, so they called in me, an expert in neuroscience, professor Richard Hoskin, a Biomedical Research scientist. Renowned for my groundbreaking work with patients suffering locked-in syndrome, I spent years mapping neural packages in the human brain for speech translation through digital synthesis.

The first time I was shown into the government's laboratory beneath Piccadilly, I expected to be filled with a childlike wonder and excitement at my first encounter with an extraterrestrial. Unfortunately, the mad-scientist atmosphere of the lab-cum-studio and the whole assemblage of unsophisticated equipment robbed the alien encounter of its charm.

I felt heavily disappointed. In its massive jar of oxygenated saline, The Martian Brain resembled nothing like the energized, pulsating super brain I'd anticipated but a gigantic, mildewed walnut instead. It was positioned on a stone pedestal, center stage, with cameras trained on it from every angle, and lit up from beneath by an eerie green theatrical glow.

The Ministry's eccentric set designer, Chevalier (looking like a sweaty eighteenth century dandy in his long ruffled sleeves and wig), complained to himself as he neurotically adjusted and readjusted the faux Martian landscape around The Brain under the stark, sweltering studio lights. I shook my head in disgust. There was something cruel about the way The Brain was lashed to hundreds of electrodes, many of which trailed off to a Sound Equipment Bank being pored over by a spurious-looking team of scientists in white lab coats. They appeared to be converting The Brain's neural signals into an unearthly twittering, the sound amplified for the viewers at home, filling one half of the lab with a noise like an aviary full of demented birds. Beside them, more technicians huddled over budget computers that monitored everything with blinking LEDs, flashing EEG screens, bleeps and alarms, as though tending an ailing patient in intensive care.

I was here to connect my microECoG grid to The Brain and run it through my patented Wernicke's Area neural decoder, but before I could take another step, I was ambushed by a young grinning blonde whom I instantly recognized as daytime TV's golden girl Miss Frilly Holly.

Her two-man camera crew shuffled in behind her like doting lackeys as the pneumatic-lipped glossy-haired bimbo pushed a microphone under my moustache.

Ah, here's the BBC's instrument of trivialization, I thought, sighing. Here to lessen public concerns by making light of them.

"Professor Hoskin," she said, reading it off the ID badge hanging around my neck, and then offered me her annoyingly optimistic children's-presenter grin. "Our viewers at home are just dying to know what The Martian Brain might be saying, if it could speak. *It* - oh pardon me." Miss Holly giggled. "I meant he or she. Is The Brain a he or a she, professor?"

Caught off guard, I felt flustered. I straightened my tie, knowing my ever-disapproving wife Linda, an inveterate newscast junky, would be watching closely. "Well, errrm, we haven't attempted to ascertain gender yet," I said with uncertain authority. "What we're doing at the moment is reading The Brain's signals, as you can see. But with the aid of my neural decoder, we should be able to convert those signals into something useful."

"What might The Brain be trying to tell us, professor? We've had lots of creative suggestions from our viewers. A Martian sonnet to rival Shakespeare. Or a new recipe for the equivalent of Martian goulash. Or is The Brain trying to gives us information that will save us all from eco-destruction?"

"It's too early to speculate," I said. "My decoder has a basic vocabulary block which works in human cases but in this case, we have to map the neural patterns from scratch."

A day later, when she ambushed me in the lab a second time and asked with sham excitement if we had any new Martian words for the home audience, I was forced to admit we didn't.

I wasn't about to reveal, though, that despite The Brain's relentless soliloquy, even my Neural Decoder was turning up nothing. For all we knew The Brain might have been telling us all to 'bog off' in ten different Martian tongues.

Then things took a decidedly nasty turn. Driving home from the lab one day, I got stuck in tailbacks because doomsayers were picketing up and down the King's Road with their Sandwich boxes announcing "Martian Heralds End of The World!" The tabloids had been stirring up trouble all week, predicting a breakdown of society with headlines like "Psionic Psychotic Martian Brain causing society's collapse".

At home, I was barely through the front door, my mind reeling after such a turbulent week, when the secretary of Sir Rupert Hines at the ministry called, demanding that I attend a meeting first thing in the morning.

"What's so urgent?" I asked. I'd been looking forward to a quiet, calm Saturday morning.

"Professor Hoskin!" The secretary's tone was a reprimand. "May I remind you that The North Korea situation is an immediate worry."

I did not need reminding that in an unprecedented move, North Korea had sent over a diplomat requesting an audience with The Brain, but a refusal by the Ministry had led to threats of war.

I hung up as my wife called me into the lounge to witness another threat.

On television, a young harassed female reporter was shouting over the noise of street battles between police and rioting protestors. Beyond, stood the indifferent Houses of Parliament.

"Those religious fanatics need shooting," said Linda, meaning the Cult of the Super Mind, a group who, according to their spokesman on TV, was fighting for the freedom of their *Martian Messiah*.

"What do these idiots think is going to happen to The Brain if it's released?" she said. "Do they think it'll get its own day time show? Or a six figure book deal with HarperCollins?"

"Publishers only offer authorship to TV presenters and glamour models," I quipped, feeling mischievously flippant after my scolding by the ministry secretary. "However, I have it on good authority that when we do finally decipher The Brain's signals we'll discover that it's actually writing a novel." A dramatic pause and a grin. "But then isn't everyone?"

Linda scoffed and folded her arms. "You think this is a joke? There's talk of the government initiating a state of emergency."

"I don't think it'll go that far."

"Really? Central London is fast becoming a war zone. And all of this anarchy is because of that bloody brain you're pandering to."

Linda had fallen under a similar spell to that of the general populace. Although she wasn't protesting for the Martian's release like some, still she squandered her evenings organizing, with her colluding neighbors, campaigns for The Martian's destruction.

"This is how the Martians will take over," she stressed. "By making us destroy ourselves. Did you know that a UFO Abduction Society just stormed the Conservative Party Headquarters, demanding the humane release of the Martian 'hostage'? I'm telling you, that brain is telepathically transmitting some sort of evil message which is causing all this hostility. Somebody should do something before we wipe ourselves out."

"Come on, Linda, it's just media hype."

"Richard, you need to get your head out of that lab. Can't you see what's happening here? The Brain's driving everyone mad. Martian fanatics will burn down London by this time tomorrow. Let's leave for my sister's up in Scotland."

I took Linda by her thin shoulders and eased her back, away from her invasion of my personal space. "I'm afraid we can't flee just yet. I've been urgently summoned to a meeting tomorrow. But don't worry. This will all blow over. A curfew will soon stop the troublemakers."

"But you've hardly been home from that lab. I'm not staying here alone with all hell breaking loose around us while you swan off again tomorrow. I'm leaving for my sister's in the morning - *with or without you.*"

With that, she ran sobbing upstairs to her bedroom. What one must understand about my wife is that this sort of thing is typical. In the heat of an argument, she makes ultimatums that she later regrets.

It was on the following morning, at the urbane time of seven forty-five am, and while all around London burned, that kidnappers broke in through the back door. The unlikely gang of white-haired distinguished-looking gentlemen claimed to be from a Masonic branch of "The Cult of The Super Mind."

They snatched me from my warm bed at the point of an incongruous looking blunderbuss. They gave me no time to change out of my blue striped pajamas. Although I did manage to grab my spectacles from the bedside table and shove them on. I was less frightened for myself than for Linda. As the kidnappers dragged me past her room, I noticed her bed was empty.

"What have you done with my wife?"

"Your wife wasn't here, Prof," said one kidnapper. His accent was old school Kensington, stiff-upper-lipped establishment.

Downstairs, another kidnapper pointed to a note on the mantel. "Looks like a Dear John letter," he said.

And so it was: Linda had packed her things and left me in the night, taking my car from the driveway too. I regretted not listening to her. Perhaps the Martian brain had driven us all out of our minds after all.

Another of the kidnappers tied a rope around my wrists. "You'll direct us to the whereabouts of The Brain and no funny business," he said. "And don't take us for fools. I'm a retired Surgeon, my learned friend here was a Lecturer at the Royal Institution, and he's a former Barrister at the Old Bailey. Now move it."

"You won't get beyond security," I cried as they shoved me out the door. "They'll have your guts for garters before you get within a hundred yards."

"Look, we've seen you on television being interviewed by that silly tart, so we know you're all working from that secret old war bunker. We just don't know where it is exactly. You're going to take us there."

Outside, riot smoke drifted across the rooftops, bringing with it the acrid smell of burning. Police sirens wailed in the distance, as the kidnappers bundled me into the back seat of a waiting blue Daimler and then jumped in as the car sped away.

"Don't bother trying to attract attention," said one kidnapper. "Nobody can see you behind these tinted windows. Besides, I think the police have their hands full, don't you?"

Since my life depended on my privileged knowledge of the bunker's whereabouts, it was a secret I planned to keep until the last.

Nevertheless, I had no choice but to direct the driver. Believing we were being followed, the driver took turns through the West End backstreets, and many of the main thoroughfares proved inaccessible, so that eventually our progress halted.

About a quarter of a mile from the location of the underground bunker, the Daimler jerked to a stop, blocked by abandoned vehicles near the fountain at Piccadilly. The roundabout was eerily silent and deserted, except for a drunken man obliviously urinating in the water.

Suddenly a sooty-browed, battle-weary individual (with a red-checkered neckerchief hanging from his chin) appeared out of the smoke and staggered up to the driver's window.

"We're all for it," he screeched. "It's North Korea. The nukes are coming. Run for the shelters." He stumbled back into the drifting smoke.

The kidnapper beside me flung open the passenger door. "Stuff it," he said. "I should be with my family. Forget the stupid Brain. It's every man for himself." With that, he jumped out and lurched away.

The first deserter was then followed by the driver, then the last remaining kidnapper, who, before leaving, apologised for the inconvenience and untied my wrists.

I climbed out, wishing I had deserted London with Linda. With little hope of escaping the epicentre of a nuclear blast, I knew my only option was to reach the underground lab before the bombs dropped.

And that was how I ended up in a riot-torn West End street in my blue-striped pajamas, amid the smoke of burning cars, screams, police sirens and the rat-tat-tat of gunfire, running for fear of a nuclear attack.

Little did I know that the nuclear threat was the false alarm of a panicked, media-brainwashed society on the verge of self-destruction, and it was happening in every major city around the world.

I heard an almighty car crash behind me and twisted around to find Linda apparently trying to drive my car through the crumpled side of an abandoned black cab near the fountain. I ran over as she staggered out, her angry waspish face lathered in perspiration. Steam hissed from the car's busted radiator.

"Linda," I cried, pulling her to the curb, "I thought you'd left me."

"Change of heart, Richard. I came back home for you and saw those awful men dragging you off into a Daimler. I tried to catch up but lost you until now. I'm so glad I found you."

I put a stop to Linda's jubilant PDA by focusing her attention on our plight.

"Get a grip," I said, shaking her. "It's nuclear war. You were right. The Brain has driven everyone mad. We need to reach the underground before the first strike."

By the time we reached the station, we were both gasping for breath. The entrance was open and deserted. We hurried past the untended ticket barrier, stumbled down the unmoving escalator, and onto the empty platform.

"Where on earth are we going, Richard?"

"Just stay close and follow me," I shouted over my shoulder as we climbed down between the lines. From there, we worked our way through the grotty tunnel. The lines buzzed electrically, with a whiff of ozone, but with no sign of a train coming. A warm and dusty apocalyptic wind blew through the hollow tunnel, whistling, as we followed the emergency bulbs behind their wire cages.

When we reached the unmarked recessed door with its inset silver keypad, I punched out the numbers The Ministry had forced me to memorize. Despite my trembling hand, I hit the right combination on my first try, the electronic lock clicked, and the metal door opened long enough for me to push Linda into the narrow corridor on the other side and slip in behind her before it closed.

"Where are we?" asked Linda, goggling around.

The place was quiet. Apparently the collapse of Governmental infrastructure had affected even this safe hold, for the announcement system was offline, nary a crackle from its wall speakers.

I had expected to meet a show of force or at least a security check, but only a skeleton staff appeared operative, a few technicians paying us no attention as they hurried down the crosswise corridor. The racket of the meeting I was supposed to attend came from one of the rooms off to our left, a red bulb flashing above the door.

Color coded arrows on the wall directed personnel to various departments. Using them as a guide, I made my way down to the lab, Linda in tow.

I peered through the little window before entering. There, in its glass jar on its pedestal, was the cause of all the trouble.

The lab was empty, no technicians or scientists, the camera crews gone. No annoying grinning Frilly Holly. I punched my access code into the door's keypad and we stepped inside.

Linda took two steps and stopped. She stared aghast at the monstrous brain.

From the flickering monitors, I could see The Brain was still sending out a mad flurry of neural pulses. The ECG formation had drastically changed, however. It resembled the encephalogram spikes of a distressed patient suffering acute anxiety or rage.

"It knows we're here," I said.

Linda blinked and seemed to snap out of her trance. "It's trying to destroy us all," she said, "but it's clever, because down here, underground, it will survive the nuclear attack it has driven us to."

She approached the platform. "Oh it's warm here," she muttered in surprise.

The green glow of the lamp bathed her sweat-dampened face as she took another step closer, looking down at the bulbous brain.

"It's huge," she gasped.

"Yes," I said, "Surely three times the size of any bog standard human brain."

"And for all we know capable of much more than mere cerebration," she said. "Telepathy even, or precognition - or even ... psychic attack!"

"Linda!" I warned. "Come away."

She looked struck silly. "I can feel *it*, or *something*, pulling at my thoughts, as if it's trying to disperse them. What are you really?" she whispered to it.

I watched the ECG spike wildly as if in answer.

"What do you want from us?" she asked.

Standard questions to any invading extraterrestrial, I suppose, but as Linda stared at the brain, the light in her eyes changed, here eyebrows drew together in suspicion, and her mouth twisted into a grimace.

"I know what you're doing," she told it. "You're the reason we're killing each other, the reason we're on the brink of destruction. You're the invasion we've always feared. The first wave of a vanguard. We'll destroy ourselves in your name like stupid children and when we've all but obliterated ourselves, others will follow from your planet to launch a conventional attack on the remaining survivors too exhausted and demoralized to retaliate."

I watched The Brain's readings zigzag wildly into spiky peaks across the monitor.

"You know, don't you?" She told The Brain. "You know that I'm going to stop you."

"Linda!" I shouted my warning this time, as she wrapped her arms around the massive jar. She hefted it from the pedestal; the electrodes lost their slack, tightened, and a few pinged off here and there.

I saw Linda's thin legs wobble under the jar's weight. She looked suddenly unsure if she could lift it above her head, as the condensation on the jar caused it to start slipping from her grasp.

Before I could step in, I heard voices coming from the corridor.

In the next instant, two armed security officers burst into the lab.

I was only peripherally aware of their guns trained on Linda from the doorway as they commanded her to put down the jar, because at that point my attention was drawn to the ECG, which was doing a wild fandango.

"Stop," I shouted. "It's frightened."

"No, it's making a final desperate effort to win," Linda shouted back.

"But the ECG, the pulses—"

"—are malicious brain waves, Richard!"

The security officers shouted an ultimatum, but Linda was defiant.

"If you shoot me, you'll kill us both," she yelled back, her voice cracking on the last word, as incredibly she found a remnant of strength to lift The Brain above her head.

In all likelihood, they would have shot her, but that's something we will never know for sure, since the standoff was interrupted by a baggy-eyed, wild-haired scientist bursting into the laboratory behind them.

He was waving a paper about and yelling, "I've done it, I've done it!"

But Linda had never in her somewhat pampered life lifted so much as a jar of pickled onions above her head let alone a twelve-pound jar of Martian brain. Her bony shoulders were trembling.

I reached Linda in two or three giant strides, and wrestled the jar from her. "It's okay, I've got it," I shouted as the security officers lowered their guns and the scientist let out an audible sigh of relief.

But the jar was heavier than I'd expected. I looked from Linda, to the security guards, and back to the scientist, in an appeal for help as the jar began its inevitable submission to gravity.

The scientist's face went from relief to horror in a split-second as realization struck.

"But I've cracked it," he whined, looking like a man about to see his winning lottery ticket flushed down the lavatory. "I've deciphered the signals. I know what it's trying to tell us. It wants us to take it to our leader!"

The awful moment came when I saw Linda cover her mouth and I knew it was too late as jar slipped from my clutches. In my mind, I heard Linda yelling her usual curse at me "You egg-headed clumsy oaf" whenever I dropped another plate on the kitchen floor.

She screamed as the jar hit the ground and exploded. Glass shattered into a hundred jagged slivers, salty water splashing our faces.

On the floor, in a pool of saline, the gooey Martian Brain lay convulsing in a death-spasm, horribly exposed and raw, like an infected organ, removed, steaming, from the body.

"…yesterday I met a young Swiss man for the first time. He had hopes for this war-ravaged land. Today we buried him. This is Dave Kite, signing off for ZBC News."

I watched my grainy image standing against boulders, scrub, dust, and sky on the screen of the laptop, allowing a moment before looming towards the screen to switch the camera off.

I rather liked the sign-off. Portentous.

It took half an hour before I found out that Scott back in DC didn't. His unfocussed face filled the laptop screen for a moment before he sat back down adjusting a headset mike in the comfort of some office. He put a cup of coffee down by the keyboard. The distorted Starbucks logo filled an entire edge of the image. It could have been deliberate; I could have killed for a decent cup of java.

"Davey, I'm sorry, I can't use this."

"Why not?"

I'd been squatting outside my tent for fifteen minutes trying to get the satellite link up and my haunches were beginning to kill me.

"It's background. It's travelogue. It's not even context."

"It's real."

"Davey, some Swiss tourist gets himself killed in a bus smash. So what? You're thirty miles from the frontline. Find a real story."

"There are real stories here too, Scott. It wasn't a bus smash. It was live fire. Civilians. And it wouldn't have happened without the mercenaries. It's about escalation."

Scott was getting impatient. "Five, ten years ago we may have run it. We'll drop the facts of the matter into a link but we're not running your piece, Davey. Get to the frontline. Check out these stories of the Chinese backing up the Taliban. The things that are happening post-US withdrawal. *That's* escalation."

He took a slurp of coffee, this time putting the paper cup down just off camera. "Nothing personal, Davey, but I've got twenty-four seven rolling news to fill and I'm too busy to nursemaid. Find me a story. Then I'll run it." He leant forward and spoke slowly, like to a child. "Keep asking yourself one question: is this a story?"

And then the laptop screen went blank. Scott was gone.

You know how well groomed, pearly toothed people forever appear on your television set telling you that they're the Moscow correspondent, or London correspondent, or Paris, Rome, or somewhere else sexy correspondent? Well, years before, when their grooming wasn't so effortless, they were the Lima correspondent, or the Senegal correspondent. And before that they covered Boise, Idaho, or whatever the left-hand armpit of the planet is. And they'd only crop up on your screens once every three years looking shell-shocked, mouthing clichés, when an airplane crashed into a train that smashed into a pick-up carrying a beauty queen, or some such. Well, that was where I was aiming to get. Left-hand armpit correspondent. And then I'd take it from there.

I tried explaining the whole hierarchy of the correspondents thing to a very pretty girl at the bar of the Intercontinental in Hyderabad before finding out that she'd just been promoted to Cairo correspondent of some West Coast outfit. I felt like everybody at the Intercontinental was laughing at me that night. In reality it was probably just everybody in Hyderabad.

The story about the Swiss, I called him that because he had a Swiss flag embroidered on to his epaulette, was more or less true.

We, or at least I, afforded him as good as a funeral as we could. I covered his body with boulders, the ground being far too rocky to dig a grave, even if we could summon the energy to do so. Then, assuming he had some Christian sympathies I stumbled over some words of contrition. The irony did not escape me: a ceremony in English for a German-speaking Swiss in some God-forsaken, war torn, unpronounceable province, the native language of which seemed to consist of vowel sounds interspersed with the retch of phlegm being brought up.

The tribesmen, huddled in the shelter of the blackened skeleton of the dead bus smoking the filterless cigarettes that kept them fluent, looked on in bemusement at me. The mercenaries that had fired on us when the driver inexplicably tried to run the roadblock had long since melted away.

Then the dozen or so tribesmen and I ascended the valley. They had wanted to bury him up the escarpment, nearer to Allah or something, but, in desperate signs, I had tried to explain the danger of planting the dead upstream. One of the words they knew and understood was 'No'.

Not that it would have made any difference as I couldn't stop them doing what they wanted to their own dead.

How the hell had I ended up here?

Ten years old. I remembered the national elation when Bin Laden was killed. I wanted to be part of it, but childhood asthma meant that the best I could hope for was to cover it. Years later I had come armed only with a camera, laptop, solar charger, cheap satellite linkage from a discount website, and those romantic notions that make men throw themselves into the furnace of battle with the belief that they'll emerge the other side. Plus an introduction to Scott at ZBC.

I like to think that I found the motley band, tribesmen without a tribe. In truth they had probably been watching me for days as I cut across the high hills to where I thought the highway to the one town with electricity twenty-four seven lay. They had let me walk straight into their shantytown encampment, hidden in a cleft up an incongruously picturesque valley, all wildflowers and burbling water.

Confused, I tried signaling my intention of fighting for their cause via twenty-four hour rolling news, whatever that may mean, if they would consider me 'embedded'. But they just laughed at me, their craggy dirty faces breaking into black-lined ridges of mirth.

I was taken through the tented village. Dark eyes under suspicious furrowed brows watched me. Smoke from cooking fires hung in the air. Goats with their ribs protruding as if they were vacuum-wrapped bleated rudely. Women washed their clothes in the stream, turning to silently watch me.

I was half-pushed, half-guided towards a tent from which the rest of the shanty seemed to spread. It was roughly in the shape of a flattened cube in the process of collapsing, its walls made of green tarpaulins and goatskins. A complicated arrangement of guy-ropes formed a lobby leading to the interior where we disturbed three tribesmen huddled in discussion, drawing on hand-rolled cigarettes. They seemed angry and shooed the lackeys away with snarled insults.

I was left standing in front of the three of them, unsure. It took more than a moment for my eyes to adapt to the cold darkness of the interior. They could see my confusion and took the opportunity to spit questions at me in their rough throaty tongue. I just stood there, scared and alone. Finally the thin lizard-like leader in the middle made what I presumed was a joke. The others laughed and by their eyes I guessed it was at the expense of my mismatch of inadequate army surplus and denim. I tried breaking the ice by laughing along.

A barked order and the lackeys that had led me into the tent re-entered and relieved me of my pack, roughly searching my pockets. The contents were tipped out onto the carpeted floor and much clucking and murmuring was made as they rifled through their booty. They ripped open the plastic bags in which I kept my dry clothes and held up my harmonica for the amusement of all. One of them blew into it creating a screeching noise. He waved it in my face, jeering something like "Sheesh, sheesh." It was passed around and they all had a go. There was little I could do other than stand there and take it, with fear drying my mouth and loosening my bowels.

It was when they found my maps that the atmosphere tensed with a sudden new interest in me. The maps were passed reverently to the leader. My eyes had become accustomed to the gloom and I could make him out much better now. He had a face like a deflated football, thick, brown and leathery. Above yellowed, exposed teeth, displayed like a braying donkey, he sported a pencil thin moustache. Imagine the severed head of Clark Gable hollowed out, sucked in, and played with in the dirt looking up at you, leering.

They kept the maps, I kept my life.

I lived with them for six days during which I discovered a number of things. I discovered they were just refugees searching for peace from the militia and the mercenaries. I discovered that if I really needed to I could stomach the way they cooked their goat. And I discovered that I wasn't really a prisoner. They returned my pack -- I think the technology was too advanced for them to barter and they simply didn't know what to make of it.

I shot some pieces, the first of which Scott liked, and the second he tolerated. The third brought the first of his verdicts of 'travelogue' that, to him, meant the highest form of damnation. Find a story, he said. So I left. The tribesmen gave me some dried meat and I walked away.

Two days later I thought I had a story.

The bus, British-made and at least fifty years old, had been making its way through the foothills. In a surreal moment in a surreal country I simply flagged it down and got on. I wasn't sure whether the people on it were refugees or this was simply some ad hoc commuter service between townships, an attempt at normality flying in the face of what was happening all around. The passengers looked like refugees, dressed in rags and carrying wildly ambitious loads, but so did almost everybody. The Swiss was sitting amongst them. We regarded each other warily and stoically exchanged nodded greetings.

When the driver decided to run the roadblock and the firing started we both managed to get off and get under cover. When the Swiss tried to get back to the burning bus to retrieve his pack I held him back, but he shrugged me off. Perhaps the tribesmen's diet hadn't done much for me. Perhaps if I hadn't tried to stop him he would have made it there and back again before the petrol tank caught. Perhaps if I hadn't tried to stop him he would have lived.

His last words to me were 'Pictures', said whilst tapping his breast pocket. I found a terabyte memory card hidden in a pack of cigarettes. It held just over a thousand photos at ultra-high definition. I guessed he was a photojournalist for one of the glossies, or a freelancer for a high-end photo agency. There must have been some expensive kit that had gone up in the burning bus. No wonder he'd tried to get it back.

I scrolled through them. Portraits of tribesmen, every hair, crease, and gap tooth brought out in infinite detail. Camp life. Landscapes of mountains at sunrise or sunset, gnarled trees, tethered goats. A charred and burnt out truck, contrasted against the yellow of the desert. Like most professional photographers the Swiss had taken ten, twenty, thirty near-identical shots in order to identify the best at his leisure later. Expertly composed and captured, even his worst were better than my best.

But one group differed from the rest. Life in one of the border towns: people, bustle, noise, narrow dirt roads, whitewashed walls with daubed slogans, street hawkers. An air of threat and intimidation. The pictures had a snatched quality at odds with the rest, as though the Swiss didn't have time to compose and position.

I flicked back and forth through the dozen or so shots. It

began with a group of women in burkas, intrusive portraits, but then the Swiss seemed to follow the traffic in the opposite direction. Following, in particular, a handcart, making its way through a mass of donkeys, pick-ups, and bicycles. Children selling cigarettes desperate to make eye contact, armed militia daring you to. At one point the handcart man's face fills the screen, blurred, too close to focus.

I guessed that the Swiss had seen something and needed to record it for posterity. But he had the sensibility of an artist, not a journalist, so what was it? He'd been allowed to openly take a dozen or so shots and he couldn't have hidden such a high-def camera -- it would normally need a tripod -- so it couldn't have been anything too controversial.

But sensitive enough to hide the card in a pack of cigarettes.

Looking again, I tried to get as much information about the handcart man as possible. The blurred face, another decent one in profile, but mainly back shots. He wore an ankle length grey robe tied at the waist with a striped sash and had straight, short black hair which probably made him look younger than he was. The way he stooped I guessed at fifty. Other than that, well, let's say if you were putting together an identity parade you wouldn't have to look long in Pakistan for a line up.

The contents of the handcart were covered with a sheet except for...and then I saw it.

Hanging below the rear of the cart, in between the handles, was a large cage, rectangular, made of wood or metal, it wasn't clear. The gaps between the bars were four, perhaps six inches. And looking out from between the bars was a...

I zoomed in to get a better look. A penguin? No, not a penguin. But not a chicken, or any kind of parrot, either. At least none that I recognized.

I flicked back and forth through the shots, now knowing what I was after. I could imagine the Swiss now, dodging through the Kasbah, pushing his way forward, trying to get ahead of the handcart, trying to get the right angle to get his shot.

But a shot of what? I joined up everything I could glean from the pictures. Two foot tall, maybe. Weighty. Flightless, surely? Its wings looked short and stumpy, but cooped up in the cage it was hard to tell. A large black head, almost spherical, which gave the initial impression of a penguin. A white line around a black eye, or just the light catching? I couldn't tell. A grey body. They didn't look like feathers, but it was a bird so it had to be. It was a bird... wasn't it?

As Scott said, keep asking yourself: Is this a story? I'd come here wanting to break exclusives about Chinese incursions into Pakistan, or US Special Forces being left behind, embedded, in direct contradiction to presidential promises and UN resolutions. But here I was, on the verge of discovering the penguin-chicken. Was this a story? Yes. But could I convince Scott?

I couldn't believe that I was taking this seriously. But if I wanted to be the ZBC left-hand armpit correspondent...

A mile or so further up the road from the now cold, black remains of the bus was a settlement hardly worth the name. Wattle and daub, and dry stone walls. Windows hung with goatskin and plastic sheeting, not a pane of glass in sight. Dung fires with nothing cooking over them for my dollars to buy. I showed the pictures of the town to the few toothless inhabitants. Finally I found one with the intelligence to realize that I wasn't just trying to dazzle him with digital pictures, but I was showing him pictures *of something*. With much finger pointing he indicated the general direction, and I guessed the level of animation equated to distance. I hitched a ride on a donkey cart climbing the hillside.

Just so Scott didn't forget me I filed another story. It managed to be both rambling and come in at under sixty seconds, pure travelogue about the people caught up in the crossfire trying to scratch a living out of the dead earth between the rocks.

I could tell, as soon as he came on the webcam, that he was about to blast me out. But he paused, blinking, brow furrowed. "Davey. You look like shit. When did you last eat?"

I paused. I couldn't recall my last proper meal, anything that had been on a plate, anything that needed cutlery or more than a moment to consume.

"I know what sleep dep sounds like, Davey. I know what malnutrition looks like. It doesn't play well. Cable viewers like correspondents to look like they haven't just stepped off the plane, but neither do they want them to have gone native. Kabul, Jalalabad, doesn't matter. Get yourself back to the city, have a shower. Have some sleep. Shave and eat a steak. In fact, almost anything beginning with an 'S'."

"I'm on to a story, Scott."

Scott leant back in his seat, grinning. "Yeah, something else that begins with an S that you need to find, Davey." He began to count off on his fingers. "Sleep, shower, shave, steak, story. And anything else beginning with an S you can get." And with that his figure blurred towards the screen and was gone.

I arrived a day later, limping with a blister. I'd slept in a crevice between rocks, breakfasted on icy waters in which I had also washed. The rest is kinda blurry. I remember patrolling the streets and the marketplace, grabbing people by the shoulders, trying to find the handcart man. Everybody began to look like him. Young, old, I kept making mistakes. I'd apologize. Mostly they shrugged me away. One or two were less accommodating. Guns and knives were revealed under robes threateningly. There were arguments. I reeled away before I got hit. I remember imitating a bird, miming a cage, waving my hands to indicate size, trying to get people to understand. A small crowd suddenly gathered, laughing at me. Me joining in with them. A headache. A blinding headache. The light hurting my eyes.

And nothing after that.

I woke up lying on straw in the gloom of a small barn or large shed. Chinks of daylight showed through gaps in the walls and roof. All around me were the clucking and scratching of chickens. My initial thought was that I'd been taken hostage.

In the gloom it took some moments to realize that the penguin-chicken was looking at me, its head cocked to one side. It was even bigger than I'd guessed, almost half my height, its thighs as thick as its wings were stunted. I was too tired to be terrified. Too terrified to move.

And then it spoke in a clipped, robotic chant, barely recognizable as English. "You are required to direct this messenger drone to those in authority. Message from the General Tu'huaht of the Mininutian Fleet, which has blockaded your planet for the last one hundred and thirteen of your Earth days. All trade between your planet and other worlds has been denied to you. Your resources are dwindling, and your resistance cannot last. But the General Tu'huaht promises leniency in exchange for your immediate surrender. The General Tu'huaht also promises that any other course will result in destruction and slavery. Message ends."

It blinked, clucked, scratched at the floor and pecked at some grain. And then it looked up again and repeated the message exactly, word for word, pause for pause, note for note. And then the chicken-penguin went on to repeat it three more times in exactly the same manner before stalking off to a dark corner of the coop. I stared into the darkness to look for any other creatures but it seemed to be alone, towering over the more familiar-looking chickens.

Then I realized that a man was sitting by me on a wooden stool, the handcart man. I had no idea how long he'd been there, whether he'd heard the message from the General Tu'huaht, whether he'd even recognized the sounds as words. He held his fingers up to his mouth to indicate food, at which point I decided that I was still a free man. I nodded.

"Dollars?" he asked, rubbing his fingers together.

"Dollars," I nodded again.

Exhausted, I fell asleep with the thought that I had to get the message, the recording, because that was what it clearly was, on video. I had no idea what it meant. The world had been laid siege by the Mininutian Fleet? Our planet was cut off from other planets? This was crazy. Utterly crazy. But it was real. And it was a story. Even Scott would have been able to see that if he could see this.

Get a video? I wasn't thinking big enough. Get the bird. Take it back to the States. This was Pulitzer Prize and Barnum and Bailey all rolled into one. My dreamless sleep was only disturbed by a single gunshot, or so I imagined.

When I awoke the coop was lit by oil lamps hanging from the wooden struts. It was night outside and the temperature had dropped by several degrees. I ached all over. I couldn't tell whether I was recovering or going down with something.

A plate sat in front of me. Rice, beans, a rough flatbread, and a chicken thigh the size of a baseball bat. "Eat, eat," the handcart man implored, pushing his dirty fingers to his dirty mouth, grinning.

In the barn the penguin-chicken was nowhere to be seen.

WELL, HARUKI, LOOKS LIKE IT'S JUST YOU AND ME, KID
BY DANIEL P. DOUGLAS

I wouldn't've noticed the drunk bum squirreled up next to my apartment building's grimy staircase, except that he mumbled, "Give us some piggy fudding," followed by a fine belch.

"Want me to roust 'em, Mr. Richter?" the scrawny paperboy yelped from the sidewalk's edge, just near his father's newsstand.

"No, Johnny, but I'll take one of those late editions off you," I said, and then pulled my damp trench coat's collar up around my neck. Rain was light for now but the wind had picked up.

"Anything worth reading?" I said, handing the boy a coin for the *L.A. Times.* "They sink the Japanese sub that shot up Santa Barbara yesterday?"

"No, still out lookin' for it."

"Thanks, kid."

"You bet, Mr. Richter."

I stepped back toward the drunk. He seemed to be swatting flies. Good chance there were some, but better chance there weren't since it was February. "Hey you, snap out of it." The bum looked up. "Christmas was two months ago buddy, so no one has any figgy pudding."

"Fruitcake?"

My lips curled. Fruitcake. Not sure of its point. Like a lot of dames, it smelled good and looked promising, but regret usually followed. "None of that either, buddy." I handed him a couple of bucks. "Here, go across the street and get some dinner at Kenji's." Best pork cutlets and noodles this side of Beverly Boulevard.

"Can't," the bum said. "They took him today, and his wife and kids."

"But…You sure of that?"

"Yeah. Feel safer?" The bum's laugh trickled off into a sigh. "Can I still keep the dough?"

I looked across the street and noticed a big sign in the front window of Kenji's meager restaurant: CLOSED. The red and white checkered curtains stood drawn behind it. The bicycle his son rode to make deliveries leaned against the bus bench out front, just like always. "Looky here, did anyone say where they were taking them?"

"Naw, just one of the places. You know, the camps for Japs."

Kenji was an immigrant, but his kids were born here. I guess that didn't matter. They were all Japs to somebody, and the Japs bombed Pearl Harbor barely more than two months ago. Now they fired on our coastline from submarines. A hazard, yes, but nowhere near the threat the Nazis posed. I should know.

"Yeah, keep the lettuce, but get something to eat. No booze. Got it, bub?"

"Yesiree."

Just then, a loud, diesel-powered truck came around the corner of the street behind me, followed by a couple of Army Jeeps and three black Buick sedans. The truck hauled a trailer that looked like it carried an anti-aircraft gun. A tarp covered it, but the cargo was a familiar shape. The Army had stuck lots of ack-ack guns in and around L.A. Heck, just down the street in the parking lot of a school, soldiers manned two .50 caliber machine guns.

One of the Buicks pulled over while the rest of the convoy drove on. None other than Dexter Jamison stepped out, but not before he had first extended his hand as a weather probe to measure rainfall velocity, volume, and density. All spit and polish, Jamison was a War Department bureaucrat on the move. Didn't know whether to trust him or not, but he was good for my private eye business. Paid the bills, and how.

"Come on over, Dex. The rain's too afraid to show itself now that you're here."

Guy must've spent a fortune on pin stripe suits. Always pin stripes, but never the same suit that I'd seen.

"I need to speak with you, Geno."

"I gathered. Where's the gun going?"

"Reinforcing MacArthur Park, but you didn't hear that from me."

Jamison pulled me away from the bum and we stepped down the sidewalk a few. He looked around, no doubt checking for unwanted eyes and ears.

"Geno," he said, "I hear you roughed up Hans Bremmer."

As a private eye, I kept tabs on some of the local, suspected Nazis and their collaborators. While the War Department paid me well for these cases, I was also my own man and didn't need Dex looking over my shoulder. I'd've joined up to fight on the front by now, but Army doctors had told me that I suffered from some sort of disqualifying medical condition. Always sounded like gobbledygook to me, but then the War Department came along waving the American flag and a whole lot of lettuce. So, I started working these Nazi cases for them. It's been decent so far, but sometimes there was just such a fine line demarcating the good guys from the bad.

"And I hear you've incarcerated Kenji Nakamoto and his family."

"Relocated. And that was done by the commander of the military district, not me. C'mon, the President authorized this kind of thing after Pearl."

"So if up to you, Kenji would still be free?"

"Knock it off, Geno. You know what we are facing. You of all people know the kind of threats that are all around us. Tough times call for tough measures."

"Exactly. Which is why Hans Bremmer ain't feeling so hot right now."

"He says he has information to share with us, but he's going to clam up if you keep at him."

"Looky here, Bremmer is German and a fisherman. He takes his boat out of San Pedro and fishes. He's not runnin' guns or smuggling saboteurs. All he's looking for is a payday, and he'll get it if you play sucker. Don't be a fool, Dex."

"Then why'd you rough him up?"

"Because he said mean things about you." He didn't, but Jamison wasn't really interested in the truth except when it suited him. And to be honest, I roughed up Bremmer because I got fed up with all of his lies. I poured it on. "And your wife."

"Oh." Jamison furrowed his brow and pursed his lips. "Why did he do that?"

"Bremmer plays the angles." This was no fooling. The guy's a schemer and, unfortunately for him, looked a lot like Hermann Göring, only twice as fat and always sweaty. "He's trying to play me against you. Said he'd share the payoff with me if I backed him up with you." Again, not exactly true, but very, very possible if I knew Hans Bremmer as well as I did. The guy was even friends with the Mayor. Brought him smoked tuna every week.

"Oh. Well, I appreciate your honesty."

"Sure thing, Dex. All in a day's work."

◇◇◇

I was having the best dream of my life. This one dame, Penny—she's from *Freddy's*, a nightclub up on Pico Boulevard—was dancing like one of those Persian belly dancers. Dreams don't have to make sense, and this one didn't. Penny's a waitress and a doll. She's put together and smart as a crackerjack. But in my dream she was dancing, and how.

That's when I had the rudest awakening of my life. Half asleep, my first thought was that the neighbors were fighting, throwing pots, pans, dishes at each other. When it became clear the racket was gunfire, I came to and crawled to the window, grabbing my Colt .45 handgun from the nightstand on the way.

My apartment window faced southwest, toward MacArthur Park and beyond that toward the Baldwin Hills. Searchlights scanned everywhere. Judging from the dark buildings and streets, a blackout order must have been in effect. With all of the air raid sirens, the order wasn't necessary. People knew to stay put and to keep things dark when the sirens sounded.

This must've been the real thing. The sky erupted. Blasts from anti-aircraft artillery fired shells overhead that burst into blinding light. Yeah, I ducked, and I covered my ears too when the nearby .50 calibers started raking the air. Whatever they were shooting at must've been close. I poked my head up just a bit past the windowsill. Tracers flew everywhere.

The phone on my nightstand rang. It sat right next to my ear so I nearly crapped in my skivvies. I grabbed the receiver and hunkered down below the window.

"Richter here and this had better be good!" Explosions drowned out the response. "I didn't catch that. Say again."

"I said this is Hans Bremmer."

"Really? That's just swell, Hansie. You know we are under attack right now so your timing ain't so kosher, *mein Freund*."

"This *is* about the attack. I have, in my very own custody, one of the invading pilots. He's a Jap, Mr. Richter. I have captured one of the enemy and I wish to have your cooperation. Perhaps you and Mr. Jamison would be interested—"

Three or four shells burst right above my building. Then, it sounded like hail hit my window. One piece came right on through the glass and landed next to my foot. Wasn't hail, but a nice piece of American-made shrapnel. Great shooting guys.

I started to get a little hot under the collar. "Looky here, do you really expect me to believe that you have captured a Japanese pilot? What'd he do, crash in the ocean and you hauled him in with one of your nets?"

"This is precisely the case."

"Don't waste my time, Hans."

"You may see for yourself."

"This is not the best time for me to drive to San Pedro. There is a war going on right now, right here in L.A." That's when I glanced out my window and saw what I think was the reason for all of the shooting. The searchlights had it lit up clear as day. All I heard was shooting, and all I saw didn't make sense to me one bit.

"I am not far, a mere ten blocks, and then you will see I am telling the truth."

"Where are you?"

"In the apartment of the Mayor's— A friend's apartment. She is an acquaintance of mine. I felt she could help me if you did not. Rampart and Beverly. We are safe here."

That's right, he was talking about Winnie. I knew all about her. "I know the area."

Of course Hans was a friend of the Mayor's mistress. What I didn't think Hans or the Mayor knew was that Winnie was a Nazi. I knew this because it was my job, and I'd had my eyes on her for some time. And she was easy on the eyes too, so it wasn't a rough deal.

"Hans, listen to me. Just stay put and don't bring anyone else into this. If you do, I swear I'll give you a black eye to match the other one."

"I shall do as you say."

I craned my neck for another look out the window. The strange metallic disc, easily as wide as a city block, was drifting south at about 500 feet off the ground. "What kind of shape is the pilot in?"

"He is uninjured from what I can see. I must say, these Japs are much smaller in person. Must be very clever, though. His head is twice the size of mine." Hans chuckled. "Very large brain in there!"

Not wanting Winnie and her Nazi infiltrators to help the pilot escape, I decided to make my way to Hans. I hung up the phone and called Jamison. He promised to send some soldiers from MacArthur Park and meet me at Winnie's, but only after the air raid ended. Until then, I was on my own. Music to my ears.

I got dressed, tucked my .45 and handcuffs into my pants, and, like a fool, headed outside. My first stop was across the street. Since a blackout was in effect, driving would have only led to jail time. I could have left the headlights off, but the brake lights were another matter. So, instead, I hopped on Kenji's delivery bike and peddled my way to meet Hans.

"Please meet Winifred Burke," Hans said, I think, as I stepped inside the apartment. I could barely hear him. My ears still rang from the artillery barrage underway outside. Fortunately, the shooting seemed to be moving away from L.A. and toward Long Beach.

Nevertheless, there she stood, not really needing an introduction, a blonde slice of splendor decked out to the nines looking ready to host a cocktail party for some of her L.A. friends. With the shades drawn, all the lit candles made Winnie and her elegant place both seem even more so.

"Pleased to meet you," I said, offering a slight bow.

"The pleasure is mine, Mr. Richter," Winnie said, extending her hand.

I accepted the offering, providing her smooth skin a gentle kiss. I included a long, deep gaze into her melting eyes as a bonus. Hansie peered away, sheepish. He cleared his throat. Winnie withdrew her hand, and caught her breath.

"Now… Would anyone like some coffee? How do you take yours, Mr. Richter?"

Without the strychnine, *Fraulein*. "Piping hot, thanks." After Winnie slinked away to the kitchen, I turned to Hans. "And if you don't mind, I'd like to see your prisoner. *Do you mind?*"

"*Nein, nein.* This way. He is in the bedroom. Blinds are drawn but we do have a small lamp on so that you may gaze upon him without difficulty."

Closing the door behind us, amid the dim light, I first thought I saw a kid sitting on the bed. I even wondered for a split second if Winnie had a teenaged son or daughter living with her.

"Behold," Hans said, pointing at the kid, "my prisoner of war."

There sat a small person. Hans was right about the big head. It was also bald. "He doesn't look well, Hans. His skin is so… Ashen. And his eyes… His eyes…"

"No doubt dilated from the low light and probably swollen from the seawater. But look, they are slanted, like almonds. He looks like Tojo himself. Notice his silver flight suit. He must be an ace or someone of high rank."

I turned to the pilot. His suit held no markings. No pockets. No zippers, buttons, or seams for that matter.

"Ask him his name," Hans said.

"His name?"

"Yes, it is the only thing that he says. It is all he says, no matter the question."

"Uh, okay. Well, what is your name?"

He spoke.

"Did you hear him, Mr. Richter?"

"I, well, I heard something. It sounded like words but I also heard a noise."

"Yes, like swirling air. I've heard that Japs talk and whisper at the same time. Very devious. Very mysterious."

"You would know." I stepped closer and he spoke again. He had tiny lips and a small mouth, almost like a slit.

"Ha ru ki."

I stepped back.

"Did you hear it that time, Mr. Richter? Sounds like 'haruki.' Definitely Japanese."

"Ha ru ki," he said again, and then pointed frail hands at the door. That's when I noticed each hand only had three fingers. Three, long fingers.

"Hans, I think he's injured. Did you see his hands? He's minus a finger on each."

Hans waddled closer, squinting his peepers. "Perhaps an Asian deformity."

"Ha ru ki."

"You see, Mr. Richter, it is all he is willing to say. Nothing but 'haruki'."

"Was he armed?"

"Why yes." Hans reached into his pocket and pulled out a silver box. It looked like a cigarette case, only thicker.

"Give it here."

"It is not that I don't trust you, I am just concerned about damag—"

"I'll damage you if you don't give it to me. Hand it over."

Hans gave me the case. It had a row of recessed buttons on its surface and blinking blue light just above them. On the back, there seemed to be a lens, and Hans noticed me looking at it.

"Be careful where you point that. It may fire accidentally."

"Get real. Does this look like any gun that you've ever seen? It looks more like a camera. A real fancy camera." I tucked it into my coat pocket.

"Ah! Then he is a spy! I have captured an enemy spy!"

I wasn't sure, but I think Hans attempted some sort of Bavarian jig. He would have danced longer, but the two gun-wielding dragoons who barged into the room spoiled the moment. Their black suits, white shirts, and red ties made them look like swastikas incarnate. And their Luger pistols meant business. Bad business. Los Angeles was crawling with these damn Nazis.

"We require your cooperation," the tall gunman said. His shorter companion only grunted. Poor petite thug was just too shy to express himself to strangers in whatever English he had picked up since the U-boat dropped him off.

"Oh yeah, who says so?" I asked. I'd been in these situations before. They seldom answered my question. Instead, nine times out of ten, they just started swinging.

That's just what the short one did. He lunged at me and took a swipe at my chops. I kneed him in the groin and pushed him back toward the other gunman, giving me just enough time to draw my .45. I hip fired and hit groin-aching shorty. But now he had a bullet hole in his chest to worry about. He didn't worry long.

I rolled across the end of the bed and ducked down the other side. To my surprise, Hans had beat me there. The other gunman dove behind a big easy chair in a corner of the room. I fired a couple of rounds into the back of that chair—and wouldn't you know it—the guy still shot back. Either I missed him or he was made of steel.

Hans screamed like the broad he was and crawled away, taking cover behind a big dresser next to the bed. It was then I noticed Haruki—or whatever—had disappeared. He must've slipped off the bed and hugged the floor on the other side.

But just then, a strange thing happened. The easy chair floated off the floor and jettisoned across the room. The Nazi gunman froze, which was perfectly fine with me. I aimed just below his slick blond hair, right at his pretty Aryan face. Without going into the details, it wasn't so pretty anymore, and was only suitable for presentation in a morgue. He slumped in the corner and bled all over the place to say the least.

I turned to see if Hans was all right, but he was gone. The window shades wafted in the wind. Yeah, he'd made a run for it—insomuch as he could run—out the window and down the fire escape. Given his physical shape, I did check. He hadn't fallen or gotten stuck. He'd made a clean getaway.

Haruki climbed back onto the bed just as Winnie burst through the door. She noticed the gun. "Oh, thank god you are safe! These men," she pointed to the floor and gasped, "rushed in and threatened me. Who are they?"

I holstered the gun and fiddled with my back pocket. "Nazi carcasses. Are you hurt, Winifred?"

She gasped again and put the back of her hand to her forehead. She stepped closer. "Why no. And you, Mr. Richter? I would feel so awful if you were hurt."

"Yeah, I think I'm hit. Caught me in the leg." I limped toward her, next to the corner of the bed. "Can you take a look? I'm feeling dizzy."

She reached out and leaned toward me. That's when I reached for and cuffed her wrist to the bedpost. "Wait here, Winifred Burke. Or should I say Winifred Burkhardt, Nazi spy." She stopped protesting after I slapped her and commanded, in *Deutsch*, to sit down and zip it.

"Well, Haruki," I said to the…person who sat politely on the bed, "looks like it's just you and me, kid."

◇◇◇

A little later, Haruki and I sat together on the sofa in the living room. By then, the ack-ack guns had ceased firing. The only sound was the ticking from the clock on Winnie's mantle.

"Ha ru ki."

"Yes, so I've heard."

"Ha ru ki," he said again, this time pointing at my coat pocket.

I reached in and pulled out the silver box. Next thing I noticed was one of his long fingers tapping the coffee table in front of us.

I set the box down with the buttons and blue light facing up. Haruki reached over and flipped it so the lens faced up. The box vibrated and the lens projected the strangest thing. It was as if watching a movie, except this movie wasn't on any screen. It was just floating in the air about a foot above this gadget. *And* it was in color.

I didn't really recognize any of the images. Some looked like star charts. Many others were geometric shapes. Some of the shots seemed sequential, each displaying an increasing number of zeros and what looked like the number one.

One image, very brief, did ring a bell. It was a large silver disc about the size of a city block. It sat on a runway in what looked like a desert. Then the screen faded to another chart, this one showing our solar system with each planet highlighted in different orbital positions.

The movie ended. Haruki pointed at the device and then at the front door. *"Ha ru ki."* With impeccable timing, in walked Dexter Jamison, followed by a few GI's.

"Hello, Dex," I said. "Hope you brought a hearse and a paddy wagon."

Jamison sniffed the room. "Where are they, Geno?"

"In the bedroom." I pointed with my thumb and the troops headed in that way. "Didn't expect to see you in person tonight. What brings you out?" I said, complete with shit-eating grin.

Jamison peered at Haruki. "Given your call, and other events, I'm glad things seem okay."

"What events are those?"

Jamison walked around the sofa, examining Haruki from all angles. During his elliptical path, he said: "Oh, you know. All these war jitters have people on edge, a little out of control you might say. Why, did you know that our gunners are firing on a barrage balloon that slipped its moorings?"

A soldier escorted a subdued Winnie through the room and out the front door. I waited for them to leave before saying, "That's a good line."

"Yes. So, I just didn't want things to go awry for you." Jamison leaned over and picked up the silver box. Without the slightest scrutiny, he pocketed it. "We can take you home, if you'd like, while there's a break in the firing."

"A break? Do you expect the balloon to come back for more?"

Jamison peered at every inch of Haruki. From his big head all the way down to his silver boots and back again. "It might. Stranger things have happened."

The other soldiers dragged the dead Nazis through the room and out the front door.

"Well then, that's quite the balloon there, Dex. I'm glad it's on our side. Just one question for you."

"What's that, Geno?"

"What's going to happen to this alien sitting next to me? You going to give it a ride too?"

When Jamison laughed, he surprised me. I was hoping for stunned silence.

"Oh, Geno, this is no space man."

"Right. He's a down on his luck Jap pilot."

"No, he is not that either. He is Japanese, but he's a mariner whose sub was sunk after attacking Santa Barbara. He is a prisoner of war now, and we will take very good care of him. Thank you for protecting him from these others. You've done a great service."

I stood up. "Looky here, Dex, he's a messenger. He brings a message. Keep the message, but let him go. He is not a prisoner."

Just then, the soldiers returned with an olive drab field jacket. They collected Haruki, draping the jacket around him. They followed their tight-lipped boss into the hallway and then outside to the street. I was with them every step of the way. At least three times, I reached for my .45, but better sense—and perhaps Germanic discipline—kicked in.

They all piled into Jamison's black Buick. Haruki sat in the back between two soldiers. Jamison sat up front next to the driver.

"Thanks again, Geno. You have no idea how much you've helped us tonight."

"Oh, I think I do." I leaned inside Jamison's rolled down window and took one last look at Haruki. He had his eyes closed and gestured with his spindly hands. It was as if he was packing an imaginary snowball in front of his face.

That's when another strange thing happened.

At that instant, the Buick's four doors flew open and everyone jettisoned out, just like when the easy chair flew across the room. I also tumbled to the ground. The doors slammed shut with Haruki and his imaginary snowball still inside. Jamison was in a heap on the sidewalk next to the silver box. It had fallen out of his pocket.

The light on it flashed, only now, it glowed red instead of blue. Looking up, I saw the Buick floating down the street. I charged after it, but stopped cold when a bright beam of white light shinned down on the car. Behind me, I heard Jamison and the soldiers running toward me.

I didn't look back. Instead, I looked up, trying to figure out what this beam of light was all about. Oh, and I figured it out all right. The metallic disc had returned, and it lifted the Buick straight up into its belly.

"Fire!" Jamison yelled, and the soldiers pointed their rifles at the craft.

I don't know how many rounds they got off. Dozens—at least—before they halted. But the light, and the Buick, just disappeared into the craft.

Then, all Hell broke loose again. Searchlights honed in on the disc, which maneuvered away to the northwest. Just as the artillery shells and machine gun fire from around the city resumed, I grabbed Dex and dragged him back into the building to take cover until the angry reverberations had subsided.

◇◇◇

The next day, all of the papers and radio stations buzzed about the air raid. Jamison called me several times to make sure I understood how much the War Department appreciated my assistance and that my bank account would see lots of lettuce very soon. I had to give Jamison credit. He knew the one thing I liked more than taking down Nazis.

But when it came to the money on this one, I told him no dice! I squeezed him for only one thing. And soon, Kenji Nakamoto and his family exited the internment camp and returned to Los Angeles.

I guess I'm just a sucker for good pork cutlets and noodles.

The Windfall
By Chris Doty

It was gone.

The oatmeal and ground beef mix for the meatloaf kept getting stuck between his finger and the ring, so he'd taken it off, set it next to the bowl on the counter while he finished. And now it wasn't there.

Joshua could swear it had been there just a second ago, before he ran into the next room to grab his phone when Maria called. She'd be home any minute now, and would absolutely lose it if she caught him without his wedding ring.

"Goddammit," he muttered as he shifted through the detritus on the speckled marble countertop: Old mail, utensils that didn't have a permanent home, the empty packaging from the meat. Nothing.

A sudden thought: *Maybe it stuck to my finger when I took it off, got put back in the bowl.* Joshua grabbed a cookie sheet from the cupboard and dumped the pre-meatloaf on it. He spread it flat with quick hits of his palm and dug his fingers into it, breaking the meat up into tiny pieces as he went, feeling for the round hardness of the ring. Nothing.

He grabbed a towel to wipe the gummy bits of meat off his hands, looking around as he did, along the counter, considering frantically where else it could have gone.

The floor.

He threw the towel on the counter and got down on all fours, searched under the soffits, running his hands along the baseboards. Of dust bunnies and bits of crumb there was much to be found, but his ring wasn't there, either.

Joshua lifted his head up, growling with frustration—

And came face-to-face with Max, their — Maria's — two-year-old black lab. Max cocked his head and wagged his tail.

There was a flake of oatmeal stuck to his lip.

Human SO mad! But just want some meat, eat little bit.

Human make drink bad water, taste like water from bad place,

place where poke and put things inside but talk nice anyway. Place human take to when say go beach.

Then human put outside, make stay out, yell more, "Bad dog! Damn stupid dog!" Then human go in, walk on other side of door while whimper and whine.

Go smell at fence, go smell at flowers, dig little bit by tree. Tree smell like raccoon. HATE raccoon. Piss on tree.

Then go back, whine at door. Human won't let back in. Just walk walk, yell more "Dumb dog!"

Stomach feel sick. So go eat grass. Crow feather on grass, so go eat other grass. HATE crow.

But before eat grass, sudden —

Biiiiig light in sky!

Then! Like bird, flying! Me! Up to light! Straight up!

Joshua paced anxiously between the living room—checking for Maria's car in the driveway—and the door to the backyard to see if Max had shat out his ring yet. He was half-way between his two lookouts when a wash of light came into the house. Maria was home. He froze, dreading the conversation he was about to have. He was already thinking through apologies when he realized that the light was coming from the back of the house, not the front.

He parted the mini-blinds on the kitchen window and squinted into the backyard, just in time to see Max's silhouette suspended in midair in a column of light. As Joshua watched, Max floated up into the open belly of a flying saucer, which disappeared at breakneck speed as soon as Max was inside.

Joshua scratched his head. "Now what am I gonna tell Maria?"

Then, inside! So scary, inside with strange things! Not my humans! Not human! Inside smell like mixed together: Burning raccoon pee and wet crow feather and under sink and bad place. Walls empty, bent like trying to eat me!

Want hide under bed. But no bed!

Still want grass. But no grass!

So make mess.

◇◇◇

"The quadruped has defecated on the deck," Mogorr flarthed, antennae drooping in the smell.

Gorrmog looked at her brood sister, exasperated. It was Mogorr's fault that they'd been sent on this worthless mission in the first place, ostensibly to make contact with the leaders of this world. But in reality, the mission was punishment for Mogorr wowpling half the Sire's brood and then telling anyone who would listen. If she'd had even a bit more discretion, they wouldn't have been forced to spend the last two-twelves rotations crawling across the galaxy to get to this backwater world—a world so unimportant that, even if they were successful, their careers were effectively falzed.

And now, while Gorrmog had been relieving herself, Mogorr had collected a specimen to begin the contact process, but a *quadruped*!

Gorrmog kluthed toward her brood sister, snarfled her on the pralt. "Why did you think that *this* creature might help us to establish ties with this world? It only has four legs! How smart can it be?" The smell finally reached Gorrmog and her antennae spornted. "Put it in the containment device. And disinfect the area."

Gorrmog snorgled at her brood sister's apologetic droop and turned to go back to the command frame, but there among the feces, the quick glint of metal caught her eye. She kluthed to the pile and settled herself down on all twelves, bringing her eye close to it. She reached in carefully with the thinnest of her tentacles — Mogorr made a disgusted flarth — and pulled out a tiny, perfect ring of metal. She held it up in the light briefly before she grabbed the tail of the specimen and lifted it — the quadruped whimpered weakly — comparing the size and shape of the ring to the animal's anus.

Mogorr knocked her brood sister aside and grabbed the quadruped by its collar, hoisting it up so she could look it in the eye. A tentacle shot out of the creature's mouth and hit Mogorr in the eye. She winced, dropping the creature. The quadruped whined.

Gorrmog turned the metal ring slowly, watching it twinkle in the light.

"Mogorr," Gorrmog said, "never mind making contact. We're

going to be rich."

Ragnarök-n-Roll: A Story of Pre-cod-nition
By David Boop

Ironically enough, the end of the world started with a joke at my retirement party from the World Oceanic Research Foundation.

Trudi, my right-hand and heir apparent greeted me at the door to our local hangout, *Compay's*. I stood in the entranceway for a moment, taking in the air rich with Cuban spices, warm bread and beer. WORF used it as their happy hour hangout and the owners gave us free use of their back room for meetings and such.

"Jahn, are you ready for this? They've been drinking for an hour already. I can make an excuse…"

I'd worked at WORF for thirty-five years, and I just couldn't get the energy to drag my sorry, sagging butt to work with the same zeal anymore. I wanted to watch the Florida Key sunsets off my patio with tall drinks and not worry about waking to an alarm clock. I had enough of traveling to dozens of oceanic-themed press conference, whaling protest or conventions on global warming year after year.

And yet, choosing to leave after so long made me feel like a warrior being carried off the field of battle for the last time. I'd fashioned my own longboat and asked to be burned at sea. The ones to roast me would be my loving team of computer techs, chemists, oceanographers…

and her.

"Jahn?"

Trudi's concern for my well-being would be the one thing I'd miss. Despite a twenty-year difference, or maybe because of it, she had always been protective of me. She bit the inside of her chubby cheeks. Trudi's hair was a mass of tight mahogany curls and her eyes twinkled like Santa's number one elf.

I harbored fantasies of waiting until I was no longer her boss to ask her out but, truth be told, her caring nature probably came from a desire to help the elderly, and I didn't want to embarrass myself.

I looked over to where the "Best Wishes!" balloons and ""We'll Miss You!" banners hung.

"Yeah, I'll be fine. As long as no one sings, 'Happy Trails,' I should survive this."

I'm really not *that* old. I'd pulled the pin early, at age fifty-five. I had investments that would supplement my pension, and I wanted to enjoy retirement while I still had any energy left to get in trouble with. The hope that trouble would involve Trudi was as much fantasy as Nessie and narwhals.

Trudi poked out her bottom lip, a sure sign she had more bad news.

"What?" I asked.

Her cheeks flushed. "I tried to talk them out of it."

"What? Talk them out of what?"

"Your gift. Just pretend you like it. Please! They said they've been waiting years to give somebody one."

My voice raised a little. "One what?"

She bounced up and down on her heels and scrunched her face. "Ewwww. I promised not to tell! Now, just come along and forget I said anything." Trudi wrapped herself around my arm and dragged me forward, oblivious to my repeated, "What? Tell me!"

It would be two hours, too many shots and a drunken debate over where Atlantis was, before I learned of my fate.

"Well," began Ferdinand, the lead IT guy at WORF, "since you're such a bleeding heart liberal… and you'd never be caught dead hunting or *fishing*…we'd wanted to give you a trophy for your wall at the old folk's home."

"Funny."

Several team members reached under a table and pulled out a big, wrapped package. Its ovular shape and bulbous front left me fearing the worst. When I pulled the paper off, there it was in all its tacky glory, the king of late night commercials:

Marlin, the Singing Fish.

Jesus! Did they still make those? Hadn't they gone the way of mullets in the Nineties? An oversized plastic bass with unrealistic eyes and a large mouth, he looked less a trophy fish and more like a child's pool toy. While I stared at my present, someone reached behind him to flip on his switch. The song could be heard over the cacophonous noise of the bar, even with local games on.

Oooga, chucka! Ooga, ooga, ooga chucka! I-I-I'm hooked on a feeling!

I wept internally. On the outside, though, I gave a full-belly laugh, one of my best performances since that time my rich uncle came over and told fart jokes all night. I thanked everyone profusely.

Other, more sentimental gifts followed and at the end of the night, I received a lingering hug from Trudi that I could swear might have turned into a kiss had my requested cab not arrived.

I stumbled through my front door, arms laden with packages and only made it to the couch before passing out. About an hour later, I shot up in stark-raving confusion when the sounds of Marlin went off unexpectedly.

Oooga, chucka! Ooga, ooga, ooga chucka! I-I-I'm hooked on a feeling!

I frantically pushed away beef and cheese packs, framed awards and other gifts until all items pressing against Marlin's trigger fell away. Silence pleasantly returned, and I made my way to bed.

The glass of tomato juice sitting on the counter wouldn't cut through my hangover any better than coffee, tea or vodka would. Still, I drank it with my daily pills; cholesterol, blood pressure, multivitamins, until they were all gone. I moved to the living room where all my retirement gifts lay strewn about. Marlin waited for me in the epicenter of the chaos.

I slowly placed the mementos received in various spots about my small, simple beach house; an A-frame with a loft just big enough for a dresser and a bed. I saw it more as a base of operations with the world's oceans as my home. Plus, working for a non-profit meant long days for a tiny take-home check. This is what thirty-five years of trying to save the planet got you. I could've gotten a job in corporate America, but why? Just to work my ass off for someone else's bottom line? Not for me.

It'd been smart to avoid romancing Trudi if all I had to offer was a body going to seed and a pup-tent's worth of house.

Oh, and a singing toy. What to do with it? One of my former co-workers might come by to visit and the damnable thing should be on display somewhere.

I picked him... isn't surprising how quickly people personify things? Well, I picked him, it, the fish... up and pressed the button accidentally. Not only did Marlin sing, but his tail flapped and his face twisted to look right at me.

Oooga, chucka! Ooga, ooga, ooga chucka! I-I-I'm hooked on a feeling!

I couldn't help but chuckle. Yes, it was cheap theatrics, but Marlin got to me. I remember laughing at the stupid Kung-Fu hamsters and "Who let the dogs out?" dogs, too. They're cute, at first, until they've been played for the millionth time. I figured that living alone would mean Marlin would rarely get pressed, so what the hell? I'd hang him in the living room.

I found a spot to mount my "catch" and after pounding in the nails and checking to make sure he was straight, I stepped back to look at my handiwork. I pressed him once more, thinking it'd be the last song for some time.

Marlin surprised me.

Go! Go, Johnny Go! Go, go, go, Johnnie B. Goode!

That was different. I had no idea that Marlin knew other songs. I pressed him again and out came Blue Suede's "Hooked" once more. Johnnie B. Goode seemed an odd choice to program in, seeing as it had no fishing theme. Maybe Ferdinand in IT figured out a way to rewrite the programming since my name was Jahn. I vaguely remember one of techs making a slurred, "Jahnnie be good!" comment as he was leaving Compay's.

After a couple presses, I couldn't trigger the additional song. Luckily, the recordings were short clips; ten seconds at the most. I decided whatever activated the second song must only happen occasionally. I left Marlin hanging and went about my day.

It must have been about midnight... No, I'm sure it was 12:15 A.M. when I awoke from a deep sleep to the agonizing off-key stylings of Marlin. In my drowsy state, it didn't immediately register that my crooner wasn't serenading me with Blue Suede, nor Chuck Berry. As I went down the stairs, the tune became clearer and as I stood in front of Marlin, my anger became befuddlement.

Marlin the animatronic fish sang...

It's the end of the world as we know it. It's the end of the world as we know it. It's the end of the world as we know it. And I feel fine.

Good thing he felt fine, because I was freaking out.

◇◇◇

I called Trudi that morning, timed to the second she was sat down at her desk with her non-fat grande chai sprinkled with cinnamon.

"You could have warned me."

"Jahn?" Caught off guard, she fumbled for words. "I'm sorry. Warned you about what?"

"That the singing fish was only the beginning of the joke."

She giggled. "Oh, that thing is awful, isn't it?"

"Awful? Try infuriating! He goes off at all hours of the night, Trudi. What did they do? Put a timer in him? Set it for Oh, God-Thirty?"

The line went quiet as Trudi, I assumed, deciphered my rant. "No, I don't think… Well, I don't know if they did anything like that. How upsetting! I'd hate to be woken to that hideous song."

Either she was completely in the dark, or a better liar on the phone than she was in person.

"It's more than one song, hon. I've heard three."

"Really? That's strange. The box didn't say anything like that when I picked it u—" I could almost see her eyes darting around her desk as she tried to decide if she could backpedal out of her slip of tongue. "I mean, when I picked it up at the bar the other night."

"*You*? You bought this thing?"

I visualized the rush of heat to her cheeks as embarrassment set in. "Yes, I mean, no, I mean, I went and bought it at the store, but it was their idea. I tried to talk them out of it. I really did!"

I took a long, deep, audible breath to calm myself. "Where did you get him, Trudi? I doubt the store will accept a return if he's been tampered with, but he's starting to creep me out."

"I really don't think they tampered with it, and we meant only the best. You know we all love you here."

We? How about you? I thought.

Trudi's disappointment resonated through the line. Did rejecting Marlin mean I was rejecting her?

"Fine. But I'm pulling the batteries and he'll just sit there until someone asks me to push the damn button. Then *they'll* get to take Marlin home."

She giggled again and we talked about the meteor shower happening that night. I bit my lip to keep from inviting her over, knowing she'd have her hands full at WORF.

We'd been tracking it for six months. I decided to leave right before the event to give Trudi's new regime legitimacy. Most of the meteors would land in the sea, which is why WORF would be on the ground floor for it. My colleagues and I had already launched tracking buoys along the coast, checking temperatures, watching for sponge migrations and the like.

Yes, that was the glamorous life I left for retirement.

I went to Marlin, screwdriver in pocket, ready to do the deed. Oddly, he looked scared as I approached him. He startled *me* half to death when he belted out…

It's a mistake. It's a mis-take!

When my heart stopped racing, I admonished him. "Men at Work, Marlin? Really? And not even one of their better songs."

Be good, be good. Be good, be good. Be good, Johnnie.

I never figured the mouth of madness would be a large mouth bass.

I looked around. Web cams? Had they planned this for a while? How could they have gotten in? Did I give anyone my keys at the party? No, I'd taken the cab to and from there, so I'd left all but my house key home. Still, I supposed, someone could have lifted it and stole away while the party ensued.

"Okay, fellows. Enough is enough. I'm not big on the whole 'punking' thing. Little too old."

I think we're alone now. There doesn't seem to be anyone a-round.

I glared. "The Tiffany version? You could have least given me Tommy James.

Marlin sang, *I Think We're Alone Now* an octave lower.

I put my hands on my hips. "Now I know this is a joke! Come on out, turn off the cams. I expect this will be on YouTube tomorrow, but I'm done. I'm pulling the plug."

I went for the fish, despite protests that what I intended to do was indeed a mistake. I de-batteried Marlin in no time flat. I set him down on an end-table, relieved that the joke was over. I plopped into a chair and exhaled.

My eyes moved slowly to where Marlin lay as, once again, he broke into song.

It's the end of the world as we know it. It's the end of the world as we know it. It's the end of the world as we know it, and I feel fine.

I checked the still empty battery compartment. I looked all over for a secondary compartment. Nothing.

I am not dead yet. I can dance and I can sing. I am not dead yet. I can do the Highland Fling.

Fuck! He knows show tunes. This could get bad.

Staying Alive. Staying Alive. Ah, ha, ha, ha. Staying Aliveeee!

I held my head in my hand. "Okay, now I've gone daft. No way this is really happening."

And I can't fight this feeling anymore. I've forgotten what I started fighting for.

I looked at him. "And what would you expect me to do now?"

Listen to your heart when he's calling for you. Listen to your heart when there's nothing else you can do.

I died. That's the only explanation. I died from alcohol poisoning the other night. Or maybe I *had* taken my car. Maybe I'd plowed into a family of four and this was *my* hell; sitting in my house, for all eternity, talking to a singing fish. The Chinese have lots of hells. Singing fish had to be right under living with your mother-in-law forever.

It's the end of the world—

"Yes! Yes. I know. End of the world. Got it. And just how do you suppose it's going to end?"

Touch me. How can it be? Believe me. The sun always shines on TV.

"The television? You'd like me to turn on the telly, Mr. Fishy?"

Apparently there were no lyrics short enough to sing just "yes" so Marlin sat there glass-eyed and motionless.

I sighed. If I was going to go mad, I might as well commit to it. I ran a hand through my graying hair and reached for the TV remote.

Still being early enough, I caught one of the morning shows in progress.

"Thanks for that update, Sheila. Bob? What can we expect from the weather today?"

The adorable and perky hostess was replaced by a fat man; still perky, but not adorable.

"Well, we can expect clear skies and moderate temperatures, which will be great for you meteor watchers tonight. There will not be a bad view anywhere this side of the Mississippi as they safely burn up in the atmosphere, except for a few which are predicted to hit the waters off the Florida Keys."

I glanced over at Marlin.

"So, the meteors. That's what's going to end the world."

You got the right stuff... baby!

Arg! God save me from singing fish that know the lyrics to boy band songs!

"Okay, Marlin. I'll bite."

Nothing.

I raised an eyebrow. "What you're the only one that can do bad puns?"

You got the right stuff... baby!

So, Marlin figured out a way to say yes. An annoying way.

"So, what's going to happen, o' sage of the sea? Will the oceans rise? Will the atmosphere burn? A cloud of steam will cover the Earth and send us back to another ice age?"

Children of the Sun! Children of the Sun!

"You're talking— singing— nonsense. We've been tracking the data for size, strike patterns, everything. There is no way we missed anything. *I* didn't miss anything!"

You had to be a big shot, didn'tcha?

My cheeks flushed. "Yes. I did. This was my baby… originally. I did all the preliminary work." I walked around, lecturing Marlin. "Sure, I may have left in the fourth quarter, but I left it very capable hands. I just… Well, I was done. I didn't see what more I could do. I *knew* what I couldn't take. Not anymore."

She blinded me with science. Science!

"What? Who?"

Secret lovers, that's what you are.

"Huh? Are you talking about Trudi? Are you trying to tell me I've been distracted by her and missed something? What? What did I miss?"

Marlin broke into a medley of songs with rock in their lyrics, starting with *It's Still Rock and Roll to Me* and ending with *You Can Still Rock in America.*

"So, either there is something off with the meteors, or you want to audition for American Idol."

You got the right stuff... baby!

"Fine. What's wrong with the meteors? Something in their composition? Something hidden?"

Children of the Sun! Children of the Sun!

I didn't know the song, so I jumped onto the computer and searched.

Children of the Sun was a 1979 song album by Billy Thorpe about…

"An alien invasion?"

You got the right stuff... baby!

"You're out of you little plastic mind. We have been looking for extraterrestrial life for decades. Thousands of us. Scientists all over the globe. There's no way we, as a species, would miss an impending alien invasion. Not in this day and age. Not with all the movies out about just such a thing."

I walked around the room. It was impossible, of course. But then, so was Marlin. Could something about the composition of the meteors hide an alien fleet?

My madness had taken a whole new direction. I wonder when I really snapped? They say the signs are subtle. I suppose singing fish are better than gunning down your office mates. I should be happy. Maybe the nuthouse will even let me bring Marlin with me.

I slapped my face, as if to wake up.

"Okay. Enough!" I pointed at Marlin. "I'm tossing *you* in the trash, after smashing you to bits, then I'm going down to the ER to be tested. Clearly, I'm chemically imbalanced. Yes, too much serotonin. I'm dreaming while awake. Or maybe that's melatonin? Can't keep the two straight. If the doctors can't find anything wrong physically, I'm going to have a nice long talk with a psychologist."

I grabbed my keys, hefted Marlin under an arm and made my way to the garage.

Cool the engines. Shut this rocket down!

"Nope, I'm done having imaginary conversations with a soothsaying salmon."

Oohwoo! Take the Trudi and run. Oh, Lord! Oohwoo! Take the Trudi and run!

I stopped. I blinked. I didn't hear that accurately, did I? He sang "take the *money* and run," right?

I held him up and looked him square in the eye.

"What did you say?"

You better run all day and run all night.

Pink Floyd seemed appropriate at that juncture. Special mushrooms in the mushroom brioche the other night would explain this bad trip.

"No, that's not what you just said, was it?"

I'm gonna run to you. Cause when the feelin's right I'm gonna **run** *all night. I'm gonna run to you.*

"No, and for the record, I fucking *hate* Bryan Adams. You need to do that bit again. Come now. Sing it. *Oohwoooooo…*" I dangled the sound waiting for Marlin to pick up the chorus. "*Oohwoooooo…*"

Nothing. I reached for the pegboard where a large assortment of tools hung. I sang, "*Stop! Hammer time!*"

Take the Trudi and run. Oh Lord.

Oh, lord was right.

Trudi wouldn't leave. She barely looked at me as she worked the buoy tracker like a game of *Missile Command*.

"Jahn, this is crazy. The meteors are going to cross the thermosphere in less than two hours. I'm taking calls from the press, monitoring field agents. Honestly, why you left before this is beyond me. They need you out there."

"They need me, or you need me? I know I need you."

She furrowed her brow, as if she hadn't heard me quite right. "What?"

"I need you."

Trudi looked up at me, her face awash with confusion and hopefulness.

Blushing, I admitted, "I love you and I want you to leave with me right now."

Reality took a hold of her again. My former assistant kicked her chair back and got in my face.

"Jahn, now's a fine time to be saying that! Are you trying to make me look like a fool? If we drop the ball on this, WORF will lose its grant. Maybe that's okay for you, you're out of here, but this is still my life and regardless of my feelings for you, I can't ju— mhff."

I kissed her.

I held her and kissed her until she kissed me back.

She came up for air. "But, Jahn…"

I kissed her again until she stopped arguing with me. Considering that most of the women in my life until that point had been dalliances, I had no way to accurately judge my romantic abilities, but with my back against the wall, I put everything I had into that kiss. I told her with my body, my heart, how I felt. Trudi responded in kind and when we finally broke away, I'd somehow hypnotized her.

"This," Trudi stammered, "This is crazy. I can't believe I'm even considering leaving."

"There are worse things than going crazy."

I lead her away from reality and into my madness. She only paused when I opened the back door of my car.

See, Marlin had called shotgun.

Trudi still hadn't bought into my "medium" catch by the time we cleared the city. So, Marlin and I showed her our act.

"Say 'Hello' to Trudi, Marlin."

Hello. Is it me you're waiting for?

"What day of the week is it, fish buddy?"

Wednesday always seems too blue.

"What's happening tonight?"

It's the end of the world as we know it.

"By the…?"

Children of the Sun! Children of the Sun!

"But how?" Trudi asked.

I shrugged. "Someone, maybe aliens tapped into his circuitry to warn me, us, I don't know. Spirit of a karaoke singer possessed my retirement gift? Doesn't matter. I stopped caring a while ago.

Marlin seems to have our best interests at heart, gills, fins, whatever."

I drove like a madman while my fish-guru spouted off songs that were more cryptic than helpful.

Head out on the highway.

"Yes, but which highway?"

I can't drive... 95!!!

"Cute."

For example, Marlin made me cut off two SUVs and a tractor trailer when he gave a sudden proclamation, *Right! You're bloody-well right!*

Trudi screamed as we missed the semi's bumper by an inch.

"Can you give me a warning next time? Like, 'The Tide is high,' or something?"

How quickly I'd been sucked into thinking like him. What had Marlin unlocked? I risked everything to save her, she risked everything to let me. I had no idea what lay at the end of this yellow brick road... an emerald city or a padded cell?

Trudi said, "Jahn, you've changed so much in forty-eight hours. What happened?"

I didn't answer. It took me two more exits before I could vocalize my thoughts.

"Marlin somehow knew the type of man I wanted to be. I could never sit idly by on a patio drinking mojitos and watching sunsets. I joined WORF to effect change, to save the oceans and, in turn, save all of us. Marlin found that in me that when I'd apparently lost sight of it."

Trudi petted Marlin's head. "Thank you, Marlin, or whoever. You do know though, if this is some sort of joke, I'll smash you to bits, torch those bits and then pee on them, understand me?"

You've got me understanding. You've really helped me see.

"Jahn, he does a better Seger than you."

"Funny."

Dusk had fallen by the time we finally pulled up to the beach Marlin directed us to. Hundreds of cars lined the roads, the parking lots and even down on the sand. All had been abandoned as indicated by their haphazard parking. We left ours and hoofed it to where nearly four hundred people gathered.

They accounted for almost all races, ages, sexes and social-economic standings. We all had only one thing in common; the items we cradled lovingly in our hands.

There were Marlins by the dozens. Also Kung-Fu hamsters, Rockin' Santas, singing cacti, and a plethora of others. Whatever reached out to us had chosen only the single most insane way to do it. It would take a special sort of idiot to believe a clairvoyant animatronics.

I said as much to Trudi.

"Or genius. You have to have a great deal of creativity and imagination to figure out the truth."

"So, all these people are geniuses?"

One person held a Kung-Fu hamster aloft and yelled, "Command me, Lord!"

Trudi winced. "Well, maybe not all."

The three of us made our way to the wharf. Many had kicked off their shoes and let the cool waters wash through their toes. Trudi and I followed suit.

I turned Marlin around.

"What now, buddy?"

Born to be kings, we are the princes of the universe!

The ground shook, the waters parted like Moses and the Red Sea. Sand slid away to reveal a stone path that led down. Luminescent fish swam up to the water walls and lighted the way into the darkness below.

"Jahn!" Trudi exclaimed, "It looks just like the Bimini Road; the one someone," she elbowed me, "theorized might be remnants of Atlantis."

"Hey, I was drunk. When I get drunk I think everything leads to Atlantis. I never expected aliens or whatever to be hiding at the bottom of the ocean all this time."

"Or maybe there is a city down there with some sort of defense mechanism to protect the human race in case of global disaster."

Our people, the last of humanity to walk the face of the earth, moved down the path, guided by unseen forces. They descended, but I held back, speculating what wonders awaited us down there. If I was truly insane, heading down that stone path meant never returning to reality or normalcy ever again.

Trudi saw my hesitation and slipped an arm through mine. "Are you ready?"

To hell with it. Reality was overrated.

"Not quite yet."

I kissed her as unbroken meteors by the thousands pierced the troposphere and then turned ninety degrees to head toward all the major cities of the world.

Because your kiss, your kiss is on my list.

We paused long enough to say, "Shut up, Marlin."

Book II

Conspiracy

My name is Gordon Dale. I'm sure you recognize the name. For many years, I hosted the morning show at WGRT, Channel 6. During the late 1980's, I was voted Pittsburgh's favorite on-air morning personality for three consecutive years. Thousands of viewers started off their day watching, *Have a GRT Morning*. I was a celebrity in the tri-state area, recognized wherever I went. People were always stopping me; at the grocery store, at the movie theater, at Steelers games, and gala charity events; eager to let me know how much they enjoyed my show. Things were good for Gordon Dale, that is, until one five-minute interview segment changed everything.

Remembering back, there was nothing unusual about the segment. A local technology firm was concerned about the scarcity of young people pursuing careers in science and engineering, and I interviewed the company's marketing director about some initiative they were sponsoring. If memory serves, Victor Brunner's company was offering some sort of scholarship to a deserving high school senior.

Immediately after signing off, I left the studio and hurried back to my office—as I always did—eager to work my way through the local newspapers and the USA Today in search of viable interview topics that might prove useful in future editions of the program. On this particular day, however, I found Victor Brunner, the man I'd just interviewed, waiting for me outside my office door.

"May I have a moment of your time, Mr. Dale?" Brunner said. He was a tall man, rail thin, with close-cropped hair that was starting to go gray. His clothes seemed to hang on him. He was, in my opinion, badly in need of a tailor.

My first inclination on seeing this odd gray man lurking outside my office door was to call Security and berate whoever had been stupid enough to allow a program guest to wander through the halls unescorted. But I smiled at Victor Brunner instead. After all, he represented one of the region's largest technology firms, and I had my well-deserved reputation for cordiality to consider.

"Please, come in," I said with a jaunty wave of my arm, "and I'm sorry, remind me again of your name."

In answer, Victor Brunner handed me his business card. I noted that, in addition to his position as marketing director, Brunner was also affiliated with Carnegie-Mellon University, a local hotbed of science and technology. And below all the other print on the business card, in bold-face type, an intriguing single word was embossed into the card. "Entrepreneur," it said.

"Well now," I said, settling down into my comfortable leather chair. "What's this all about, Mr. Brunner? I'm afraid I only have only a few minutes to spare. They keep me pretty darned busy around here, and I have an important program meeting to attend in just the next few minutes." I glanced at my watch to reinforce the point.

"Oh, don't worry," Victor Brunner said. "This won't take much *time* at all." He chuckled nervously, as if he'd just made a little joke. Brunner seemed jumpy, even more nervous then he'd been in front of the television cameras. "I can assure you with one-hundred-percent-certainty, Mr. Dale, that when we are finished talking, you will be glad we spoke."

He sat down in the chair across from my desk, and I noticed that he was carrying a black leather valise which he struggled to slide next to his chair. The case appeared to be quite heavy.

"You might be wondering how I can be one-hundred-percent certain of your future happiness, Mr. Dale," Brunner said. "Well, the honest truth is, I can be certain of that happiness, because I've seen it first-hand."

I smelled a sales pitch coming and cringed in anticipation. Victor Brunner was no salesman, that much I was certain of. He had all the natural charisma of a rock. His presentation was smarmy and stilted, and as I've said, his clothes didn't fit.

Before I could raise an objection, Brunner stood and hefted the black leather case onto the surface of my desk. The case fairly bristled with padlocks, three of them. Two of the padlocks opened with a key, and the third was a combination lock. Brunner began enthusiastically spinning the dial on the combination lock while I attempted to repair the damage he'd done to my carefully stacked pile of newspapers.

"Mr. Dale, I am here today to present you with a unique opportunity, an opportunity to change the world as we know it." Oh my God, I thought, Victor Brunner is one of those dreamy-eyed, academic do-gooders, probably some kind of ecological nutcase. Carnegie-Mellon was full of them at the time.

Brunner snapped off the first of the locks, and leaned forward over the top of his valise. He caught me staring at the lock, and snatched it off my desk, stuffing it into the pocket of his sports coat. He was speaking in a whisper now. "For the past twenty years, I have been working with the world's foremost scientific minds, tackling one of the most perplexing questions ever to confront mankind."

Nutcase, I thought again. I leaned forward in my chair and began inching my hand toward the phone, thinking that I might need to call Security at any moment.

Brunner went on. "The pursuit of this intriguing question started out as hobby for our little group, an exercise in mental gymnastics, a lark really." He laughed like some kind of gawky shorebird. "But you know how scientists are, Mr. Dale. Eventually wagers were made, and soon our little question was all anyone could talk about."

Brunner reached into the breast pocket of his jacket, and when the hand emerged, it was clutching a key ring with two small keys. The fob was gold and etched with a mysterious insignia; three ancient-looking, incomprehensible runes.

"Let me be honest with you, Mr. Dale," Brunner said. "I am no intellectual match for the other members of the group. Frankly, I'm not even sure why I was asked to join, except that I have the unique ability to get things done. I am a can-do person, Mr. Dale."

"I can certainly see that," I said a little nervously, "and it sounds like you've put together a real crackerjack team of scientists there, Mr. Brunner. Now I'm afraid I..."

"Crackerjack, oh I'll say," Brunner said. I noticed for the first time that he had the faintest vestiges of a foreign accent, "I can assure you that our group encompasses a wide range of scientific and engineering disciplines. Werner Von Braun insisted on that. He was one of the founders of the group."

I must have given Brunner a strange look, because he said, "Werner Von Braun, the rocket scientist, Mr. Dale? Of course, you're familiar with Von Braun's work with NASA."

Once Brunner mentioned rockets, of course I remembered Von Braun. "Yes," I said, and then added emphatically, "NASA."

"And Carl Sagan," Brunner said.

"The guy on *The Tonight Show*?" I said incredulously.

Carl Sagan, who'd hosted a successful science program on PBS—if there really *is* such a thing as a successful program on PBS––was a frequent guest on *The Tonight Show*. Johnny Carson was always mocking Sagan's drawn-out New England accent, and the way he had of saying, "Billions and billions."

"That's the guy," Brunner said brightly. The tempo of his speech had begun to accelerate, his hand gestures growing ever more frenetic. It reminded me of a coal train starting down a long grade without any brakes.

He pounded on the top of the leather case with an open palm and held out the key ring. "The contents of this valise are so important that they must be protected with two different varieties of lock. Even if someone were to pilfer the keys, or take them from me by force, there would still be the combination lock to contend with and vice versa."

I nodded. "Couldn't someone just cut a hole in the bottom of the case, Mr. Brunner?" It seemed quite obvious to me at the time.

Brunner chuckled as he opened the last of the three locks. He thumped the side of the case with a tightly clenched fist. It made a dull, leatherine thud.

"Mr. Dale," Brunner said. "The skeleton of this case is constructed of the latest space-age titanium alloys. You couldn't break into this case even with a laser."

Although I didn't have a laser, I was still skeptical. I let my hands drift back to my desk, allowing my left hand to rest squarely on the telephone handset.

"Mr. Dale, I see no reason to keep you in the dark any longer," Brunner snapped the top of his case open. "I have earth shattering news for you." He dangled the final lock in front of my face like a hypnotist. "My associates and I have unlocked the secrets of time travel."

Instinctively, my hand wrapped around the telephone receiver. Brunner saw it.

"Wait," he screamed out, reaching forward frantically. "I can prove it."

I'm not sure why I didn't pick up the telephone. Maybe it was all those science fiction programs I'd watched as a young boy or maybe it was my intellectual curiosity, but whatever the reason, for the briefest of instants, I allowed myself to consider the ridiculous possibility that Brunner might be telling me the truth. My odd guest must have detected the glint in my eye, because he withdrew his hand away from mine.

"Think of it, Mr. Dale," he said. "Being able to move effortlessly through time, knowing what's about to happen before it actually does. Think of the incredible advantage such a thing could provide a person in your position; actually knowing what tomorrow's big News story will be today. You could arrange to be at the site of every momentous event. Your journalistic instinct would be faultless."

I had to admit it; the notion appealed to me. I'd begun my television career as a news reporter, and even done a two-year stint at the anchor desk before being relegated to *Have a GRT Morning*. Since my demotion, I'd resigned myself to the fact that I'd never be able to work my way into the news end of the business again, but Victor Brunner's improbable revelation struck me like a sunbeam breaking through a leaden sky; providing an unexpected ray of hope.

"Consider the ancillary benefits for a moment," Brunner said. "Want to know which stocks are going to increase a thousand-fold in value next year? Want to know who will win the Kentucky Derby, the World Series, the Super Bowl? You must admit, the possibilities are positively captivating."

Something about Brunner's presence, his breathless voice, his darting, electric eyes, his squirming fingers and flailing hands, mesmerized me. I forgot completely about the ill-fitting clothes, and found myself daydreaming about the myriad of possibilities an entirely certain future might provide. Absurd, I know, but I couldn't stop myself.

My reverie was interrupted by the appearance of Chuck Mellenak. Chuck was the director of *Have a GRT Morning*, and he miraculously appeared in my office doorway, which is to say, he'd probably been standing there for quite some time, and I just hadn't noticed him. Instead of offering one of his usual derisive remarks, Chuck just stood there, mute, outlined by the door frame. He wore a ghostlike smile.

That's when realization hit me like a baseball bat. "Chuck, you sleazy bastard," I thundered, waggling my finger at him. "I know what the hell you're up to." (Back in the Eighties, you could still speak your mind in the office without being sent to Human Resources for sensitivity training.) "You may think you've pulled the goddamn wool over my eyes, but you haven't."

Obviously, Chuck had put Brunner up to this whole sham performance in order to make a fool of me, something he attempted to do on a daily basis. At the sound of my voice, Chuck disappeared from my open doorway, and I had to lean out beyond the edge of my desk to shout at his rapidly retreating form. "Coward," I screamed. "Asshole." Then I turned my attention back to Brunner.

"I'm afraid I'm wise to your little scam, Mr. Brunner," I said amiably. "You're a friend of Chuck's, aren't you? Come on, fess up."

It occurred to me that Chuck was a CMU graduate— something he lauded over me whenever he got the chance—and Brunner's business card had noted an affiliation with the university. The guy is probably with Carnegie-Mellon's School of Drama, I thought, but Brunner regarded me with incredulity, like *I* was the one who'd escaped from the asylum.

"I'm afraid I'm not familiar with anyone who goes by the name of... Chuck," he said, "unless you're talking about Chuck Yeager, the test pilot. He was a member of our group for a while. We had intended to allow Yeager to make the first to journey into the time-space continuum—a brilliant P.R. move, my idea really— but with all the production delays and the bickering between scientists, I'm afraid Yeager became discouraged and left our group. He is a man of action, after all."

"Chuck Yeager?" I chortled. "Who are you trying to kid? I didn't just fall off the turnip truck, you know?"

Brunner leaned his long, thin frame across my desk until our noses were nearly touching. "That's good," he said in a near whisper, sneering like a serpent. "You view the world with a certain amount of skepticism. You refuse to accept matters at face value. That could prove extremely valuable."

He jumped to his feet. "Mr. Dale, it's quite clear to me that you are a 'show me' sort of person, and therefore, I am prepared to offer you a little demonstration." Brunner caught the edge of my office door with a wing-tipped toe and swung it closed. "I'm afraid, however, I must insist on complete privacy before proceeding any further." He took a step toward the closed door, and snapped the deadbolt shut. All right Chuck, I thought, let's see how you're going to play this thing out. I meant Chuck Mellenak, not Chuck Yeager.

Brunner began glancing around the walls of my office, obviously looking for something. "That lamp there," he said, pointing to a green-shaded banker's lamp that decorated one corner of my desk. "Do you have any idea how many amps of current it draws?"

The question threw me off-guard and all I could think to say was, "It's a seventy-five watt bulb, I think."

"Seventy-five watts," Brunner repeated thoughtfully and glanced over my head. He pursed his lips as if he was doing mathematical calculations. "That *should* be fine. I don't want to blow any circuit breakers, and as you can imagine, my power consumption needs are fairly substantial."

He pulled the yellow end of what looked like an electrical extension cord from his case, and plugged it into the wall outlet on the far side of my desk. From inside the valise, a low, throbbing hum began. Brunner smiled at the sound, which gradually grew in volume. The case began to pulse and creak, and there was a rattling noise that reminded me of a kid's toy drum. I believe my desk lamp dimmed slightly. After a few moments of this racket, a thin bell sounded, just once, like one of those wind-up oven timers.

"The device is ready," Brunner announced. He took out a pair of stereo headphones, heavy-duty ones, and clapped them onto his head.

"Where's the cord on those headsets?" I said.

"No cord needed," Brunner answered. "These are wireless headphones. We designed them to utilize the latest infrared technology."

"Yeah, right," I scoffed. "Wireless infrared headphones. Who's ever heard of such a thing?"

Despite the preposterous cordless headphones, Brunner seemed intent on playing his practical joke out to its inevitable end. His enthusiasm for his role had not flagged one little bit, in fact, if anything, he became even more possessed by manic energy. He reached into the mysterious case, and his hand began spinning phantom dials and flipping switches. I rose to my feet, trying to see what he was doing, but Brunner slammed the lid closed before I could catch a glimpse of anything inside.

"I'm afraid I can't let you see the guts of the thing," he said. "It's all highly hush-hush." He blanketed his lanky form over the top of the valise and did not move. It seemed pointless to remain standing, so I sat back down and once I did, Brunner settled back into his chair as well and adjusted his headphones.

"I will not lie to you," he said. "There is a certain amount of danger involved in time travel, especially for novice chrononauts. Fortunately, I am quite accomplished at the techniques by now, so there is almost no danger of my arms or other appendages flying off." He laughed as if he'd just made a little joke, which I guess he had. I marveled at just how earnest Victor Brunner seemed. He was definitely giving the performance of his life.

"I won't even try to explain the theory to you," he said, "except to say that it has something to do with the wormholes that connect different sections of the time-space continuum. You see Mr. Dale, all times, past and future, occur simultaneously, occupying space in different dimensions in the fabric of time."

Brunner re-opened the top of the case and reached a hand into the shadowed interior. A single clear tone—A above middle C, if I'm not mistaken—drowned out the other rumbling, clattering and whirring of the mechanism.

"Imagine your life as a run down a football field," Brunner said. "You're sprinting from one end zone to the next, from your birth to your death, but what you don't realize is that there are an infinite number of similar football fields above and below your own, each one slightly shifted, temporally. With this device, the chronoscope, I can travel through the wormholes that connect these different plains in time. I can move forward a hundred years into the future, or go back to last week depending on how far I travel in the wormholes."

"Wormholes," I said. "That's an interesting term."

"Yes. Isn't it though? I believe Stephen Hawking first coined the term. He's a member of our group, you know."

A Brief History of Time had been a best-seller just the year before, and while it wasn't the sort of book I would ever read, I was still aware of the book's existence and Hawking's reputation as a top scientist.

"Do you mean the guy in the wheelchair?" I said.

"Yes," Brunner hissed conspiratorially. He patted the now throbbing case. "How do you think he ended up in that wheelchair in the first place?" Brunner waved his hand impatiently. "But enough talk. Why don't we get on with a little practical demonstration of the device? How about if I jump ahead into the future? Would that convince you?"

He didn't wait for an answer, but reached into the case once more. The musical tone was pinched off, and a darker, more ominous one began. The deep, bass rumble grew in intensity, and soon I could feel it all the way down to my fillings. The mysterious leather and titanium case began to vibrate back and forth, pulsating so quickly I could barely follow its movements. The shaking became violent, blurring the edges of the chronoscope until they seemed to dissolve away. Brunner smiled as his eyes drifted shut.

Eventually, the movements of the chronoscope became so pronounced that the thing began walking across the surface of my desk of its own accord. It looked to be headed for a tumble to the floor when I reached out and grabbed it frantically. The moment my hand touched the case, vibrations traveled up my arm like a bolt of lightning. My arm shook so violently that I was afraid my elbow joint would shake loose. The vibrations traveled down my spine, and soon my legs, my feet, and even my toes were shaking like a rogue washing machine gone berserk.

Brunner's eyes popped open suddenly. "And I'm back," he said. The suitcase began to throttle down. All the whirring and wheezing and wobbling of the case ceased, and except for the odd feeling that I'd been running a jackhammer for eight hours, I felt fine. Victor Brunner took off the headsets and set them down on my desk.

"Hold on just a second," I said. I was reminded of that old magician's joke. "Want to see me disappear? (Blink.) Want to see it again?"

"You didn't go anywhere," I said. "You were right there in that chair the whole time."

"It might seem that way to you, in this time-space continuum," Brunner said, "but in fact, I moved three days into the future. I watched you do your show this coming Friday." He nodded amiably at me. "You did a nice job," he assured me.

I stood up, intent on throwing Brunner out of my office when he said, "I'm afraid I have some bad news for you, Mr. Dale, terrible news as a matter of fact. In three days' time, you will be involved in a serious car accident. You could be severely injured, possibly even killed." The revelation stopped me cold.

"I'm going to die in three days?" I said, completely flummoxed.

"I said you might *possibly* die, Mr. Dale. Even though I saw it happen in the future, that doesn't necessarily mean it will come to pass. Armed with this knowledge, you could, for example, take steps to prevent the crash from happening."

"Steps?" I said. "What kind of steps?"

"Well, you could call in sick on Friday, for example. You could lock yourself in your house, and refuse to get into an automobile for any reason."

A chill ran through me and shook me about as thoroughly as Brunner's chronoscope had. In my mind's eye, I saw the crash happen in slow motion, saw the broken glass, saw the blood, the crumpled metal, my damaged face. And then, reality hit me like a ton of bricks.

"Damn you, Chuck Mellenak," I said aloud. Suddenly, I knew *exactly* what was going on. The whole complicated deception became clear to me. Chuck didn't want me coming to work on Friday, and I knew exactly why.

The new head of our corporate News Division was scheduled to make his first visit to Pittsburgh on that day, and I'd been informed that he planned to watch *Have a GRT Morning* upon his arrival at the station. It would be his first chance to see me in action.

And it just so happened that Chuck's new girlfriend, a young, pretty, air-headed news reporter who'd been at the station less than a year, had recently been assigned as my back-up on the show. Whenever I went on vacation, or called in sick, Chuck's girlfriend would slide into my chair and take over the hosting duties. If I called in sick on Friday, *she* would be the one who got plopped into the host chair. The bigwig from corporate headquarters in Atlanta would get to meet *her* and not me, which would provide her the perfect opportunity to steal my show. That's how it works in television; miss one day on the job, and your entire broadcast career can end just that quickly.

"That's it," I said, jumping to my feet. "I've heard just about enough from you, sir. Leave my office, now." Victor Brunner seemed surprised at my sudden explosion. He began winding electrical cords hurriedly, and stuffing them back into his valise.

"I will be right here at work Friday morning," I shouted, "and both you and Chuck can take that to the goddamn bank." I pointed emphatically toward the door.

Brunner looked dismayed, perhaps even a bit frightened. "I'm begging you, Mr. Dale. Whatever you do, please be extremely careful this Friday, especially behind the wheel. Your life hangs in the balance, and we need you, Mr. Dale. The world needs you." And then, he was gone.

That Friday afternoon, on my way home from the station, a fast-moving Camaro ran a red light and t-boned me at an intersection. My car was totaled. Fortunately, I saw the Camaro approaching in my peripheral vision, and instantly recognized that the car was not going to stop. Instead of hitting the brakes, I stomped hard on the accelerator and the car hit me in the rear quarter panel, avoiding a more direct collision with my door. The impact spun my vehicle one complete revolution through the intersection, and once the car came to rest, it burst into flames. Luckily, since my door had missed being damaged by inches, I was able to unclip my seatbelt and get out before my vehicle became engulfed in flames.

Once my heart started beating again, and I was officially pronounced unharmed, I had the police deposit me back at the television station. I rushed to my office and immediately began fumbling through the stack of newspapers on my desk, searching for Victor Brunner's business card. I couldn't seem to find it anywhere. Maybe I'd swept the card into the trash, I thought. I upended the wastebasket on the floor and began frantically sifting through the candy wrappers and interoffice memos, all without any luck. Then the phone rang.

"What do you think about the efficacy of time travel now, Mr. Dale?" It was Brunner.

"You heard about my car crash?" I said.

"Heard about it?" he said. "I was there."

"You were there?"

"Well, Mr. Dale. I knew when and where the crash would happen, so it was a simple matter to be in the area at the appointed time. I'm glad to see you survived."

The realization of what had just happened to me struck with roughly the same force as the Camaro. "You saved my life, Mr. Brunner," I said. "Without you, I guess I wouldn't even be here now."

"Oh, believe me," Brunner said with an off-hand laugh. "The future holds many a great things for Gordon Dale. Or should I say, Gordon Dale, network anchorman."

Maybe it was because of the car crash, but I found myself unable to speak.

"How about if I come by your house this evening," Victor Brunner suggested, "so we can discuss your incredible, shining place in America's future."

Just after sunset, there was a knock on the door of my townhouse. Victor Brunner stood out on the front porch dressed in casual attire, gray dress slacks several sizes too big for him and a golf shirt with the Oakmont Country Club logo sewn into the breast pocket. He was carrying the chronoscope with him, and the weight of the case caused his spindly frame to list badly to one side. He seemed anxious to get off the street, and hurried through my front door. As he set the case down in front of my couch, I noticed that all three locks were securely fastened again.

"I don't suppose you'd go for a drink," I said.

"Then you'd be mistaken," Brunner said, dead serious. I went to fix us both a martini.

"Are you a golfer, Mr. Brunner?" I asked, making small talk while I mixed the drinks.

"Oh, perhaps a bit of one," he said, with his oddly accented, somewhat lilting voice. "I am definitely a fan of the game, however."

I pointed at Brunner's shirt. "I've had the chance to play Oakmont course a time or two," I said as I slid in behind the bar in my living room. Oakmont Country Club is Pittsburgh's most venerable golf club. "Every year on Media Day, they allow some of us TV hacks out on the course to try our luck."

"How fortunate for you," Brunner said. "I've never actually had the opportunity to play the course. I picked up the shirt at the U.S. Open."

"When was that?" I said, straining my memory. "At least five years ago, wasn't it?"

"Oh, I'm not talking about the 1983 Open," Brunner said. "I attended the 1994 U.S. Open. It was a classic, went to two playoffs. Do you want to know who wins?"

Brunner looked at me slyly, and I handed him his martini.

"Mr. Brunner, one question has been bothering me all day," I said as I settled down next to him on the couch. "Why exactly are you approaching me with this invention of yours?"

"It's simple, really," he said. "Someday, we'll need to tell our story to the world, and we need influential, charismatic people to do that."

"Influential," I said laughing. "You flatter me, Mr. Brunner, but honestly, although nearly everyone recognizes me here in Pittsburgh, beyond the tri-state region, I'm really a nobody."

"That's just not so," Brunner said, holding me tight in his gaze. "I have it on good authority that, ten years from now, you will be America's top-rated network news anchor. As I think I alluded to earlier, America will come to love Gordon Dale, they will trust him implicitly, the public will hang on your every word, Gordon, and that will qualify you to be our spokesperson. At the proper moment, one word from you will afford our little enterprise instant legitimacy."

Brunner took a long draw off his martini, draining the glass all the way to the olive. He set it decisively on the coffee table and stared at me with a piercing look. "That is, Gordon, *if* you decide to join us."

"Is there some question about that?" I asked.

"Well, of course there is," Brunner said. "Our chrononauts have identified three journalists who might fit the bill for us. We've approached the other two fellows as well, hoping to find… (he allowed his voice to swell) the Walter Cronkite of the New Millennium. It's a bit like searching for the next Dalai Lama."

"Enough about South America, Victor," I said, a little frantically. "Just who are these other two guys?"

"I'm afraid I can't say, Gordon."

"And how will you decide which of us gets the job?"

"Oh, we won't pick you, Gordon. You will pick us."

My heart began to race. I tumbled to my feet and began pacing about the room. Suddenly, the evening seemed very warm. I started to perspire, something I try never to do. Even though it was ridiculous, I couldn't help thinking that those other two guys were conspiring to steal my spot on the network news, snatch away my chance at immortality.

"Think of it, Gordon," Brunner said. "Yours will be the face every American turns to in times of crisis. War, famine, civil unrest, from Iran to Oklahoma City, from the supercollider to the twin towers, you will be trusted, revered, a national treasure."

Oklahoma City, I thought? The twin towers?

"And don't forget the other benefits," Brunner continued. "Every stock you buy will go through the roof, every real estate investment you make will magically sprout condominiums, every time you buy a coin, a stamp, an autographed baseball, a Christmas ornament; it will inevitably become the most sought-after of collectables. Midas didn't have a golden touch, Gordon, he had a chronoscope."

"Then, how about giving me one of those stock tips right now, Victor," I said and laughed. The martini was starting to make me feel good.

Victor Brunner laughed. "All in good time, Gordon," he said as he stood up. He hoisted the chronoscope onto my coffee table, and then began searching in the pockets of those baggy clown pants of his until he found the key ring. He sat back down on the couch and started removing the padlocks.

"How would you like to take your first journey through time, Gordon?" Brunner said as he worked the locks. My pulse pounded in my forehead, and I sat back down on the couch. I had the uneasy feeling I was about to pass out.

"I would like that very much," I said.

Brunner spun the dial on the combination lock back and forth so quickly it blurred my vision. Once the case was open, Brunner glanced up, a look of concern crossing his face.

"You're looking a bit pasty there, Gordon," he said. "Perhaps another drink would buck you up a bit." He got to his feet. "You stay right there. This round is on me."

Before he carried my empty martini glass to the bar, Brunner found an electrical outlet and plugged the chronoscope in. The thing began to make the same series of outlandish squawks it had before. Clanks and clatters emerged from the case, bells and musical tones.

With Brunner occupied all the way across the room, I tried to catch a glimpse inside the black leather case. I eased myself forward on the couch, placed my hands on my knees and craned my neck to see inside. But just as the dials and lights and wires revealed themselves, Brunner returned to the couch with two more martinis. He drank his hurriedly, which surprised me. Somehow, I had him pegged as a teetotaler.

"As I told you before, Gordon," Brunner said, "Time travel is difficult. Both body and mind must learn to adapt to shifts in the time-space continuum. Perfecting the technique can often take several temporal voyages. Your first voyage will, by necessity, be a modest one, and regardless of what happens, you must remember that relaxation is the key. Above all, you must not be anxious, Gordon." I realized my body was as tense as a tightly wound spring. Brunner patted me on the knee paternally, and held out the headsets.

"Ready?" he said. I quickly drained the last of my bitter martini and took the headsets. The chronoscope began to throb expectantly. I could feel its power the moment I touched the headsets. Brunner leaned in close to me, like a football coach advising his quarterback before a big game.

"Now, listen carefully," he said. "Whether you are traveling to the past or the future, you will be entirely invisible to the people there, unseen and unheard. The experience is somewhat like watching a movie. Eventually, you'll be able to get up and move around, but you cannot physically affect any object in the future or the past."

"So, I can't bring any souvenirs back with me?" I said.

"No souvenirs and you can't leave anything behind." he said. Brunner's golf shirt caught my eye and he quickly added, "At least not as a novice. For you, I'm afraid, time travel will have to be an entirely voyeuristic pursuit." He pointed to his ears, indicating that I should put on the headsets. I did, and immediately felt like I was inside a bee hive. Brunner shouted over the din.

"What will it be, Gordon? The future or the past?"

A good question. Where did I want to go in time? I immediately zeroed in on the girl's locker room back at my high school, hopefully, right before swim class was about to start. But that didn't seem like a fitting thought for America's most-trusted anchorman, so I quickly banished it from my mind.

"I guess I'll try the past," I said.

"Good choice," Brunner said, "far less jarring to both body and mind." His hand disappeared into the case, and he began spinning dials on the chronoscope. The box began to rumble. The rumble turned to a roar.

"There's nothing to worry about, Gordon," Brunner mouthed to me. "So, for God's sake, enjoy yourself."

A high-pitched squeal sounded in my headphones, like a thousand fingers scraping across a blackboard. The chronoscope began to vibrate on the coffee table, and I felt like I was vibrating right along with it. The squeal in my ears became bone-rending. I felt like the sound was emanating from inside me and radiating out into the room.

I began to feel groggy, even a little sick to my stomach. My living room walls started to look fluid, like they were bed sheets on a clothesline, undulating in a soft breeze. I glanced down at my hands, and noticed that my vision had become hazy. I couldn't seem to bring anything into sharp focus. The martinis churned in my stomach, percolated, bubbled up, until I was certain I was going to vomit. I gritted my teeth, trying to hold the feeling at bay, but then I remembered what Brunner had said about relaxation. But where was Brunner? I glanced left, glanced right and did not see him. I looked around frantically, wanting to tell the guy to turn off the machine before I lost my lunch all over his precious titanium valise. But then, I felt his hands gently removing the headsets. He was right there behind me. The room was quiet. The chronoscope thrummed contentedly.

"I'm sorry," I said. "I had to stop. I thought I was going to upchuck. I guess I'll have to make my first voyage through time some other day."

Brunner laughed with delight. "You are suffering what we chrononauts refer to as TDS," he said, patting me on the back, "Temporal Displacement Syndrome. Time sickness. It's quite common."

"But, I didn't go anywhere." I said.

"Au contraire, my good man. You traveled exactly one day into the past. Were you able to get up and move around?"

"Nothing changed," I said, objecting. "The room remained exactly the same. You must have stopped the machine before I was able to travel anywhere."

Brunner gave me a look of consternation. He brought his face close to mine, reached out a hand and examined the whites of my eyes.

"Well," he said, drawing the word out to great length. "I'm assuming this room looked pretty much the same yesterday as it does today. You just failed to notice any of the subtle differences." He completed his impromptu examination and settled back down on the couch. "Next time, we'll send you into the future and then, once you've returned, we'll move the couch or something, so you'll know."

"I don't think I could stand any more time travel right now," I said. "I feel sick as a dog."

It was true. Every nerve ending, every internal organ, every brain cell was still vibrating, turning, spinning. It was like being trapped in the world's worst hangover. I was barely able to get to my feet, and Brunner had to help me to the bathroom.

"The first time I ventured into the void, I couldn't think clearly for a week," he whispered unnervingly into my ear. I immediately responded by throwing up into the toilet. Brunner left me there, hugging the cool porcelain for what seemed like hours.

When I finally emerged from the bathroom, I was barely capable of independent motion. I crawled as much as walked back to the couch. Victor Brunner was standing in the corner of my living room with his back turned to me, talking on my phone.

"Is our guy on-board?" he was saying. "Good, good. Glad to hear it. Keep me posted." Then, he glanced back over his shoulder, saw me and stiffened.

"I've gotta go," he said quickly. He unwound the long cord and hung up the phone. He turned back to face me. "Hope you don't mind," he said. "It was a long-distance call." Even if he'd called China, I was in no position to do anything but nod weakly. I collapsed onto the couch, feeling like there was nothing left inside me, which was true, since I'd barfed it all up.

"So," Brunner said in a voice that struck me as entirely too loud. "It's time to make a decision, Gordon. Are you buying in or not?"

"Victor," I said. "I'm really in no condition to make a decision like that. Maybe after I've seen a little more of what your device can do."

Brunner flung a hand into the air disgustedly. "Everybody wants to ride the roller coaster, but nobody wants to buy a ticket," he said. "Unfortunately, your free ride is over, Gordon. Either you buy in here and now, or this honor goes to somebody else. It's just that simple."

Thoughts spun through my mind. I considered my life in Pittsburgh and what it had become. Then I thought about what my life could be. I imagined sitting on the set of the CBS Nightly News, seeing the red "On Air" light go on, saying good evening to all of America.

"All right," I said. "I'll be your spokesperson."

"Then you're buying in?" Brunner said emphatically.

"Absolutely," I said with as much enthusiasm as I could muster.

"Great to hear," Brunner said, jumping to his feet and pumping my hand excitedly. "Now, where do you keep your checkbook?"

"My checkbook?" I said.

"What did you think I meant by buying in?" Brunner looked at me with incredulity.

"But why would you need my money?" I said. "You can travel through time, and what about all those stock tips you were telling me about?"

Brunner looked at me like I was a third-grader. "Gordon, we learned very early in this process that people who are not invested in the program, have an alarming tendency to drop out. I already told you about Chuck Yeager, right? The only people who remain truly committed to our little project are the ones who've made a substantial sacrifice to be part of it."

I nodded with bewilderment.

"Remember, Gordon, we are still years away from making our breakthrough public. When we finally *do* go public, you'll get your money back, a hundred-fold, a thousand fold, a million-fold perhaps, but in the meantime, we need to insure that no one backs out, or sells us out to the government, or the military, or blackmails us. You can understand what I'm trying to say can't you, Gordon?"

"I guess so," I said, my vision swirling and my ears ringing like my head was still inside that toilet bowl.

"Look at it this way, Gordon. Let's say I told you I wanted to bring another guy into the fold. The first thing you'd ask me is, 'How do I know we can trust this new guy, Victor?' And my answer would be, 'We can trust this new guy because he *bought* his way in.' It's called earnest money, Gordon. It keeps everybody honest."

Warning bells began to go off in my head. "I don't know, Victor," I said. "I'm going to have to think about this. Just how much money are we talking about here?"

"Gordon, Gordon, Gordon," Brunner said. "You disappoint me. I had such high hopes for you. For God's sake, man, I saved your life. Stop blathering and put a price tag on that for a minute."

I still felt so nauseous that I wouldn't have put a plug nickel on the value of my life. "Victor," I said weakly. "Can't I have just a little time, say a couple of days, to think this thing over? Anyone would take a little time to consider a decision this important."

"Our other two potential spokesmen aren't delaying *their* decisions. They're both proceeding full-speed-ahead. That's why I was just on the phone. I was getting a progress report."

This immediately silenced my objections. I sat quietly, unable to find anything to say.

"Where do you want to be in ten years?" Brunner said. "Hosting a morning show in Pittsburgh? I don't think so." He took both my hands in his and squeezed them. "Don't miss the chance of a lifetime, Gordon."

"All right," I said and struggled to get up off the couch. "I probably have a couple thousand dollars in my checking account," I said, "Maybe twenty-five hundred."

"Gordon," Brunner said, as if he were speaking to a disobedient, young boy. "That will do fine for starters, but I've been to the future, so let me just clue you in on how this thing is going to work. In addition to the three-thousand from your checking account, you're also going to write me a check for ninety-seven-thousand dollars from your brokerage account. Do that, and your new life begins immediately. And let me assure you Gordon; it's a beautiful life, a life where you are the toast of the town, America's top-rated anchorman, the first person to appear on the cover of Time Magazine as 'Man of the Year' for three consecutive years."

"But that money is all I have in the world," I said. "Well, that and my good name."

Brunner leaned forward. "I hate to be the bearer of bad news, but fame and fortune is not the only possible outcome for your life, Gordon. You *could* end up as America's top-rated anchorman, or you *could* end up a broken, defeated man. I know for a fact, that if you choose *not* to join us, within a year, you will no longer be employed at WGRT. You will be out of the broadcasting business forever. It will be only a matter of time until no one even knows who you are. You will disappear into the fog of time, never to be heard from again."

Given those two options, how could I choose to do anything but write the checks?

"This is a decision you will never regret, Gordon," Brunner said as he packed up his case. "You are now part of the greatest technological discovery in the history of mankind. Next week, just as soon as your checks clear, I'll be back, and you can take your first voyage into the future. Prepare yourself, Gordon Dale, because in the future, you will be a God." He patted my hand gently, nodding as he stared into my undoubtedly bloodshot eyes. "Now, try to get some sleep," he said.

Victor Brunner didn't return the next week. I never saw him again. I called the switchboard at Brunner's company, and was told they had no Victor Brunner, and never had. They even claimed that their company offered no scholarships to high school engineering students.

I took a videotape of Victor Brunner's appearance on *Have a GRT Morning* to Carnegie-Mellon University, where I met with the Dean of the College of Engineering and the head of the Physics Department. I played the tape for them.

"Do either of you know this guy?" I asked, searching both men's faces for signs of recognition. Neither man looked happy, probably because I'd gotten them to agree to the meeting in the first place by implying that my television station was planning to honor their contributions to Pittsburgh's academic community with an award.

"The guy claimed to be affiliated with CMU," I said, pressing my case. "He claimed to be working on a project with some of the world's greatest scientists; Carl Sagan, Stephen Hawking, Werner Von Braun."

The head of the Physics Department eyed me suspiciously. "I think Werner Von Braun has been dead for over a decade," he said.

"Maybe in this time-space continuum," I shot back, which shut them both up immediately.

"What about Chuck Yeager?" I asked, desperation creeping into my voice. Not surprisingly, once the two academicians started to realize that there wouldn't be any heroic interviews on Channel 6, featuring their wives and families, they both turned somewhat peckish.

"I've never met Chuck Yeager, Stephen Hawking or Carl Sagan," the engineering dean barked at me, pointing at the television, "and I've definitely never seen that guy."

I leaned forward and fixed both professors with my most sincere, camera-friendly expression of concern. "Do me a favor, will you?" I said, tapping the monitor "Give it one last good look, all right?"

I lost my job at the television station just before Christmas. Management claimed that the whole Carnegie-Mellon flap had nothing to do with their decision—something I still don't believe. I was told there was a downturn in the economy, and positions had to be eliminated. So, in the end, Chuck's girlfriend ended up taking my spot on *Have a GRT Morning* after all.

It took me a long time to get over the pain and disgrace of losing everything; it took years as a matter of fact. I'd been scammed, I'd squandered my life savings, and I couldn't bring myself to tell a soul about it for fear that people would think I was an idiot. From that time forward, whenever someone was named an anchor at one of the network news programs, someone like Tom Brokaw, I found myself wondering if maybe *he* was the one who'd stolen my job. Humiliation turned to bitterness, and turned again to misanthropy.

I had to start my life over again, from the ground up, and although I never saw Victor Brunner again, he left me with a hundred-thousand dollar lesson in life to remember him by. I came to understand that anyone who measures their worth based on other people's opinions is standing on rapidly shifting sand. Fortunately, it was a lesson I learned early enough to make a difference in my life.

I'm content with my own little niche in the time-space continuum now. I know I wasn't meant to be a network anchorman, I wasn't even meant to be a morning show host. I'm just a simple man, leading a circumspect life of obscurity. I remind myself of that fact every morning when I roll out of bed. Then, I put on my flip-flops, and head for the beach. And that's the real reason I'm a happy man today. Well, that and the fact that I followed up on that little stock tip Victor Brunner gave me all those years ago and sunk all my remaining cash into a little outfit called Microsoft.

SUITE FOR THE LADY IN RED
BY SUANNE SCHAFER

Langley, Virginia, 24 February 2013

"Eliminate her, Mark."

My ulcer began a slow burn as soon as Caulder gave me the assignment. I ignored the pain. He'd interpret any reaction as a sign of weakness.

Caulder joined the CIA in 1985. A couple years later, I mustered in. I'd been active military in a clandestine DCS outfit longer than he'd been CIA. Bottom-line—who had actual seniority? Back in 2008, we were candidates for the same promotion. He took credit for my breakthrough in a tough assignment and yanked the position from under my nose. I'd been treading water since, trying to survive until retirement. Our professional relationship remained strained. Our friendship ended.

Five years ago, Caulder recruited the target, Sarah Griffon. I knew her by reputation only.

"What's your theory?" I asked.

"Sarah, uh, Dr. Griffon, came to see me three months ago, wanting out, *begging* to be released." His eyes darted toward me, then away. "Wouldn't give a reason. Said it was personal. For Christ's sake, I couldn't let her go. We'd spent months embedding her in the Fatah al-Islam refugee camp. She'd successfully seduced Baroodi. He was beginning to trust her."

His fingernails drummed on his desk, irritating the hell out of me.

"Why take her out? Everyone's entitled to some time off."

Caulder stood and paced. "Damn it. I told her she could go when she completed this assignment. Said she couldn't wait. Then disappeared."

I took Griffon's dossier from Caulder's extended hand. As I scanned the pages, I raised my eyebrows. Sarah Griffon. Born Arlington, Virginia, June 16, 1983. Unlike me, she had an enviable pedigree. Her father, a career diplomat, was a handsome blend of wealthy white Anglo-Saxon Protestant and French-Moroccan. Her Lebanese mother was a world-renowned cellist. Griffon spoke half a dozen languages. The only thing we had in common was classical guitar.

Rather than compete with her illustrious parents, she attended medical school. A respected physician, her forthright stance on human rights and her work with Doctors Without Borders put her at the forefront of international political debates. Her patrician background allowed her to hobnob with world-class movers and shakers. With her medical credentials, she easily accessed places the organization couldn't, such as refugee camps where terrorists bred like mosquitoes.

Caulder, recognizing both her potential and her connections, had pulled her into the fold. After training her personally, he used her for hand-picked missions which she carried out with aplomb. Some stateside staff resented the fact that Griffon got the plum assignments, leading to rumors of a *quid pro quo* sexual relationship between Caulder and Griffon. I didn't doubt the rumors. Though they remained unsubstantiated, the scuttlebutt continued, spread by office-bound assholes who had no fucking idea how difficult Middle Eastern missions could be. Often the only clue to whether you faced friend or foe was how a man draped his *keffiye*.

As proud of his protégée's meteoric rise as if he'd hatched her himself, Caulder had obviously taken her defection quite personally.

I passed her documents back to Caulder.

He sat down again. After extending a photograph to me, his fingers resumed their staccato percussion on his desk. "This is the first time she's been seen since she vanished."

I sucked in a breath, staring at the close-up long after memorizing the image. A woman to die for. Black curls. Olive skin. Luscious lips. I got lost in her chocolate eyes. Seconds passed before I remembered to exhale.

"She is lovely, isn't she?" Caulder asked. His voice betrayed his emotion though his face remained expressionless.

I nodded, though in my opinion, good spies preferred anonymity. Like me. Gray hair, gray eyes, unremarkable features. Griffon's beauty and outspokenness made her unforgettable.

He tossed me the next photo as if the paper were too hot to handle.

The second I picked it up, I knew why. Looking like an illustration from the *Sports Illustrated* swimsuit issue, Griffon walked on a beach hand in hand with a man I vaguely recognized. Her hair was wild and tangled by the wind, her face luminous. A tiny bikini top barely covered perfect breasts. A damp sarong clung like plastic wrap to her hips revealing parts of a female I hadn't seen in years.

Clearly Caulder had the hots for the woman. Hell, who wouldn't? Just looking at her image, I was half in love with her myself.

"Who's the guy?" I handed the photos back to him.

"Ariel Chabat. Some kind of musician."

No wonder he seemed familiar. Not just any performer. A virtuoso. The best classical guitarist in the world. I had a couple of his CDs at home.

"He's a Spanish Jew. A real Zionist. Moved to Tel Aviv six years ago." Caulder growled his irritation. "By consorting with him, Sarah's undermined everything we've accomplished in the Gaza Strip."

"She's probably in love."

Caulder snorted. "She knows better. We all do. When was the last time you let a woman interfere with your duty?" He stopped short. His gaze flicked to mine and then away. "Sorry, Mark. I didn't mean—"

I waved my hand to cut him off. I knew where he was heading with that remark and had no desire to go there. "Why me?"

"You're our most experienced operative."

"You've been around longer," I countered.

He shook his head. "Can't be objective. I trained her."

"You mean you fucked her."

Caulder gave me a nasty look, suggesting I'd overstep my bounds. "I wish," he snorted. "Hey, I retire July one. Karen's planning a second honeymoon. She'd kill me if I took off now hunting for a woman half my age." He stood before his office window staring out at the compound.

"Where's Griffon now?" I asked.

"Chabat performs with the Madrid symphony orchestra the nineteenth. We think she'll be there."

I sat upright. "That's tomorrow."

"Short notice, I know. We can't let her vanish again." Caulder swallowed hard and looked down, avoiding my gaze.

As I witnessed his discomfort, I doubted he'd told the truth about not fucking Griffon. In the past he'd had more than one May-

December affair but never with such a gorgeous woman. If he had any feelings for Griffon at all, how he could he have ordered her to seduce Baroodi? I decided a man who'd screw his best friend out of a job wouldn't think twice before sending a woman he loved into harm's way.

While Caulder seemed sufficiently virile to keep two women happy, I suspected Karen finally put her foot down about his philandering.

He stopped pacing long enough to pull a packet from a desk drawer and pitch it to me.

I snatched it in midair. My name, Mark Kuhlmeier, had been scrawled across the envelope with a thick black marker. I ran my finger under the flap and removed Spanish and French passports, train and plane tickets, an employee ID for the Auditorio Nacional de Music and a fat stack of Euros.

Caulder stuck out his hand, terminating our little chat. "Take her out, Mark. She's a loose cannon."

I gave him a lukewarm shake.

Over the past thirty years, I'd brought down dozens of enemies but really didn't like killing. Taking out one of our own rankled me. Somehow, I'd bet this assignment had more to do with Caulder placating his wife than Griffon's defection.

On the overnight flight to Madrid, I drifted into an uneasy sleep in which memories of Judith resurfaced. Nightmares I'd thought long buried had been stirred up by Caulder's comment.

Tel Aviv, December 27, 2008

A steaming cup of coffee in one hand, Judith opened the door to the balcony with the other. Still wet from sex, clad only in love, her belly rounded with our child, she stood outside watching the morning traffic in Tel Aviv.

"Call in sick," I begged.

"I can't. There's a war going on."

"Come inside. Someone will see you."

"You just want to have your way with me again." She turned to watch me dress and laughed. "Going commando?"

I ignored her as I tugged my jeans up my thighs, focused on getting the zipper over my latest hard-on.

Crash! Something shattered on the floor. Shards of coffee cup skittered across the terrazzo toward me as a whine passed my ear.

Surprised, I looked up.

Judith's mouth opened several times. She staggered, took one step and collapsed to her knees. Blood pumped from her chest, a massive hole where her left breast used to be. A bullet whizzed past my shoulder. I dropped to the floor and crawled toward her. Another round zipped by me and embedded in the wall. The next struck Judith in the back of the head. Bits of brain and droplets of blood splattered me and the walls of her apartment.

I stood and raced to the balcony railing. Across the parking lot, a man, features hidden by a baseball cap, dropped from the roof of the building to a nearby tree, then to the ground. Knowing I moved too slowly, I ran to the bedroom. Last night I'd been so eager to get Judith into bed that I hadn't put my firearm in its usual place. Valuable seconds passed as I dug through discarded clothing and rumpled sheets to retrieve it. By the time I raced barefooted down the stairs to street level, the assassin was gone.

As always, I woke up at that point, sweating, out of breath, heart racing, regretting my inability to save the woman I loved—or avenge her.

Since Judith's death, I'd been celibate. And impotent. After seven years of self-imposed abstinence, I doubted the old dog would ever rise again.

Madrid, 25 February 2013

The next morning, I wandered up the *Calle del Príncipe de Vergara* to the auditorium. With a point-and-shoot camera around my neck, a *Fodor's Guide* in one hand and a worn backpack, I followed a docent through the concert hall, listening to him lecture in badly-accented French.

My Madrid contact, "Emilio" according to his name tag, caught up with me in the toilet. We pissed in unison. The roar of our streams drowned out our whispered conversation.

He said, "I tracked Chabat to the Hotel Ritz. No one's seen Griffon yet. He's ordered dozens of roses and an elegant dinner for after his performance tonight. So either she's coming in, or he's got himself some fancy whore."

"It's her." Only true love could drag a woman like Griffon out of hiding.

Emilio and I exited separately. I continued my reconnaissance while he disappeared backstage.

When the tour ended, I exited with the other tourists. I found the main concert hall, the *Sala Sinfónica*, perfect for my needs. Twenty-two hundred seats circled the stage except upstage which was occupied by a large pipe organ. There were no dark wings with heavy curtains Griffon could hide behind while enjoying her lover's performance. Anywhere she sat she'd be visible. From the catwalk above the nosebleed seats, I'd get a clean shot.

Hours before the concert, I swiped my ID into the auditorium's card reader and walked in like I belonged. Dressed in the gray coveralls of an electrician, I climbed to the catwalk. Security would be tighter at the time of the performance, so I smuggled my weapon in early. Pretending to adjust lights, I duct taped my Colt to the underside of a lamp housing. Minutes later, in the bowels of the auditorium, I snagged a janitor's pushcart. With broom and dust rag in hand, I checked out Chabat's dressing room. Then I wandered around with the cart, keeping busy enough to avoid second-guessing the project.

Show time approached. From stage left I watched for Griffon as seats filled. I'd begun to think Caulder's intelligence was faulty when, at the last minute, she appeared. Dressed in a scarlet gown, she sat front row dead center. She couldn't have made herself a more obvious target.

In the first half of his program, Chabat, accompanied by the orchestra, worked his way through an astonishing repertoire, highlighting two centuries of works for guitar. Under the spell of the music, I relaxed.

Patrons mingled during intermission while the stagehands cleared the orchestra's chairs preparing for Chabat's solo pieces. As I moved toward the catwalk, my right foot hit something slick. I slipped and nearly fell. I looked down to investigate. Someone had dropped a program. Without bothering to look at it, I picked it up and stuck it beneath my overalls into my shirt to read later.

In the catwalk, crouching low to avoid being seen, I pulled the Colt free from its tape, attached the suppressor, then slid the pistol into the voluminous pocket of my uniform. The cartridges, DRT frangible hollow points, contained a compressed powder that disintegrated into a fine dust when they struck a target, causing massive internal damage. One shot should take out Griffon without passing through her to harm innocent bystanders. The final explosion of clapping just before Chabat's encore would mask the report of my firearm.

The second half of the performance included Chabat's exquisite rendering of Tárrega's *Recuerdos de la Alhambra*. The piece always jerked my heartstrings and suited my melancholy mood.

God, I envied Chabat's skill. With more bravado than talent, I'd played guitar in high school and college. Peer pressure made me hide my love for classical music by cranking out rock and roll on a beat-up Stratocaster. Years had passed since I'd plunked out a tune. Maybe I'd take up playing again when I retired—if I lived that long.

Thunder shook the theater. The audience stood, clapping wildly. "Bravissimo!" and "Encore!" echoed off the rafters.

Shit! The sudden burst of noise jerked me back to the moment. I'd gotten lost in the music long enough to jeopardize the assignment. I refocused. My fifty-six-year-old knees creaked as I knelt on the catwalk. Obscured by the brilliant stage lights, I slid the forty-five from my pocket, flipped off the safety and made sure a round was in the chamber. After popping a couple of Tums to calm the fire in my gut, I took a deep breath, steadied my hand against the railing—and waited.

Ignoring two thousand people, Chabat played for Griffon alone. Mesmerized by his performance, she blew him a kiss at the end of one spectacular number. Neither her affair with Caulder nor her seduction of Baroody could compare with the obvious chemistry between her and Chabat. No wonder she wanted out.

After Chabat's final note reverberated into nothingness, he stood, leaned his guitar on the edge of his seat and bowed elegantly. Behind him, stagehands brought in another chair, footrest and a second instrument still in its case.

He swiped long fingers through wavy brown hair, stepped to stage front, bent toward Griffon and motioned for her to join him.

A demure Griffon stood but held back.

Chabat wiggled his fingers again, cajoling her.

People in adjacent seats playfully pushed her forward.

Griffon's lover took her hands and lifted her onto the apron.

After a fierce kiss, Chabat wrapped one arm around her and said to the audience, "*Mira!* Look, everyone. We got married today." He raised her left hand and flashed her ring to the audience. The patrons responded with louder applause accompanied by whistles and cheers.

Chabat strutted with manly pride. Griffon glowed.

Fuck. I would have to take her out on her wedding day. I couldn't do it. I started to walk away, but Caulder's voice echoed in my head. *When was the last time you let a woman interfere with your duty?*

I turned back, rubbed my burning gut and wondered why Griffon had worn red.

Chabat tucked a curl behind his wife's ear, revealing a delicate pink shell. He had unknowingly cleared my target for me, but something in the way he'd caressed her stole my breath. To block his gesture from my mind, I closed my eyes, refocused on the job at hand, and inhaled deeply. When I opened my eyes, I raised the pistol until the laser sight kissed Griffon's right ear, and exhaled.

As I squeezed the trigger, Chabat swept Griffon off her feet and swung her in a joyous twirl. The bullet entered the back of his head. Instant kill. Wrong person. *Major fuck-up.*

Like a Rube Goldberg contraption, Chabat tilted into Griffon in slow motion, knocking her backwards. She stumbled into his instrument. Stepped on it. Dissonant notes ripped the air. Her high heels tangled in guitar strings. She crashed into his chair. He fell on her. Her anguished scream soared above the noise of the spectators.

Instantly silent, the stunned audience was paralyzed.

Griffon lay on her back beneath him, calling his name, begging someone to help him, frantically trying to lift him off her as his blood poured out. A haphazard pile of chairs, instrument stands and sheet music partially obscured my view of her. I could still see the desperate waving of her reddened hands. The debris didn't block her screams.

Seconds later, the crowd went berserk. People leaped on the stage to assist her.

Too many spectators surrounded her. I couldn't get a clear shot anymore.

Now fully aware of what had happened, the onlookers began scanning the auditorium trying to figure out where the attack had originated.

Taking advantage of the ensuing pandemonium, I escaped before anyone saw me.

On the *Calle*, I hopped on the first bus leaving the area. Half an hour later, in the bus station toilet, I tore off the coveralls and stuffed them in my knapsack along with the Colt and name tag.

Slipping out a different door, I grabbed a taxi to the train station. There I placed the backpack in a locker. Minutes later I entered the men's room and dropped the key into the tank of the second toilet on the left. Emilio would recover everything in a few days.

With seconds to spare before its departure, I caught the overnight train to Paris.

Paris, 26 February 2013

By the time I reached the City of Light, morning editions of *Le Monde*, *Le Figaro*, and the *International Herald Tribune* had made their way to the Gare d'Austerlitz station. I picked up the *Trib* and read it while taxiing to Charles de Gaulle airport.

Chabat was dead. *No shit.* I'd killed an international treasure. And destroyed a $60,000 Hermann Hauser guitar. Griffon survived but remained hospitalized mourning the dual loss of her husband and her unborn child. *Double fuck.*

I tossed the newspaper in the garbage and entered the departures terminal at de Gaulle. When I presented my passport to buy a ticket to D.C., I discovered the playbill I'd picked up in the Madrid auditorium. Tucked inside the booklet, an errata page revealed Chabat had changed his program at the last minute. He planned to premier his newest composition, *Suite for the Lady in Red*. Griffon would have made her musical debut in his duet for two guitars.

Langley, February 27, 2013

Caulder's secretary had said, "Go on in," but I stopped outside his office and swallowed a few antacids before knocking.

"It's open." Caulder's voice penetrated the oak veneer door.

His back to me, he stared out the windows of his corner office but pivoted the second my foot stepped on his carpet.

"Mark, what the fuck happened?"

The room crackled with tension, his and mine.

"Circumstances beyond my control." Despite the Tums, acid chewed my stomach. Seemed like it never stopped anymore.

"The collateral damage was too great," Caulder said. "You fucking took out an innocent bystander. The State Department is up in arms."

"You ordered it."

"I expected you of all people to be competent."

I dug my fist into my smoldering abdomen. "Caulder—"

He interrupted me, slamming his fist on his desk. "Ambassador Griffon moved Sarah from Madrid to some ritzy convalescent hospital in Switzerland. He's hired the Swiss-Security Agency to guard his daughter around the clock. Find her. Take her out."

In my cubicle I scanned international news reports. In the Middle East, tensions had escalated to the boiling point. Ambassador Griffon blamed Baroodi, his daughter's ex-lover. Israel attributed Chabat's death to Hezbollah. The United States pointed its finger at the PLO. Baroodi held the U. S. responsible, claiming Griffon had been a spy, a Mata Hari sent to seduce him.

When I arrived in Bern the next morning, I found no trace of Griffon. Once again she'd vanished. The Ambassador held the Swiss police and Swi-Sec responsible for her disappearance. But I knew she was a woman who didn't want to be found.

Langley, 30 April 2013

For two months, as I followed every conceivable lead, Caulder grew nastier, fuming constantly about my incompetence.

"What the fuck have you been doing with your time?" he bellowed. "Do you have any idea the flack the department will take, that *I* will take, if it comes out we killed a guitar player while trying to dispatch an ambassador's daughter? I'm not letting you jeopardize my reputation—or my retirement."

"It's not my fault. You taught her every trick she knows."

"She switched sides, Mark. This is a simple targeted killing."

In training we learned that assassination equaled murder. The U.S. Government did not condone the killing of someone who disagreed with policy. On the other hand, a "targeted kill" was more akin to self-defense in advance than murder. In Caulder's mind, Sarah had become an enemy combatant and fair game.

"You're letting the fact that she's a woman cloud your judgment." Caulder's voice seethed with venom. "This all harks back to Judith. Do I need to put someone else on the case?"

I shook my head. "I can handle it. Just a little more time."

"One month. I plan to retire with a clean slate."

Back in my cubicle, I searched my desk for another roll of antacids. That bastard would bring up Judith again.

Dragging my thoughts from the past, I stared at the photos in Griffon's file. Recently I'd spent so much time staring at her picture I felt I knew her. I no longer called her "Griffon." She'd become "Sarah." At night I'd wake up drenched in sweat, tormented by a recurrent dream in which Judith had Sarah's curls and wore a red dress, stained darker with the blood of husband and baby.

The burn in my belly grew to a steady blaze antacids couldn't touch.

In the end, I found Sarah by chance.

Some stupid college kid, returning from a summer slumming in Europe, got caught smuggling a kilo of hashish into New York's JFK. The Feds ran the photos on his digital camera through their facial recognition software. He'd snapped an image of a beautiful woman eating *tapas* at a Spanish cafe. Our missing agent. I traced her to the *Realejo Barrio*, the old Jewish quarter of Granada.

Sarah and I had never met, so I didn't bother with a disguise. Over the past several months I'd let my temples silver and allowed a beard to proliferate, which I trimmed to a neat goatee. I projected the persona of a middle-aged man going through a midlife crisis. The role suited me.

Granada, 14 May 2013. D minus 16 days

The first few days in Granada, I stayed in a hostel near the cafe where Sarah had been photographed. Every day I ate there, hoping she'd return. When she did, like a lovesick pup, I followed her up a steep hill to her home. A sign on her front door advertised a room for rent. I smiled. Things were finally looking up.

I easily charmed the landlady, a frail, black-garbed grandmother, with dollars, if not my rakish grin. She introduced herself as Señora Chabat.

A chill climbed my spine. "Are you—"

Before I finished the question, tears trailed down her cheeks. With a lace handkerchief, she dabbed her eyes. "Ariel was my great-grandson."

Fuck. I added her to my expanding list of casualties.

The Señora patted my hand. "I'm ninety-seven years old. Death and I are good friends. We become more intimate every day."

She gave me the keys and sent me upstairs to check out the apartment alone. Though her villa was elegant on the outside, the upper floor had been converted to four *pieds-à-terre* with thin walls and cheap furnishings.

I climbed the stairs to a tiny foyer, turned the key in the door on the left and walked in. Fair-sized living area. Adequate bedroom. Microscopic bath. Past those, a kitchenette with French doors. I opened the doors and stepped onto a balcony furnished with a bistro table, two chairs, a chaise lounge and a breathtaking, unobstructed view of the city. Mid-rise buildings squatted in prayer beneath the distant cathedral. A pair of louvered shutters divided my half-balcony from Sarah's. I unlatched them and crossed into her territory. Her outdoor space had identical furniture. I peeked through her windows. Her place mirrored mine.

Quickly I descended the steps and told the Señora I'd take the room. Then, staked out next door to Sarah, I awaited the perfect opportunity to win her confidence.

Every night before Caulder went to bed, he texted me with the number of days I had left to accomplish my mission. *D minus nineteen days, D minus eighteen days, D minus seventeen days . . .* I wondered if Karen actually reminded him to text me or if the act of crawling into bed with his wife stimulated a knee-jerk reaction.

Over several days, I familiarized myself with Sarah's routine. She cared for the Señora with genuine affection and ran the house with military precision. After breakfast, she left for the market with a basket on one arm to do the daily shopping.

At the morning and mid-afternoon meals we tenants shared with our landlady, I watched Sarah. The simple acts of eating, drinking, and conversing together lulled me into a sense of domesticity I hadn't known since Judith.

Once I could predict how long Sarah might be gone on her errands, I picked the lock on her door, slipped on vinyl gloves and snooped.

Not much in the living area. A utilitarian sofa. No phone to tap. No radio. No television. A black leather bag sat by at the front door, filled with her stethoscope and medical paraphernalia. A guitar lounged against the wall. I opened the case and groaned with lust. A Ramirez. As good as the Herman Hauser ruined when I killed Chabat. I ran my fingers over the strings. Badly out of tune, the guitar hadn't been played recently. I wondered if the instrument was Chabat's or Sarah's. Next to the guitar, a CD player.

The bedroom didn't yield much either. Books in three languages. Lacy underwear stowed in a drawer made my heart race. The armoire held three pairs of jeans. Six T-shirts. One black dress. When I stroked the length of her silky white nightgown, I shivered.

Beyond learning Sarah's favorite toothpaste and soap, the bathroom gave up only her fragrance, *Azahar*. With a twist of the lid, I opened the bottle. The smell of orange blossoms spiraled through the air. I envisioned Sarah touching the golden perfume on her wrists, the pulse of her neck, then swallowed as I thought of the scent lying between her breasts. I always knew when she'd been on the stairs that led to our rooms, the aroma lingered there laced with her ever-present sadness.

After placing a couple of discrete bugs, I slipped back to my own apartment.

At night the sounds of her toilette penetrated our thin shared wall. I felt a peculiar intimacy with her then, imagining being married to her, sharing a bedtime routine and sleeping spooned together after love-making. As she prepared for bed, she hummed a wistful tune I didn't recognize. Like *Recuerdos de la Alhambra*, its poignant notes made me long for something I couldn't name.

D minus fourteen days. Two weeks left. Despite Caulder's order to eliminate her, I still hadn't killed Sarah, though I could have taken her out at any time. By now, she and Judith were so twisted together in my head, I knew if I killed Sarah, I'd be no different than

Judith's assassin.

◇◇◇

Granada, 29 May 2013, D minus 1

A week later, at lunch, the Señora said, "Sarah, perhaps one of our guests might escort you to the concert tonight."

The old woman appraised each of us tenants before her eyes settled on me.

Realizing I'd been "volunteered," I said, "I'd be happy to." I understood the woman's logic. Her Sarah would be safe with an old man.

"*Abuela*, are you ill?" Sarah knelt before the Señora, immediately taking her pulse.

Señora Chabat protested as Sarah fussed over her. "Dear girl, I'm fine. I simply fear the evening will be too stressful for me."

"I understand." Sarah kissed the old woman's wrinkled cheek.

At 7:15, Sarah descended the stairs, wearing the black dress from her closet, a *mantilla* draped over her shoulder. Her ringlets, precariously pinned with chopsticks, would tumble like a house of cards were one chopstick removed. She was stunning but pale and taut with tension.

As I helped Sarah out of the taxi, the poster for the event caught my eye. *Fuck.* A musical tribute to Ariel Chabat featuring guitarists from around the world. My head swiveled searching for an escape route.

Sarah noticed. "*Abuela* didn't tell you?" With an apologetic shrug, she added, "Classical guitar isn't everyone's cup of tea."

"It's fine. I'll enjoy it."

"I hate this sort of thing." She grimaced. "But Ari was my husband. I have to stay. You don't."

"The Señora would be upset if I left you alone."

She shrugged.

Inside, Sarah listened to the performances, facing dead ahead, her hands so tightly clasped in her lap that her knuckles bleached. Her closed eyes dammed tears threatening to spill.

I knew the moment the music reached through her sorrow. She leaned back in her seat. Her hands relaxed and separated, her fingers twitched, and then flew, playing the intricate notes on an imaginary guitar.

Afterwards, audience members and performers gathered around Sarah, acknowledging Chabat's extraordinary talent.

Someone called Sarah's name.

The crowd parted for an ancient gnome.

"Maestro." She greeted him with kisses on each cheek followed by a warm embrace.

He patted her hand. Tears streamed down his cheeks. "Ari was like a son—"

"I know." Her lips trembled. Her dammed tears overflowed. With the touch of a finger she captured a droplet and transferred it to the old man's cheek, blending their sorrow. "We share every tear."

When he tottered away, Sarah clutched my arm. Wild-eyed and trembling, she said, "I've got to leave!" At a near run, she dragged me out of the theater.

In silence we climbed the long hill back to the Chabat villa, Sarah a step or two ahead of me. Though the evening was muggy and warm, she wore the *mantilla* as tightly wound around her as her sorrow.

At the top of our stairs, she leaned her forehead against her door, her eyes so full of tears she couldn't insert the key into the lock.

"Allow me," I said, taking the keys from her hand. For a brief instant, she leaned into me and rested her head on my chest, seeking comfort. I wanted to taste her hair. Her *Azahar* swirled around me. With a deep breath, I wrapped my arms around her.

She pulled away.

"You could use a drink." I held the door for her. "I have a bottle of sherry, but no glasses."

She shook her head. "Thanks anyway." She half-smiled. "But I can lend you a glass."

"Don't make me drink alone."

Her lips twitched in surrender.

I dashed across the hall, found the bottle and returned to her apartment.

She handed me glasses. I poured the sherry.

"Give me a minute," she said, returning to the kitchen. "I'll put together *tapas*."

Over the tinkle of cutlery and plates I heard her humming that haunting melody again.

I wandered the apartment until, unable to resist, I lifted the guitar from its case. After picking a few sour notes, I began tuning it.

"The high E is still flat," she observed as she came into the living area carrying a tray of olives, peppers, a sliced baguette, slivered ham and dried apricots. She settled on her sofa and pulled the chopsticks from her hair releasing a tangle of loose ringlets.

More than anything, I wanted to become entrapped in those curls. Instead, I kept tuning the instrument. "Do you play?"

She shook her head.

"I thought I'd be the next Eric Clapton when I was a teenager."

"007 for me." She grinned. After a pause, she added, "But I suppose, in reality, a spy's life isn't all that glamorous."

To change the subject, I ran my fingers over the guitar strings and asked, "What's that song you hum all the time? I can't place it."

She looked puzzled.

Damn. The tune was so ingrained in her she wasn't aware she vocalized it.

"It goes like this." I played a dozen notes.

"No!" She burst into tears and ran into the bathroom.

For a few minutes, I waited to see if she'd come out. When her sobs showed no sign of subsiding, I chugged both our sherries, grabbed the bottle and retreated to my apartment.

The night remained muggy. I headed to the kitchen, dropped off the sherry and cracked the seal on the bourbon. I opened the French doors, praying for a breath of cool air. Sitting on the balcony, I started drinking straight out of the bottle. The first gulp burnt my esophagus, lit a fire in my gut, then settled into a golden glow. The alcohol left me maudlin, morose, and drunk enough to admit that I'd fallen in love with Sarah.

My cell vibrated. The daily text from Caulder. *D minus one. Eliminate the problem within twenty-four hours, or your career is over.*

Fuck him! With a flip of my wrist, I tossed the phone on the chaise then dropped down next to it.

I was screwed. If I didn't kill Sarah, Caulder would send someone else to do it. She'd be dead anyway, and my career would be *kaput*. If I did murder her, my life would be over. *Double fuck.* Suddenly, I wanted to screw up Caulder's life like he was fucking up mine. To make his retirement a living hell.

After a shower, I looked at myself in the mirror, noting the grizzled hair that surrounded my cock, the slack ball sack that dangled beneath. *You're getting rather long in the tooth, Mark.* I gave the old dog a stroke or two, but he didn't bother to rouse.

During the night, guitar music floated in from the balcony and awakened me. Sarah must have been too upset to sleep. The amber eye of the clock blinked 2:00 A.M. I stripped the sheet from the bed and carried it outside to the chaise. There, naked and half-asleep, I listened to Sarah play. At first, not having practiced in months, she fumbled, cursed and started over multiple times. Finally muscle memory returned, and she ran through several songs flawlessly.

The music changed to a recording of a lone guitar, a plaintive melody in A-minor, reminiscent of Sarah's tune. A man missing his lover.

Plink. Plink. Plink. With a shuddering sigh, Sarah tuned her instrument up a third before playing along with the recorded music, her guitar a woman replying tenderly to her man.

I recognized the tune Sarah always hummed.

Suddenly I realized I was hearing the duet Chabat wrote for their wedding, *Suite for the Lady in Red.* He had recorded his part so she could practice while they were apart.

In complex counterpoint, the two tremolo-laced melodies intertwined in the most intricate guitar piece I'd ever heard

Sarah paused, and then began the second movement where the joy of lovers reunited segued into what I could only call fuck-me music. The male guitar led with a pulsating bass, the female replied breathlessly. They climaxed together in a crescendo ending with simultaneous thumps on the soundboards of the instruments and a three beat pause. Afterglow followed, a series of descending arpeggios.

Finally, the third part in A-major reprised the opening but with a sweet, uplifting resolution.

I moved to the shutters, tilting the louvers so I could see Sarah. She sat on the chaise, instrument in her lap, replaying the second movement, her mouth open, her foot tapping like a metronome, her body responding to the thrusts of the male guitar.

In her white nightgown she looked pure. But, like me, she'd played the game. Like me, she'd followed orders. I bet she never told that new husband of hers what she did for a living. Never told him Caulder had fucked her. Never told him she'd fucked Baroodi.

Since Chabat's death, she'd drowned in misery. She needed someone to ease her pain. Someone with blood on their hands. Someone who understood what it was like to lose a lover and a child to an assassin. Someone who knew how living a double life could make you forget who you were. Someone who understood what it's like to whore yourself for your country. Someone to love her. Someone like me.

Before I could open the shutters to go to her, she stopped half way through the movement, laid her guitar on the floor, stood, walked across the balcony.

The recording continued, Chabat playing alone.

With her head bowed, Sarah leaned on the rail and peered at the city lights. For a moment, I thought she might jump, but with a sob, she ran both hands through her curls. Then she tilted her head back. Her fingers meandered down the front of her neck and chest before arriving at her breasts. Her pelvis undulated to the throbbing of Chabat's guitar still playing on the CD. With a whimper, she pulled her gown off and threw it on the chaise.

My heart raced.

In the moonlight her olive skin seemed gilded.

Sarah turned from the balcony railing and restarted the second movement before sinking to the chaise, caressing herself, teasing her nipples into peaks.

Stunned, I adjusted the shutters for a better view, then inhaled sharply at the unfamiliar sensation of my cock stirring.

Watching Sarah, I grew harder. Painfully hard. Teenage boy hard.

As her fingers slipped past dense curls into the valley between her thighs, she moaned.

I reached for my cock, reveling in its power.

For the first time that night, a cool breeze stirred, carrying toward me the intoxicating fragrance of orange blossoms mixed with her desire.

Keeping time with Chabat's fuck-me music, her hand moved faster between her legs. Her breath grew ragged.

To keep from groaning, I bit my lip. Seven years of long-buried semen jetted into the shutters. I staggered with the intensity of the release.

"Yes, Ari!" she cried, arching her body with her orgasm.

My heart stopped. Seven years of waiting—and she called out for another man.

With my head resting against the louvers, I watched Sarah till her breathing slowed. Lying on her back, one arm curved upward, one beneath lush breasts, she slept. A satisfied smile graced succulent lips. Black curls cascaded over golden skin. Her body echoed the curves of the guitar on the ground beside her.

Seven years.

My abdomen tensed. My stomach blazed into an inferno. I went inside and grabbed the antacid bottle in the bathroom.

Two Tums, then four, didn't knock out the burn. Twelve Tums later, fire still raced up my esophagus. I tasted blood. *Hell must taste like this.*

Seven years, and she'd never be mine.

After retrieving my pistol from the nightstand, I opened the shutters and stepped toward Sarah. I looked down at her, then fired one shot into her heart.

"Ari," she breathed, and then her body went limp.

Seven years, and her last breath carried another man's name.

Plink. Drip. Plink. Drip. Drops of her blood sounded the guitar strings before falling into its womb.

I sank onto the chaise and lifted Sarah's head to my lap. With my left hand, I twisted her curls like Chinese finger traps around my fingers, determined to bind us forever. With my right hand, I brought the Colt to my mouth. I swallowed the barrel and squeezed the trigger.

THE GARBAGE MANDALA
BY DENNIS MOMBAUER

Something stuck out of the garbage, and Vasto immediately recognized its strangeness. This week alone, he and his coworkers had cleaned out hundreds of bins, bags and containers, fed their contents to Devora and delivered it all to the Facility, but they had never come across a thing like this.

"Do you see that?"

"Do I see what?" Irakov, another of the garbage men, entered the narrow alleyway. "Whatever it is, just leave it. We're late already, and if some asshole has thrown glass or syringes into the trash again, it's his problem, not ours."

Irakov's breath condensed in the air, barely visible in the traces of brightness that trickled down from the streetlights. The hours before dawn always seemed to be the coldest, perhaps because they were furthest from the sun, perhaps because the men themselves were still at their most vulnerable.

"It's some kind of mechanical device, like nothing I've seen before." Vasto advanced further into the alley, slowly walking toward the garbage bin.

The thing looked similar to a watch, but lacked a face or hands: round, with a pane of glass covering a convex hollow space. Something inside it began to move, like a mechanical animal that had been startled by Vasto's presence: a small metal blur ran round the edges, then in a tighter circle, followed a spiraling path toward the middle, like a spine curved in on itself. It reached the center and disappeared through a small hole, so fast that it completed its entire trajectory in the time Vasto made another step. As it vanished, he stopped dead, watching for any further movement – but the watch-thing, as big as Vasto's palm, remained motionless.

"Come on, just leave it. You can look for garbage treasures on your own time."

Vasto reached out and tapped lightly against the glass, feeling a strange, plastic-like surface, almost body temperature despite the cold weather …and there was something else behind the bin, barely visible in the gloom of the receding night. There were lines drawn on the wall that formed a complicated graffiti pattern all over the concrete, spreading out in both directions in a wing-like fashion. Its coloration was one of extremes: a stark white, shimmering like the crystals of some sun-dried salt lake, crisscrossed by lines and circles of such absolute blackness that they seemed to seep into the wall and become part of its underlying network of cracks and structural fault lines.

"Come on! I can hear the engine starting, and Sedon won't wait for us much longer." Irakov was always rough and wild, always impatient, but he would never leave one of his crew behind. "Whatever it is, look for it again tomorrow."

Vasto took one last glance at the graffiti and the not-quite-a-watch, turned away, changed his mind, turned back and quickly pocketed the thing.

The other workers stood resting around old Devora, their garbage truck with the outdated loading mechanics and the slightly erratic engine. The driver's door was open and the heat from inside turned into steam in the cold air, as if the vehicle would breathe and shiver together with the men in their orange overalls.

Now that the shifts had been extended even further and the days grew shorter, they both went to work and got home in freezing darkness, and still there was so much to do, so much garbage quelling out of the pores of the city, as if it were suffering a feverish infection.

"All aboard?" Sedon's voice from the driver's cabin didn't sound any more urging than usual, and the men gave short grunts of confirmation as they climbed up on the footboards.

Vasto clasped a handle with one hand while the vehicle rumbled along the streets, its fumes and engine noises enveloping him like the warmth of a giant animal. They stopped at house entrances and street corners, gloomy alleyways and the brightly lit portals of subway stations, collecting trashcans and feeding them into Devora's rear.

The sun finally rose, the streets filled with cars and people, slowing the progress of Vasto and his coworkers to a crawl and surrounding them with honking and annoyed voices. There wasn't another watch-thing anywhere in the trash, but one time, Vasto thought he saw a similar graffiti to the one in the alleyway as they passed a construction site.

"Time to go home, boys." Sedon heaved his body out of the truck at the parking lot, like a humanoid crab ejecting from its hard shell. For all his ponderous corpulence, Sedon had always reminded Vasto of a Buddhist monk, his fat body radiating a meditative tranquility. His eyes above the heavy pouches moved like badly lubricated ball joints, but their gaze seemed to capture everything, even the tiniest detail of their surroundings. "Same time tomorrow?"

"Same time tomorrow."

Vasto stripped out of his work uniform – gloves, boots, the orange vest with the reflector stripes – and put on his own clothes, which made him feel even more vulnerable to the cold. Gusts of icy wind tore one of the newly planted garbage bags out of a trashcan and made it fumble through the air with plastic fingers, as if it wanted to find and touch Vasto.

He made his way home, but his thoughts circled around the thing he found, the strange, indicator-less watch resting in his pocket. He couldn't imagine what purpose it might serve and what the moving thing had been, fast and tiny like a frightened animal. It was something that didn't belong here, something that was at the same time foreign and familiar to Vasto, as if it had been specifically designed just for him.

The bus was overheated, and the illumination accentuated the tiredness in the other passenger's faces, their flaccid skin, the eyes staring bluntly into the distance. The engine vibrated under Vasto's seat, and in every curve, he was pushed slightly to the side and away from his incipient sleep. Outside, lights and darkness drifted past and mixed in the window with his own reflection, until he couldn't distinguish himself from the landscape anymore and finally dozed off.

It was nearly a full week before Vasto found the second object.

Devora clattered down the streets in different parts of the city, far away from the dark alleyway, collecting more and more garbage without ever reducing it. Vasto looked out for something similar to his first find, which he had locked away at home, but he discovered nothing except the usual.

Maybe that wasn't exactly right: it was the usual, perpetual flood of household waste and roadside litter, but there were odd things scattered across it. Vasto noticed an increasing number of disturbing and rare objects in the trash, the dismembered heads of dolls, wooden boards with ritualistic arrays of nails, spider-like constructs of black rubber, reminiscent of jellyfish washed ashore after a high tide. Small glass-blown bubbles drifted to the surface of the waste mass in Devora's bowels, accompanied by baby shoes, little clay tablets and exotics masks jingling with threaded shards and colored seashells.

At night, he saw vague resemblances of the graffiti symbols float through his dreams, trying to connect and form a bigger pattern – but the edges and lines didn't match up, and it all fell apart again. He almost sensed a kind of plan in it, a system of occult instructions, but their meaning constantly evaded him, and he couldn't follow them.

The second find surprised him nearly as much as the first. He and his coworkers were trotting alongside a slowly crawling Devora, their reflector stripes glittering in the headlights of oncoming traffic: and there it was, a painted spider web of lines and circles, just a few steps into a lesser-used side street.

"I'm gonna get the cans here. Why don't you take those ones?"

Irakov mumbled some obscenity under his breath in response, and then trudged away with the other garbage men. Vasto studied the graffiti for a moment and tried to memorize it before he began opening the cans, rifling through them. He wasn't sure what made him hope there might be something worth finding, that the graffiti was more than it appeared to be, that it was a hidden sign– until he saw it.

The second thing looked completely different from the pseudo-watch with the spiraling movement, but it evoked the same sense of extraneousness, of not-belonging, and it was made from the same material, not new and clean, but also not as dirty and derelict as everything around it. Its shape was that of several light metal joints in a line, linked by smaller bars and pistons, as long as Vasto's forearm, although thinner and more flexible.

There was nothing moving this time, so he put the object under his vest and continued to work, feeding Devora until she could make the next trip to the Facility.

"Come on, that's enough. Traffic is easing up." Vasto and the others followed Sedon's voice, and Vasto got in the front seat. The truck began to jolt with the starting engine, trembling under him like an excited riding mount.

"Here we go." Sedon released the handbrake, engaged first gear and slowly accelerated along with the cars before him, trying to blend in and merge with the herd.

On Vasto's way home, the traffic lights felt off, as if they had somehow changed their rhythm, forcing Vasto to stop when he was picking up his speed, to hurry when he was instinctively slowing down. They turned red at times he wasn't used to and when he least expected it, making his entire path to the subway station awkward and straining.

He walked down the stairs into the subway and passed a control lamp that flickered with an unsteady orange, as if a fire was smoldering inside the wall. Maybe the city was changing, or maybe Vasto only imagined it … it was possible that the Administration had indeed reprogrammed the lights, reacting to some invisible change in the traffic it had unearthed from its data.

As Vasto waited for the tram that would carry him through the tunnels, past a construction site where workers had torn open the street, and to the bus station back on the surface, he let his fingers wander across his second find.

It was clearly mechanical, but at the same time, it had a weirdly organic feel to it, becoming somewhat malleable under Vasto's careful pressure. It appeared to be neither metal nor plastic, and there were several tiny hooks and holes, as if it was a part of something else, not a whole.

The cold crept out of the gaping blackness of the tunnels on pitter-pattering rat feet and made Vasto shiver. In the glow of the tube lights, the subway station seemed eerily bright, as if it was part of the moon or some mist-shrouded nether realm, color- and lifeless like a painting in monochromes.

The display panel had shown the same arrival times for hours now, and the minutes till the next train seemed not to count down, not to count up, not to count at all. Below the display, a woman appeared to be watching Vasto while her manicured claws pressed a phone to her ear, but when he returned the look, she averted her gaze.

The tiled walls made the station look like a public pool or a slaughterhouse, and for a short moment, Vasto imagined how all the people waiting here would bleed out, their turbid red sloshing back and forth between those walls, trapped in a prison of coldness and slick, unassailable surfaces.

Vasto took another look at the display panel, and this time, it changed: and simultaneously, he could hear the train entering the station from behind his back.

Snowflakes drifted over the city, and the garbage accumulated in powdered white heaps next to the containers. Devora and the crew worked their way along the streets, collecting plastic bag after plastic bag in the vehicle's clamoring bowels, while the cold trickled in through their gloves and work vests.

At every intersection, identical streets stretched away into the distance, lined by garbage and increasingly shrouded in white fog, as if the city was being swallowed whole by the snow, and Vasto and his coworkers were the only ones still struggling.

Sometimes, Sedon flashed the headlights when another garbage truck came toward them, otherwise the outside world drifted past without any point of contact. They stopped, jumped off Devora's footboards and brought back to her new sustenance in bags and container loads.

At noon, the sun little more than a dim shape on the clouded sky, the crew took a break, standing together in a semi-circle next to Devora, watching the streams of traffic and passersby. A tram glided silently past them like an enormous moray eel through murky water, appearing out of the white mist and disappearing into it on the other side.

Vast had found five of the objects by now, and he was sure that there were more, that they were all connected. Whenever Devora stopped, he tried to get away from Sedon, from Irakov and the others to search for more – and sometimes, he made a find.

The thing was some sort of small bag or bellows, with plastic rings and wires that ran across it as veins would through a living body; it had protruding connections and also a tiny display, covered by arched glass. Something moved under the glass, a metal blur too fast to recognize, which curved into a spiral and dissolved without Vasto being able to tell how or where.

When he returned to the truck, he saw the men standing together in a tight circle like a pack of animals trying to share their warmth, turning outward to him as he left the alley. No one showed Vasto a smile or a nod, they all just averted their eyes and scattered as soon as he approached them, as if he had disturbed some kind of private meeting.

An astronaut coming back after a mission alone in space might feel the same way: everything had become different in his absence, and new relationships had formed among his friends and family, a subtle web of social connections that he could neither perceive nor penetrate.

On Vasto's commute home, the tram slowed down at the construction site, and Vasto took a long look outside the window. Cables ran through the whole site in thick black lines, shimmering like frozen oil under the streetlights, crisscrossing a cold island carved out of the sea of nightly black.

The workers turned when the train passed them, always facing Vasto, as if their backs had to stay hidden from sight, as if they were hollowed out and full of engine parts, of cords and levers that reached into them from the ground. The lamps filled the space behind the workers with deep shadows, and only the edges of the digging pit were illuminated by their light, making it seem like it had no bottom and no end.

At home, until late in the night, Vasto worked at putting his finds together. He didn't know what he was building or what any of the individual parts were, but it became increasingly clear to his probing fingers that they fit together, that they matched up and would form … something. There were hooks and lugs with corresponding sizes, cogs clicking against each other, shapes that seemed to be able to interlock... if only Vasto had all the pieces to this puzzle.

There were parts missing, bridges and joints that needed to be there, no matter how hard Vasto tried to put it all together, guided only by his tactile sense and the half-remembered graffiti dreams. The more parts Vasto added, the more familiar it all seemed – but he was certain that he had never seen any of these things – nor their slowly growing accumulation – before.

He found further objects during the days that rushed by in a tired haze of darkness and falling snow, and he experimented with them in the evenings and at night. The shifts were lengthened again by the Administration, from the dark of the morning hours to the increasingly early dawn of the hibernal nights.

Vasto didn't understand how they could work so long and still have so much garbage left, how the bins and containers filled themselves so rapidly. The city's population had stayed the same, but now, the short shifts of the old days would have never been sufficient, and the Administration pushed for more and more, so the streets wouldn't clog up like calcified arteries.

The snow stopped falling, and there weren't any free spaces left for it to fall on. The city was coated white, the streets covered by icy slush, and Vasto made steady progress in putting together his private project. More and more, he felt alienated from his coworkers, alone in his days and nights, and this isolation weighed heavy on him.

"Sedon? Irakov?" He had watched for an opportunity during one of their breaks, when Sedon had come of his seat and seemed to meditate in the rising steam of a coffee cup. "There's something...something I've found in the trash, several things actually, and I'm building something else with it, I don't know what."

Vasto paused and tried to rearrange his thoughts into coherent sentences: "The things I've found, they are pieces of something greater ... and there were graffiti symbols at every place I found them. Don't you think that's strange? I'll show you, if you want ... I just needed to tell somebody, to talk with you about it. Come, I'll show you one of the graffiti nearby."

"That isn't necessary, Vasto. We believe you." Sedon's eyes seemed like dull glass in the cold cones of the streetlights, as if he had been replaced by some perfectly lifelike robot. "You have found some garbage and seen some graffiti."

"You don't want to look at them?"

"You shouldn't worry about such things. There is always something strange to be found in the trash, but it doesn't have meaning or importance." Sedon's voice seemed changed, had become as grey and shapeless as the coffee steam through which it was spoken.

"I don't worry, I want to know! The things I've found, they are not normal … there's something wrong with this city, you must have noticed that."

Irakov, who had always been a fighter, a challenger, never taking shit from anyone, with anger that was quick to arouse and easy to appease again, seemed utterly uninterested in what was going on. "Just leave it be. You are tired. We all are, from the long shifts, the hard work."

"Right." Sedon nodded slowly, as if his head was being jerked back and forth by invisible strings. "Let's get on with it."

Vasto wandered through the snowbound city, and his coworker's words haunted him. Was he obsessed with random bits of garbage and some pieces of street art, or did they just not see the bigger picture: a pattern of changes, a mutation of the city, some sort of urban sickness that was silently spreading with more and more acute symptoms.

He crossed a corner and suddenly realized that he had lost all sight of Sedon, Irakov or Devora, of the street, even his own tracks. A strong feeling of danger surged through him, as if someone were watching him, as if something were happening behind his back, in his blind spot – but there was nothing, no matter how much he turned. He felt a mixture of intense fear and aggression, his primal instincts telling him alternately to stand and fight, to run, to hold his ground, to flee as fast and far as he could.

He strayed along an empty alleyway, past a manhole cover under which he could hear the rush of flowing water close to the surface, as though a rainstorm in another part of the city had flooded the sewers from floor to ceiling. Vasto wondered if he had become delirious and was losing his mind, or if there was some rational explanation for these perceptions and feelings, if he truly was in danger.

A small paved plaza opened up before him, little more than an indentation of the alleyway, with an unused flowerbed that had been covered with snow and frozen dirt. There was no one to be seen, no one entering or exiting the plaza, no chairs, no tables, no workers, nothing.

Vasto felt as if he had made a grave mistake, as if he had run into a trap that was about to snap shut around him. The surface of a tiny puddle, unfrozen despite the cold, rippled under a passing wind, even though the house walls provided nearly perfect shelter, and Vasto couldn't see anything else moving. There was a soaked warning vest just lying there, forlorn, without an owner… but who would leave his clothing behind in this weather?

Sweat congealed on Vasto's forehead, made his hands greasy and his clothes damp on his skin. Suddenly, his legs weren't strong enough to support him anymore, and he collapsed against the wall, brushed aside snow, and slid down.

There was graffiti leading out of this blind end, half-hidden under the white coating, but clearly recognizable in its tangle of zebra lines, its esoteric patterns that Vasto's dreams had so often tried to unlock.

Just looking at it seemed to calm his mind, to make his heart go steadier, his breaths deeper. He followed the familiar patterns with his eyes and then his body, along the walls, away from the paved plaza and its invisible horrors: and he escaped.

The lights became sparser outside the windows as the bus left the inner city, slowly accelerating toward the outskirts. Although it grew darker, Vasto had the paradoxical feeling of ascending from a deep black ocean, away from all the glowing spots that could only be anglerfish on the hunt for prey.

What he had found under the furthest branches of the painted graffiti tree was something that he believed to be the final part, a malformed connecting piece of ports and clamps: and if he was right, it would give shape to everything else he had assembled so far.

On the way home, Vasto couldn't get the strange reaction of his coworkers out of his mind, Sedon's detached stare and Irakov's empty robot eyes... they hadn't been themselves, almost as if someone was remote-controlling them... and by the time he arrived, Vasto was certain that they were already part of it, whatever "it" was.

He prowled around his rooms until he arrived at a radical decision: he had to get out of the city. It wasn't safe to be here anymore, neither for him nor for the thing he was building: and they both needed to escape.

The next bus to the train station left in ten minutes, so he grabbed a few of his belongings and began to pack his project into a garbage bag. Part of him wanted to insert the final piece right now, but the same feeling of danger as on the small plaza overcame him, overwhelmed him, and he needed to flee.

As the bus left the suburb with Vasto's home, it passed two police cars and an ambulance speeding in the opposite direction, without sirens, but very fast and determined. Was this the city coming for him?

There were no police officers at the train station, and Vasto could board without complications: but what did that prove, except that he might have acted just in time, before it would have been too late?

The train reached the neighboring city in the middle of the night, and Vasto exited it onto an almost empty platform. The few people getting off with him quickly dispersed down the stairs and into the coldly lit passageways, and Vasto followed them like a sleepwalker.

No one knew where he was now, nobody could find him... he had paid for the ticket with cash at the machine and left no record of his destination. It was secure here, no one was watching him, and the feeling of imminent danger had subsided down to a manageable base level.

Vasto put down the garbage bag outside the passageway, unpacked its contents and looked at them. When he added the last piece, it snapped into place with an almost inaudible clicking. Vasto's focus suddenly changed, his perception shifted, and he finally realized why it had all seemed so familiar: The last piece was literally the heart, and it made sense of all this, transformed a bunch of random artifacts into a greater whole.

It had been difficult to see under the displays and valves and mechanical additions, made of metal and plastic, not from flesh: but what Vasto had built were organs, entrails, a replica of the human heart, lungs, stomach, liver and kidneys, all held together by elastic rubber bands, tubes, and an artificial spine.

It was almost too alien to be the result of Vasto's work, and just looking at it here felt wrong, as if he had brought a contagion into this other city, a foreign virus that would spread and spread until it permeated this place, just like the snow had suffocated Vasto's home.

With quick, sudden movements, Vasto stuffed everything into the garbage bag again, looked out for observers and started to walk. He turned the corner of the empty station yard, and there it was: a graffiti shimmering from out of the darkness of a distant alleyway, easily picked up by Vasto's attuned eyes.

As he approached across the abandoned nightly street, lined with discarded litter, Vasto saw that this graffiti was unfamiliar, done in the exact same style as the others, but with different lines, different patterns, a different plan. New instructions… a new blueprint for new parts, to complete what Vasto had started, to build something to support those organs, something that would form a new body… a new being born from the city's sickness.

September 10, 2012 8:40 P.M.
Arkham, Massachusetts
"I just don't know if we should do this."

The words had barely left Charlie's mouth before a chorus of exasperated groans and sighs filled the small, dimly lit living room.

"Yes, Charlie, we are doing this," Emmerick responded through gritted teeth. "And quite frankly, I'm starting to wonder if 'we' should still include 'you' anymore."

"Hey, no one wants to stop this thing more than I do!" Charlie snapped back. "In case you've forgotten, I had an uncle who would still be alive if 9/11 never happened!"

Emmerick's face softened with a mix of embarrassment and regret. He was well aware of the loss Charlie experienced that day, but a decade of ridicule and scorn had worn his temperament down to the last thread of grace he had left. The thought of someone he trusted like Charlie becoming a sheep like all the rest was more than enough to send him over the edge.

"Sorry, Chuck," Emmerick finally exhaled in a low voice. "It's just—"

"—it's just that now is not the time to be getting cold feet, hun." Michelle interrupted. "I know your uncle was like a father to you, but most of us got family we stand to lose now if this thing doesn't go how it's supposed to." She reached over and put a hand on Charlie's shoulder before continuing. "Why don't you just take a deep breath and tell us what's troubling you about tomorrow...besides the whole changing the course of history part, of course."

Michelle's warm smile set both Charlie and Emmerick at ease. Getting the group settle down was something she'd always been good at doing. Charlie figured her talent for remaining calm in the face of chaos was from her time as an Explosive Ordinance Disposal expert in Afghanistan. After disarming bombs with bullets flying around your head, diffusing a shouting match between two middle-aged men was probably a piece of cake.

"Well...for starters, no one here is an engineer," Charlie began. "I know everyone here is intelligent, but for something this big, we should probably have at least one person with us who can confirm our theory."

"All the proof is already out there," Joseph chimed in from the other side of the room. "You've read it just like the rest of us. Any engineer who doesn't see something that obvious is either not worth their salt or too scared of being ridiculed by the world…or worse."

"Hun, I've seem more things blow up in my lifetime then you can imagine," Michelle continued. "Trust me; there's no question that was a controlled demolition."

"And even if it wasn't, Dr. Marsh is one of the smartest folks you could ever hope to meet," Emmerick added. "He may not be an engineer, but I'd still trust his word on just about any subject over anyone else's."

Charlie glanced over to the window where Dr. Marsh stood, peering out towards the street and acting as if the people inside his living room didn't exist. Marsh claimed he was watching for signs of government surveillance, but it appeared to Charlie as though the professor just didn't want to converse with them. It was one of the many reasons he didn't care for the old man despite all he'd done for them. He always felt like Dr. Marsh looked at their group with an air of smug contempt, as if he were observing rats locked in a cage rather than people who he considered to be his peers. He also always smelled like fish; not in a strange 'old man' way, but like a full sea of them was constantly following him wherever he stood.

"…and that's another thing," Charlie said, looking back towards Emmerick. "You know I trust you with my life, E…but you gotta understand how hard it is for me to accept that a geology professor from Miskatonic University created the world's first working time machine."

"You watch your tongue, whelp!" Dr. Marsh bellowed while continuing to stare out the window. "There are powers and forces found within this earth far greater than your over-medicated brain could hope to—"

"—but I saw it, Charlie," Emmerick interrupted. "Dr. Marsh took me and Ray ten years into the past a few weeks ago…watched the Red Sox lose to the Yankees in Fenway back when we still had Ramirez."

"Then why didn't we try to stop it before it happened?!" Charlie blurted out. "I know getting on the planes in mid-flight would've been impossible, but we could've killed the hijackers or something."

"Then no one would have known that our government was behind it," Emmerick sighed. "They'd just find another way to murder American citizens and justify the Patriot Act. We need to get the proof that's inside the tower basement."

"But when those planes hit, people will still die...including my uncle," Charlie said in almost a whisper. "We could've stopped it. Maybe if we'd just gone back a few days earlier and warned people—"

"We've been trying to tell people about what really happened on 9/11 for years!" Raymond grunted. "If they won't listen to us now with all the proof right in front of them, do you really think those sheep would have listened to a bunch of folks claiming to be time travelers from the future?"

"We gotta go down inside that basement and get the explosives, hun," Michelle stated firmly. "I'll disarm it; that'll save plenty of lives along with giving us indisputable evidence about what really happened."

"...and we gotta do it that morning." Raymond added gruffly. "The building will be too well guarded while they're setting everything up."

"That leads me to my last problem with all this," Charlie said after a deep breath. "If time travel exists, then it stands to reason that it would become a more refined, efficient, and widely used process in the future...so why hasn't anyone from our future gone back and stopped what happened on that day already?"

That last statement was the first one met by silence from the rest of the group. After a few moments, Dr. Marsh's low, growling voice finally answered.

"There is much about the act of traveling through time that neither I nor a whelp like you can possibly comprehend. Perhaps others have already traveled back in time before us, spinning off a new line of existence in which that horrible day brought forth a people's revolution rather than a government boot upon our necks. Others may have simply failed. But we do know that we have the means to travel back to that day ourselves...which means that tomorrow, we shall alter history ourselves."

"And we have to do it tomorrow," Emmerick added. "The device that Dr. Marsh built can't be set to a specific date and time; it takes you back 10 years from the present. Tomorrow is the anniversary, so we need to act now."

Arkham Police Department Missing Persons Report
<u>Reporting Officer</u>: Lt. Detective Swinburne
<u>Date Investigation</u>: September 12, 2012
<u>Missing Persons</u>
Emmerick Alexander Jones
Michelle Johnson Berger
Joseph Edward Stevens
Raymond David Griffon
Charles Phillip Valentich
Dr. Allen Franklin Marsh
<u>Officer Notes</u>
On the evening of Sunday, September 11, the Arkham Police Department received multiple calls between the hours of 6:00 P.M. – 8:30 P.M. in regards to the subjects listed above. The spouses of Mr. Jones, Mrs. Berger, Mr. Stevens, and Mr. Griffin all reported that their family members had not been seen or heard from since the evening prior. Charles Valentich's roommate, William Klass, called to report him missing at approximately 11:15 P.M.

On Monday, September 12, Dr. Marsh did not appear at Miskatonic University to teach his 8:00 A.M. Geology class. By this point, more than 24 hours had passed since the previously mentioned subjects were last seen by their cohabiters.

After speaking with the subjects' families and friends, the unifying factor found among them was that they were all part of a local 9/11 Truth Movement chapter which communicated regularly. Neighbors of Dr. Marsh reported a large gathering of cars at his residence on the evening of Saturday, September 10. They were all gone the next morning.

Toll records and traffic cameras show their vehicles heading into New York City during the early morning hours of September 11. NYPD is working with our department to locate their vehicles and the missing subjects.

◇◇◇

September 11, 2001 6:35 AM
New York, New York

"You look nice, hun," Michelle said while straightening Charlie's tie.

He wanted to tell her that she looked nice as well, but his labored breathing made it impossible to do anything but nod and catch his breath. The miles of walking, combined with the events of the last 12 hours, had left Charlie feeling so dizzy that he could barely stand up anymore.

The group had driven in the middle of the night up to New York, eventually stopping at Fort Tilden Park. It was chosen due to its low security presence and lack of visitors. Unfortunately, that meant they would have a long trek to get to the World Trade Center once they arrived in 2001.

Upon entering the park, the entire group had changed into professional-looking business attire to go along with their forged World Trade Center entrance passes. The heavy, formal clothing seemed to be weighing down on everyone except for Dr. Marsh, who already dressed that way on a daily basis, and Michelle, who looked strikingly beautiful in what she referred to as her "Agent Scully Pantsuit."

Dr. Marsh then hastily assembled the time travel device, which looked like a miniature street lamp attached to a small electric generator. Inside of the long, vertical cylinder were various slots, all filled with bizarre looking green and blue stones. Charlie's eyes had still been transfixed on them when Emmerick motioned for the group to huddle close together near the device.

"Have we got everything we need?" Raymond asked.

"Yep," Joseph responded, holding up a collection of laptop bags. "And I'd really appreciated it if you guys could take these now because they're heavy as hell."

The group all reached over and took a bag while Dr. Marsh pulled a book out of his left coat pocket. He immediately turned to a page near the middle and began reciting something in a language unlike any Charlie had heard before.

"G'aas Oftg Onat! Sang iat san xaa't lats tu shas xuia' ghuftft su iangu sha ftungt ur shut ghu'ftg nax fta naga thunlftasa!"

The group stared at the professor nervously except for Emmerick and Raymond, who both made quick motions with their heads not to gape at the professor while he read. Before they could look away, however, the stones inside of the long cylinder began to glow brightly in the early autumn night. Within seconds, the blue and green light enveloped them a force so brilliant, it felt as though they were wrapped inside of a warm, ethereal blanket.

That briefly pleasant sensation ended just ask quickly as it began, spilling them back out onto the ground in what appeared to be the exact same place they had just been. Charlie wanted to look for any sign that they'd succeeded in traveling to the past, but he was too busy vomiting to do so.

"Easy now," Ray said while helping him back up. "I did the same thing when Professor Marsh took me and Emmerick back for the first time."

Charlie looked over to see that everyone aside from Ray, Emmerick, and Professor Marsh were keeled over and vomiting on the ground.

"Just be glad this ain't like the version of time travel they used in the Terminator movies," Ray added while clapping him on the shoulder. "Otherwise, we'd all have to see E naked…although that might not be such a bad thing with Michelle along for the ride."

"Eat a dick, Ray," Michelle coughed between heaves of bile.

While the rest of the group continued to struggle through their debilitating bouts of nausea, Emmerick helped the professor dismantle the device. He then instructed everyone to place one part of it in their laptop bags. Charlie was about to protest that it would be caught by security, but he then remembered how different the world was before 9/11. It was a time when you weren't under constant surveillance or feeling a security guard's hand go down your pants. America was a country that had yet to exchange its freedom for a false sense of security.

As if on cue with his ruminations, Charlie's eyes glances ahead to where the World Trade Center towers used to stand…only now they were still there. Two beacons of a time gone by when life was better and he still had his uncle.

Charlie had wanted more than anything to start running right then towards Albany…to knock on his uncle's door and hug him. To tell him how hard the last ten years had been without him there to talk to when he missed his father or life felt too hard to continue living. Emmerick's voice snapped him out of it, though, barking at them to start heading for the World Trade Center.

By the time they were a few blocks away, the sun had begun to rise. Charlie's feet hurt from the dress shoes he was wearing. His left shoulder also ached from the surprisingly heavy bag that hung around it. He'd already felt weak from vomiting when they arrived; now he was moving forward solely on pure determination, the knowledge that what they were doing that day had a chance to bring his uncle back driving his tired body forward

After Michelle complimented Charlie and straightened his tie, Emmerick explained that they'd need to space out their arrivals at Tower One so as not to look more suspicious than they already did. Copies of the floor plans that Ray had reconstructed were handed out, but each of them had memorized the path to the basement level a long time ago.

Emmerick and Dr. Marsh entered first, followed a few minutes later by Joseph. Next was Ray, then Charlie and Michelle. By 8:15 A.M., they had all made it into Tower One, gathering in the stairwell near the location Ray had pinpointed as the most likely to be rigged with explosives. Emmerick didn't like cutting things so close, but it had been Dr. Marsh who convinced him to leave such a slim margin in their operational timetable.

"There can be no chance of interference by those of this time period," he'd said during one of their final meetings. "The longer we stay, the greater the chance we will be found and stopped from completing our mission."

Right now, however, that mission was in danger of not being completed due to an entirely different and unexpected reason.

"Where the hell are the bombs, Ray?" Emmerick asked as Michelle unloaded her equipment.

"I…I don't know. By all accounts and measurements, they should be right here. This area was large and isolated enough to contain them. It also makes sense with witness accounts of where the lower level explosions were heard."

"Well hun, you better let us in on your back up theory soon," Michelle said after standing back up. "Because if you don't have one, this party's gonna be over before it even gets started."

"You idiots…"

Something in Dr. Marsh's voice caused a chill to run down Charlie's spine. He'd always found the professor off-putting, but the mix of glee and malice with which he spoke now truly terrified him.

"You're not helping, doc," Emmerick hissed. "We need—"

"Oh, I've actually helped quite a bit, but not as much as you," Dr. Marsh interrupted as his mouth spread into an impossibly wide grin. "You see, the evil in this world had always been such a simple thing before today. There are terrible men and women who wish to do terrible things in the face of overwhelming good. Sometimes, they succeed. Most of the time, however, they do not. Today, however, they will achieve not just their own ends, but also birth a cycle of mistrust and division that—"

"Doc, we don't have time for—"

"The planes were enough for those evil men, but you are the key to the Great Old Ones' plans!" Dr. Marsh interrupted in a loud whisper. "All here is as it should be by your species' hand, but it is you who brought the seeds of division inside this place!"

"Holy shit!" Michelle exclaimed.

Everyone turned. Michelle had unzipped the front compartment of her laptop bag and was peering down inside of it. When she looked back up, her eyes were wide with fear and rage.

"You put thermite in these!"

"…and inside the device which you helped carry inside," Dr. Marsh said with a slight gurgle in his voice. "Not enough to bring down the building, but enough to plant the needed seeds of doubt and madness."

Charlie's brain had yet to process what was happening when the professor moved with a quickness that should have been impossible for someone his age…or anything that was human. He latched onto Michelle, opened his mouth at a sickeningly wide angle, and bit down into her neck. Before she had fallen to the floor, Dr. Marsh's right hand shot out and violently plunged through Joseph's chest.

Ray, Charlie, and Emmerick all screamed as they turned and tried to escape. Two long back tentacles burst forth of Dr. Marsh's mouth and wrapped around Emmerick and Ray's feet, tripping them so that they fell hard onto the floor. A third tentacle attempted to wrap itself around Charlie, but he managed to reach the stairwell in time to begin barreling back up towards the lobby.

Behind him, Charlie heard screams which were silenced in a wet, horrifying crunch. Immediately afterwards, footsteps far too rapid for those of a man pounded behind him, gaining ground faster than his mind could concoct a way to escape. Adrenaline and fear allowed him to get to the third floor before something wet and terrible wrapped around his neck. In the next instant, the world went black.

Dr. Marsh yanked Charlie's body to a nearby utility closet and shut the door. He wasn't sure who might have heard him, but none of that mattered anymore; the plan of the Great Old Ones had once again been fulfilled.

"And now the chain begins anew," he thought with a wicked grin.

He had been shown long ago what the future held for his actions here in the past. The thermite, Charlie's body inside the closet, and others working from the present time would send this species of false rulers spiraling towards madness. In a matter of years, many of them would consider every possible act evil by a malicious few to be the work of many. Years later, even natural disasters and weather phenomena would be feverishly twisted into weak excuses for revolutionary dissent…and eventually, violence.

"Thank you, Yog-Sothoth, for allowing me to be your vessel," Dr. Marsh prayed in his native R'lyehian tongue after reaching the basement floor. "May their madness be their undoing…and allow the Great Old Ones to rule over this planet once again. I sacrifice myself willing to see this brought forth."

As Dr. Marsh's prayer ended, a terrible sound followed by an explosive crash could be heard many floors above him…

…and to this day, 1,115 victims and 7,930 body fragments from the World Trade Center attack have not been identified. While sound scientific reasoning and the consensus of structural engineers indicates that a controlled explosion played no part in bringing down the World Trade Center towers, the evidence of trace amounts

of nano-thermite in the building's wreckage continues to be a hotly debated issue.

The Harvest Consortium
By Dean H. Wild

The line where the night sky met the sea was something Rook
Jeffries was always able to pick out, whether from the shore or from
the foredeck of a runner like this one. Most guys in his unit couldn't
pick it out, not without night vision headgear, but he homed in on it
like a precision instrument. It was not only the line he was meant to
watch now, but that's where his eyes kept returning, darting to the
black and foamy chop of the ocean to check for smaller, stealthier
vessels and then scanning the sky for gliding, predatory craft in
between. Nothing in his sector, he thought and clutched up on the
carbine in his hands anyway— always thinking, always ready— a
thousand miles of seawater under his watch for only a few minutes
more. He wanted a smoke. He supposed Eckles, who stood watch on
the port side, wanted one worse since it was hard to find him without
one smoldering in his fingers or dangling unlit from the corner of his
mouth. Once this maneuver was over, they could both light up, clink
a few beer bottles in honor of one another's health, and put this night
behind them. Once the divers finished their work, and the shrouded
shape of a man was pulled up from the sandy bottom, they could all
put this seething tension behind them, tuck it away, make it into
nothing more than a secret.

     The cryo-crate sat only a few feet from him— a dull gray
coffin with a single blinking light in the lid, which seemed like a red
beacon in the dark declaring ready-ready-ready for its cargo. And the
question rose into Rook's head again, breaking the surface of his
thoughts, as unwelcome and expendable as an unauthorized diver
would be showing up inside of the maneuver area just now. His
orders were to shoot any suspicious personnel, blind and clean, and
worry about their identity and their motive later. The question was
not so easy to drown out, however, because no matter how many
times he dispatched it, it came bobbing up again. The question was
why?

     The guy down there (how many fathoms by now?) had been
buried at sea either by Pentagon order or some type of international
protocol, of that he wasn't sure, none of the four of them on deck
watch were sure: him, Eckles, Brimhall, Wirtz. But the fact
remained, Special Forces took out his scheming, death-dealing,

terrorist ass and his miserable carcass was dumped out here. And twelve hours later, under the guise of a security patrol to keep those who might wish to either defile or martyr the corpse in its watery grave, he and three other sharpshooters, and a team of divers, a medical science team and two big-boned bruisers who were tagged only as the men from the HC (and showed up in a type of ops gear he'd never seen before), came out to retrieve the body once again.

Why?

Eckles and Brimhall were of the opinion the official autopsy was either fucked up or was done against the bastard's religious edicts. That meant we had to move in, make it right and put the corpse back before anyone could get their hands on the evidence. The cryo-crate meant the whole patch job was going to happen off-site, which in turn meant there would be another maneuver, just as rapid and covert as this one, to plant the body back at rest once the repairs were made. A lot of fuss, Rook thought and scanned the sky-to-water line again, since the guy was dead, the whole world knew he was dead and ninety-eight percent of the world was relieved for it and didn't care if he was buried in hallowed ground or chopped up and used to slop the hogs.

He wondered, his hands tightening a little more on the carbine grip, if he'd be called back for the return maneuver.

The first underwater explosive charge came to him as nothing more than a thump, sounding gentle and far away. With it came a light in the water off the bow on his side, a soft green pulse lensed by countless feet of seawater. A mushroom cap of displaced water swelled over where the light pulse had been, and it broke the surface with a muddled, gargling boom and a rush of foam. And then all else broke loose. Gunfire stuttered from the stern, Brimhall judging from the location, and it was immediately followed by a volley from Wirtz. Someone was shouting "Drones! Drones! Drones!"

Something glided over Rook's head, nearly silent, like a massive kite. Feet pounded the deck. Another charge lit the water dead ahead. Then one of the divers surfaced, splashing madly. He was screaming. Personnel poured out from below-decks, some armed, some bewildered. And there were others, men who swooped in from above like predatory birds, releasing their gliding apparatus upon landing on the deck to free their hands and wield the pistols from their belts or the grenades from their flacks. Not drones, Rook thought as he watched an abandoned glider splash into the sea like a wounded bird. Not even close.

One of the glider men was a few feet away, executing a trot-style landing as he pulled two canister grenades from his jacket. Rook brought his carbine up without a second thought and planted a single bullet in the man's gut- nowhere that would immediately kill him and send his thumbs off the grenade triggers. Then, with a running leap, Rook shoved the sole of his boot into the man's chest and sent him overboard. The ensuing explosion sent a splash of seawater and blots of red onto the deck.

He could see Eckles firing into the night sky above them, picking off dark vague shapes—only a few more now—sailing overhead. The diver was still screaming in the water, his words hoarse but more defined now. "Pull me in, for Christ's sake. I've got the payload. I've got the frigging payload."

Brimhall, too, was screaming. "Get off me you son of a whore." He screamed this twice, followed by a thunderous detonation which rocked the runner, and then Brimhall was quiet.

Rook took aim at another glider man, this one with a pistol in each hand which he fired repeatedly like a performer in a wild west show, relying on sheer luck to guide his bullets. Rook's shot was clean. The man dropped and revealed another intruder directly behind him. Rook took him down, too.

Three personnel rushed past him. He recognized one of them as Colonel Sinclair, who had boarded this mission with the quiet removal of someone just along for the ride. Sinclair was attended by the two bullish men in the weird HC gear.

Sinclair fixed his gaze on Rook and stepped up to the cryo-crate. "Cover us, soldier." Then he turned to the HC men. "I'll do this, you pull in the payload. Get to it!"

Rook clutched his gun, at the ready, as instructed. It was the way things needed to go, no matter how hard the question *why* hammered at your skull. He looked across the deck at Eckles who took down a glider man, did a harsh 180 on instinct and took down another who was rushing up behind him. Blind and clean. Damn, they were a good crew. From the corner of his eye, Rook watched Sinclair press his thick fingertip against random spots on the lid of the cryo-crate. The top opened with a jump and a hiss and a few tendrils of escaping icy white air. The body inside the crate was wrapped in coarse muslin, a male body well over 6 feet in height. Rook could not help but stare, since his expected purpose for the crate was to take a body back, not bring one out into the ocean. But it did no good to question. Ever.

"Give me a hand, soldier," Sinclair said as he worked his hands under one side of the shrouded body.

Rook shouldered his carbine and slid his hands under the other side, and together they lifted the corpse (and yes, it was a corpse, not a dummy or decoy, the cool, organic weight of it was unmistakable).

"To the railing. Starboard. Now," Sinclair barked.

Something below decks made a massive billowing sound which could only be flames. The runner rocked. Someone screamed from below. Rook followed Sinclair's lead and they shuffled with their cargo to the starboard side until their hips rested against the railing. They tossed the body over with a type of hurried disregard, each of them taking a moment to evaluate the actions of the HC men who worked a few feet farther along the bow.

A rescue line trailed from the hands of the HC man on the right to the diver, who bobbed ten yards out. A small, blinking floatation device was tethered to the line and the diver grasped it desperately with one hand. His other arm stayed below the surface, weighted down by something unseen. The payload, Rook thought. He was very pale, this diver, his face poking out of the black cowl of his diving suit like a watery moon. The HC men pulled him in, slowly, despite the flying bullets and the grenade discharges and the licks of flame that darted out of the below-decks stairwell to sniff at the topside deck. The diver at last reached the boat and was pulled up, helping himself along with his one leg— the other had been blown off in the underwater blast, leaving a ragged stump that spurted dark crimson along the hull as he climbed. And on a braided tether, his payload rose out of the water behind him; a body wrapped in whitish fabric, male, a little over 6 feet tall, linked to the diver's straining arm.

Everything seemed to converge at that moment. Rook saw the remaining glider men move out across the deck. He heard Wirtz cry out from the stern, a plaintive yelp that ended with a thick gurgle. Then a bullet tore into Rook's side, just below the ribcage. It felt like a hot finger boring into him and worming around restlessly. He clutched at it and dropped to his knees. One of the HC men went down next, clutching his throat around a gout of spurting red. The diver was down, too, a leaking red hole between his eyes. The runner began to pitch drastically to one side-taking on water somewhere below-decks. And above Rook, another, newer dark shape loomed, this one blasting them with air stirred by massive rotors, all sound drowned out by the rapid-fire stutter of chopper blades. Another underwater charge detonated, this one so close to the bow that he felt a spray of hot ocean water wash over him followed by an equally hot gust of air that reeked of flint and sulfur. He dropped to the deck, pain spreading from his bullet wound and occupying every inch of his side from his neck to his knee.

"Get that payload in there," Sinclair roared at the remaining HC man, his hands on the open cryo-crate lid, "Ten seconds before that whirlybird dusts off. Ten seconds."

Hands fell on Rook as the runner pitched further, a howl of surrender echoing from its wounded hull. "Hang on, Rook," Eckles said to him. "They're tossing down some rescue lines now, but we gotta move fast. We'll patch you up back at base. Just hang on."

Rook saw the cryo-crate lift away from the deck in a mesh of rescue lines, its red light once again blinking importantly. He attempted to get up, but pain doubled him over and sent him sprawling back onto the deck. Eckles wrangled one of the few remaining rescue lines and lashed the attached harness around him. He would have to buy Eckles a beer when this was done, he thought, and a whole pack of smokes.

As he was lifted from the deck, the pain flared again and backhanded his already slipping consciousness. Suppressing gunfire came from above him. Another explosion ripped through the runner below him. He searched the night for the horizon, for that reassuring line, but before he could be sure it was there, the pain flared again, and he blacked out.

It was not the base infirmary. It wasn't any infirmary. Rook was sure of that. The room was too small, too bare, and there wasn't enough light. He rolled off of the cot set against the wall, and clutched at the broad, hastily-applied bandage under his shirt. It wasn't a very professional patch job, but it offered some small comfort. It took him a moment in the dim, single-bulb light to determine the way out of the room. Everything was white except for the keypad door latch, which at first seemed to float like a silver tile in the fog. He was at the door within two paces and he waited there, sharpening his ears.

"Anybody there?" he called out.

He evaluated the silence, not quite ready to test the touchpad, not quite sure he liked the feel of any of this. His carbine was gone, of course. So was his belt with his canteen, utility pouch and knife. The buttons had been snipped from his shirt and the laces were gone from his boots.

"I need to talk to a commanding officer," he shouted. "Now."

Another moment of silence. Then something crashed into the door on the other side, hard enough to make it jump in its frame. He leapt back just as the door burst open. The first man fell backward into the room, clutching the field knife jutting from his chest. He released his last breath as he hit the floor, his uniform shirt already dark with blood. The other man slouched into the doorway and gave a weary smile. It was Eckles.

"No commanding officer, but I'll have to do."

"What the hell is going on?" Rook restrained himself from shouting at the top of his lungs.

"Weird shit, that's all I know. Come on, let's put this dickhead on your cot and then get out of here. It'll buy us some time if they think he's you at first."

Rook gave a disparaging glance at the dead man. "He doesn't look anything like me."

"You're a dickhead too," Eckles said with a half-smile. "All you dickheads look alike. Come on."

They moved quickly, not speaking again until they were in the corridor, which was as white and dimly lit as his room.

"There's no surveillance in this sector," Eckles told him and led him off to the left. "Not like closer to the Consortium."

"The what? Where are we?"

"Nowhere good," Eckles said. His gait was very loose and weary, like a runner at the end of a grueling marathon. "I've been checking the place out for the last hour, and there's something you've gotta see before we try to get out because I need someone else to see it. Somebody else to back me up."

"See what? And what's that in your hand?"

Eckles held up the small black cube with a narrow glowing strip across the front. Liquid crystal letters swam in the glow. DETAINMENT, they spelled out.

"They're not big on signs around here, but I guess that makes sense. This isn't a place for visitors. I took this off the guard at my door right after I put his lights out."

"Blind and clean."

"You know it. This little gem tells you what part of the complex you're in."

"Complex? This place is that big?"

"From what I can tell, it's huge."

"Military?"

"Not exactly. Come on. Take this cube thing and tell me where we're at."

Rook clutched the smooth black box in both hands and glanced between it and the path ahead as they walked. Eckles was in front. His buttons and bootlaces were missing as well. And there was a miniscule but deep hole in the skin just behind his right ear. A thread of blood leaked from it. Rook wanted to ask about it, and he wanted to comment on how he would feel better if they could find him a gun, or had at least taken the knife out of the body of the guard back at the room. All his thoughts were shoved aside when the display in the location cube changed.

He squinted at it.

"What the hell is Pentagon Elemental Psych Storage? Is that in code?"

"I don't think so. I saw a lot of stretchers in a lot of rooms while I was looking for you, buddy, so the word Psych doesn't surprise me at all. The stretchers were all empty, but—"

Red lights suddenly began to pulse high on the walls every ten feet or so like awakening eyes. Rook could hear distant squawking sounds from multiple communication devices. He could also hear running feet not far away, and doors opening and closing. "They know we're out, damn it."

"We've got to get out of the mainline," Eckles said and broke into a run. "The next door we come to, whatever it is, we're taking it."

Rook followed. As he ran, his bullet hole sent a sharp stitch of pain across his side, and the words "push it in deep" shot across his subconscious. Hasty words. His own or the memory of another? He wasn't sure.

They came upon two doors on facing sides of the hallway. Both doors were secured by touch pad mechanisms. Rook checked the black cube and the readout indicated *Vatican Global Behavioral Studies-Inquisition Sector.*

"Vatican?" Rook heard himself say. "Inquisition?"

"No time to figure out this amusement park," Eckels said, and indicated the stretch of corridor behind them. From the sound of it, a group of people was hustling toward them, double-time. "So far, door codes are all seven-seven-six. Split up or take it tandem?" Eckles asked and reached for the touch pad on his side.

Rook was closer to the other door. "Split up," he said, "for now."

He punched in the code. The door jumped open with a baleful hiss. He slipped inside and closed it again without looking back at the corridor, or at Eckles. The room was a dim and cool box, and he was immediately aware of two things. The first was the sound of people rushing past outside, a tinny voice from one of their communication pads instructing them to "report to Harvest Tissue Banks for security watch Beta." The other thing he came aware of was the man seated near the back wall watching him.

He recognized the man at once, and the words were out of his mouth before he could consider keeping quiet. "Colonel Sinclair?"

Instinct made him evaluate the room for any usable defenses and any secondary exits. A series of long metallic instruments, like dental picks and drills, hung on the wall near Sinclair. All of them were attached in some way to an access panel, either by hoses, slim cables or electrical wires. The only other outlet was a drain in the floor near the man's chair.

Sinclair was bound to the chair with nylon straps, except for his right arm, which he'd managed to work free. A dark bruise covered half of his face. Blood flowed from somewhere on the back of his head and stained his shirt collar dark red. He blinked at Rook, momentarily stunned.

Rook rushed over and tore one of the larger implements from the wall, one with a stout barrel and a sharp pointed end. He used it to saw at one of the straps binding Sinclair's arm.

"What the Hell is going on, Sir? I thought that chopper that came for us was one of ours."

"It was," Sinclair said with a barely concealed scowl. "And last I heard, it was reported lost at sea with no survivors. That makes us dead men, solider. What is it? Jefferson?"

"Jeffries, Sir."

Sinclair nodded. "Jeffries. I'd heard about how the HC couldn't be trusted, damn corpse-grinders. Ghouls really, boxing up dead bodies like that. But I thought, how tough could a bunch of grave robbing bio-techs truly be?"

The peaked instrument wasn't doing a very good job on the nylon, but Rook kept trying. "HC, Sir?"

"The goddamn Harvest Consortium. They deal in brain slices and adrenal glands, DNA and gene samples from some of the world's most notable criminal geniuses. Bone fragments, tendons and cartilage. They hold auctions every spring in Dubai. Every faction that can afford to come shows up. The world is overrun by those attempting to create a new master race, Jeffries. The next super-soldier. The perfect, ruthless yet capable leader." Sinclair shifted in his chair, his expression taking on a type of urgency. "Forget those straps. The dirty bastards micro-chipped me before they shut me up in here. Tracking, mind control, I don't know what the Hell it's for. I was working toward dislodging the damn thing when you came in."

Sinclair bent his head down to offer a good view. Rook stared at the hole bored into the muscle just behind the other man's ear lobe, and he thought of how Eckles suffered a similar wound. "It's deep, sir."

"Dig, with that thing in your hand," Sinclair demanded and clamped his jaw, his teeth colliding like stone blocks. "I want it out. Do it."

Rook gulped and pressed the pointed tip of his instrument against the edge of the wound to pull it open. Faintly, a white light pulsed inside the bloody tissue, no more than a grain of illumination.

Yes, Rook thought as he pushed the needle-like point further in, *I'd want it out, too*. The light was housed in a miniscule black disc, and Rook managed to pry the whole thing closer to the surface of Sinclair's skin. A freshet of new blood coursed over his work. Sinclair made a soft moan in the back of his throat. Then the light pulses picked up in pace. Rook felt the need to hurry. The blinking became a solid glow. From the hole, a curl of smoke and the scent of frying blood make him choke back a groan.

"Colonel," he said, "I don't think I should—"

"You will do this, soldier." Sinclair spat through clenched teeth. His eyes were squeezed tight. "Those bastards might have a world full of evil in their freezers and a silo full of money, but they aren't going to have me any longer."

The chip sprouted black threads that tunneled rapidly, like hungry roots, back into the wound. Rook's instincts took over and he backed away as a wire-thin buzzing sound emanated from the chip, accelerated, grew in pitch.

Then, detonation.

Blood and tissue jetted simultaneously from the back of Sinclair's ear and from between his gritted teeth with a wet coughing sound. Rook pressed the combination on the door latch and was outside again before Sinclair had fully slumped over, lifeless, in his bonds.

Hands clamped on his shoulders. He whirled around, his fist clenched tightly on the drilling instrument still in his hand, ready to plunge it into whichever member of this nightmare establishment might have caught up to him, but he instantly relaxed when he looked into the face of Eckels.

"What's shakin'?" Eckles asked him. "You find trouble over there?"

He motioned to the door behind him. "Sinclair is in there. He's dead. Some kind of micro-explosive in his head." It made him think of the small hole behind Eckles' ear, but he decided not to draw parallels, not just yet. He gave Eckles a chance to peer inside before he went on. "This place is a goddamned den of body snatchers, according to the Colonel. They deal in brain parts and bone chips, selling them to the highest bidder. I'd have a hard time believing it, except Sinclair knew he was as good as dead, and dying men don't—"

"Believe it," Eckles said, his eyes very intense beneath their weariness. "It will help you cope when we get down to the tissue bank. I didn't realize it earlier, but not only is the tissue bank something you need to see, it's the way out of the Harvest Consortium. Have a look."

Eckles opened his door across the hall so he and Rook could duck inside. The room was as small as the one occupied by the now-defunct Colonel Sinclair, but instead of being festooned with strange instruments designed for drilling and piercing, the walls held mops and brooms, loops of unused hose, sprays of cut wire. Rook shrugged. "A maintenance closet?"

"And backdoor access," Eckles said and stepped over a stack of tarnished buckets to get to the back wall. He indicated a door there so non-descript Rook barely recognized it, not even when the other man pointed to the keypad, and then to the floorplan schematic bolted onto its face. Eckles traced his finger along lines in the schematic as he spoke. "A tunnel connects this closet to another maintenance area for the tissue bank. On the other side of that same room is a secondary door, another tunnel and then—" he pushed his finger off the edge of the schematic and made a broad grin, "—fresh air, baby!"

Rook sought out the line where the sky met the horizon outside these walls. To his relief, he sensed it, even in the depths of this Consortium complex, felt connected with it and found a type of peace knowing it was still there. "Then let's hit the back door running."

Eckles opened the door and the two of them stepped into the unlit throat of the access tunnel. They crept along slowly, side-by-side in the pitch black, feeling for sudden turns or drops in the floor. Eckles eventually took the lead, and Rook made grim note of the faint pinkish light pulsing in the blackness, coming from a spot behind Eckles' ear. So much like the cryo-crate back on the runner, quietly declaring ready-ready-ready.

"Hey, Eckles," he rasped. "About that micro-explosive that took out Sinclair. I think—"

"Clamp it," Eckles shot back, "we're there, and I can't see the goddamned keypad. I'm going to have to wing it. Use my radar. Isn't that what you do when you make your horizon checks? Use your radar?"

"Yeah," he said, and waited.

When the keypad lit up, filling the tunnel with ghostly light and harsh shadows, Rook jumped. His bullet wound sent out a complaint from the sudden movement and he clutched at it while he stepped in closer to evaluate the readout on the door release. It was not requesting a code, but a thumbprint verification. "What do we do now?" he asked Eckles.

Eckles did not turn away from the keypad, but calmly put out his right hand in a thumbs-up gesture. "This," he said, and pressed his thumb against the pad.

Rook tensed, ready for alert sirens to blare and security lockdown clamps to rattle at the door, to perhaps even see the keypad display the word "Unauthorized" in accusatory red. Instead, the door popped open with a slight hiss. His hand tightened on the piercing tool. "What the hell is going on, Eckles?"

"We're still on-mission, that's what going on, soldier. And now that Sinclair is dead, you're my second. No more bullshit. So let's move out."

The man rushed through the door. Rook followed him into another maintenance storage area, this one bedecked with spools of cable, a large wall mounted circuit-breaker box, metal tanks resembling hospital gas canisters, and dangling hazmat suits. There were two other doors, and Rook's recollection of the schematic made it apparent which was the secondary door—the way out. Eckles, however, strode toward the other.

"This way." Rook pointed. "This is the door we want, Eckles."

"Commander Eckles," the man said and punched his code into the keypad at the other door. "We'll get to that in a minute. Like I said earlier, you need to see what's over here before we're done. It will add some clarity to the mission."

Rook had to admit, a little clarity at this stage would be welcome.

He followed Eckles through the door into a high-ceilinged chamber, much like a warehouse. Instead of crates and boxes, however, the place was lined with row after row of stainless steel coffin-like containers, each with a singular blinking light on the top. Cryo-crates. There were hundreds.

"All of them are occupied, aren't they?" Rook asked as they stepped in, both of them keeping a watchful eye for any type of security personnel. There were cameras, no doubt, and they might have already disturbed a dozen body sensor lasers, but for the moment all was quiet, the tissue bank remained a peaceful environment for those who rested in their cryo-crates.

"Every last one," Eckles said. "Small-time serial killers that barely make the headlines of their local news to mastermind terrorists. Battlefield geniuses and political juggernauts. Some of the more popular ones have been parceled out regularly over the years. Those sleeping dead are down to about half of their former selves, and they've made the Consortium millions of dollars."

"Monstrous," Rook said, glancing at the nearest crate. A metal plate bearing a bar code was mounted to the top. Instinctively, he pulled out the black cube, which he'd stashed in his pants pocket while he attempted to help Sinclair, and set it directly on top of the code. The readout flashed "Tissue Bank and Raw Material" and then changed to *"Edward Simms, London, 1889 WC."*

"WC? Whitechapel?" he said. "They've got Jack the fucking Ripper in that box?"

Eckles nodded and took him to the other side of the room. "What's more monstrous is what's over here. Fetal stasis."

Vault doors, like morgue compartments, filled the far wall. Eckles opened one to reveal a glass tube containing a tiny knot of tissue afloat in a bath of yellow gel. Rook stared at it with sick evaluation. "Fetuses. Raw materials. For all those auction attendees who need something impressionable to graft their newly purchased tissue onto, or impose their freshly acquired gene samples."

"Exactly." Eckles said and led him back toward the maintenance room. "And so far no one has been able to defy nature, to successfully construct a super-human or a mega-brain military mind. So the experiments go on in country after country and the Consortium continues to thrive."

Rook wondered what else was in store. As Eckles said, they were still on-mission, and a mission never consisted of simply getting out.

After a moment, Commander Eckles went on. "I've been working undercover for years, passing myself off as an enlisted man with some intuitive talents who worked his way up to sharpshooter.

Every phase of our efforts to take down the Consortium has been carefully planned every step of the way. Every man on that runner tonight was deemed exceptional enough to fill in as a second if something should happen to Sinclair or myself. That includes you, Rook. Tonight was our night to put a stop to the greed and the debauchery. Still is."

"On-mission," Rook thought. The next instant a guard in dark-colored uniform swept up behind Eckles, rifle in hand. Rook traded imperative looks with Eckles, which confirmed he had an assailant of his own to deal with. He jabbed the piercing tool backward without turning around and the man behind him let out an airy snoring sound. Rook felt his weapon grind into muscle and bone, and he let it go when the guard fell over. Blind and clean. Then he spun around, stooped and pried the man's rifle from his hands. The man looked up at him , dazed by the sensation of ebbing life, his face a mixture of insult and fright. Ironic, Rook thought and glanced away, how it took so much death to thwart the gross mishandling of the dead.

Eckles grappled with his guard, simultaneously flipped the man flat on his back and wrested his gun away. He smashed the butt of the rifle into the man's face, once, twice. The third blow had more effort in it, and Rook heard a muffled crunching sound deep inside the man's skull.

Eckles looked around. "There will be more any minute. We've got to do this. Assholes and elbows. Let's get to the secondary door."

Rook followed him back into the maintenance room. "We're leaving?"

"That would be the case if you believe the schematic," Eckles said and punched seven-seven-six to open the door that promised freedom.

Beyond the door was no tunnel leading to eventual escape, however. There was only a blank wall holding a number pad at eye level. A master shut down control, perhaps. Something to kill the power to the cryo-crates and the fetal stasis tubes and transform the whole tissue bank into an assortment of ruinous rot. Eckles gave it a lingering stare, and then looked back toward the door leading to the tissue bank, which they had tightly closed. He looked like a man nearing some long-sought fulfillment, and it made Rook think of the hole behind the man's ear again, and the hazard it posed.

"Eckles," he said, pointing at his own ear, "they've micro-chipped you. Just like they did Sinclair. It's something bad. Something explosive."

Eckles didn't seem to hear him. "It's a two-part system. Each component, on its own, is harmless. You can play with it, even take it off the wall, and it looks like so much inactive junk. An unfinished project of some type."

A low, buzzing alarm began to sound. Through the door, Rook heard it echo inside the tissue bank like the honking of a huge, imperative beast. Running feet were approaching. Many running feet. "Eckles, it's behind your ear."

"It takes two people," Eckles went on. "Your part is behind that breaker panel on the wall. You better take it down now, Rook."

Rook hurried over and did as he was asked, hoping compliance would incite Eckles to listen. The panel came off easily, and the rows of electrical circuit breakers looked unremarkable. Too unremarkable for a complex such as this. A ruse, indeed.

Eckles crossed over to the tissue bank door and depressed a sequence of numbers on the keypad. He muttered the words "Jam code," with satisfaction. A moment later, the door jumped in its frame as it was pummeled from the other side. Next, gunfire came from outside, aimed at the door latch. It sounded like a series of small pops. "We've only got a few minutes," he said and went back to the secondary door.

Rook followed him, and then confronted him. "Eckles, they might be able to activate your chip remotely."

Eckles gave him a mournful look that blended eerily with his anticipation, and placed his hand behind his ear. "I think they already have. Mine. Yours."

Rook blinked at him. "Me?"

"They had to make a hole for mine," the man said, his glance traveling down to the crude bandage visible under Rook's shirt.

Rook tore the gauze padding from his wound and exposed the neat, maroon hole in his flesh. He cupped his trembling hand around it to put it in shadow. The light pulsing in there was faint, but undeniable. The blinking seemed rapid to him. Push it in deep. Goddamn. Goddamn it to hell.

"It's the bottom breaker on the right," Eckles said, his face hard now, ready for the inevitable. "It's spring loaded so no dummy playing around with it could activate it unintentionally. There's a similar failsafe on this keypad, so when I hit the final number in the code, I have to maintain contact. That's when you trip the breaker and hold it. It will send a wireless command to the main detonator. Then the whole damn complex, and everything in it, becomes vapor hanging over one big-ass crater. Are we still on-mission, soldier?"

Fragments blew inward from the door near the latch as bullets finally chewed their way through. Guards began to ram the door with their shoulders, and the hinges started to give, the gap between door and jamb growing inch by inch. Rook aimed his rifle at the gap, ready to fire should any threat come to Eckles before they could enter his code. He thought about evil and brilliance and high intellect gone sour, and he thought about how any one man should be allowed only one chance to tread the earth and make it count. It was only fair. It was only natural. A weak, crawling sensation crept through his wound, and he envisioned the thread-like grippers burrowing from the microchip into his skin. He thought he felt the ticking heat of the chip's light blinking harder, faster, nearing its apex.

He said, "We are on-mission, Sir."

A guard poked his head in, a pistol raised toward where Eckles was just pressing the first digit of his code. Rook fired. A spray of red shot into the air from the man's temple and he dropped. *Death to right the mishandling of the dead.*

Eckles finished, his finger pressing hard and white against the last number, and he gave Rook a hardened glare. Another guard was struggling through the partially opened door, this one toting a carbine.

Rook dropped his rifle and twisted around to the breaker box. He tripped the breaker without looking at it. Held it, blind and clean.

He squinted at the air, and found the line where the sky met the horizon. He wondered what lay beyond that line, and thought it was a fair question.

Then, detonation.

Maestro
By Jamie D. Wahls

He remembered yesterday's tennis match with the same intensity he recalled his marriage, or the birth of his son, or his wife's death, or the death of his son. And that was troubling, because it meant he himself had been tuned.

What was worse, when he slipped away to the tennis court that night, he found he had no ability whatsoever, which meant he had been receiving tune-ups for the entire six months he thought he'd taken to tennis.

It was an amateur mistake, inadvertently stimulating the amygdala while implanting a memory. It turned what should have been a banal half-remembrance into a flashbulb episode, of which he would recall every false detail in aching precision. He knew the process behind that error well. He had committed it himself, long ago, in his second year at the Corps.

He rose from his narrow bed, aching, and tucked the thin white blanket back into place behind him. The privacy of his single room was a symbol of status he no longer trusted. He splashed gray water onto his graying face with sure hands. In the mirror, he contemplated himself, documenting the progress of his wrinkles with unflinching scientific precision. He usually combed his hair back, to cover the implants, but today he brushed it forward, leaving his Hippocamplus visible like he used to do as a young man. Some of the young techs shaved their heads—even the women—to show their mods, but a man of his stature had no need for such flashy maneuvers.

Today would be crucial. He must give no indication he knew his architecture had been modified, and he must tune himself from now on. Being scanned would reveal anxiety which he should no longer have.

The day's work was unremarkable. The usual mind-numbing chores. A mid-level programmer who complained of an inability to focus. A political prisoner to be turned automata. Routine cases.

He let himself enter the calm, easy flow state he used for work. He was early enough that no other technicians would be present, and he had the most private tuning apparatus to himself.

A firm hand gripped him above the elbow and he nearly shouted in alarm. But it was only Bergstrom, the sole architect senior to him and his direct superior.

"You all right?" Bergstrom asked, with a sly grin. He had a haughty bearing but a workman's manner of speech; it left the impression that his smiles were to manipulate. He had the discomforting habit of pausing a moment before replying, as if he was choosing his facial expression from a rack, deciding which would best elicit the desired response.

"I'm fine," he told Bergstrom, with as relaxed a smile as he could manage. "Just not enough sleep last night."

Bergstrom smiled gently, and studied his face with the merciless interest of a master soul surgeon.

He turned back to work, feeling Bergstrom's eyes on his back the whole time.

He stimulated the reticular formation to induce a light coma before he began work on his staff technicians; it was a standard precaution when working on someone with knowledge of the system, and the motions to do so were as comfortable and ingrained as turning off a light switch. He found a blossoming sexual perversion in the youngest apprentice, and, with a small frown, destroyed it.

He mapped the brain regions which the apprentice used in her craft—still poorly developed—and stimulated them gently, the patient gardener. He left, with a knowing smile, the nascent attraction he found to another apprentice; he remembered well his own time as a journeyman.

He walked down the plain cement hallway, past two automata performing some electrical repair. He had long since tuned himself past thinking of them as people, and any reaction to them, convivial or revulsed, would only serve to embarrass him before his colleagues. He could not afford the attention, today. It was time to finally use the plan he had set in place ages ago. Part of him was terrified, and he made a mental note to kill it.

He sent a courier automata with details of an communications channel, signed with an anonymous encryption key. His sister would know who was sending the message. She would find him a way.

◇◇◇

"It's dangerous business, tuning yourself. You're more likely to end up crazy than find godhood."

His wife had smoked in the room of the master tuning apparatus, a breach of protocol so vile that it would have brought a reprimand and a rebuild had she done it during the daylight hours. He loved her.

She had smirked gently at him, mouth quirked in a half-smile with the cigarette in the corner, and whispered hotly, "Would you like me to co-author?"

She thrilled him.

She was dead now. He remembered it like a tennis match.

◇◇◇

The journeymen quarters were empty this time of day. It would be another hour before those in the morning shift of training would return to change out of uniform.

He sat uncomfortably on someone else's bed as the communications channel flicked on.

"What's the emergency, Maestro?"

His sister had been calling him that for ages, and in the long years his feelings towards the diminutive had mellowed. Her picture came through poorly in places, but he could tell she was lit by some red, actual-fire glow, and she was grimy with the blood of whatever machine she was working on today. He coveted her circuits, itching to get her into the tube so he could find out what her expert brain looked like. She had always refused. She had built herself completely independently, and remained in her job underground with great fiery engines and hollow-eyed automata on the condition that she never be required to submit to anyones' well-meaning mental-ministrations, even his.

"Someone's altered my memory, Hanna. I need to get out."

Her eyes narrowed in a sudden flash of what he hoped was protective sisterly instincts. "How did you find out?"

The question rubbed him the wrong way; he was gripped with a sudden paranoia—she had sold him out for her perpetual mental amnesty, she was working with them, she was trying to cover their tracks and plug the leak and by tomorrow neither this conversation nor tennis would be remembered. "It's not important," he said.

"Okay," she said.

"Can you send the boat?" He asked calmly. If she had betrayed him, she shouldn't know that he knew. And if she hadn't, then this was what he came to do.

"Of course." She frowned a bit. She told him a place and a time, neither very far away. "Be safe, okay?"

She showed nothing but concern. He doubted that even a master architect of wills such as himself could tune out a loving childhood spent together; love was hard to remove. He had considered removing memories of his wife, but his love for her saturated them, and would likely float freely as paraphilia's were they denied their proper grave. So he continued to ache.

He terminated the connection and headed to the room of the master apparatus, stray recollections rising unbidden as he went. Here he and his wife had gone through their memories together, selectively removing the hurt from their arguments and leaving the lessons, writing over their myriad petty jealousies and his strange, stupid dalliance with a woman whose name was scorched from his mind. If she had had other lovers, too, he had deleted even the memory of deleting them. But he would have loved her anyway, of course. That was just how he was made.

He activated the machine. The massive power drain would have signaled an alarm, but he had long ago written exceptions into the automata responsible for resource allocation. He slid himself into the tube and locked his head into place, and activated the optic interface.

Even after all these years, he still felt a giddy rush of power as the information flooded into him. He held in his metaphorical hands the transcendent mind of a physical being, and the sheer sense of power was no less thrilling when the mind in question was his.

When he was younger, he had played pranks on his fellow apprentices, giving them attractions to animals or planting memories of murders in their minds. He had ceased such diversions after a similarly playful architect was found guilty of rape and sentenced to automata.

The readout of his mind flowed over his vision, and he pursed his lips. He was more unsettled than he'd realized. A less experienced and more vicious technician could have recommended him for complete rebuild, with care taken to preserve the expert circuits. He soothed himself as well as he could without going subconscious.

"It's like a massage." he had lectured once, in the vaguest terms. "Don't try to force things. Many gentle passes, with soft, purposeful stimulation. Not a wasted stroke." He didn't remember the students' faces as more than young, curious smears, but he recalled each of their brains. He had regarded them as affectionately as a sculptor regards clay, and cut away the parts that had no purpose or beauty.

He rose from the tube, bleary. He had lived a comfortable, routine existence for many years now, and reacted like an old man when deprived of sleep. Although he was an old man.

He stiffened in surprise when he saw a large male silhouette standing near the doorway—but it was just an automata. He squinted and approached. It was the automata that his wife had commandeered for her personal use years ago, a muscled male specimen that they had named Spot, for a pale birthmark on his dark belly. It was odd now to see Spot again, on the janitorial detail. He shook his head and tried not to view the coincidence as anything but. He had yet to fully eradicate the weeds of superstition and their deep roots inside of him.

He knew that he had only perhaps another five hours before an automata at Compound Security found his transmission and correlated him to it with enough statistical significance to warrant an investigation. Here in the compound, with such a high availability of architects, there would be no shortage of curious colleagues and jealous underlings eager to take an incisive peek at his closely guarded soul. With any luck, he wouldn't remain even an hour.

He considered his options and what tools he would need, and said, "Spot."

Of course it didn't respond. It no longer had a name.

He sighed, snapped his fingers, and pointed to his badge. Its eyes glanced over MASTER ARCHITECT and it nodded, granting him command privileges.

"Come with me," he told Spot

He walked swiftly through the compound with Spot in tow, alone save for the other janitorial automata that emerged at night. It wouldn't do to take any of them; their absence would be noted in the morning when the floors weren't clean enough. But he would need more for his plan. He didn't recall formulating the plan, perhaps it had arisen when he was in his trance of self-improvement. Or…

He froze, and then sighed. He had long since realized that paranoia in this department was simply useless. If he was his own enemy, he certainly wasn't going to let himself find out.

He walked into automata storage, using his pass to get past the guard, and crept quietly along the stalls. Many of the automata here weren't sleeping, but just laying fallow, eyes open, until they were needed. There had been no shortage of human resources since the war began.

His eyes roved over each of their placards, studying. *D-786, Metalworking. D-787, Heavy Labor. D-788, Translator.*

He scanned the work details. A younger architect was scheduled for work in the city tomorrow, to serve as a judge. Two bodyguards were allocated.

They would do perfectly. He snapped, and they came to his side.

He exhaled. He needed to go to the city anyway. One last service wouldn't kill him.

He struck the architect's name off the list.

◇◇◇

When he was a young technician, he had seen one of his mentors killed, in a way, by an enemy soldier.

A captured enemy soldier was being taken in for a correction of loyalty. "One of ours originally, I think," mused Master Architect Reba. "I wonder how many times we've passed him back and forth now."

They stuffed him into the tube together, and his mentor took the controls. The soldier was drugged unconscious, of course.

The trap was clever enough that he wished he had designed it himself. A tiny capsule bomb snorted into the sinuses was triggered by the magnetic fields of the tube, blasting a fireball through his mentor and the tuning apparatus.

A medical team of automata and one person had rushed in, of course, but there was no saving his mentor. So they hurried the top half of her to the nearest tuning apparatus to take an imprint of her brain before cell death cracked the stained-glass masterpiece inside her head.

Reba clutched his hand urgently as she died, clinical despite the massive trauma. Neither he nor she looked at her legs, where they lay against the wall.

"Have you ever taken a death imprint before?" She was serenely calm--she had probably programmed herself with a death routine, sparing herself and onlookers some horror and ghastly questions of afterlife, in favor of beautiful utility.

He shook his head mutely.

Her eyes, already a little glassy, focused on him. She recognized him, forking the death routine into a personalized message. "Oh, you're here. I have great hopes for you, my boy. You're going to do me proud."

She was perhaps about to begin on a longer and more tailored oration to him, but she stiffened in surprise, and died.

He performed the death imprint flawlessly. Even years later he acknowledged it was good work. It got him promoted to full architect, and for years he modeled the growth of his own expert circuitry on the final snapshot of hers.

He stormed down the hall, burly guard automata and Spot in tow, bracing himself to snarl at the guards at the edges of the compound. He had never bothered to learn acting, since it was inferior to being.

He stepped outside, and the night was black, cut through by searchlights. The great gray wall of the compound loomed oppressive between him and freedom. Military automata, some of whom he recognized as his work, paced tirelessly atop the wall, one command or unauthorized action away from ending his fledgling escape attempt with what he knew was impeccable accuracy.

One of the two real guards held up a hand authoritatively. "Halt."

The maestro slowed down, fidgeting impatiently. "There's been a murder."

The guards shared a glance.

"In the city," rattled off the maestro exasperatedly. It was even true. "They want me to verify guilt before they execute. I'm taking these as my bodyguards. Move, please."

A flicker of recognition passed over a guard's face. "I think I heard something about that." He said, slowly. The guards tentatively stepped out of his way.

His nails were digging into his palms so much that he might bleed. He nodded imperiously at the guards, and strode past.

He entered the courthouse, and people parted before him. He was surrounded by raw, unworked product.

They were unsettling. Their eyes darted around chaotically, with no clear goal. He could spend months trying to streamline any one of them. He could make them so much better.

An interchangeable civilian meekly showed him to the questioning chamber.

The maestro sat down behind the controls of the tuning apparatus. He closed his eyes, and let himself enjoy the tiny note of euphoria that he had written in as an incentive for beginning his work.

This apparatus was old. He chewed his lip while he watched the system load. Eventually the screen settled into the familiar government background of hands clasped in prayer. He listened to the soft humming of the machine readying itself, and he gestured at the automata to bring in the prisoner.

A pause, and he blinked and looked up. None of the three had reacted to him. These three weren't built for that.

He scowled, and raised his voice. "Bring in the prisoner, please."

The man was ugly. He was yelling.

The maestro liked to listen to music while he worked, so much so that he'd inadvertently connected his auditory tract to his expert circuits. His wife had teased him mercilessly as they tried to untangle that. He had no music now.

Attendants fumbled slightly with the straps in the tube. They locked the man's head into place. He was screaming and crying. The maestro watched.

The man's head came into view on the screen. He was moving too much.

"If you keep moving, I will kill you." said the maestro.

The man stopped, and so did the attendants. They were watching him. Their faces were tight.

The maestro hesitated. "I didn't mean it like that. The... any probes that I make will be less precise if you move. I might accidentally hit the pons and disable your breathing. You might not notice in time to breathe manually."

The maestro brought his gaze down to the screen. "What is your name?"

The man said something. This was a calibration question.

"Describe the events which took place as you entered this room."

The maestro's eyes darted over the screen, hungry for data. So that's where he kept short-term recall...yes. Extreme emotionality, extreme volatility. The maestro briefly strengthened the man's willpower. "Describe the events which occurred the night of the murder."

Fear, spatial positioning, long-term recall, social modeling. Language processing. Medium-term recall. Fear... Imagination!

The maestro nodded. That was a lucky break.

"Did you kill her?"

Fear, long-term recall.

"Why did you kill her?"

Fear!

He blunted the fear response, disabled most of the frontal cortex.

"Why did you kill her?"

Anger, directed at him. Ah, so the current idea of the maestro was in that little node of social modeling. He stunned it.

"Why did you kill her?"

Imagination. Medium-term recall. Social modeling. Empathy. Anger, not directed at him.

"What kind of person was she?"

Despair. Happiness. Despair.

"What did she do?"

Medium-term recall. Long-term recall. Anger. Despair.

"And you're not the kind of person who can tolerate that."

Surprise. Anger. Fear again. The maestro frowned, and numbed the fear response more thoroughly.

"What were you unwilling to lose?"

Despair. Medium-term recall. Happiness. Imagination.

"It hadn't happened yet?"

Anger.

The maestro exhaled. He'd verified guilt in the first five seconds. Now he was just giving rein to his curiosity without Bergstrom looking over his shoulder.

"What did she deny you?"

Imagination. Happiness. Anger.

The maestro pursed his lips. This wasn't basic sexual jealousy. The recurring flashes of anger were equally at the wife and at someone else, someone...

The boundaries weren't mapping to anything in the visual cortex. This wasn't someone he had ever seen—a rumored rival? No, he would have more mirror neuron activation...

Ah. This wasn't someone, this was something.

"The State?"

Anger. Yes. Or close enough.

He called up the file on the woman. Aged 32. No criminal history, no rebuild. Mind imprint on file; stable. Average emotionality. Low ambition, average intelligence. Profession: Mother (Public).

The maestro glanced down at him. "You wanted a child? One you could keep?"

Happiness. Despair.

"That was very irresponsible of you."

The maestro looked at the man in the tube, looked at his face. Whatever part of his personality was currently reacting, it was managing a distant, troubled smile.

The maestro sighed. Nothing else for it, then.

He turned up the power far past what he would ever allow one of his students to use. The system flashed an alarm at him; he dismissed it.

He burned out the center for fear, scorched it so permanently that the man would never know fear again. He burned away the portions of the brain that kept the endogenous painkillers from working; the man would know soaring euphoria for the rest of his days.

The maestro burned away a specific spot in the motor cortex, one he burned from a lot of prisoners. The man's face suddenly drooped. He may know euphoria, but it would be well hidden. He would never again smile.

At last, the maestro called one of the people over. "Guilty."

The attendant took the guilty man away.

The maestro sat back. His shoulders drooped. He was alone.

It was barbarous. He could have fixed that man. In three months he could have eradicated jealousy, discontent and the possessive pull towards fatherhood. He could have done it in three weeks, if maintaining intelligence or preventing seizures weren't a priority. The man liked his life. The maestro could have fixed him.

But the peasants demanded execution. Blood for blood. Barbarous.

The maestro stood up. His calm was leaving now that he wasn't watching a mind through glass. He could feel the anxiety knotting up his shoulders. He shook his head.

He snapped his fingers, and the automata fell into formation behind him. He took a deep breath.

He walked alongside the machine, looked in the tube. Like many, this one had leather straps on the inside. The immobile headpiece had a tiny bead of blood on it, from where the guilty man had thrashed and cut his forehead. The maestro wiped it away. Blood smeared on his fingertips.

He stared at it.

He bent double and vomited into the tube.

His body heaved. He jerked back too quickly and slammed his head into the top of the tuning apparatus. He let out a long, whimpering groan.

He blinked. His vision was blurry. Carefully, minding his tender head, he extricated himself from the tube.

He righted himself. The automata waited. He gave a short and self-conscious little laugh as he glanced around to see if anyone saw.

The door and freedom beckoned. To lead his automata away, he tried to snap his fingers, but they were still bloody.

After a short walk and a very stressful wait, a boat arrived for him in the harbor, maneuvered by autopilot without automata crew. He boarded with his retainers following. He fumbled with the controls. Not his skillset, but he got the boat out of the harbor, and from there he let the machine do the work.

He settled in the cabin. The automata stood before him.

To his grandparents, they had been a horror. To him, a necessity. To the children in the street they were appliances.

"What am I going to do with you?" he said. "I would send you back, but you have my location written inside you. You're like little missiles that work in reverse; I fire you back, and it blows up in my face."

He paused.

"I don't sound lucid. I've had a lot of experiences I wasn't expecting today. I should retune."

The things watched him, waiting for a command.

"You and you, jump overboard and drown."

They did, both. He stopped the boat and, to be sure, waited until there were no more bubbles coming.

He hesitated for a moment longer, looking at Spot. He sighed.

"Spot, jump overboard and drown."

It didn't respond. It no longer had a name.

"Oh. Oh, that's right."

He sat for a few moments, alone with the sound of the boat motor and his thoughts and his dead wife's toy.

He embraced it.

He was awoken by the rays of the setting sun and many real people climbing onto his boat. They were talking amongst themselves. Before he had the time to consider a furtive thought about violent, ill-equipped self-defense, a loud, hairy man with wild eyebrows had taken his hand in a firm grip and was shaking it vehemently.

"So this is the maestro that Hanna talks about, hey?" he yelped. "Pleased to meet you!"

The maestro nodded.

"The name's Corbin!" boomed the man, still shaking his hand. "Do you have any luggage we can gather?" Corbin laughed with great self-satisfaction.

People swarmed onto the boat, a dozen of them, a bewildering number of unknown entities. Their chatter set the maestro near panic. He had no idea what their brains looked like or what they were capable of.

"Who's this?" asked Corbin, looking at Spot. And then, "Aw, shit."

The maestro made an attempt at a smile, but Corbin's face had gone sour. He was talking heatedly on a radio.

"...never told me that he'd be bringing one of their robots with him. I've half a mind to throw them both over right now...Yeah? And why does a composer need a slave?"

They had marched him and Spot off the boat and into the earth; they entered narrow reddish tunnels cut into the side of a mountain. It had been a mine at one point, the maestro figured. What it was now he couldn't tell, save for a repository for dirty, well-armed people, improbably busy inside a cave.

A group of grimy men were sorting bullets and cleaning guns. As he approached, they turned, friendly, but as soon as they saw Spot their eyes went hard.

It wasn't better elsewhere. Women building some vast bronze machine watched him with open contempt. A child, no more than seven and working in an assembly line with adults, saw Spot and bared her teeth at the maestro.

He tried smiling, at first, but that seemed to draw more ire, until word of his passing preceded him and faces were closed and hateful even as he arrived.

He and Spot descended into the mountain.

"You brought him here?" Hanna asked. "Why?"

"It was my wife's," said the maestro, uncomfortable with the question and her pronoun. "I brought it on a whim, and I couldn't bring myself to get rid of it on the boat."

"Christ." She shook her head. "That'll earn you no love here. I told them that the nickname was literal, you might've heard. If they knew what you really did...well, I doubt I could have gotten you in alive."

She brushed at his forehead. "You've got something there—"

He slapped her hand away. "It's an implant. I got it years ago."

"Fine." She said, rolling her eyes in the way he remembered. "Want to see what I've been working on?"

The assembly line made tiny objects, not much bigger than a pea. And they all came from this workshop.

She held a finished one up to the light, and in its shiny surface his reflection was tiny and upside-down.

"...and so once scanned, the implant will detonate."

He was getting chills. "Hanna, that's awful."

She put the smooth, pill-sized metallic capsule back down on the workbench, careful not to lose it amidst the shadows and the tools. There wasn't much light in here.

"Look," she said, testily. "I know you can give me a lecture about how science itself isn't evil and that your craft isn't evil *per se.* We've had that conversation. And I know that the retuning process has killed a lot of problems that I just don't know about because they just don't happen anymore—"

"Depression, schizophrenia, existential doubt--" the maestro interjected.

Hanna bulled over him. "But your regime's applications are evil. You've created--okay, not you--*someone* has created the most total and inescapable form of slavery ever to exist. " She gestured at Spot with quick stabbing motions. "This is an abomination. You've taken human beings and turned them into, into what? Killing machines, surveillance robots, fucking Roombas!"

"Fine, fine." He waved his hands in front of him, as if to shield against her argument. "But there are good applications too. Unprecedented automation of complex systems that is just too complex for anything *except* a carefully made autistic savant, with human reasoning, human values and inhuman focus. And okay, I'm sorry that you don't think that the price is worth it, that you don't want to live this way for maybe a century or two until we--or rather, our engineer automata--can get AI smart enough that we can keep every human instead of sacrificing the worst and the best to the cause of progress. I'm sorry you can't see past your basic, stupid human revulsion to that which looks-like-but-is-not-human. But…" He gritted his teeth. "But putting these things in soldiers is not a humane solution. Once a man gives his life for his country and signs up to be a soldier automata—"

"We've never been putting these in your soldiers!" she shouted. "These are for us! People who would rather die than be one of your slaves!"

"One of…" He paused. "Hanna, do you have one?"

She stared at him.

"Shoot." He deflated. "I was so curious."

"Of course I have one," she muttered, heat leaving her words. She cocked her head at the sounds of commotion in the hall, some argument. "You've always known how I felt about tuning. That's why I joined the abolitionists."

He nodded, and then stopped with a jolt. He did a double take, but her face was deadly serious.

"You joined the abolitionists?" It came as barely more than a whisper.

She regarded him, puzzled. "Where do you think we are now? Biggest base in the world, and a total secret. I told you six months ago I had joined."

He shook his head. "You didn't. I—"

It hit him like a gut punch. "Oh." he said. "Oh, no."

Hanna knitted her brows in concern.

The sounds of commotion in the hall grew louder, and more violent.

The door burst open, kicked in by a masked military automata. The maestro dropped to the ground with his hands on his head.

Hanna shot the automata once in the head, and once again to be sure, before she turned to the maestro, angry.

"At least *try* to escape?"

He shouted. "I led them right to you! They wanted the abolitionists and I led them right to you, you've got to run! You can't trust me, my mind is turned against you and I never played tennis after all!"

She blinked, and then her mouth formed into a familiar disapproving line. "You've been self-tuning again."

"Yes!" he shrieked. "Yes! I have. But I'm not the only one in there. Ha! You really can't trust me. I might be programmed to…to…to kill you or something grim if it looks like the abolitionists are going to win. Or maybe I'm supposed to escape with you and lead them…right back to the new base wherever you end up. You can't take me with you! All right? You can't!"

He fell backwards against the wall, sliding down it and curling into a ball.

Hanna dragged a workbench until it barricaded the door, and she knelt next to him.

"Shhh," she said, "It's all right. Shhhh."

And she brushed her hand across his furrowed brow, and whispered something, and the words didn't matter.

He remembered a time, years and careers and revolutions ago, when he was six and she was eleven, when she had sat with him in his bedroom and he had sobbed. And she had stroked his forehead and told him that the storm would pass and that he was safe. And he couldn't hear her words over the thunder but the words didn't matter. All that mattered was the closeness, and the peace, and her, the only family he had ever known.

And now, as everything was dull ringing noise and his eyes were clenched shut and he could feel the tears spilling out, once more his world narrowed to the brushing of her fingertips on his forehead, to that bare touch, and he let himself hurt.

Brush. Brush.

"It's all right," whispered the only family he had left, over and over again. "It's all right."

"You have to leave me," he said. "You have to."

"I know." She said. And then, "I love you, Adrian."

Adrian laughed, just a little. "This is what it takes, huh?"

She stood up, pulled away. "It was a one-time thing," she said, hiding her eyes as she turned away from him. "I'm not dropping a perfectly good nickname for anything." She reloaded her gun and turned back to him, her face composed. "We can find you a new name when we meet again."

"Sure," said the maestro. "Sure."

She pulled the workbench away from the door. She gave him a last fleeting glance and strode out. The door slammed shut behind her.

The room was empty except for the maestro.

And Spot.

Gunshots rang out in the hall and a body hit the floor, and he wouldn't accept the possibility.

Low voices outside. And then...

The door banged open. A flat-eyed bodyguard automata entered, gun trained on the maestro. Behind him came Bergstrom.

Bergstrom nodded to the maestro, as if meeting for lunch. His gaze traveled around the room, a quick examination of the rudimentary workshop. A second bodyguard automata entered behind him, and this one the maestro recognized as his own work.

Would that he had left himself a backdoor. He laughed, high and manic. Bergstrom elevated one eyebrow and walked over.

Bergstrom squatted in front of him, and those pale eyes flitted about, searching his face.

"I won't thank you," Bergstrom intoned, "because you had no choice. But you did everything perfectly. Just what we needed."

Bergstrom sighed, and his eyes didn't change. "You know, I voted for you to just have a memory wipe after all this was done, buddy. Maybe a rebuild, tops. I told them we didn't need to bust you all the way down to auto. But you were with your sister a whole lot longer than you should've been, and now that's right out. It'd be a complete pain in the ass to try and make you forget that, you know?" Bergstrom smiled, and it was vicious. "You do know. But hey, bud, I'll imprint your brain and use it as a textbook for years to come. You'll be immortalized, a hero of the field, because," he glanced to the more dangerous of his bodyguards, "because, well, you do some really good work. You deserve to be remembered for that, too. So when the time comes for you to be auto'd, I won't let some green tech do it and kill you by accident. I'll be doing it personally, okay? Does that help?"

The maestro looked up. "Did you kill her?"

Bergstrom paused. "No." he said, his voice neutral. Then he said, "You." He pointed to the inferior of his bodyguard automata. "Stay here and make sure he doesn't leave before we can retune him."

And Bergstrom left.

The felt very empty again, save for the guard and the maestro.

And Spot.

The maestro looked around. The bodyguard automata had the gun trained on him, and wouldn't be getting tired. The stone walls were thick and would muffle any noise. The single light in the room was on the workbench.

Ah, the workbench.

The maestro saw an option, and smiled. This plan was unmistakably his. His mind wouldn't be going in any textbook.

He walked to the workbench spreading his hands on its hard surface. The bodyguard watched him, gun still leveled.

The maestro paused. And shouted to Spot, "Spot! Kill him!"

It didn't respond, of course. It no longer had a name.

The bodyguard turned immediately and fired twice on Spot, spraying blood across the wall.

And Adrian snorted a smooth, pill-sized metallic capsule.

BOOK III

SPACE OPERA

All was going quite well aboard Captain Quasar's star cruiser, the magnificent Effervescent Magnitude. Quasar and crew were moving right along through star-punctured black, on schedule for their rendezvous with the exalted king and queen of Planet Brociliamide, a peaceful world where the captain had once helped to end a civil war. All in a day's work for a star faring hero such as Bartholomew Quasar.

The coordinates were laid in, and Hank sat at the helm, his four furry arms moving across the console languidly, adjusting the heading as necessary to avoid random space debris: asteroids, meteorites, derelict privateering vessels with frozen crew drifting nearby—that sort of thing. The other members of the bridge crew were also at their stations, catching up on reports and other duties often neglected when facing emergency situations.

In the absence of pressing matters that usually demanded his full attention—conflicts with toll collectors or attacks by bounty hunters, for example—Quasar leaned back in his deluxe-model captain's chair and stared at the view screen that consumed the fore wall. But he didn't really see the frosty streaks of starlight they passed at near-lightspeed. Instead, he was catching up on some much-needed z's.

He'd long ago perfected the art of sleeping with his eyes open. Back at the academy as a young cadet, such an incredible ability had not earned him any credits—nor had his bravura at wooing young female cadets. Nevertheless, it had been time well-spent, and now he reaped the rewards. Sleep, glorious sleep, whilst still appearing to be in charge of the bridge.

"Captain." Commander Wan suddenly stood at his elbow.

"Ho there!" Quasar sat up straight with a sharp intake of breath. His first officer had a bad habit of sneaking up on him when he least expected it. He could never tell if she did it on purpose, enjoying his reaction. She was a stoic sort. "Status report, Commander?"

"No, sir. I…need to speak with you. In private, please."

"Very well." He peered at her expression—or lack thereof—hoping for a hint of some sort. No such luck. "Is the conference room to your liking?"

She nodded, and he led the way, leaving the bridge in Hank's capable hands—all four of them—for the time being. Once the door to the conference room slid shut, Quasar and Wan were left alone with a long glass table, cushioned swivel chairs, a blank wall screen, and a wide viewport looking out onto the silent void of space. Commander Wan cleared her throat and spoke up, hands clasped behind her back and spine erect.

"We have an intruder on board, Captain."

"Really?" He broke from staring vacantly out the viewport, which is what he did anytime he was in the conference room. His crew might have thought he looked pensive—or so he hoped—but in actuality, he was, to quote an ancient Earth phrase, *spacing out*. "Wouldn't the ship's computer have notified us if such were the case?"

"According to the latest duty roster, she is a member of the crew."

"She?" Quasar raised an intrigued eyebrow.

"Our communications officer on the bridge. A Lieutenant Jones, sir."

Quasar's eyebrow sank, wrinkling toward its counterpart. "We don't have a communications officer named Lieutenant Jones."

"Precisely, sir."

"Yet she's on the roster?"

Wan nodded. "I did a little digging and was able to ascertain she was assigned to the bridge last week. By you, Captain."

"Preposterous. I don't remember assigning a communications officer. What does a communications officer even do, anyway? I thought you handled that sort of thing—communication transmissions and whatnot."

"I do, sir."

Quasar narrowed his heroic gaze at nothing in particular and strummed his clean-shaven chin, one of the more prominent features on his chiseled face. "I'll need to get to the bottom of this."

"May I suggest that you exercise caution, Captain? We don't know who we're dealing with, and it appears that only you and I don't believe she belongs aboard the Magnitude."

Quasar frowned at that as he and Wan exited the conference room. Returning to the bridge, he leaned toward her and lowered his voice, speaking out the side of his mouth.

"Which one is Jones?"

"Right there, sir." Wan indicated the rather attractive brunette seated at a console toward the rear of the bridge. The woman seemed immersed in her work. Professional. Yet she was the only member of the bridge crew in a skirt three sizes too small.

"I'll get her on uniform violation if nothing else," Quasar quipped.

"You approved her…unique uniform, Captain. It's on record."

He stopped himself from throwing up his arms with incredulity. He didn't want to draw any unnecessary attention to a situation that was conspicuous enough as it was—even though no one else on the bridge seemed to notice there was a half-dressed imposter in their midst.

"Lieutenant Jones," Quasar said, approaching the woman's side and hoping to startle her just a bit.

"Yes, Captain?" Jones swiveled toward him with the most gorgeous pair of legs he'd ever seen. She batted luscious dark eyelashes and graced him with an equally fabulous smile. Her emerald eyes were easy to lose oneself in, which the captain did— lose himself, that is.

Commander Wan cleared her throat abruptly at Quasar's elbow. He did his best not to look startled, even as his pulse lurched.

"As you were, Lieutenant," Quasar said.

"Yes, Captain." Jones returned to her duties, smile intact.

"Well, sir?" Commander Wan whispered as Quasar headed toward his deluxe-model captain's chair. "What do you plan to do?"

"Get in a little nap." He yawned. "Wake me up when we reach Planet Brociliamide."

Wan took him by the elbow, politely escorting him back to the conference room. There, he found himself in the presence of a very frustrated first officer. According to her, he and his bridge crew—all except Commander Wan herself—were currently under some sort of spell. The witch in question called herself Lieutenant Jones, and her sphere of telepathic influence seemed to extend fifty meters beyond her present location, where it ended abruptly. (That was the distance between the conference room and the bridge, so it seemed safe to assume such was the case. However, there was that

185

ancient Earth adage about assuming things—)

"So you're saying this is the <u>sixth</u> time we've had this conversation?" Quasar scratched his head in bewilderment.

"Sixteenth, sir." Wan paused, composing herself. "In this situation, it would appear the only solution is to relieve you of command and order a security detail to escort Jones—or whoever she is—straight to the brig."

"Sounds like a plan, Number Wan. I'm relieved." Quasar frowned all of a sudden, deep in thought. "Why is it this witch's wiles don't affect—"

"I never said she was a witch, Captain. I don't believe in magic."

"Nevertheless, why don't her wiles work on you—when she apparently has everyone else on the bridge under her spell?"

"Perhaps it is due to the rigorous mental exercises I undertake every morning prior to reporting for duty. I may be immune to telepathic suggestion."

"Mayhaps." Quasar mused, stroking the cleft in his chin. "Very well, Commander. You seem to have the situation in hand. Notify me as soon as this Jones woman is locked up. I have more than a few questions for her."

With a crisp salute, Quasar headed to his quarters and his deluxe-model bunk.

When Commander Wan contacted the captain later from the brig, she did not sound happy.

"Is our witch in custody?" Quasar rolled out of bed with a yawn and adjusted his rumpled uniform.

"No, sir. I am in custody."

Quasar paused before his mirror, hands frozen where they had been smoothing down his close-cropped blond hair.

"How's that, Commander?"

"I am in the brig, sir. Lieutenant Jones somehow managed to convince the security detail on duty to lock me up. She must still be somewhere in the vicinity, because her influence on their minds has not waned."

Quasar clenched his jaw until the muscle twitched. "Our

intruder is at large? This situation has gone from bad to even more so. Very well, I will resume command and head down there in person to set those security officers straight."

"Captain, we can't risk it. She may be waiting for you. If she were to…influence you to change course, she could take over the ship by proxy."

"By proxy? Right." Quasar nodded without knowing exactly what it meant. "Well, we can't have that."

"For now, sir, remain locked in your quarters. As soon as she's out of range, the guards will release me. Then—"

"Hang tight, Commander. I've got everything under control."

"No—Captain, wait—"

Quasar jerked his head to terminate the transmission via the comm link in his collar. Activating his desktop intercom, he announced, "Attention all decks, this is your captain speaking. As if you didn't already know." He winked at no one in particular. Because he was alone. "We have an intruder aboard going by the name Lieutenant Jones. Apparently a communications officer, though I've never heard of such a position aboard a star cruiser. Regardless, she is an imposter and will soon be brought to justice. Until then, remain at your posts, but notify your superiors should any of you see a raven-haired, green-eyed vixen in a skirt far too short and obviously not part of a standard regulation uniform. I will keep you apprised of the situation as it unfolds. Quasar out."

Next, he called the brig.

"Sentinel, this is your captain speaking. Again. But this time, I'm only speaking to you, not the entire crew. So pay close attention to what I'm about to say."

The sentinel paused. "Yes, Captain?"

"Release Commander Wan immediately."

"I'm sorry, sir. I can't do that."

"Didn't you hear the ship-wide announcement I made a moment ago?"

"Intruder alert? Yes, sir. But as matters currently stand, Commander Wan attempted a mutiny after locking you in your quarters, and she must be detained. So therefore, in other words, sir, until I see you in person, request respectfully denied."

"How would you like latrine duty for the foreseeable future?"

"Sir?"

Quasar collected himself. "Who told you all that nonsense?"

"Lieutenant Jones, sir. She said you were suffering from temporary amnesia—"

Quasar shut off the intercom and drew his Cody 52 Special. Storming out of his quarters, he headed straight for the brig. In his mind, he saw the scene play out as it undoubtedly would: with him scowling at the sentinel on duty, pointing his gleaming pulse pistol at the beguiled idiot, and ordering him to release Wan from her holding cell.

But that's not what happened.

Instead, Captain Quasar found himself back in his deluxe-model captain's chair with a beautiful woman standing beside him. They both stared at the view screen on the fore wall as a massive, hazel planet came into range.

"Standard orbit, Hank," Quasar ordered as if this had been their destination all along. It had not, of course, for this was not Planet Brociliamide. Captain Quasar had no idea what this planet was called. Nor had he any idea how they had arrived at this strange world.

"Home sweet home," the woman murmured.

"Lieutenant Jones," Quasar began. "What—?"

She smiled at him with a finger on her lips, and he fell silent, hushed by her magical influence. He had never seen a pair of eyes so mesmerizing, a head of hair so gracefully flowing, or a uniform with a skirt so short—let alone a skirt at all. She was captivating, to say the least.

"The captain would like you to ready a transport pod, Hank," she said, and that sounded like a good idea to Quasar, so he didn't object. As Hank vacated his post at the helm and trudged toward the rear exit of the bridge, following orders without question, Lieutenant Jones patted Quasar's hand. "Soon we'll be home, my love. It's been so long. Has it changed, I wonder? That is the only constant in the universe, I suppose: change. They tried to keep me away with their drugs and their prisons. Little men afraid of a woman with powers they could not begin to fathom. But you're not afraid of me, are you? Oh Captain, my captain?"

"Not at all." He felt his chiseled features break into an enamored smile, even as uncertainty squirmed in his bowels. Was he afraid? Anxious?

The exit door slid shut, but not before Commander Wan had stepped inside with a fully charged plasma rifle. Without giving Lieutenant Jones a chance to appreciate the situation, she fired a beam that struck Jones in the shoulder, driving her to the deck with a short cry—not to mention a burst of blue light and the mingled aroma of charred uniform and sizzled flesh.

The smile dropped from Quasar's face as the witch's spell on him evaporated, and he leapt from his chair with his Cody 52 Special at the ready.

"Don't move!" He aimed the muzzle at Jones. That's what he'd intended to do. But instead, the muzzle pointed at Commander Wan, now standing behind the intruder where she lay on the floor.

"Shoot her, my love!" Jones gasped, wincing at the pain from her scorched shoulder. "She is the only obstacle in our way!"

Quasar's grip on the pulse pistol tightened, but he hesitated, once again finding himself lost in her incredible emerald gaze. That moment was all his first officer needed to bring down the butt of her rifle, cracking Jones—or whoever she really was—across the back of her skull.

"No!" Quasar fired.

It was a good thing Wan's reflexes were so fast, or the pulse round that erupted from the captain's pistol would have fried a lethal path from her right eyeball straight through her brain. Instead, it slammed into the starboard side of the bridge and fizzled with sparks of blue light.

"Sorry about that, Commander." Quasar shook his head to fight a sudden wave of both dizziness and nausea. "She had quite a hold on me, I'm afraid."

"Humph," grunted Hank as he reentered the bridge. "Where was I going?"

"To ready a transport pod," said Wan. "I'll take our intruder to the surface—alone. We'll let her own people sort this out. Whatever this is."

"Good idea." Quasar holstered his weapon. "I'll notify whoever's in charge down there that you're on your way. But judging by the impression she's made here, I doubt you will receive a warm welcome. So we'll cover you as you make your approach. Full complement of plasma torpedoes standing by."

With a nod, Commander Wan bent to one knee and tossed

Lieutenant Jones over her shoulder like a limp, life-sized doll—and a ravishing one, at that. Without a word or a glance back at the captain, she followed Hank to the nearest launch bay.

◇◇◇

Captain Quasar and Commander Wan once again stood in the conference room, but this time there was no Sirilian intruder on board with highly evolved telepathic powers, and the Effervescent Magnitude was back on course, headed to Planet Brociliamide.

"Mental exercises, eh?" Quasar regarded his first officer with a raised eyebrow as well as unguarded admiration as they finished their debriefing on the day's events. "Perhaps you can teach me a few of those sometime."

"Perhaps," Wan replied, as stoic as ever.

"And whatever move you used on that poor sentinel in the brig—Dr. Yune said it could be a week or so before he has the use of his hands again."

"He was a stubborn one," she said. "As were the Sirilian chancellors. They did not want Jones back on their planet, but there was little they could do about it. Apparently, she plans to rule their male-dominated world. Providing education for female Sirilians is her first priority."

"Jones. Also known as Jeruzabel, if our translation software is correct. Which I can never be sure of, truth be told!" Quasar chuckled until he realized he was the only one doing the chuckling. "Can't believe I was that gullible. Enlisting her when we made that stop on an otherwise forgettable supply planet whose name currently escapes me. Won't make that mistake again, I can assure you—unless you enjoyed being captain for a day?" He winked.

She almost smiled. He caught the brief curve of her lips before she quickly straightened them out. "All in the line of duty, sir."

He saluted her. "Thanks for saving the day, Commander. Now back to work. I believe you have communications to monitor, among other things?"

"I believe I do, sir." Nodding once, she exited the conference room.

Once the door had slid shut behind her, Quasar stretched out on the table with a yawn, glad his mind was his own again.

Fortune Awaits You on Mars
By Michael McGlade

As young Aaron Adams, whose disgraced parents had dispatched
him to the colonies, thrustered into New Cydonia space harbor on
this lumbering starship, he watched the Red Planet swirl and heave
like the vortex of some rusted snow globe, the northern hemisphere
storming beneath a massive dust cloud. Bound for the capital city,
which would have been visible from this distance were it not for the
blood-red clots of sand, young Aaron's new life awaited once he
stepped through the door of his uncle's apartment. Aaron had turned
seventeen on the lonely month-long journey to Mars.

Passengers crowded the deck and jostled for a view of the
planet and this crush shoved Aaron farther and farther away from the
point of disembarkation until he trod on a shoe and was yelped at by
a man he had been acquainted with.

"Aren't you getting off?" the man said. "Gangplank's that
way," and he pointed his eyes toward the throng.

"I didn't think it would be ever so red," Aaron said. "It's just
like the pictures."

"Couse it's bleedin well like the pictures. Think the
commercials would've lied to us? Fortune awaits you on Mars."

It was a play on the popular immigration commercials: *Your
fortune awaits among the stars.* They were always trawling for
people with no prospects who thought five years on a colony planet
was better than what they were leaving behind.

"You think it'll be as crowded when we get down there?"

"New Cydonia's bigger than Paris, London and New York,
all rolled into one. Best place for a scut like you to make his way in
the world."

New Cydonia was built around the "Face on Mars." Aaron
really had wanted to see the face before shuttling to the surface.

The man eyed Aaron. "Where's your travel card?"

It wasn't clipped to his suit lapel, an old suit his father had
given him, which was a couple sizes too large. Everyone had their
travel cards in plain sight. You couldn't get off the starship without
it.

"Must've left it in my room," Aaron said. "Had it there, know I did. Say, will you watch my luggage a tick, while I pop back inside for it? Won't be a tick. Promise."

And Aaron forced his way into the stream of people gushing out the door and salmon-like wriggled his way inside against the flow, oblivious to the disgruntled sigh of the man left to watch over his luggage, all the possessions he owned in this world.

The way he knew to his room had been barred, the door he should've taken locked. He took an unfamiliar route, one he had never gone before. He hurried through a long series of small rooms, down short staircases, one after another, through winding corridors, past the open door of a voided room with an unmade bed and a deserted desk, until finally Aaron was utterly lost.

At a dead-end, the wheezing boy found himself before a grubby door unattended to or cleaned in years, as if maintenance had purposely avoided it. Aaron heard music from within and in a blind panic knocked and rapped the door for he would never find his way out of this gargantuan starship with its warren of corridors, and this fear of loss and isolation seized him, manifest in his pounding on the door.

"It ain't locked."

Aaron threw open the door and stumbled into the quite tiny, casket-sized room, which contained a man clutching a letter in his trembling hands who upon seeing this wheezing huffing strange boy stuffed the letter in his uniform pocket like it contained bad news, the kind you were ashamed for others to know about. This man in his forties had salt and pepper razored hair and an intricate swirling tattoo on his face. A tribal tattoo. Hands, red raw and black stained.

"I'm lost," Aaron said.

"Who isn't?"

The man's voice rumbled like a propulsion engine.

"My travel card, I left it... It's in my room."

"Lost your luggage, too?"

"It's up on deck. Left it in the favor of a man—"

"He a good friend?"

"I've spoken to him a few times before."

"Boy, New Cydonia will chew you up and spit you out."

"But the man – what's his name – he was ever so kind when we spoke, met him last night and he even ordered me a brandy."

"How old are you?"

"Seventeen and a day."

"And he paid for those brandies?"

"Well, now see here, he'd forgotten his wallet and I settled the bill but he promised to get the next one."

"Was the luggage important?"

"Everything I own is in it…"

Aaron's shoulders bunched. He slumped on the bed, brushing past the tattooed man, no way to avoid him in this cramped room. Aaron hung his head in his hands.

"I'm in room 634. Do you know where—?"

"You a rich boy?"

"Not particularly."

"Second class. Ain't cheap."

"It was a farewell gift, I suppose. I'm to make my own way in the world, now. Can you help me find—?"

"Room 634, Second Class. Well, for a poor-boy-in-a-rich-room like you, I guess I could find time in my busy schedule. If the pay's right."

Aaron reached for his wallet. It was gone. Stolen. First his luggage, now his wallet. All he had left was the travel card and without it he'd be in port jail until his parents wired him new visas, which had already cost them more than they earned in a year. Maybe they'd leave him to rot in the brig. No more than he deserved.

Aaron scratched at his wet eyes, turned away from this stranger, didn't want him to see the tears. Felt like a child.

"Course I'll help you find your bloody card. Don't want no money, neither." He put a hand on the boy's shuddering shoulders. "Thing about those visas, may cost an arm and a leg, but they're non-transferrable. No one's gonna nick it. We'll get it back for you."

"Promise?"

"Course I do."

He passed the boy a napkin and Aaron wiped off his cheeks. Even managed a smile.

"I went away at your age, boy. Know what it's like."

"Sent away?"

"No. Chose to go. Wanted to make my own way. Your fortune awaits among the stars."

There was a jaded lilt to the way he said it that the boy could not mistake.

"But you've got a decent job."

They both glanced around the casket-sized room.

"Yeah," he said. "I guess I made it. Fourth Engineer Zirilli."

"I'm Aaron Adams. Say, Zirilli – that's a Tritian name."

"Second generation Tritian. Frigging stigma that's been. Born on a Triton colony, never shake it off. Not that I want to. I'm proud of who I am. Never ran away from nothing in my life. But sometimes, just sometimes, I wish I could start over, have a different beginning."

"Can't be that bad. You're an engineer on the fifth largest star cruiser in the galaxy."

"Eighth largest. They keep building them bigger."

The Tritian exited the room and Aaron followed.

Zirilli was tall, over six feet, but his legs were stumpy in comparison with the length of his body, short because of the peculiar gravity on Triton, and instead of being blessed with super strength when off-planet, a peculiar effect occurred in which Tritians tended to move clumsily, giving them the appearance of impairment because, when their muscles were not taxed by immense gravity, they degraded to normal human strength. The facial tattoo and the strange body shape, it was hard not to judge a Tritian unfairly.

The starship shuddered to a halt and the engines wound down to a low drone.

Passengers' feet drummed and vibrated the bulkhead while they disembarked. Whatever desire Aaron clung to in the hope of being reunited with his luggage evaporated. It would be gone by the time he arrived on deck, a place he couldn't go without first retrieving his travel card, for without it he wouldn't even get to Mars. Better that he arrive in a dirty shirt, twice mended by his mother before departure from earth, than to not arrive at all. He couldn't return to his home planet, that much had been made clear. No, Mars was where he would make his way. Earn enough to pay for his child, a child he might never see, and send such monies back each week without fail, the details of which had been brokered in a contact between Aaron's family and the maid who seduced him – as long as she was provided for, no details of the illicit child would appear in the gossip columns to tarnish the family's name.

Aaron said, "I've seen plenty of Zargs as stewards, porters, engineers, officers. Even Captain Liebling's a Zarg. Seen a couple of Martins, though not so many as I thought there'd be. Even saw a few Centorians. Do all you Tritians work below deck?"

"I'm in the minority, boy. Just me. Only Tritian on board."

"Must get lonely?"

They ascended a short staircase and followed a slew of access corridors that had walls barely wide enough to stand straight.

"I'm interested in engineering and technology," Aaron said. "Had I not left Earth I think I'd ever so much have liked to study to be an engineer."

"You're Earth born?"

"Yes."

"Engineer's a good job, then."

"I don't understand."

"Twenty-three years doing space hops. Been working on this rig six years and, every time I get to go for a promotion, I get a citation or a reprimand and someone else gets the job."

"Always?"

"Only Zargs get promoted."

"Isn't that against the rules?"

Zirilli laughed like it was the funniest joke he'd ever heard and so infectious was the man's laughter that Aaron joined in and minutes later, with several more twisting helix turns and stairs climbed and having passed through even more, Aaron no longer recalled what the joke had been.

Zirilli paused outside Room 634. The engineer respectfully knocked at the door, waited, heard no one inside, and entered. Aaron's room was the cheapest of the second-class berths. It was a small room with a single bed, much like the engineer's. Aaron had spent a month here and it felt like home, saw the lighter patches on the walls where he had hung some movie posters, and the bed neatly made, so that the maid would not have to do it.

Beyond the porthole, where Aaron had spent much of his time gazing at the black cushion of space, and the pinpricks of endless stars, the boy now saw two immense warships cross each other, yielding to the sway and swell of Mars' gravity as it buffeted them, buffeted as much as their vast tonnage allowed. Two powerful shots reverberated through the hull. Salvos, probably fired from those warships. Already, Aaron noticed sleek, elongated shuttles knife the atmosphere after departing the harbor with expectant throngs of tourists and newly minted citizens.

Zirilli lifted the travel card off the writing desk and inspected it. The card belonged to Aaron. Full citizenship. He was on Mars for good, not just some rich kid on a gap year travelling the stars.

"OK, young master, here's your travel card."

"Thanks, Zirilli."

Aaron reached into his pocket of loose change but Zirilli stayed the boy's hand.

"There's good in you, boy, just don't let nobody take advantage of you when you get to New Cydonia."

"My uncle's coming to collect me. Uncle Merrow. He'll help me find some suitable labor."

Aaron extended his hand. Zirilli shook. Smelt the oily blackness of hydraulic oil on the man's work-worn hands.

Here was this man who had no home, this ship was his life. It was all he had. Couldn't a better life be made? Couldn't someone rise above their station, leave their mistakes behind, get on with making something of themselves?

Aaron said, "You believe you've been unfairly discriminated against?"

"This very day, the promotion I'd been promised, and earned…"

He passed the letter he had been holding when Aaron first saw him. The letter said:

"Due to unforeseen budgetary constraints, we must inform you that the position of Third Engineer is no longer tenable. We shall however keep your name on record. You may be eligible to apply for another position when it becomes available. We appreciate your dedication and diligence. Chief Engineer Sheddon."

"What was the reprimand?"

"None this time. Just a simple flat out categorical 'No.' Budgetary constraints is their way of saying you will never be promoted."

"There's no other avenues?"

"Find another tub to work on? What's the point? Here's the same as everywhere else."

"Speak to the captain."

"People like me don't speak to the captain. Doesn't even know I exist. Plus, he's a Zarg. They all stick together."

"Not Captain Liebling. I've heard him speak, been at the captain's table. He's an honorable man. I know it. He'd be duty bound to do the right thing. He has to. Why, if we could just somehow speak to him, tell him your side of things, I know he'd promote you in an instant. There'd be no question of it."

He ruffled Aaron's hair. "Thanks, boy, but dreams like that never happen."

"I promise to get you a fair meeting with the captain."

"You're a decent boy, but a boy is all you are. Stay out of this."

If the Duty Officer or this Chief Engineer Sheddon had his way every one of the officers would be a Zarg. There'd be no Tritians, no Martians, Centorians, nothing. Every one of them would be a Zarg.

A door had been shut on Zirilli. The boy had to repay the man's kindness by ensuring another door opened.

Zirilli led Aaron toward the deck. Ascending, they passed through larger quarters. Places where the officers roomed. Higher. Brighter. Full-size windows, not portholes.

Aaron passed a door marked Bridge. He entered. Zirilli grabbed at the boy but it was too late.

Sitting at a table engaged in conversation were four men, three dressed in khaki naval uniform and the other wearing Mars Harbor Authority red and black. A square-shouldered attendant sitting nearest them at a control panel also had his back to the door.

Two officers were standing at the far end of the bridge, near the window which overlooked the still swirling, hiccupping Red Planet. They spoke in low tones and both wore navel uniforms, but the older of them, though not by much as they were each in their forties, as he gesticulated, imparting his opinion which the other did not dare interrupt, his animated monologue caused light to blink off his heavy row of medals. Aaron knew this to be Captain Liebling.

But the boy had dithered too long and the attendant sitting at the control panel with his back to them had turned and, upon seeing them, stood and interposed his body between them and their goal.

"Leave here at once!"

Aaron fainted to the left, dodged beneath the attendants' grasp, and ran clear across the bridge, past the table of officers, toward the captain.

The whole room came to life. The officers at the table sprang to their feet. The captain watched this entrance and seemed unperturbed by the boy in the ill-fitting suit. Next to him Second Officer Rasmussen glared at the officers to see which of them would first draw their weapons.

Aaron was before the captain and had in his hand his travel card which he offered. Captain Liebling stayed his officers and, taking the boy's travel card, went to a large desk and sat. Aaron stood opposite him.

Zirilli, who had waited patiently at the door for the moment when he was needed, now moved next to the boy after the captain beckoned him forth.

Captain Liebling regarded them both, and then turned his attention to the boy's travel card which lay on the table. He flicked it aside as if it didn't matter. Considering the introduction concluded, Aaron lifted the travel card and placed it in his pocket.

"I was seated at your table," Aaron said.

"You were?"

"We spoke."

"I suppose we did."

"I come here to bring to your attention a grave matter of injustice—"

"What are you doing with this boy?"

Zirilli was tongue-tied. His neck flushed crimson.

Aaron couldn't help but think that it was possible he had been too trusting of his new friend, Zirilli. What if the man had not been forthright with him? And this moment of hesitation, which Zirilli displayed, added weight to the problem of his never being promoted, if indeed the man's story had been true at all.

Aaron made a mistake coming here. After all, he was a nobody, an Earthling, yes, but no one of any importance. This obvious truth was compounded when Second Officer Rasmussen moved next to the captain and placed his hand on the butt of his holstered sidearm.

He meant to eject them, forcibly if need be. The hard look in his eyes contained more than a trace of disdain for the Tritian.

"In my opinion," the boy said, "Fourth Engineer Zirilli, has been done an injustice. There is a Sheddon on board, Chief Engineer, who for the past five—"

Zirilli shook his head.

"…for the past six years," Aaron continued, "has elected this engineer be passed over for promotion."

Captain Libeling regarded the young man's confident patter with a grin.

"Why, he just this very day," the boy continued, "before arrival in New Cydonia harbor singlehandedly repaired the starboard pulse propulsion ramjets."

The captain raised an eyebrow and said, "A job that on any starship would have earned you a promotion." He checked the maintenance roster and confirmed the statement. "That repair alone would have saved the company enough to warrant you being promoted to a higher pay bracket." He studied the boy and the Tritian. "I expect you shall receive notification when you are eligible for promotion."

"Show him the letter."

Reluctantly, Zirilli passed the captain his rejection letter. Captain Liebling read the note, placed it on the table, waited.

"Is there anything else?"

"He's a good man. He's a good worker. Can't you see your way to at least reconsidering the rejection of his promotion to Third Engineer?"

"Does the boy always speak for you, Zirilli?"

"He makes a fair point, captain."

"The decision has already been made."

Aaron said, "Then overturn it."

"Oh, if only life were that simple."

"But I tell you this Sheddon has it in for my friend, Zirilli. Six years he's been passed over. Never once complained, just buckled down, did everything asked of him. Captain, won't you at least say that if he maintains his good work and a position becomes available then he will instantly be awarded it?"

"How dare you, Zirilli," Second Officer Rasmussen said. His face was crimson and the vein in his neck pulsed. "That you cannot come to terms with Sheddon being your superior and following his orders, that you've the gall to come to the captain with this, bypassing the chain of command, and that you dare bring this boy with you, having trained him to parrot on your behalf—"

Captain Liebling said, "We must get to the bottom of this. I'm not familiar with your work record, Zirilli. So I shall send for Chief Engineer Sheddon and he will explain why it is you have been passed over for promotion. I am sure there is a reasonable explanation."

The captain went to the intercom and spoke, leaving Aaron and Zirilli at the far end of the room like unwelcome visitors.

"I'm done for," Zirilli whispered. "Done for. That record is Sheddon's savior. He'll have it all in there. Every petty thing he's made me do will be in there. It's airtight."

"Nothing's airtight. No door is ever shut without some other one opening."

Presently, the door knocked and Sheddon entered. A squat man with thick eyebrows and a hint of an overbite. He approached the captain and held clutched to his chest, like it were some cherished possession, a thick dossier.

"Captain Liebling, sir," he said, "I have come here as requested to attest to my innocence. That this engineer is accusing me of some impropriety is unfathomable. Captain, sir, and all present, I can substantiate my good name and character, and refute all charges made against me by this … man. And to do so I have brought documentary evidence, the ship's log, and if necessary can have all and any statements made by myself verified and corroborated by impartial and unbiased witnesses who I have assembled outside the door."

Sheddon had come prepared. Hardly the actions of an innocent man.

"What about the ramjets?" Aaron blurted.

"Who is this urchin?"

"Answer him."

Sheddon faltered. Eyes darted around the room.

"Is Zirilli purporting to have fixed the ramjets without informing the Chief Engineer, namely me, that he did the repair without consultation, permission, or proper safety regards?"

Zirilli hung his head in shame. Cheeks crimson beneath the heavy black lines of his facial tattoo.

"We were entering harbor," the captain said. "The pulse propulsion ramjets are the only means by which to slow our approach for docking. Repair is imperative. It overrides all protocols."

Sheddon inhaled to speak but Captain Liebling silenced him with the flick of his finger. He had a petty officer bring him the dossier. The captain scanned through it, then studied Zirilli. He returned to reading the file. Minutes passed.

Sheddon stood tall.

Zirilli squirmed.

"To read this report, I would think you were an uncouth, abrasive, negligent man, Zirilli. Someone more suited to working a boiler room as a stoker than a Planetary Class Star Cruiser engineer. If so, then why repair the ramjets? Why go on a space walk into obvious danger at your own personal peril?"

"Because he's a rat, sir. Vermin. He did it to save his own neck. If the ship crashed, he'd die."

"He could have informed you," Aaron said. "You'd have made him fix the problem then cite him for some trivial breach of protocol and record it in your thick dossier. Does every officer bear as much scrutiny as Fourth Engineer Zirilli?"

"I resent your implication. This is not a Class thing, nor a Race issue."

"Why mention his race, him being Tritian, unless it is of importance?"

The captain acknowledged Sheddon's slip of the tongue and furrowed his brow. He thought for a long moment, studying Sheddon's face, his perspiring forehead, the dark rings which had formed at the pits of his khaki shirt.

"I will remind you, young sir," the captain said, "that you do not speak unless asked to do so. I am affording you a privilege and the benefit of doubt to allow you to be present in this restricted area of my ship."

"Sorry, sir. But you heard him, didn't you? He as much as admitted it was down to Zirilli being, well, not a Zarg."

"Youthful petulance is your undoing. Have the boy escorted from my ship."

Two officers approached Aaron. Zirilli, whose head hung down like his neck was a slinky, couldn't meet the boy's eyes.

It was over.

Nothing else remained to be said.

The captain had been offered a simple way out, that of righteous indignation.

The intercom buzzed. Captain Liebling lifted the receiver and listened. A few words into the conversation he stayed the officers who were escorting the boy, and his steely gaze fell on Aaron. He replaced the receiver in the cradle.

"You are to meet your uncle, Merrow?"

"Yes, sir. I was delayed and Zirilli helped me find… How did you know my uncle's name?"

"Your uncle is Senator Merrow?"

"Yes."

"Why didn't you just say so?"

"Because I know you to be a man of integrity and I knew if you heard the truth you would act on it accordingly."

Captain Liebling chuckled.

"You have a good friend here, Zirilli. Pity it's all for naught."

Senator Merrow entered the bridge. This short, wedge-shaped man, trundled toward the captain with luggage in tow.

Aaron's uncle was here. His uncle would save the day. Uncle Merrow. Senator Merrow.

He kissed Aaron on the forehead and in return received from the boy a kiss on the cheek.

The luggage belonged to the boy and Aaron noticed the shape of his missing wallet in the front compartment. Neither of his possessions had been stolen. The man hadn't run away with it. There was hope. Always hope.

He blurted out in staccato the details of Zirilli's injustice.

Uncle Merrow met the eyes of all concerned, first the boy's then Zirilli, and lastly Captain Liebling.

"This is indeed a sticky situation, my boy," he said to Aaron. "Had these men known the precarious details surrounding your departure from Earth, they may not have been so receptive. But I see you have taken this man's case to heart, and who am I to stand in the way of justice?"

He took Aaron by the shoulders in a fatherly grasp and stared into the boy's eyes, and the boy felt the first fluttering in his chest of the great new life he had ahead of him, with someone who stood for justice and rights.

"However, one must know what fights can be won. There is the matter of ship's discipline to take into account. Pursuing a plea for justice might shut the door altogether on Zirilli's future. My boy, you have interfered too much already. We must depart."

"But what will happen Zirilli?"

"He will get what he deserves, no doubt, the captain will see to it."

"But…"

He didn't get to finish. Uncle Merrow ushered the boy from the room, uttering an apology to all concerned.

Aaron broke free and returned to Zirilli, took the man's hand in his and met Zirilli's eyes, if only for a brief moment before his uncle grabbed him by the scruff of the neck and dragged him toward the exit.

One final pleading glance toward the captain.

A decision had been made, Aaron saw that now. Captain Liebling had shut the dossier and pushed it aside like it meant nothing.

Facing the boy, who was in the threshold of the doorway on his way to Mars under his uncle's care, the captain offered a reassuring grin to him and to Zirilli.

"Three units in the beta quadrant have gone missing in the last week. Two the week before that, and another four over the previous month."

Harold Brant slipped his traveling case from the overhead compartment and checked the seals. Over three hundred shuttle flights on company time, and no one had ever tampered with his luggage. If the bio-locks didn't deter a potential snoop, the ICS logo stamped into the brushed metal surface certainly would.

The recording continued, replaying the mission statistics. "Nine missing bots since the first, and every one of the rogues loaded with the new, state-of-the-art, ICS compassion program."

The company's shining achievement was causing one hell of a mess, and that mess had dragged Harold to the backwater reaches of the system on a cheap shuttle flight with only a few hours' notice. He tucked his case under one arm and returned to his seat.

"Initial contact: Newt Maxfield, colony manager, purchaser of one hundred and fifty ICS synthetics, model 215C straight off the belt."

What the recording didn't add, Harold could guess well enough. These outlying colonists considered the company a necessary evil. They liked the products just fine when they worked, but he'd be facing anti-company hostility if the bots had actually malfunctioned. Even with the ICS record and the fact that ninety percent of bot breakdown was eventually deemed user error.

They'd be dying for a crack at the mega corporations, at ICS and at Harold as well. He'd be landing with a target on his back…again.

He switched off the recording and removed his glasses long enough to archive the file. This far out few passengers remained. What had begun as a crowded flight ended with Harold, a slim kid looking for work in the outlands and a family relocating after what the woman had assured everyone was just a bad financial investment. Her husband slept most of the way, but their six-year-old daughter had bounded between the seats whenever the artificial gravity allowed. Now she curled against her mother's side and grinned at Harold.

The light on his glasses blinked and he shoved them back on. The job worked for him. He reminded himself how just how much while the family slept their way through the pre-landing announcements. Forty-five minutes to touchdown, enough time to listen to his notes again.

"Incident report, Dirlane colony, beta quadrant. Nine bots currently unaccounted for. Colonists report compassion malfunction...highly suspect. Probable cause, user error." Harold memorized it while his shuttle tipped forward and began its descent. "Three units in the beta quadrant have gone missing in the last week..."

"You must be Brant." The man thrust out his hand mechanically, like a bot. "I'm Newt. Newt Maxfield."

"Call me Harold."

Maxfield had thinning brown hair and a round midsection. He wore the rough, utilitarian garb that marked him as a colonist. Still, his grip was firm, and he shook Harold's hand without any overt hostility. His gaze was steady and as unflinching as his grip, but softened when Harold endured the handshake without breaking eye contact.

"Well, Harold. Your bots are causing one hell of a ruckus out here."

"My report says you've lost nine so far."

"Eleven."

Maxfield didn't catch the inflection, the adjustment to his wording and the implication that it was the colonists who lost the bots and not the other way around. Good. They'd set that precedent right out of the gate. It would make the shift to user error much simpler in the end.

They took an open-air skimmer from the ramshackle spaceport. Dirlane boasted a rocky surface too poor in valuable minerals to warrant commercial mining, but rich enough in agricultural soil to allow the colonists to eke out an existence between the jagged, blue-tinged mountain ranges. They flew along the base of one of these, twisting over ground that barely showed enough dirt between the ridges to grow a weed let alone crops.

The colony had still managed to establish itself, to twist the natural hostility into a sort of security measure. No matter that no one wanted anything Dirlane had to offer, the paranoia of those who sought the colonist lifestyle made that deficit into a perk. Whatever the reason, Dirlane was only sparsely populated, with few roads and those barely wide enough to allow the passage of the few cargo liners and trade merchants that the residents allowed to land.

Harold watched the blue rock, the lines of passing stone and growing shadows. He had to squint. They'd put down only a few hours before sunset in this hemisphere and the skies already drifted toward deep purple. While Maxfield drove, he prattled on about the bots. He blamed the compassion function, the new baby that ICS wore proudly on its corporate sleeve.

Harold should have taken the opportunity to deflect the accusation. He should have grilled the manager on his maintenance schedule, dug up any unauthorized modifications that might take the blame, but his eyes caught movement between the rocks. He spied a slim silhouetted darting from one stone crest to the other, and it moved far too fast to identify.

"There's something out there."

Maxfield spat over the side of the vehicle and nodded grimly. "The damned dogs."

"Dogs?"

"Native species. Sneaky bastards, always slinking around the rocks."

"Are they dangerous?" The shadow hadn't looked that big, but Maxfield's voice trembled at the edges.

"Destructive mostly. Diggers. The longer we're here the less distance they think they need to keep."

"I see." Harold had heard the story before. Native species and farmers had been clashing for centuries. If the dogs had gotten used to the colonists then crops and livestock would raise the stakes. He doubted there'd be anything in the shadows on Dirlane for long.

As if to prove his point, Newt Maxfield waved one pudgy arm toward the backseat and flashed Harold a nasty grin. "There's a mag-rifle under the tarp, businessman. You feel free to take a shot at 'em."

"No thanks."

"Didn't think so." Maxfield spit again and flashed his teeth. "Businessmen got not stomach for colony life."

"I suppose they don't." Harold stared out at the rocks. The shadows took on different shapes, moved of their own accord. Dogs slipping upslope, between the stone fingers and away from the hollow echo of Newt Maxfield's laughter.

"Amend record. Set missing bot count at eleven." Harold spoke to his glasses and stared out the thick, well-streaked window. Maxfield's skimmer still waited in the middle of the road, squarely between the hotel where he'd dropped Harold and the quadrant's only tavern. "Arrived at beta quadrant and scheduled bot observation for oh-six-hundred hours."

That gave him one night to recover from the trip. His room had only sparse furnishings. The bunk had no electronic features, though the bath suite was well fitted. He'd have to rough it, but judging from the shape of beta quadrant's other buildings, he'd scored the best room in town.

His travel case lay on the bunk, still sealed. Harold crossed the room in three steps and pressed his fingers against the bio-pads. The lock heated, bleeped and then clicked open. The case lid lifted, revealing an interior of padded compartments exactly the shape of Harold's tools.

He took inventory, checked the charges on each item's indicator and removed them one at a time for examination before tucking them safely away again.

Eleven bots missing. It had to be user error. Still, should they have an actual situation on their hands, eleven rogues might be more than he could repair alone. He considered sending a transmission, but shook off the idea. Too early. Most likely Newt Maxfield let one of his colonists fiddle with the programming.

These colonists never learned.

Harold placed the last item back into its nest and triggered the lock with a voice command. The lid lowered, sealed again, but the final click was lost in the sound of shouting outside. He recognized Maxfield's voice, but the screamer was definitely a woman. He told himself to ignore it, to focus on the job and let the colonists' world go on around him.

Somehow, he still ended up back at the window.

His room was on the second level, but the windows worked. In the home worlds, nothing above the ground floor had functional windows. He pushed the glass out and leaned into the open. Maxfield stood beside his skimmer. His voice rolled like soft thunder, but the woman facing him raised her voice for the purple skies to hear.

"Shot three more last night! At this rate they won't make it another year."

"Quiet, Marta. We've got a company man here." Maxfield glanced nervously toward the hotel. It only guided his adversary's gaze straight to where Harold spied on them.

"Good!" The woman threw her hands wide and turned her attention to Harold. "Company man, is it? Well, how does the company feel about the extermination of natural species?"

"I," Harold sputtered. He felt his face warming, and his throat dried up, choking him on each word. "It's not really our business."

"Oh no?" She put her hands to her hips, including him in her wrath now by lumping him in with people like Newt Maxfield, native dog slayer. She wore the same colony drab as Maxfield, but it looked a great deal better on her slender frame. Dark hair riffled over her shoulders and who knew how far down her back. A sharp chin thrust forward, illustrating her ire as much as her volume did. "Let's talk business then, company man."

"Marta!" Maxfield raised his voice at last, but it didn't even slow her down.

"Did he tell you he had his man fiddle with your fancy bots?"

"Shut up, woman!"

"Messed with their programming, didn't you, Newt?"

Maxfield deflated and cursed under his breath. He kicked the side of his skimmer hard enough to rattle the doors. "Go home, Marta, for land's sake."

She'd done her damage, but Marta grinned up at Harold once more just to prove it. Then she spun on her heel and marched toward the tavern, leaving a muttering Newt Maxfield alone in the street. He might have deserved the woman's fury, but Harold felt a stirring of pity anyway. The man knew he was sunk. He *should* have known better than to modify an ICS bot.

"I'd have been able to tell anyway," he said.

Maxfield grunted, nodded and didn't look up to the window. "I suppose so."

Harold waited. He watched the colony manager with a mixture of pity, distaste and company-groomed offense. You didn't fiddle with a product that was already perfect. The last part won out in the end. When Maxfield finally climbed into his skimmer, Harold Brant called down his sentence. He had to say it, even though he was certain, Maxfield already knew.

"Unauthorized modification of any ICS product renders your warrantee null and void."

Maxfield cursed again, loud enough to reach the window and then some. He brushed a fat hand through his hair and sighed. "They were protecting the dogs, businessman. The damned dogs."

"ICS is not responsible for the application of its product in non-standard situations." He saw Maxfield's shoulders sag and relented, veered from the standard script a little. "That being said, I'll see what I can do."

"Do what?" Maxfield sounded more skeptical than hopeful, but he sat up a little straighter.

"I'll do what I can." Harold leaned back inside. He shouldn't promise anything. ICS merchandise agreements were iron-clad.

When Newt Maxfield started his skimmer and moved on down the street. Oh-six-hundred hours seemed a lot closer than it had a moment before. Harold needed sleep. He needed to sort out what the compassion function had made of Dirlane's wild dog situation and he didn't believe for one minute that Newt Maxfield would be happy with the ICS standard explanation.

"Compassion my ass," Maxfield waved his hands toward the yellow fields, and the skimmer drifted toward the edge of the road. "It's a damned nuisance. What do they need compassion for?"

They passed a line of alert, ICS robots. Each synthetic waited at the end of a long row of fluffy grain. Each pair of glowing, near-human eyes carefully followed their movement.

"Why?" Harold cleared his throat and continued to examine the waiting bots. "The compassion function is a safety improvement, Mr. Maxfield. A bot with compassion would never turn on its owner, for instance. It would never kill, could never be used as a weapon."

Maxfield grunted. The skimmer bobbed along, slow enough that Harold could watch the eyes watching them. The bots waited for orders, as they no doubt waited every morning. Powered up, but without direction until someone triggered their next action. Their silver bodies had grown dim under a layer of Dirlane soil. He'd have to make a note about maintenance too. Optimum service life depended on regular cleanings.

"So how many have turned?" Maxfield's question pulled his attention away from the bots.

"What's that?"

"Before compassion, how many bots turned on their handlers?"

"Oh. None really."

"None."

"The ICS has always stressed proactive measures. It's policy."

Maxfield grunted again. He pulled the skimmer to a halt and killed the engines, parking beside the only structure they'd seen since leaving town. It faced the fields, and behind it the same jagged fingers of rock lifted toward the distant mountains.

"Here?" Harold eyed the corrugated metal shed skeptically. "This is your facility?"

"Yup." This time Maxfield grinned. He hopped out of the skimmer, and Harold scrambled to follow suit.

As soon as his feet hit the soil, however, a gunshot echoed through the morning, splitting the quiet and sending Harold to his hands and knees.

"Where'd you go?" Maxfield's voice called, but gunfire still rang in Harold's ears, and his heart hammered. "Brant?"

"I'm here." Kneeling in the dirt like an idiot. Harold heard the crunch of Maxfield's boots, the chuckle at his own expense. He'd overreacted, and the colonist would never let him forget it. "Just dropped…got…"

A heavy hand landed on his arm. Harold sat back and looked up at a familiar, ICS designed face. Glowing eyes blinked down. "Are you satisfactory?"

Harold knew that voice. He'd helped program over two hundred unique ICS approved personalities. "I'm fine."

"Let me help you up, sir." The bot cupped its hand under Harold's arm and lifted, pulling him gently to his feet.

"Thank you."

"No problem, sir." The metal hand released him, and the bot stepped backwards, reversed its motions and ended standing in perfect position beside its row, eyes glowing, as if it had never moved.

"See, that's just creepy," Maxfield said. "Compassion my ass."

"It's a miracle of programming. ICS has broken new ground in artificial personality." He sounded like a commercial, exactly like a commercial.

"Rubbish." Maxfield shook off the spiel. "I just need the damned things to work."

The gun boomed again, more distant this time. Harold only flinched and turned his gaze to the rocks and the slope that hid Maxfield's "damned dogs. "He glared at Maxfield, but the man only flashed him his teeth and chuckled.

"You can't build fences?"

"They dig right under them." He crunched toward the shed, stopping only when he reached the door.

Harold tore his gaze from the hills, but when the third shot fired, he saw the bots flinch too. He saw the glowing eyes turn to the rocks. How much of this would their compassion function tolerate?

"Brant," Maxfield called. "We doing this or not?"

"Yes." Harold trotted away from the skimmer. He kept his gaze forward, away from the rocks and the line of bots.

Maxfield waved him into the building. They had strip lighting set in the ceiling, but it didn't hide the filth. Some old crates had been fashioned into a table, and sitting on one end of this was a skinny colonist with red hair on every part of his body that wasn't covered in the dull, colony-issued cloth.

"Jared," Maxfield barked as he ducked inside. "This is Harold Brant, ICS man come to sort out our bots."

Jared grinned and nodded his head until the hair on the top of his head danced. He had a wire driver in one scrawny fist, and he tapped it absently against the side of the crate he sat on.

"Are you the one that modified our products?" Harold asked.

Jared's grin faded. His eyes darted to Maxfield waiting by the door.

"It's all right." Maxfield stomped his way to the table. "Marta already told him."

"I'd have known anyway."

"I only tried to tone it down a little," Jared had a whiny voice. He spoke too fast and at too high a pitch. "Just so they'd let us alone about the dogs."

Harold sighed. He'd heard a thousand reasons for tampering with a bot. Nothing should have surprised him. He gave Jared a patronizing nod. "Show me what you did."

They traipsed back outside. Harold opened his case on the front of the skimmer and waited for Jared to herd one of the bots over. The synthetic obeyed without hesitation, stalking over with the stiff gait that the engineers just couldn't quite make look natural.

"I jus' turned it down," Jared insisted.

Harold gave him a look and pulled out his analyzer. The device would scan the bot's circuitry, compare it to the initial schematics and tell him in less than forty seconds exactly what the hicks had screwed with.

"Display cranium port, please." He ordered the bot, and its silvery head spun in a half circle. Bots were easier than people, in Harold's thinking. They never asked questions and, so long as you left their programming alone, always behaved in a neatly predictable fashion. "Prep for scanning."

"Confirmed." The bot's speaker blared the recorded response. Harold heard static, but that would be the lack of proper maintenance. The indicator lights on the back of the metal neck flashed, and his analyzer picked up the signal and went to work.

"It'll just take a second." He watched the screen and the flow of data instead of the two colonists. "What did you say you did to them?"

"Turned that compassion thingy down."

"You didn't." The readings indicated no change in the personality matrix whatsoever. "The Compassion program is completely functional. You've haven't changed anything."

"Well," Newt cleared his throat. He pushed in beside Harold and Jared shuffled away to make room for him. "Maybe you could show him how to do it then."

"Excuse me?" Harold switched off the analyzer.

"Your bots are killing our productivity. They ain't working right."

"Are you asking me to perform an unauthorized field modification?"

"Well," Newt rubbed his hand over his head again, scrubbing at the sparse hair. "I wasn't really asking, but…"

"Stop!" The shriek had a familiar ring to it. They all turned to the hillside, watched while Marta huffed her way down the slope carrying a limp, dark form in her arms. Even the bots looked. "You stop this instance or…I'll file a…report."

Harold tucked his analyzer back into its compartment. He tried not to notice the dead dog, the dribbles of blood Marta left in her wake as she carried the carcass across the rocks. The case sealed again at his touch, and he heard Maxfield's muttered curse. The man, Jared, spat on the ground.

"These bots are colony property," Marta shouted again. She reached the bottom of the hill and trudged forward. The dog's legs swung in a ghastly rhythm on either side of her arms. "Paid for with colony funds, Newt Maxfield. You don't have permission to do this!"

"Do what?" Newt shrugged, but he exchanged a look with Jared, and the slower witted mechanic chuckled openly.

"You!" Marta turned her ire on Harold. He stepped backwards, flinched when she dumped the animal's carcass on the front of the skimmer. "I'll file a report. I'll have your job if you so much as tweak a wire."

"I have no intentions of doing any such thing." Harold leaned as far from the dead animal as he could. It had glossy black fur and an elongate shape, slim and fast. He'd seen them move like liquid shadow between the rocks.

"Oh." The woman tossed her hair back and it fell like a wave over her shoulders. It shimmered like the dead dog, even with the hound's blood staining the front. "You see what they're doing, then?"

"No." Harold didn't want to see. He wanted to put as much distance as he could between himself and the colony.

"But you're not going to help them?" She leaned over the carcass, placed a delicate hand against the animal's coat. "Are you?"

"No."

"Be reasonable, Marta." Maxfield pleaded. He stepped in front of Harold and reached for the dead dog. "They're tearing up the crops!"

Harold flinched when Newt picked up the body. He turned his gaze away, fighting down bile. If he hadn't, he might have missed the bot's reaction. He might have missed the shift in the stiff pose, the glow of blue eyes and the tightening of two, metal fists that were programmed never to cause harm.

"Eleven bots unaccounted for, but no discernible tampering in the units. No modifications made." Harold paced his hotel room, talking to his glasses. "Local dispute over native species, colony manager claims bots are interfering with extermination of nuisance animals."

He closed his eyes, but the image of the dog carcass loomed too clearly. He needed a drink, needed off this rock.

"No malfunction witnessed." Hell, the eleven units could have been stolen for all he knew. They could have broken down or Maxfield could have hidden them. He could be fishing for replacement funds. "Current reports suspect. No evidence of erratic behavior in units."

He tried not to remember the look, the bot's blue eyes when Maxfield picked up the dog. "Compassion program fully functional."

The door to his room thumped and Harold dropped his glasses. The knock came three more times while he bent to pick them up.

Maxfield's voice hollered from the other side of the panel. "Brant! Wake up, Brant! Your damned bots got Marta."

Harold stumbled across the room. He hadn't slept yet. The day cycle on Dirlane was shorter than Home-world standard, and even though the moons were well up, he hadn't been able to nod off, had gotten up three times to record more details.

Now Newt Maxfield was trying to break down his door. He slid it open and stared at the colony manager. The stink of alcohol backed Maxfield's words. They didn't slur yet, but Harold guessed Newt had been drinking at the tavern since they'd returned from the fields.

"Marta's gone."

"What?"

"Bots got her. Come on an' see for yourself."

"The bots cannot have 'got' her, Mr. Maxfield. They are programmed to be incapable of harming…"

"Just get your fancy case and come on, Brant."

He headed back down the hallway and Harold was forced to rush, to scramble for his traveling case and hustle to catch up with the man. *Bots got her.* Was it even possible? ICS synthetics could not harm a human. In all his cases, in all anyone's cases, no one contested that fact.

Maxfield had his skimmer fired up by the time Harold shuffled out of the hotel. They drove straight between the low community buildings without conversation. The metal habitats made dark silhouettes to either side, passing at the skimmer's top speed.

They scooted between tiny domed houses, leaving the thicker bulk of town behind. Newt muttered something he couldn't make out, steered the vehicle between two rows of pre-fabricated homes and then pulled it in sideways beside the one that had to be Marta's.

The entire side had been ripped free. The metal peeled back in strips, curving in the dark like sharp fingers. Debris, what was left of Marta's furnishings, trailed out in a lumpy swath across the artificial lawn.

"Bot tracks everywhere," Maxfield commented. "Nothing else strong enough to do this."

"No." Harold shook his head and climbed out of the skimmer. "Synthetics cannot cause harm. They didn't do this."

"Like hell they didn't." Maxfield growled and kicked at a cracked chair leg. "Damn company bullshit. Those things are dangerous, and you know it."

"ICS is not responsible for situations caused by non-standard synthetic utilization." Harold imagined the glow of the blue eyes, the way the bot flinched when Maxfield dropped the dog's carcass to the stony ground. "If illegal modifications have been made—"

Maxfield lunged at him. The only thing that kept Harold's neck from landing in the man's fat grip was the chair leg. Newt tripped over it and fell forward, still reaching murderous fingers for Harold's throat.

Harold shuffled away. The skimmer hummed idly beside Marta's ruined home, and the moonlight reflected off the torn metal, the rocks and the hillside behind it. Something else gleamed in the low light. It stood taller than the stones, waiting in the open and bathed in soft moonlight.

Harold's arm came up, pointed out the bot before Maxfield could recover enough to throttle him. "Bot." He blurted it. "There's a bot."

Maxfield's head swiveled around. He dropped his fists, and his voice lowered. "Is it coming for us?"

"Ridiculous," Harold said. No synthetic had ever harmed a human being, excluding a few cases in the records that were clearly labeled as user error. He squinted at the bot on the horizon. It raised one metal arm and then turned and vanished over the hillside. "We should follow it."

"You're out of your mind." Newt stood up, however, and he climbed into the skimmer and waited for Harold to join him.

"It's perfectly safe." He recited it.

Maxfield didn't answer. He gunned the skimmer, and they rocketed after the bot, off-road, sliding between the rocky spears with far less grace than the native dogs. The synthetic moved faster, however. It kept at least one hill between them, appearing just as they'd top an incline and waving one arm to make certain they knew which way to go.

The skimmer slowed to a crawl, and Maxfield shook his head. "It's a trap. This feels like a trap?"

"Not possible." Harold eyed the bot waving from the far peak. "It's just trying to show us something."

"You trust that thing after what you saw at Marta's place?"

Harold eyed the bot and frowned. He pictured the dead dog, the blue, glowing eyes and the metal fingers peeled back from Marta's habitat. The company manual played over his doubts. He'd spent eight months memorizing it. *A synthetic is incapable of…*

"Yes, I do."

"Fine." Newt moved the skimmer forward again, accelerated, still shaking his head. "It's on you, then."

They drove down the next slope and up the far side. When they crested that peak, however, their guide did not appear on the far one. Newt piloted the skimmer down and stopped it halfway between ridges. He sighed and climbed out of the vehicle. "What now, businessman?"

Harold got out and took a step away from the skimmer. He eyed the high ridges around them, the rocks tipped with moonlight and the shadows where the dogs hid between them. "I'm not sure. We could check…"

Newt Maxfield had a mag-rifle in his hands. Harold stared at the muzzle and tried to register why it might be pointing at him. The shiny barrel didn't waver, and Maxfield flashed his teeth. "Just hold very still, businessman. They'll be along in a minute."

"What? Who?"

"Hand over the glasses, please," Maxfield said.

"Glasses?"

"Now!"

The mag-rifle shifted position, and Harold scrambled to take off his glasses. He held them out, but Maxfield shook his head. "Put 'em on the front of the skimmer, real carefully."

Harold did as he was told. When he'd laid the glasses down, Newt's gun waved him away again. "What do you want with them?"

"Evidence," Maxfield said. "You recorded it yourself. *No modifications made.*"

"You're after the money?" Harold backed away from the skimmer. Behind Newt, he could see the bot's return. He swung his gaze from side to side and counted. They lined up at the rim on all sides, eleven missing bots bathed in moonlight and shadows.

"Do the math," Maxfield said. "One hundred and fifty synthetics completely covered by your standard, ICS, warrantee."

The math added up to far more than Harold wagered his life was worth. He watched the circle of blue eyes closing in and fought back a wave of panic. Bots on all sides, moving in that stiff, automated gait that never quite looked natural.

He'd had nightmares that started like this. Every time he landed to investigate a report, he dreamed of metal death. His memory chanted the ICS assertion, *no synthetic can harm a person, no synthetic can harm…*

"Wait!" His knees wavered now. The bots kept coming and Harold relived every doubt he'd ever had about the ICS manual. "Be reasonable. Please, we can work something out."

"On your knees, businessman." Maxfield grinned and waved the mag-rifle.

Harold dropped to the hard ground. He shook all over, and his eyes moved from one oncoming bot to the next, trying to imagine which one would tear his head off. Which pair of metal hands would circle his throat and squeeze the life from his body.

He almost missed the smaller figure, the slim form standing between the bots. When she strode forward, Harold's relief flooded through him. Marta. Here was the woman, unharmed and walking among the bots without fear. Harold let out his breath, but it caught again when she snarled at Maxfield.

"Why is he still breathing?"

"Waiting for you." Maxfield growled back.

Marta laughed, high and echoing. "These company men never learn."

"Wait!" Harold connected the dots. "The bots haven't malfunctioned at all."

"It's almost cute," Marta said. "The way he tries so hard."

The insult combined with the realization that he wasn't being attacked by murderous synthetics brought Harold back to his senses. The whole thing had been a setup, the dogs, the inspection. They'd played him for a company fool, and he'd behaved as predictably as any bot. What would they have done if he'd agreed to make their modifications? He swallowed a dry lump of nerves and eyed the woman glaring down at him. She was smart. This was most likely her plan.

"They won't pay you." He said it fast, spoke in a rush and prayed they didn't shoot him before he could explain. "Eleven bots missing and I'm the only corpse? They'll never believe it."

"Shut up, businessman." Maxfield stepped closer. He lowered the gun's muzzle until Harold could see all the way inside. Any minute now and it would all be over.

"He's right," Marta said.

"What?" Newt jerked around, confused for the second it took her to blow him away. The pistol was small, tiny enough that Harold hadn't even seen it in her palm. He heard the boom of it, though, and he saw Newt Maxfield's body jerk to the side and fall.

The mag-rifle hit the stones first, but too close to Marta's foot for Harold to see any hope in that. Newt crashed to the ground beside it, and Marta stepped over him, laughing. She aimed her pistol at Harold now and shrugged. "Poor Newt, but it's for the good of the colony."

"What about the dogs?"

"What?"

Harold put his hands on the ground behind him. He leaned back and looked up at the colonist. "I thought this was about the dogs."

Behind her, Harold could see the metal heads swivel. Blue eyes glowed in the moonlight.

"The dogs!" Marta waved her pistol toward the rocks. "We just needed an excuse for the malfunction, a reason that compassion crap could turn nasty."

"You killed it, didn't you?" Harold held his breath. He might have imagined the incline in the bot's posture, the tilt to the silvery head.

"Who gives a damn about dogs, company man? I killed a dozen of them, and I'll kill a hundred more if it gets me the…" He words squeaked away, clamped shut in the grip of thick, metal fingers. They flexed, and Harold heard the cracking of bones, the snap as an ICS synthetic twisted the woman's neck.

It dropped her, and she lay lifeless against the stones. The bot backed one step away and froze, stiff and at attention, as if it hadn't moved at all. Its blue eyes glowed and it spoke in a voice he'd hear in his sleep.

"Are you satisfactory, sir?"

Harold Brant left the colony skimmer at the spaceport. He boarded the shuttle with only his traveling case, a pair of company-issued glasses and a tiny, unregistered pistol.

The shuttle had few passengers. A young couple heading for the home worlds to start a new life, a few teenagers heading for university in hopes of making something out of their future.

Harold stowed his silver case and took a seat near the window. The light on his glasses blinked, and he recorded his final statistics.

"Situation on Dirlane fully investigated. Warrantee null and void." He closed his eyes, saw stone and bodies and a ring of glowing blue eyes again. "While no field modifications were officially detected, synthetics were subjected to non-standard use and severe circumstances resulting in aggressive…"

He stopped and removed his glasses. The dogs had swept in almost immediately, had taken care of the bodies while the synthetics waited for orders. Harold sent *them* back to the fields where they belonged.

"Circumstances resulting in erratic behavior," he amended. "Two casualties."

He'd checked them first, had made absolutely certain that no modifications had occurred, that all systems were standard. Then he'd pocketed Marta's pistol.

"Official investigation complete. Final determination: User Error." He'd taken the gun, and Harold doubted he'd ever be without one again. *Synthetics are incapable of causing harm. Ninety percent of bot breakdown…* Harold Brant archived his recording and sent in his report.

SPACE PARTNERS
BY RICHARD W. BLACK

The alarm woke Susanna Angela Mathews. She pulled the covers around her body and begged the universe for more time. Then her hand found Marc and another idea took shape.

"Alarm off," he said but he did not move and she knew the day, or at least the morning, had potential.

He touched her and she felt the sensation start. Skillfully, his fingers were under her nightgown and explored her body while locating every spot that elicited a pleasurable response. Eventually, he eased over onto her and gently brought her to the point of ecstasy. Oh, what a morning, she thought as she blissfully cried out.

But it was still morning and he popped out of bed with his usual energy and she moaned, there would be no additional sack time, no second ride into the land of pleasure.

She heard the sanitation spray start and swung her legs over onto the floor.

"Are you coming?" Marc called from the other room.

"Yeah, yeah," she muttered.

By the time she peeled off her nightgown and entered the sanitation room, he was in the spray compartment.

Stepping in with him, she felt the burst of warmth, the temperature was set to her maximum comfort, and she soaked in the pleasure of the shooting mists.

The sanitation spray units were modeled after the old water showers humanity employed for years. However, the sanitation units captured H2O from the air and transformed it into a soothing but powerful mist. For five minutes, the unit sprayed their naked bodies with a soapy mixture designed to clean but safe on any orifice including the eyes. Then it would automatically switch to a cleaning mist. They were facing each other and she enjoyed his hands rubbing her back and limbs and all the special places that he knew to touch and sanitize. Oh how she loved being sanitized. Then she reciprocated until the unit switched off and the heat blowers turned on.

Their standard morning sanitizing took thirteen minutes and twenty seconds, standard time.

She had need of another unit in the sanitation room and, by the time she was finished, he was dressed and probably in the kitchen. It always bothered her that he managed to dress before her. Was that chauvinistic of her? And, as usual, he had her favorite breakfast ready. On the other hand, he ate a power bar designed to maximize his metabolism. She had a similar option but she still preferred real food made in the old ways. By old ways, she meant on a self-cleaning hotplate using kitchen utensils used by surface dwellers on Earth. Most on Phoenix Station had meals of prepackaged foods prepared in special dishes inside microwave oven units and they opted to eat with their fingers.

Some might call Sam an old-fashioned girl but she liked the reputation. There was a rebellious side to her, an unconventional piece to her makeup.

While they ate, Sam and Marc watched the morning news beamed across space from Earth. It was the usual mixture of infighting among this people group and that people group, a lost animal or child found and the happy-to-be-alive section to close out the broadcast and leave the viewer with a sunny perspective on the world.

"Thank the stars and the Universal Space Consortium that we work in space, Marc," she said with a raised coffee mug.

Marc tapped his mug to hers. He did not drink coffee very often but his morning brew was a syrupy concoction that he developed which he said did more for him than her coffee did for her. She wanted to argue but the science was unquestionably on his side so she resisted. Like most couples, it paid to pick her battles especially when dealing with an intellect that just might be superior to hers.

"What is on the agenda, today?" he asked when she finished her coffee.

He was intelligent enough to know that nothing of consequence should come between a robotic systems engineer and her morning coffee.

While she cleaned the dishes, she considered the schedule she had rolling in her brain. With her eidetic memory, it was like seeing the list of tasks roll past on a electronic pad screen. Also, she insisted on always cleaning up the breakfast dishes since her food made most of the mess and she always felt guilty about how he just did the chores around their living quarters without complaining to leave her more time for her work. That could be maddening because she was a constant complainer. Perhaps that was why they got along so well.

Dr. Susanna Angela Mathews, nicknamed Sam in college by her classmates, lived with her companion on Phoenix Station, a space station on the rim of the asteroid belt between Mars and Jupiter.

Space was the wild frontier of humanity but it was also relatively peaceful compared to Earth. There were twenty assorted countries that had their own space programs or were part of an alliance of smaller nations who combined their resources to venture into space. And, for the most part, there was a live and let live mentality among those who worked on what was referred to as the rim, out beyond Earth space. Unlike the continual conflict that plagued Earth's surface dwellers.

There were dozens of space stations like Phoenix around the asteroid belt that mined it for precious materials sent to the factories in the stations on the Moon or those rotating around the Earth. The resources in the belt were so plentiful that, once a people group made it out this far, there was no need to fight over them. Like low hanging fruit on a tree, all that remained was to harvest the resources and fighting over them was a waste of time and energy. Nevertheless, there were the occasional conflicts as humans would be humans. In those circumstances, those involved were generally on their own to solve the problem; whether that meant peacefully or violently. Companies who worked in deep space had their own security forces to protect their interests. The only law was the law of might makes right.

Out on the rim, robotics was the field in most demand as corporations interested in cost-effective operations preferred robot labor as opposed to the more expensive human kind. The use of robots on Earth and in the colonies of the Moon and Mars were heavily regulated to the point that self-contained robotic units in the shape of humans were illegal and experimenting with android or cybernetic technology could result in heavy fines. But out in space, there were no laws restricting the development and use of robotic technology.

That freedom brought Sam to Phoenix Station. She was at the top of her field and specialized in creating mining robots.

Owned by Universal Space Consortium, Phoenix Station launched Sam's creations into the belt to mine for a variety of minerals then returned with their cargo to waiting freighters that carried them back to Earth. The freighters had a dual purpose. They not only transported the raw material but also served as processing plants so that, once the materials reached their destination, they were ready to be used. The corporation gave Sam a free hand to do anything she wanted so long as the minerals flowed and the profits mounted.

Her contract with the consortium had already made more money for Sam than she could spend in a lifetime but could not care less. She lived and worked in the most exciting place in the universe without constraints and she had Marc to share it with her. What more could a woman want?

"Sam?" he prompted her.

"Oh, yeah. Sorry Marc." What was the day going to look like? She signed, "Well…"

The intercom link beeped and interrupted her. Commander Tom Wilson's face appeared.

"Good morning, Sam, Marc," he said.

"Tom, this can't be good news," she responded.

Protocol on Phoenix Station was very familiar, first names only and usually nicknames were the preferred manner in addressing others. VIPs rarely visited so most understood the culture and accepted it. Dr. Susanna Angela Mathews loved that out here, she was Sam. Commander Thomas Wilson ran the station and commanded the security team there to protect the company's interests. But to everyone on the station he was Tom.

"ARMS 080 is having problems so we need you to take a team out and look at it," said Tom. "And before you ask, we tried to recall it for maintenance and it is not responding. Every protocol has been tried and nothing has restored communication."

"Oh," responded Sam in that female sarcastic manner she knew she could get away with, "aren't you the messenger with all the answers. What's wrong with it?"

"If we knew what was wrong with it, we wouldn't need to send our prettiest and shapeliest roboticist out to look at it, now would we?"

Tom knew that Sam hated those who thought that women were less talented as engineers and loved to rub it in by referencing her extremely good looks. Though, Sam sometimes wondered if it was a game or if he really was hitting on her. Ah well, she had not yet invented a device that could read minds. Although, she wondered if Marc could. He was extremely intelligent and, in her opinion, understood the human mind better than anyone she knew. A question for another time.

"Well, I guess I know what I'll be doing today," she said.

"Pick your team and I'll see you both at the briefing."

Tom was about to end the communication when she quickly asked, "What makes you so sure that Marc will be on the team?"

For a brief moment, Tom looked at her as though staring through the viewing screen then burst out laughing. With that, he ended the link.

Sam was not sure if she had just been insulted.

"Marc, am I that predictable?"

He regarded her for a minute then turned and walked to the front door to wait for her.

As she passed him on their way out, she glared at him, "I could say something about men but I won't. I'm above that sort of thing."

While Sam was in Tom's office going over the mission parameters, Marc went to the shuttle launch wing to prepare Shuttle Fred. Its official designation was Interplanetary Shuttle Vehicle F-0891 but as happened out on the rim, as it was with people, machines were given nicknames to facilitate communication. Traditionally, the pilot to whom the craft was assigned gave it its name and Interplanetary Shuttle Vehicle F-0891 was assigned to Nicholas. He was already supervising the maintenance crew as they changed out the fuel rods. For any mission into the asteroid belt, standard procedure was to equip the shuttlecraft with fresh fusion fuel rods that powered the engines and all the systems. Going into the belt was dangerous enough without risking a power failure.

On any other station, Shuttle Pilot Nicholas McGregor would have been Nick, maybe even Mac. But Phoenix already had four Nicks and a Mack so, he was just Nicholas.

"Marc," Nicholas greeted him. "Ready to surf the rocks?"

Pilots since the biplane era have had a language all their own and a tint of cockiness about them and rim shuttle jockeys were no different.

"Hello, Nicholas," replied Marc. "It is always agreeable to have a change in the normal routine of life."

Nicholas laughed, "You crack me up. Talking to you is like talking to one of Sam's robots. I guess that's why you're Mister Lucky."

"Monogamous relationships are not required on the station, Nicholas," said Marc.

In response, Nicholas glanced over at the crew working on the port fuel rods then lowered his voice, "But the lady doctor has made it painfully clear that she is not interested in anyone other than you. The most beautiful woman on the station and she only sees one man, that raises a lot of questions about what you're packing."

Marc shook his head with a slight grin.

"Why is it that men assume a woman is attracted to another man because of his sexual prowess? I like to think that I stimulate Sam intellectually, culturally, socially…"

Nicholas stopped him, "Yeah, I get the idea. You're the complete man."

Marc shrugged then handed the pilot an electronic tablet.

"I noted that three scratches on the hull were not repaired after the last mission," Marc said. "And your port engine was barely within spec."

"What?"

Nicholas grabbed the tablet and read over the maintenance logs. Then he looked helplessly at Marc, "How did you…?"

"I have learned to interpret what I am reading," Marc responded. "Since coming to Phoenix Station, I discovered that the maintenance crews have methods for relieving their workloads by manipulating the maintenance logs. Oddly enough, they use the truth to cover lies."

"Is there anything you don't do well? How does one become the perfect man with the perfect woman?" Nicholas asked angrily before marching over to the crew chief.

Everyone on the station knew the story. Dr. Susanna Mathews arrived at Phoenix Station on a private space cruiser. She brought with her an assistant that also turned out to be her lover. To the disappointment of the men of Phoenix hoping for a shot at the new and beautiful scientist, they proved to be a devoted couple.

Reba and Sam entered their security codes for the clerk then gathered up the helmets, gloves and life-support packs that would transform their one-piece jumpsuits into environmental suits.

They then took the long walk down the corridor to the shuttle wing of the station. As they did, they passed several men who did not hide their leering gazes. Reba was her usual perky self. She and Sam had been friends from the first day Sam arrived on the station.

"I will never get tired of that," Reba said as she bounces along. "I love having men look at me."

"I will never understand this station's preoccupation with sex," remarked Sam with a frown.

"Come on, Sam. Just because you found Mister Right, Mister Perfect, don't force the rest of us to settle," chirped Reba.

Reba was a female space engineer in a field dominated by males. She was cute, personable but would never be a contestant in a beauty pageant. However, out in deep space where men outnumbered women 10 to 1 or even 20 to 1, she was very popular. The two were old friends from university days.

"Not that I'm complaining, mind you," Reba continued. "The fact that you're not in circulation just leaves more for the rest of us."

"You're greedy, Reba."

"I prefer cheap. I haven't had to use a credit for a meal or bar tab since I got here." She cannot contain her cheerfulness, "I have two years left on my contract and I intend on going back to Earth a very rich woman."

Sam was puzzled, "You're planning to go back, why? Out here, there aren't the laws and regulations. People can basically live the way they want, so long as they do their jobs. I mean, even the outback Martian colonies have become over-regulated societies."

"Seriously Sam, what can you do out here that you can't do back on Earth?"

They reached the door to the shuttle wing but neither woman entered her code. For a moment, they stood facing each other as Reba waited for an answer. It suddenly seemed important to her to have her friend respond.

"What is there on Earth?" Sam asked. She had one reason for escaping and it was the same reason that she intended on remaining in deep space. But such dark secrets were always best left as dark secrets. So her hand eased over and entered her security code.

The light whisper of the door opening started Reba and she jumped.

Sam hurried on and the other woman had to rush to catch up.

Nicholas and Stark piloted Shuttle Fred with Sam, Marc, Bart and Reba in the back. They were following the homing beacon to where ARMS 080 sat dead in space. ARMS stood for Advanced Robot Mining Shuttle and the consortium's robots were the best in the business thanks to Dr. Mathews.

Universal Space Consortium had discovered a cluster of asteroids with a healthy deposit of nectron ore. It was one of the most sought-after raw minerals discovered in the belt. Refined, it was used in most electronic equipment. Consequently, the consortium kept the location and the extent of the find a carefully guarded secret. Only a few in Phoenix Station knew which ARMS were programmed to mine nectron ore and where they went. Therefore, Sam kept her team compact. Nicholas and Stark were cleared to know the particulars of the mission as was Marc. Bart and Reba, however, knew only that they were going after a mining shuttle that had broken down. The two space engineers were the best on the station and, given the importance of the mining robot, she thought it best to have the best with her.

Working in space was a skill unlike any other. There was the weightlessness, the environmental suits with the gloves and the helmets that restricted movement and vision. The smallest tasks could take hours and fine adjustments were difficult at best. Added to the pressure was the sensitivity of working on robots. Sam's artificial intelligence units were the most sophisticated yet developed.

An ARMS was a composite machine. There was the shuttle aspect of the machine that performed the actual mining which looked like a cross between a spacecraft and a backhoe. Then there was the brains of the machine, a human-like robot. Once humans wearing environmental suits rode in the mining shuttles but when roboticists, and particularly Dr. Mathews, perfected practically human-like robots to perform these types of dangerous tasks, it was only prudent to use them. At first there was an outrage over the loss of skilled manual labor jobs but the politicians had very little control over what happened on the rim and the companies working out in deep space gave assurances that humans would always be needed to service these robots. Universal Space Consortium touted Dr. Mathews as the perfect example. There she was, the foremost creator of robots working in space.

"Sam, we're closing in on the beacon," said Nicholas.

Sam moved up to the cockpit. She did not know how pilots did it. Weaving in and around the asteroids in the weightlessness of the shuttle craft caused her to have motion sickness. She would have taken a remedy for it but she did not want it to affect her work.

"It's not there," said Stark.

Normally, Stark would be commanding his own shuttle mission but Sam wanted the best so she requested him as the co-pilot. It was debatable as to which pilot was the best but it the shuttle was issued to Nicholas so he had command. If Stark resented it, he did not show it. That was unusual given the tensions that sometimes flared up on a space station over the least little incident.

"What do you mean, not there?" Sam asked.

"It's the opposite of there," snapped Stark.

Nicholas shook his head. "I'm looking at the beacon signal right now. It says the ARMS is two degrees off the starboard and twenty meters away.

"I'm looking two degrees off the starboard and there is no visual," the co-pilot insisted.

"That is not possible," remarked Sam. "There is a homing beacon in the shuttle unit and one in the robotic unit. If one is disabled, the other one takes over."

She looked closer at the signal on Nicholas' screen. "And that is the robot's signal."

"All I can see is an asteroid," Stark said.

"All right, get us as close as you can," Sam said. "Marc and I will take a walk and see what we can find."

A few minutes later, Sam and Marc nudged their self-propelled packs and flew to the small meteor from where the signal emitted. It did not take long.

Reba and Bart waited in the doorway of Shuttle Fred in case they were needed. Spacewalking was dangerous business and the fewer people doing it the better. In the cockpit, the two pilots were also in their complete environmental suits. Once the door to the shuttle was opened, a number of bad things could happen so regulations said to play it safe.

"Found it," said Marc over the comlink.

Sam sailed over. The beacon was lodged in a small crevice in the asteroid.

"How did it get here?" wondered Sam.

"It was not meant to be here," surmised Marc. "I think someone thrust it in this direction in hopes that it would clear the field and drift off into deep space."

He studied the beacon closer. "Someone forcibly removed the device from the robot," he said casually.

"So how do we find my robot?"

"Geometric positioning." Marc said it nonchalantly. "Using distances and reference points to determine the relative position of an object."

Sam would have slapped him but for the suits, helmets and the fact that he was already working out the math on his electronic pad. He had the location before they reached the shuttle door.

"Nicholas, Marc has a new course for you," Sam said to the pilot over the comlink.

Using Marc's calculations, Nicholas and Stark piloted the shuttle into the asteroid belt. The pilots were giddy. Shuttle jockeys love to run the belt, they were by their nature adventurers and risk takers.

"That's deeper into the belt," said Bart looking at his tablet with the new course and was not happy.

"Can't help that," Sam said as they settled in. "That's where the ARMS is located."

Bart wanted to protest but the craft was already moving forward.

The beacon had traveled in a straight line, as there was nothing to push it off course, but the shuttlecraft had to weave around the small rocks floating in space. That pleased Nicholas and Stark. This kind of flying was why the two pilots had come to the rim.

In the back, Bart and Reba held on while Sam and Marc concentrated on the beacon.

Marc looked into Sam's eyes so she could see the shift in his expression. "I can only think of one reason why it would have been purposefully torn out."

In an instant, she understood and raced to the cockpit.

"Ease off the throttle, Nicholas," she ordered the pilot.

Initially, Nicholas was perturbed. They were having fun.

"We might not be alone out here," she added.

The two pilots comprehended immediately and the ship abruptly slowed.

Tension filled the shuttle as it crept through the asteroid field. The pilots and Sam swept the space beyond the windshield. After a standard hour, Stark saw it first.

"There it is," he whispered, as if anyone beyond the craft could hear him.

In the distance was the mining unit floating in space near an asteroid. Not far from it was another vessel.

"Russian mafia," breathed Nicholas. "We have to hide."

He steered the shuttle behind an asteroid blocking the line of sight with the other craft. Then he started to switch off the unnecessary systems.

"What?" Sam did not understand.

"Rumor has it that the Russian mafia took over Blue Moon Station. That's one of their shuttles," Nicholas explained. "Bad people. They play by their rules and their rules are not nice." He continued to work furiously. "We need to power off as much as possible."

"What are they doing?" was Stark's question.

"My guess is that they are trying to access the memory of the worker robot," said Sam. "Somehow, they managed to intercept a miner and they are more than likely trying to find out where it has been working."

"Is that possible?" Nicholas was confused. "I thought that was impossible."

Before Sam could reply, Stark added, "Yeah, I thought the memories automatically wiped if someone tries to tamper with them without the right codes."

The two pilots looked to Sam to confirm their beliefs but they were unhappy when she did not.

"Given enough time and opportunity, I can break into any robot's memory," she said carefully. "We have to stop them."

"No way," Nicholas said immediately. "Those guys out there you do not mess with, not a chance."

"Universal Space Consortium makes a ton of credits off of the deposit of nectron ore," she said slowly. She did not like what she knew they had to do but that was the price of having her level of clearance in the company. "If another group finds where we are mining, there will be a war over the deposits, especially with these mafia types in the mix. Do you want to get in the middle of a space turf war?"

Nicholas shook his head inside the helmet, "No and that is why we go back and report the incident."

Sam hesitated. She did not want to say this but her highly organized mind ran the scenarios and none of them worked except one so, "I'm afraid that I have to pull rank on you, Nicholas."

Shuttle Fred was running silent, no communication with Phoenix Station was allowed. Therefore, Nicholas could not run around her by calling Commander Wilson. Nevertheless, she knew that not even Tom could override her decision. Part of her agreement to take on the Phoenix job was a stock option clause. Dr. Susanna Angela Mathews owned a piece of the company as a shareholder. Anyway, Nicholas knew who was ultimately in charge of the mission.

"What do you want to do?" he sighed.

"I don't know," she said. "Let me talk to Marc and the space engineers."

"Swell."

But Sam had already gone to the back. Marc, Bart and Reba had heard everything over the comlink so there was no need to explain the situation.

"Suggestions?" Sam asked Marc and the space engineers.

Bart and Reba said nothing. Sam believed they were too terrified for coherent thought. Great, working in space was not something Sam was very skilled at doing. She needed the help of those who did.

"Bomb it," Marc said quietly.

"What?"

Sam waited. She could see through his eyes that he was thinking.

Marc spoke slowly as though forming the plan as he was speaking the words, "We push an asteroid into the mining unit. If nothing else, it will destroy it and the robot. However, we might catch a break and the asteroid or ensuing debris will also damage the opposition's shuttle."

"What's to prevent them from flying away?" demanded Bart. "We can't possibly get an asteroid to move quickly. They'll see it coming and jump out of the way."

"They're powered down to conceal their presence," said Nicholas over the comlink. "That's why we didn't know they were here. It will take them several minutes to fire up their systems."

"Okay," said Sam, "how do we push an asteroid into them?"

Marc opened the emergency locker to reveal spare environmental suits.

"We take the life support packs from these and attach them to two asteroids, aim and fire," said Marc.

"Two?" Bart did not understand and his voice expressed his animosity. "Why two?"

"To increase the odds of success." If Marc was insulted by Bart's angry tone, he did not show it. "If one misses or only does a partial job, the other might succeed in finishing the job."

The two target asteroids were chosen. They were no larger in diameter than the height of a person. Any smaller and they might be seen while they worked, too large and the life support packs might not be able to push with sufficient force. Marc estimated the coordinates for the mining unit and programmed them into the units. Sam and Marc would take on one asteroid while Bart and Reba would work on the other.

Sam could barely contain her excitement. This was the adventure she had come into deep space to find and the added bonus was to experience it with Marc. It would have been faster to go directly from the shuttle to the asteroid but that would have exposed them so they flew a circular path to avoid line of sight. Using an adhesive, they attached two life support units in a central location, smooth enough for the glue to adhere. Across the field, they could see Bart and Reba working. They had agreed to keep the verbal communication to the minimum to prevent it from being intercepted and their presence discovered. Marc gave her the thumbs-up and she waved over to Bart and Reba.

At the same time, Nicholas positioned the nose of Shuttle Fred out from behind the asteroid they were using as cover so that the pilots could watch the Russian craft.

They gave the rock a push, the momentum nudged them backward but the equal force started the asteroid forward. At the rate of travel, they had about ten standard minutes until it made contact.

"Rockets!" The alarmed voice of Nicholas blasted over the comlink.

The first rocket rushed at Shuttle Fred but the aimer had not anticipated the asteroid moving. By the time the rocket drew in on the ship, the asteroid had moved into its path. Wham, it glanced off the side of the rock and exploded.

Had not Marc reacted quickly by grabbing Sam and spinning her around, she would have taken the impact of the shockwave. Instead, he absorbed the blow and a piece of shrapnel hit his life support unit on his back. His head and feet snapped back, his body stretched like a bow.

The explosion changed the forward motion of the asteroid, shoving it to the side along with Marc and Sam which cleared the way for the second rocket. It missed Fred's nose but hit the asteroid shielding the ship. Nevertheless, because of the size, the shuttle did not move.

Bart and Reba panicked. Had they stayed put, the huge space rock they had propelled toward the Russians would have concealed the two space engineers but their only thought was to return to the safety of the shuttle. Consequently, they exposed themselves by flying into the open and gave the Russians visible targets.

Cradled in Marc's arms, Sam fought to clear the fog from her brain.

"Marc? Marc?" she called but he did not respond. She twisted around and saw his eyes were attempting to focus. "Marc!"

Gradually, his eyes regained life. "My spine," he managed to say, "has been snapped. I'm paralyzed."

"I can get us back to the shuttle," she assured him.

"Two of them," shouted Stark over the intercom, "outside of the ship with handheld rocket launchers…"

Wham, bam, the third rocket hit the asteroid hiding Shuttle Fred and blew pieces of rock everywhere, some hitting the shuttle and others tearing Bart apart. His shredded body somersaulted off into the field. Reba screamed but, for the most part, she was protected from the blast by Bart. With two small exceptions; a piece of stone ricocheted off of her helmet and another destroyed the control panel for her life support unit, shutting it down. She was helpless in space. Reba looked up at the crack in the face shield of her helmet.

"We've been hit," Stark announced.

"Mayday, Mayday," Reba called over the comlink.

Sam was moving toward the shuttle with Marc's body cradled in her arms. The additional weight made her progress slow.

"What is your status, Reba?" asked Nicholas.

"My life support unit is inoperable and I have a crack in my helmet." Reba's voice was weak and shaky. She was afraid to move or speak loudly for fear of growing the crack. "I need someone to come get me quick before the crack worsens."

"That last blast blew out our power. We're trying to restore it," said Nicholas.

Stark's voice came over the comlink, "I can manually open the exterior door but it will take a few minutes."

"I don't have a few minutes. Sam, Sam, I see you," cried Reba. "You can reach me."

"Leave me, Sam," pleaded Marc. "Save your friend…"

"No!" Sam interrupted. "I'm going to save you first then I'll get her."

"It is not right to save me at the cost of…"

Another rocket slammed into the asteroid. The force of the impact pushed Reba further away. Sam heard her sobs over the comlink.

"You can still reach her, Sam," said Marc. "Leave me, it is the right thing to do."

However, Sam kept moving toward Shuttle Fred and refused to look at Marc.

As Sam and Marc approached the shuttle, she heard Nicholas' excited cry, "We have power!"

Shuttle Fred pulled out from behind the asteroid and the exterior door opened. Sam hefted Marc inside and glanced back at the Russians, fearful that another rocket might find them this time. Instead, she saw the rock put in motion by Bart and Reba slam into the mining unit.

Pieces of the mining shuttle flew into space. Inside the cab, the robotic unit shorted out and broke apart as motors inside the titanium shell blew apart in mini explosions. While this was happening, the mining unit was pushed back against the Russian shuttle attempting to put space between itself and the unit. But as Nicholas had surmised, it had powered down and the lack of power kept it to a crawl. The port engine took the blow as the mining unit spun around. The protection around the engine of the Russian shuttle was not as good as the mining unit and a fuel rod ruptured. There was a small explosion then a chain reaction created larger ones until the oxygen tanks blew. It took less than a standard minute from the time that the asteroid hit the mining unit until the Russian shuttle exploded into little pieces.

Inside Shuttle Fred, Stark rushed back to help Sam put Marc in a seat.

"Go, go!" Stark called up to Nicholas.

The shuttle slid up beside Reba where Stark and Sam could pull her into the craft. The co-pilot closed the door and raced forward all the while telling Nicholas to kick it. Sam fought the impulse to help Marc and turned her attention to Reba. But it was too late. Her helmet visor had cracked open and her body abruptly exposed to the vacuum of space. It was a terrible death. Within her soul, she was happy that she did not have to care for the other woman and rush back to Marc.

Shuttle Fred limped back to Phoenix Station with one engine damaged. Nicholas and Stark nursed the wounded ship under the constant threat of power outages, an engine stalling or another critical failure. The two pilots did not have the time to worry about Sam and Marc in the back with Reba's body. They did not see how she was working furiously on him. The shuttle was a sight, banged and beaten as it bounced into the shuttle wing.

Nicholas and Stark were astonished to find Marc standing when they emerged from the cockpit, though very unsteady on his feet.

"Marc, you are a sight," exclaimed Nicholas. "I thought you had bought it."

"I am a little sore," said Marc stiffly.

"He's going to have some bruises tomorrow," Sam chimed in nervously. "I need to get him back to our quarters and clean him up."

"Quarters?" Nicholas was surprised by that. "You don't think that, maybe, he should go to the infirmary and have Doc look him over?"

"He'll be fine," answered Sam. "He'll be just fine."

It took all the effort Marc could muster, along with Sam's assistance, to walk to the exit as the dumbfounded pilots and maintenance crews watched.

In their quarters, Sam took Marc into her lab, laid him on her work table then cut off his clothing. The gaping hole in his back where she had performed her robotic triage was seeping fluid when she removed the makeshift bandage she used to plug it. Using a scalpel, she further enlarged the access hole to the damaged parts but with a cleaner incision then she clamped it open.

As she worked, she was reminded of the voyage from Armstrong city on the Moon to Phoenix Station. Part of the signing bonus from the consortium was a private cruiser to the station. While the executives who had negotiated the deal thought it was a vanity request, Sam wanted the privacy to work on her ultimate project, assembling a Mobile Artificial Robotic Companion. She had secretly worked on the android for two years, creating it in pieces she concealed in a variety of lab equipment. The cruiser had a crew of five with orders not to disturb Dr. Mathews in her quarters or the lab she set up in the cargo bay.

Marc took shape during the long trip. Once assembled, she had a month to fine-tune the programming. It was love at first sight when she switched on his systems and he became alive. He was everything she could want or ask for in a man. The first time she made love to Marc she knew she had accomplished her goal of creating the perfect partner, her space partner. For what she had done would not even be accepted on the rim, deep space was not that wild.

But he was worth it; she thought then and still thought the same thing. Marc was worth any risk to have in her life.

When the cruiser docked with Phoenix Station, the crew thought Marc was part of the station crew helping to unload Sam's equipment and personal luggage while the station crew thought he was a part of the cruiser crew. When the cruiser disembarked, Sam and Marc formally presented themselves to Commander Wilson, Dr. Mathews and her assistant, Marc.

"What does it look like?" Marc asked.

"It's not as bad as I originally thought." She exposed the spinal structure. "Your number twelve vertebra is completely smashed by the impact of the blast. Eleven is twisted but the rest are in good shape. Just to be on the safe side, I think I'll replace ten and thirteen."

The station's comlink chimed. Sam ignored it as she worked.

"That will be Tom," noted Marc. "We should be in debriefing, right now."

"You're in no shape to be debriefed."

The comlink continued to chime.

She removed the damaged parts and his limbs went limp.

"You realize that, logically, Tom will come to our quarters when he eventually loses patience?"

Sam sighed, "He will not find anything to be concerned about if you let me concentrate and finish."

"I continue to be disturbed about your decision to save me instead of rescue Reba," Marc said as Sam worked quickly on his skeletal structure. "It defied the three laws of robotics."

"First of all, you're not a robot…"

But Marc did not allow her to complete her sentence, "Sam, call me an android or artificial intelligence, I am a robot made to appear to be human."

"No!" Sam was angry. "I won't hear talk like that. I love you. You are my lover, my friend, my companion."

"I can never love you in return, Sam," Marc said in that even toned manner.

"I hate it when you use that tone with me. Can't you, just once, get emotional when we're alone?"

Meanwhile, she had installed the new parts and was packing the area with the soft spongy substance that Marc's system used to give his body definition. Then she closed the hole and, using a clear glue, sealed it. Movement returned to the android's limbs.

"How does that feel?" she asked him.

Marc flexed both his arms and legs.

"Everything seems to functioning within acceptable parameters," he replied. "The spine has a slight squeak."

"Once your system lubricates the new parts, that will go away," she said as she took out a small hand sander. "I need to buff away the seam so your skin can revitalize…"

The doorbell rang.

"That will be Tom."

Sam wanted to swear. "Why couldn't he have given me five more minutes?"

The doorbell rang again.

Marc's even toned voice drove her insane, "You have to answer the door. He knows we are here."

Fighting back the string of expletives she had on the tip of her tongue, she washed her hands then hurried from her lab to the living room. Releasing the door, it slid open where Tom Wilson stood, his angry expression said it all.

"Sam, what do you think you're doing?" he demanded. "Standard company procedure after a mission, any mission and especially one as screw-up up as this one, is for the participants to debrief."

"Sorry, Tom. I was focused on making sure Marc cleaned up and settled in."

"Yeah, about that," Tom interrupted, and he was annoyed. "From what Nicholas, Stark and the maintenance crews said, it appeared that Marc was seriously injured. Why isn't he in the infirmary?"

Before Sam could respond, Marc walked in wearing a bathrobe. "It is like I told Sam, Tom. I am fine, just a bit banged up. My partner, over there, is a bit too protective."

Tom was visibly relieved to see Marc up and walking. "I was concerned, Marc. Two deaths on a mission and potential third, you had me worried."

Marc smiled, his voice had a touch of humor. "The reports of my demise were slightly exaggerated."

"All right, well Sam, you and I have to report the incident to headquarters."

"We managed to thwart industrial theft and stop a corporate war," Sam said. "At best, we should get a performance bonus."

"I heard about how you saved Marc." Tom shook his head sadly, "Too bad you were also unable to get to Reba as well."

"She was just too far away for me to reach."

"Yeah, so Nicholas said. Okay then, ten minutes and I want you in my office. Marc, you sleep it off but I expect you in my office first thing in the morning with your report."

"I shall be there," Marc replied.

Tom left and Sam dropped into a chair. For a moment, she fought to control her breathing. Marc waited. Once she had composed herself, she stood.

"That was close," she sighed in relief.

"You should be happy that my programming does not require me to speak the truth to humans. You really need to be honest," said Marc. "You cannot maintain this charade forever. Eventually someone will discover the truth."

"What do you expect me to tell corporate or people in general? Hey look, I've developed a Mobile Artificial Robotic Companion because all of you suck and I'd rather live with an AI. I call him Marc for short. We stay together like any other social partner, make love and enjoy life together." She paused, as though expecting a response but the mental processing unit determined that the question did not have an answer so he remained silent.

"If I tell anyone that I've broken the laws against android development, they will take you away from me, forbid me from ever working in robotics again and probably send me to prison."

"You sacrificed a human life to save a machine," Marc said. "You have lost your moral compass."

She kissed him. "I love you, Marc. I would sacrifice a thousand lives for you. Rest. Tonight I'm going to clean up your back then we'll have a romantic meal and make love."

With that, she was gone.

Without a function to fulfill, Marc sat straight in a chair, flicked his operating system into sleep mode and his eyes lost their focus.

Sensing that there was no human presence in the room, the station's computer system controlling the environment in Sam's quarters switched off all but the security lights and dialed back the temperature to conserve energy.

ID: Thomas James Saber
Rank: Pilot, 1000-00 OLYMPUS I
Personal EWord Journal: Saber-066

Log: 4-9-2019

Very few people could claim witness to the wonders that I, pilot-astronaut Thomas James Saber, beheld today.

The black event horizon always left a massive impression on me, but even more so now that we had set foot on the lunar surface. Seeing it through the glass of my helmet made me desire complete silence while witnessing the eternal darkness above me.

When I saw Earth, home, for the first time from the space station, it changed me forever. Now, while observing my planet from the surface of the moon, I felt so powerful and yet, somehow very small. Earth appeared as a sugarcoated blueberry, the kind of treat my mom made me when I was a kid. I reached out and held the entire world in the palm of my hand.

As we stood on another world, a world I had dreamed of visiting since I was a kid, my perception escaped full comprehension. Fifty years since the first men set foot upon the moon's surface, I created similar footprints and witnessed worlds beyond. Few words existed to describe my emotions as I stood on the ghostly surface of the moon.

The immediate surface impression reminded me of a desert dune some high school friends and I had motor-biked through in Arizona, except, in that adventure, there existed fewer craters - as in none - and the sand was not ghostly gray. Anticipation overwhelmed me as I wondered what more awaited us in our exploration of the lunar surface.

The Ares VI dropped us at our coordinates with no damage sustained during the landing. We had five days for this initial OLYMPUS mission. Though our mission entailed gathering lunar soil and rock samples, I knew our real objective was to stake out better landing and site coordinates for the follow-up OLYMPUS missions in the coming years. The ANNO Corporation remained far

243

more interested in potential mineral resource sites than understanding the history of the lunar surface. Regardless, I considered myself fortunate because the corporation had already selected me as a pilot for future missions.

The landing took a toll on our respective strengths, so we decided to explore the lunar surface more after we reenergized with some rest. The cheers from ANNO Corporation headquarters certainly made it worth the long hours.

In dreamlands and fantasies, children see the stars and the universe beyond. I wished my daughter had accompanied me and observed the alien existence – the grey stone and soil, black sky, and cratered landscape – I saw up close today.

Log: 4-10-2019

The moon appeared so empty, but in fact, it held much to offer.

Dahlmer and I explored craters for most of the day and collected abundant regolith samples. We all noticed how different the lunar soil was from what we were accustomed to on Earth. Though I couldn't feel it in my fingers when I first examined the soil, I grew a sense for its texture. It grinded up like sand and, yet, it puffed away like dust.

Once we established precise coordinates for the Altair module—our home base—we geared up the rover for exploring and charting as much of the surrounding landscape as possible. The Altair's surrounding landscape contained a series of mountains and massifs, towering masses of lunar rock and dust. Holding sufficient cataloguing of the surrounding surface formations, our lunar map model appeared accurate, but Dahlmer , Archer, and I intended to scout out and gather additional details.

This was especially important, as our lunar model held one uncatalogued mountain. Every other natural formation in the region seemed accurate and detailed, save for this one mountain. Its massive shape rose above the lunar surface in a series of steps on all sides.

We made a rapid approach to this divergent mountain. Since neither NASA nor ANNO had any catalogued details about this mountain, the three of us decided to give it a name: *Noctis Mons*, Latin for "Night Mountain."

The name was Archer's idea. Honestly, I didn't have much input into the matter. I'm not very creative in that way. Noctis Mons seemed fitting, though. It absorbed the nocturnal shade of the lunar atmosphere, embodying the night and the darkness as its own.

Less than two miles from the mountain, the wide base of Noctis Mons, with its symmetrical edges, loomed closer. The region around the mountain lacked craters.

Strange.

Craters great and small littered the moon. Why their absence around this mountain?

We completed a full circle around the mountain perimeter. After exiting the rover, Dahlmer , Archer, and I decided to acquire more documentation of our mountain. Our visual equipment functioned as it should and we obtained good data. Headquarters expressed interest in the images of the mountain, but Hachet and Logan, who monitored events from the Altair module, remained unimpressed. I'm sure their enthusiasm and interest would sway if they supplemented our explorative effort first hand.

Soon, however, strange, confusing reporting from Dahlmer about structures interrupted our survey efforts of Noctis Mons that neither Archer nor I comprehended.

Until we saw them for ourselves.

Oh, my God! Holy shit!

Less than a quarter mile east of the base of Noctis Mons stood unfathomable objects: structures symmetrically edged and constructed with an intelligent eye.

Ruins.

Ruins of a lunar city?

What was I thinking? This evaluation could not possibly be accurate.

The bosses didn't seem to believe it, either. They extended our personal-cam live feeds to gain a panoramic view of these lunar ruins – megalithic structures, built not formed. Something other than random acts of galactic nature must have constructed these objects.

An arch-like structure occupied the foreground area, which, at first glance, appeared natural. However, closer observation revealed its smooth edges and syncretic formation. Passing under the arch exposed a series of stone formations comprised of a series of cylindrical structures. They stood well over forty feet high and one-hundred feet long. These formations contained a series of perfectly carved slits in them, each placed in layers of three spread evenly about.

Above this oblong megalith was its strangest feature: a carving that resembled a bent line, like a squirming worm. Archer commented that it appeared rigid, like a long-division symbol, but to me, it looked more serpentine.

But this discovery was just the beginning.

Many more edifices laid about this area, including three pyramid-shaped structures, comparable to those in the deserts of Egypt, but with a dome-like feature in the center between them.

Encircling the pyramids and dome stood a series of tall, flawless, carved pillars, well over twenty feet tall. At the foreground of these structures rose two carved figures vaguely similar to human heads. Two carved, oval shapes on the tops of these figures gave the appearance of eyes, but the megalithic objects had no mouth, nose, or ears. The two lunar heads also contained odd symbols – squiggles and dots – carved into them, with no apparent relation to any type of writing.

Preliminary examinations revealed these structures were moonstone carvings. The symmetry and clean patches demonstrated a very sophisticated design. The three pyramids stood 200 feet tall and 400 feet wide. The dome in between them was of similar size.

We all felt awe and astonishment in their presence. Frenzy engulfed the ANNO Corporation's CEO and its other executives over the images streaming back to them. An imperative question now overwhelmed the entire mission: Who built these ruins and why?

We all believed we would make history by returning to the moon and today's discovery exceeded anyone's expectations about that. Noctis Mons consumed our thoughts and answers to innumerable questions eluded us.

A nagging thought, one that I kept to myself, crept into my consciousness: I hoped this discovery and mission would not turn out to be more than I bargained for.

Log: 4-11-2019

ANNO Corporation Headquarters finally acquired all of the images we obtained of the lunar ruins. There's no telling what will happen next. For now, the bosses said to continue with the current mission guidelines. However, that no longer remained an option for us. For better or for worse, the OLYMPUS I mission had changed.

We all discussed our next move, something very uncertain for us. We knew ANNO was up to something. After all, you don't make a universe-shattering discovery and then go back to business as usual. Something was brewing, and I wished I knew what it was.

The five of us concluded our next priority would be a closer examination of Noctis Mons. The ruins existed very close to the base of the mountain. Perhaps a detailed search of the perimeter would reveal more about our discovery. I just hoped we would understand the nature of what we find. Everything witnessed and discussed within the past twenty-four hours previously existed only in the realm of cheap science-fiction books and Syfy Channel movies.

But this was not pretend at all.

Once into our renewed exploration of Noctis Mons, Archer discovered the most astonishing feature of Noctis Mons: a crevice with vast interior chambers. These chambers held precisely carved ramps and walkways leading up and down. After we illuminated the interior chambers, we also discovered numerous carvings in the moonstone walls.

Noctis Mons was not a mountain, after all. It was a pyramid. One giant pyramid! Perhaps the largest megalithic structure ever built.

I felt uncertain just how to comprehend this lost piece of code of life. Some sentient beings built this structure eons ago. No longer could we view life merely as an earthly ideal. Something once lived upon this ghostly lunar surface. Something built these ruins and this massive mountain-mausoleum. Who, or what, left these ominous footprints of moonstone behind knew many details about the universe that we were only just beginning to discover.

Moonstones, metallic mechanisms, and pillars held the pyramid's interior together. Appendages like rotted-out gears hung from several chamber walls. Perhaps they operated the chamber mechanics, once upon a time. Much of the inner chamber looked built to handle complex machinery. Some of the mechanics, though clearly rotted out, seemed more advanced than human technology.

Carvings occupied both metal and moonstone alike, all depicting different designs more mysterious and confusing than the last. The carvings in the chambers of Noctis Mons included some type of hieroglyphic outline and were unlike any human form of writing.

Images of vaguely humanoid subjects also appeared in the carvings along with various squiggles, symbols, and dots. One wall contained a chamber that contained what appeared to be a model of the solar system: concentric rings, carved with a massive orb in the center, each with nine other orbs circling around each other. The chamber wall may have also contained something behind it.

Perhaps this black alien world held ominous hidden treasures.

Log: 4-12-2019

The exploration of Noctis Mons and its inner chambers prompted a quick end to our deeper discoveries. We had no choice. We uncovered a large inner tomb, decorated heavily with carvings and oddly-spiked monoliths. In the center of the tomb laid what seemed to be a sarcophagus, at least in appearance.

I wanted to be cautious in approaching the center of the tomb, or touching anything. Dahlmer , however, was all too eager to grab whatever he could. Once he set foot in the center of the chamber, some ancient mechanism activated, showering the entire area in a cloud of dust and debris. The chamber closed its way in, nearly crushing Archer as a result.

Additionally, Dahlmer soon felt dizzy, disoriented. It was then that we headed back to the Altair module, concluding our explorations of the Noctis Mons site until another day.

Our immediate health was a concern. Dust that showered us in the interior chambers covered our suits. Logan decontaminated them and cleared us of any possible toxins. NASA could be proud of their protective suits, as none of the excessive amounts of moon dust penetrated them.

Headquarters had told us to remain on current mission guidelines. However, seeing as they were aware of our latest discovery, they expected us to transfer all information gathered about the nature of Noctis Mons and the ruins beneath it, but they wanted our discovery kept quiet, despite the media spectacle surrounding our mission.

To think that it took eight months just for Congress to vote on basic funding for NASA. Instead of nations exploring the cosmos, private companies like ANNO took the lead in the name of discovery for the sake of profit. ANNO has paid me well, so I couldn't complain. They also sent me to the moon faster than today's NASA ever could. Congress fought like monkeys over appropriations funds, and yet, somehow believed they could take credit for our mission just because we maintained a link with NASA.

Because of our situation, however, ANNO guarded our great discovery as a secret and kept it from the world. You would think that after having made perhaps humankind's greatest discovery, it would immediately make headline news, but it didn't work out that way.

Regardless of what ANNO planned, we still had to come to terms with our discovery. So, Archer, Logan, and I reviewed our video footage. Logan seemed the most fascinated with the ruins and vast inner chambers of Noctis Mons. He held a background in classical archaeology and remained glued to the computer screen, carefully watching every angle of the footage.

What fascinated Logan more than the megalithic structures were the various carvings he dubbed "cryptoglyphs." He referred to them in this manner because of how vaguely similar the lines, dots, and squiggles resembled writing patterns. Accurate identification of the style escaped Logan, though it seemed to mimic an intelligent record of some kind.

After reviewing a substantial amount of video footage, Logan noticed a tract of cryptoglyphs that repeated on several different structures. Although the tracts looked similar to ancient human writings, none of us could make any sense of them. Honestly, how could we? It was clear that whoever built these structures and carved the cryptoglyphs was not human and shared no discernible earthbound connection.

Yet, the pyramid structures appeared similar to what humankind built on Earth thousands of years ago. These ruins may have existed as remnants of humankind, but only if ancient man found a way to travel to the moon and live without oxygen – and this assumption was clearly absurd.

There was no telling what cosmic entities had once sprouted and flourished on the lunar surface, but they were most certainly intelligent life forms. What race of sentient beings could possibly have lived or even sought to live on a place like the moon? The moon stood out as more useful as a meteor repository than a flourishing land of life.

We were exceptionally confused. How anything, let alone advanced megalithic builders, could have existed on this barren space rock escaped our understanding. The possibility that these remnant structures could also give us a glimpse into humanity's origins arose as an even more disturbing prospect. Perhaps I've read *Chariots of the Gods* too many times, but the question felt worthy of inquiry.

Logan continued examining the footage and samples, while Dahlmer and Hachet carried on the fieldwork. A sudden and unexplainable tiredness overwhelmed me. A mysterious exhaustion also laid claim to Archer. Perhaps tomorrow would bring the two of us renewed energy and a better idea of what we faced during the dark lunar days.

Log: 4-13-2019

Even as my tiredness persisted, I couldn't sleep properly. Something was wrong, and I felt it, but Hachet checked me over twice and said there was nothing wrong with me. Archer and Dahlmer also complained about ailments, but they, too, checked out fine.

My ailment defied specific explanation other than it included a creeping feeling under my skin, itchiness, and various stages of moodiness. These unsettling feelings seemed to grow worse over time. I didn't care what Hachet said - a sickness grew within me.

Further unexplainable symptoms engulfed me, including sporadic irritating pain that felt as if something ate away at my back and thighs. Knives drove into my flesh. Six more hours into my symptoms, itchy red rashes appeared and they burned with insatiable passion. Nothing served to halt the quick spread of these eruptions. My symptoms progressed before my eyes and an unexplainable metamorphosis overwhelmed me.

Only two days remained before we returned to Earth. Through the intensifying pain and sickness, I found it amusing that as much as I had wanted to come to the moon, I now desired to go home.

Beyond my own affliction, Archer and Dahlmer deteriorated even worse than I did. Dahlmer grew immobile and withdrawn, while volatile hyperactivity engulfed Archer. Because of Archer's status as our commanding officer, his erratic state created a massive problem for the remainder of the mission. Dahlmer, clearly sick, would have assumed command, but he hadn't moved or spoken a word in sixteen hours. His ailments included fever, growing skin rashes, and white boils.

This forced Logan to take charge of the OLYMPUS I mission. Only he and Hachet appeared healthy and unaffected.

The situation grew all too clear: a horrible sickness compromised us while exploring the Noctis Mons ruins, but that seemed impossible. How could any pathogen survive on the lunar surface? More importantly, how could it have penetrated our helmet and suits?

More than ever, absolutely nothing made sense.

The CEO and other ANNO executives, fully updated on our situation, offered nothing, but a loss of words, for our predicament. Anticipated treatment on Earth following tomorrow's withdrawal from the moon stood out as our only hope.

Unfortunately, though, Archer worsened by the hour and began uttering incoherent, delusional statements about a "monster." He described it as a swift humanoid creature that had long talons, shrieked while it circled around, and clawed at the Altair module. How Archer heard anything shriek in the vacuum of space was beyond me.

Logan assured him of the obvious: nothing lived on this lunar surface.

But then again, we found those ruins. I didn't know what to believe anymore. None of us did. Our unanticipated experience defied explanation. We opened a door into a mystery of the universe, but our greatest discovery had become our worst nightmare. We were breaking apart, turning against each other. Departure meant salvation, hopefully.

A growing, unfamiliar strangeness consumed me. Dreams and reality became indistinguishable. I saw fairies, moon fairies that floated by, grinning and laughing. Moon fairies. Yes, sickness absorbed me.

The mission no longer held any concern for any of us. All we wanted was deliverance from this place, from our conditions.

Log: 4-14-2019

What the fuck was happening?

Violent, murderous, and destabilizing insanity had completely taken over Archer! Whatever inflected us overwhelmed him more than any of the rest of us.

Archer destroyed the Altair module's communications equipment, compromising our satellite links with headquarters. He damaged the onboard computer's motherboard, hacking it with an emergency axe.

But that wasn't the only thing he attacked with the axe. He used it on Dahlmer too, chopping his head clean off.

He kept going on about the monster and Dahlmer was "One of them!" He shrieked, claiming that all of us had become monsters, including himself. Trapping us here to die was how he intended to "save the world!"

He nearly killed Logan and me, but we managed to fend off his attacks.

Archer now ran wild on the lunar surface, escaping into a galactic dreamscape of terror.

The only communication equipment still operating were the units within our suits. We had no way to contact Earth unless someone repaired the Altair's onboard computer. Hachet, the engineer among us, said he could possibly rewire the communication equipment, but even so, we couldn't lift off, as Archer had also destroyed the launch controls. Archer had very well killed us all.

Logan went in search of our insane, murderous commander. Not the best idea and I requested to accompany him. He insisted I stay in the Altair, due to my illness.

But I needed to break out of here.

While Hachet busied himself with a futile effort to fix things, a mysterious, unexplainable desire for freedom burned and swelled within me. The darkened lunar landscape beckoned.

A secret existed there . . . and . . . in the symbols we witnessed.

A hidden coded message within the cryptoglyphs finally revealed itself to me. I understood the lines, squiggles, and dots for the first time and the wisdom of an ominous cosmic age spelled itself out to me.

Insanity surely consumed me, for the message was unreal. It spelled my name. Beings of ancient eons past knew my name, perhaps even before humanity existed!

Surely, in that moment, I existed in the clutches of either insanity or a nightmare.

Wake up! Wake up! Wake up!

Log: 4-15-2019

I performed the necessary actions and killed Hachet. He called me a monster and attacked me with an axe, but I got the best of him. I didn't have a choice. I neither needed nor wanted to die.

Now, alone, on the lunar surface, I searched for Logan, to tell him what happened. I hoped he and the others would understand.

As I searched, more strangeness enveloped me. I grew weaker and distortion morphed my senses. My visual perception shifted through phases of normalcy to overwhelming color barrages. My skin numbed and I felt deep, burning itchiness within.

Walking alone, I found the rover, but no sign of either Logan or Archer. The communication unit in my protective suit remained quiet, despite repeated calls out from me. I hoped Archer wouldn't get to Logan before me.

The need for rest and renewed pains overpowered me. As I sat on a rock for over an hour, resting, labored breaths plagued my respiration. I had to start walking again, soon, to find Logan.

What end awaited us here?

I was not a killer. The real killers, the monsters, existed out here, in the darkness.

Archer was right.

Shrieking, swift shadows of transitory terrors grew closer. Even in the vacuum of space, I heard them. Entities lived on the surface of this rock. We should have never returned to the moon. Luck blessed our predecessors. A nightmare hid here.

My daughter, Alice, was the most beautiful girl in the world. I loved the way she smiled and twirled her blonde hair. She loved her

Barbie dolls and their houses. Horseback riding with her near the lake brought joy to us both.

I loved her.

I knew sorrowful tears would be unavoidable when they told her about me.

Don't cry, Alice, don't cry.

I discovered the moon's secret.

Don't cry, Alice.

I wanted to remember her beautiful smile. The sweet memory evaporated into the void. My subconscious mind pushed thoughts about Alice out of the way, forcing sadness into my heart and recognition of another coded message within the cryptoglyphs.

The message read: "I live again."

Darkness and isolation engulfed the moon and me more than ever. I counted stars. Losing count, I started over four times.

Pain, nagging and seething, ebbed and flowed within me. My helmet held in my screams. Memories of home, and of who I was, faded into obscurity.

But I progressed on.

Rocks and shadows followed me. The fairies, ephemeral entities, guided me and I followed.

The moon mocked me.

Help me, Alice.

Log: 4-16-2019

The transmutation neared completion and death embraced Archer.

Logan, too.

Archer killed him and then he tried to kill me, too, but I got to him first.

Before smashing the glass of his helmet's faceplate with an axe, I got a good look at what happened to both of us. Archer's face held altered features: black eyes, peeling skin, and sharpened teeth. He also lost his hair.

In his garbled voice, he laughed and taunted me through the communications link. "Look at us! What we are cannot exist. We belong dead! We are dead!"

"No, you belong dead. I live again!"

Then I smashed his faceplate with the axe. He died from the blade and exposure to the lunar atmosphere. In his faceplate, I also I saw my reflection.

An awful beast, a monster, peered back at me with one black alien eye and one bloodshot human eye. My face shed its skin.

The secrets of this rock remained all mine now. The megaliths with their cryptoglyphs appeared more and more numerous. They led me to something great. They led me to where all the moon's secrets awaited me.

Every cryptoglyph revealed its hidden messages to me and I read them clearly. Noctis Mons called me forth! The great mountain of madness, the great idol of the darkest of all ages, showed me the old race I rebirthed.

All power and knowledge of the Ancient Ones, who once congregated this dark space, was mine alone. I held the secrets of entire galaxies and the dark powers of the unseen.

I was the resurrection of the race from the Outer Stars, the chosen one for rebirth, the vessel for their life.

Noctis Mons, Noctis Mons! I will not die. You will not let me.

I needed to break free, and so I removed all restraints. Then, I lived again.

Noctis Mons!

Alice.

Final Log: Saber-066

Saving Internal Data: files//1000-00afxZ78cEdRQ9910000…thomas_james_saber066
Power Loss in: 5…4…3…2…1

PIT STOP
BY REBECCA A. DEMAREST

The mass of tangled wires on Maevis's workbench twitched as she yanked a capacitor out. "Oh hush, you'll be right as rain in a moment." She had just picked up the soldering gun and wire to put in the new part when the alert on her long-range communicator pinged. Touching the activator patch on her right shoulder, she smiled and answered. "You've got Mama Maevis, refueling station Airco. Who's the rascal on my frequency today?"

"Mayday, mayday. God, is that even right, do you say that on a spaceship?" The link was tinny and breaking up, but Maevis could hear the panic in the male voice on the other end of the connection.

She dropped her tools and launched her chair across the room to the company computer array, earning a displeased yap from the Jack Russell terrier that had been sleeping in the middle of the floor. "Good enough, partner. What's your location and status?" She typed in a few commands to access the map of who was in the area.

"I...I don't know where I am exactly. Janice was navigating, and she's...she's hurt pretty bad. I stopped the bleeding, but she won't wake up. God, I'm a dead man."

Whoever was on the line, he wasn't one of their long-distance haulers; they didn't hire people as shakable as this. "What's your name, son?"

"Tim. Timothy. Please, can you help me?"

"Okay, Tim, take a look at the board in front of you, you should see a line of numbers somewhere on the console. Do you see them?"

"No, I, yes, yes, there they are." He read them off to Maevis and she charted them into the system. He was not on any of the approved flight paths, but was pretty close to her refueling station, less than a day by thrusters.

"Very good, Tim. Now, can you tell me what happened? Do you have atmospherics, control?"

"I'm not sure. The alarms stopped sounding right before I figured out how to make this stupid radio work. I've never even been in a spaceship before this, Janice was the one..."

"All right, I gotcha. Just listen to Mama Maevis. We'll get you down safe. I'm going to give you a list of things to try. Do you think you can do that for me?"

He agreed readily and Maevis closed her eyes, envisioning a standard navigational panel. Running him through a checklist of specs, she determined he was in one of the high speed runners, designed to carry people fast and who didn't need to bring much with them. It wasn't a company standard, but she thought she could talk him through resetting the auto-pilot. After a half hour of instructions, she had the ship locked onto her beacon and coming in for a landing. As she hurried out to the refueling dock to prep the catch pad, Maevis convinced Tim to get his shipmate Janice down to the autodoc.

"Have you got the doc activated?" she asked him.

"*What seems to be the emergency?*"

Maevis grimaced at the memory the quasi-human voice woke in her, but she gritted her teeth, hauled the fueling cables over to the enormous anti-grav net, and started hooking them up.

"Her leg, it's just been...crushed."

It seemed morbid to be listening in on the kid's conversation with the machine, but Maevis didn't want to disconnect her link until she had them safely planetside. There was no telling if she'd be able to get the connection back.

"*I see. I will do what I can.*" Maevis knew that line. That was the line the docs were programmed to respond with when the situation wasn't great. She remembered hearing the same thing right before the damn butcher had taken her right arm and a good chunk of her right ribcage. At least the technology had improved since then. Maybe this one would be able to save the girl.

The last fueling cable didn't want to engage, but with a flick of her carbon-steel fingers, it snapped into place. "Tim, I need you to go back to the control room for me."

"But Janice—"

"The doc is taking care of Janice. I need you to give me your coordinates again so I can get the net aimed." She didn't, really, but she did not want this boy watching Janice get her leg amputated and the standard cyber-interface installed. They didn't carry limbs shipboard, but every ship carried the interfaces because accidents happen, and the faster the interface was installed, the more likely the cybernetic prosthesis would work.

The boy read out his coordinates again and Maevis hurried

back to her workstation to get the net up and running. Whatever ship these two were in was *fast*. A lot faster than anything in the company's fleet.

Maevis had just gotten the emergency net up and active when she heard the proximity alerts sound. It was a good thing she didn't have any company ships docked right now or she'd have had to clear them out for this. There was no telling what shape this kid's ship was in, or whether it would hold up to the impact of landing, or how much damage it would do to her little asteroid. She crossed her fingers and prayed silently to whatever gods would listen to get her through this one alive.

"Tim, buckle yourself in, I don't know how rough your landing is going to be. I'm going to lose our connection here as you enter the approach path because of the net, but I'll be waiting for you on the dock. I'll have a lei in one hand and a mimosa in the other."

"Sounds good, see you..." His voice crackled out and Maevis hurried to the window and raised the bamboo shades to watch as his ship streaked across the sky and fell straight towards the net. The terrier that had been asleep on the floor leapt to the bench at the window to watch with her.

"Better take cover, Angus," Maevis whispered, but the dog ignored her as usual. The two of them watched the ship tumble until it hit the anti-grav net and slowed, just enough that when it finally hit the water, it was hardly more than a love tap.

Maevis decided to leave the field on until she could determine how badly the ship was damaged and hurried down to the docks, though not before snagging her long-sleeved shirt and gloves from the hook by the door. The haulers joked that she was trying to protect her pretty skin from the harsh sun of her pit stop, and she never bothered to correct their misconception.

She struggled into the extra clothes as she skidded down the trail to the docks, and hit the boards just as the hatch popped on the ship and a young man in his late twenties tumbled out. She steadied him, gave him a once over, and took his chin in her hand to study his face for any signs of trauma. Satisfied he was in one piece, she leaped through the entryway and ran straight to the control room to ensure that the ship wasn't getting ready to blow and take them with it. Getting to know Tim better would just have to wait.

"So, Tim, can you tell me what happened?" Maevis studied

panel after panel, but couldn't see anything amiss in the sensors.

"We were going along just fine…Janice had it all under control when we had an alert about something in the engine room and she went to check it out. All of a sudden I heard this really loud bang and ran back to check and found her pinned under a giant canister."

"Show me."

She could tell by the way he moved through the tight corridors that he was used to the big open hallways of one of the central planets: he huddled and shied from the bulkheads, unsure where they actually were in relation to his body. Maevis stood tall; they hadn't made a corridor yet that could challenge her five-foot-two height.

The engine room was a mess; she couldn't believe that there hadn't been any alarms or alert lights on in the cockpit with the amount of chaos she was seeing. But as she looked more closely at the primary drive mechanisms, it became clear that what she was seeing was mostly spare parts that should have been stored around the room. The drive itself was still contentedly humming away in standby. As a precaution, Maevis shut it down completely before heading down to the autodoc's bay.

While they walked, Tim kept up a stream of commentary of theories that Maevis mostly ignored, since he obviously couldn't explain what had happened any better than she could figure out. She'd spent years tending these ships on long-haul supply missions before her accident and they weren't much different now. But for the life of her, she couldn't tell what had happened in that room. There was no sign of a failure on the part of the engine—it was fully intact, but the room had definitely suffered some sort of explosion.

When the two of them reached the bay, Janice was already lying sedated in one of the recovery bays, a blanket neatly covering her up. Even with the blanket, it was obvious that one of her legs was much shorter than it should have been. Tim went to the patient's side and took up one of her hands, anxiously stroking the young girl's hair. There was almost ten years difference between the two of them and Maevis couldn't help but wonder why the two of them had been on the ship together, alone, and she prayed the young girl was Tim's sister.

"Doc, how is she?" Maevis couldn't bring herself to lift the blanket and check for herself.

The screen on the autodoc flickered to life. "*Successful amputation and implantation below the right knee. Small contusion on back of head, presumably suffered in a fall after being struck in the leg. Stable, no concussion, expect a full recovery.*"

Of what's left, Maevis thought. "Is it safe to take her off ship?"

"Off ship? Why do we need to get off the ship?" Tim looked panicked and tightened his grip on Janice's hand.

"*She is stable and is secured for transport.*"

"Thanks, doc, I'll take good care of her. You, get the gurney up and running. We need to secure the ship and get landside 'cause I don't particularly feel like hanging around a ship that just had an unexplained explosion, do you?"

"Point taken. I'll get her up." He hesitated as he reached to tuck his arm under where her shin should have been, but then swallowed and picked her up, ever so gently, and placed her on the hovering plank at his side.

Maevis led the way back out of the ship and onto the dock, helping Tim maneuver the unwieldy anti-grav gurney. After they were cleared, Maevis punched in the code for a high-level stasis field, just in case anything else on the ship felt like exploding. She'd rather not have to rebuild her refueling dock...again.

She gave a piercing whistle and waited as the trees along the shore thrashed before giving way before Bessie. It was a good thing Maevis had a hand on the gurney, because Tim shouted and just about knocked Janice into the water at the sight of the island's five-foot-tall robot arachnid caretaker.

"Yes, Mama Maevis?" Bessie's voice was much more natural than the autodoc's since Maevis had programmed it herself, modeled after old-world actress Marilyn Monroe.

"Bessie, love, can you go get guest rooms one and two all open and aired out? Make sure the good sheets are on the beds."

"Sure thing, Mama Maevis." The machine briefly scanned the gurney, then turned back to her maker. "You'll be needing your scanner and kit then?"

"Thanks, Bessie, you're a doll." Maevis started dragging the gurney up the dock and Bessie kept pace long enough to reply, "And you're a peach!" before clattering off up to the house.

"What the hell *is* that thing?" Tim had recovered himself well enough to steady Janice's head as they started the hike up from the beach to Maevis's home and the island's command center.

"Well, it was the island's repair drone when I got here. But it was just so depressed with the limiters on it, so I took off the AI dampeners and gave her the legs. She picked the voice herself though. Her name is Bessie." Maevis smiled, remembering the robot's first teetering steps and excited giggling.

"And she picked that name herself as well?"

"Oh, no, that's just a shortening of her designation, Build and Servicer, Series E."

Tim stopped as they reached the top of the trail, frowning. "Isn't it illegal to remove AI limiters?"

Maevis made a rude noise. "They're like intentionally brain-damaging a child. I won't stand for them. Besides, what kind of harm could Bessie do out here on the ass-end of the galaxy? She's more likely to commit suicide out of boredom by leaping into that forsaken ocean covering this asteroid than she is to try and take over humanity. Now, let's get your girl here inside and comfortable, shall we?"

Her reasoning didn't seem to comfort the young man, but that didn't bother Maevis. She'd been questioned by the company before regarding her decision, but they seemed more interested in watching the robot's development in this controlled environment than they were in fining her for her indiscretion.

Bessie had just finished prepping the guest rooms when they reached the house, and she graciously bowed them into the room nearest Maevis's own. "I'll just go run and get your kit, b-r-b!" she trilled, and off she went again.

"Here, on three..." Maevis held Janice's shoulders, making sure to support her head on her forearms, and the two of them gently placed the girl on the bed. Tim started to adjust the blanket to more fully cover her, but Maevis stopped him. "I've got to start by taking some measurements."

She steeled herself a moment before pulling back the blanket. The girl's whole left leg, from just below the knee, had been completely severed. "Well, the good news is, she can still work on a ship if she wants to." Maevis took the bag that Bessie brought in and pulled out her holo-scanner.

Tim paused in his anxious pacing in the doorway. "I'm sorry, what?"

"Less than ten percent'll be mech. If she wants to work shipboard, the company will let her. If she passes the tests, that is. And if she still wants to after this."

He laughed, harsh and hard. "If her father ever lets her out of his sight again. But I doubt he'd have let her fly for the company even if she hadn't pulled this stunt."

Maevis carefully didn't look up from her scanning. "So who's she to you then, if you're not her father?"

"Not what you're thinking, I promise you that." Tim slumped into the wicker chair at the window. "She's my student."

"Your student." The holo-scanner beeped and she flicked on the display to get the measurements for Janice's new leg.

"She is the daughter of Viceroy Collins of Theseus. I'm her tutor. And right now? Her hostage." He groaned and slumped forward, dropping his head into his hands. "I am so dead. Take her to see the shipyard, he said. Maybe it'll show her ships are big and dirty and not for little girls, he said."

Maevis pulled a carbon-steel rod from her bag and started marking lengths on it. "Considering you're all the way out here and she was piloting a ship, I take it that didn't go over so well?"

Tim snorted and ran his hands through his hair. "She talked them into giving her a ride on the new prototype courier vessel. Then, as I'm throwing up in the toilet like the terrible spaceman I am, she knocks the pilot out, barricades me in the bathroom, and doesn't let me out until she's already launched the poor sap in an escape pod with a note to her father informing him that she's running away."

"Wait, if you were just up for a trial run, did you guys get swept for hydrogen ticks before you left?"

"Hydrogen what?"

"Well, shit. That's why you had an explosion. You left Theseus without a tick sweep. Hold on a minute." Maevis let out two separate whistles and within moments both Bessie and Angus were in the doorway. "We've got a tick ship at dock. Angus, guard." The little dog ran off, barking until he was answered by several other canine voices. "Bessie, can you get the rest of the crew and sweep the island? Full spectrum."

"Yes, Mama Maevis, right away." Bessie took off at a trot and a few moments later was followed out the front door by an assortment of mechanical beasties.

"Were those...more Bessies?" The look on his face was begging for a "no" answer, and Maevis was tempted to say yes. She never understood why people found the poor machine so frightening. She was sweet when you got to know her.

"No, those were other bots I've got programmed up to help around this place. I think the chef, the landscaper, and the maid, so it looks like dinner is going to be my responsibility tonight. Hope you like omelets, 'cause that's about all I'm rated to cook." Maevis went back to the task of measuring and cutting the carbon-steel rod in her lap. As soon as she had it trimmed down, she mounted it in the socket of the interface on Janice's leg. Using the holo-scanner for a quick measure, she confirmed it was the right length to form the skeleton of the girl's new leg, then took the rod off and gathered her tools. "Come on, let's let the poor girl sleep and I'll make us something to eat."

Tim didn't eat much of the omelet Maevis made, but she wasn't too offended. It seemed like the man had a lot on his plate, and her appetite probably would have deserted her too, if she was in his place. When it was clear he was going to fall asleep over the dining table, Maevis led him back to his room and ordered him to bed, offering her usual array of sleeping supplements. It was sometimes hard for the company men to fall asleep landside after being accustomed to sleeping in the reduced gravity of their ships, so she had quite the selection. But he refused, thanking her before closing the door. Maevis went back to tidy the kitchen, then headed to her workroom with her kit and worked late into the night on Janice's new leg. She only took one break to go out and check on the status of the tick hunt.

Stretching on the front porch, Maevis let out a sharp whistle and it didn't take long for Bessie to respond.

"We seem to be clear, Mama Maevis."

"Excellent. Could you please keep scanning tonight? I just want to be entirely sure. I'd hate to be the epicenter of an outbreak."

"Absolutely, Mama Maevis."

"Thanks, you're a peach."

"And you're the bee's knees."

Maevis chuckled as Bessie rustled off into the forest again; she was never sure what endearment the machine would dredge up from the movie archive next. Making her way down to the docks, Maevis shed her long-sleeved shirt, reveling in the feel of the tropical breeze on her bare arm and shoulder again.

"Angus, how's it going?" The Jack Russell terrier was surrounded by a pack of mutts on the docks, all of whom were sprawled across the boards, mostly asleep. Angus let out a grumble and lay his head down on his paws.

"Nothing? Well, I'm sorry. But that is good for us. I'm going to run a sanitization on the ship, and then you guys can go in to clean up whatever's left, deal?"

Jumping to his feet, Angus let out a sharp bark, his tail going mad. Maevis went over to the stasis control panel and sent a diagnostic wave through the ship, followed by a sanitization wave. It should kill anything of a biological nature on board, but having dogs trained to sniff out parasitic creatures was always a good backup. As soon as the waves had dissipated from the stasis field, she lowered it and opened the hatch for the dogs. They flooded in, all barking and baying for the hunt, but they were only inside for about ten minutes before they started trickling out.

Angus was last and spat a charred hydrogen tick at her feet. It was apparently the one that had exploded during flight. If that was the only one, then they should be good. Maevis dropped the carcass in the dock's incinerator and started back up the path, calling for the pack to come get their dinner.

The wave of fur at her feet kept her concentrating on her footing on the way back up to the house, so she didn't notice Tim standing on the porch until she was already at the front steps.

"So, that's what you meant about percentages. What are you, eleven, twelve percent?"

Maevis paused, her breath catching in her throat. She fought the urge to run, and instead just put the long-sleeved shirt back on. "Almost thirteen. Three ribs as well as the arm."

"Wait, are you *that* Maevis? Maevis Stanton? From the Icarus?"

"Why they had to name a ship after that idiot...you'd expect the whole damn thing to explode. Well, it nearly lived up to its name."

"I can't believe it! You're a living legend—no one knows where you went. Well...I guess now I know." Tim followed her as she shoved past him and into the house. "You were one of the best test pilots in the 'verse. Why are you hiding all the way out here?"

Maevis went to the kitchen, poured kibble out for the pack, and then turned back to Tim. She waved her arm in his face. "Thirteen percent."

"So what, you can't fly anymore. You're a legend. People would pay money just to have their picture taken next to you. You have inspired whole generations of pilots and mechanics. They made a movie about you."

"I know. I donate every one of their damn royalty checks to cybernetic rights." Maevis put the kibble back in the cabinet and slammed the door.

"But don't you want to help people, tell them your story? I mean, even Janice loves you, your story is why she wanted to be a pilot."

Maevis ripped off her overshirt again, brandishing her metal arm, making her fingers wiggle so he could see the pistons and wire tendons flex. "You want me to encourage young people to do this? To sacrifice their very bodies to a company who doesn't give a shit about them, to be banned from the only job they were born to do just because they have one percent too much metal in their body? You want me to teach flying? How can I do that when I'm never allowed to pilot another vessel in this 'verse because the company lawyers are concerned that my presence on said ship could start a riot? Because you meat people are too fucking scared that I have the advantage?"

Maevis brought her arm down on the granite countertop of the kitchen island, cracking it down its center. She knew she was crying now, but there wasn't anything she could do to stop it. She used her meat hand to wipe the tears away, angry at herself for getting carried away. And on top of everything, she'd have to source a replacement for the counter now. She blamed it on the adrenaline rush from earlier in the day and lack of sleep now.

"I...I'm sorry." Tim was cowering in the corner of the kitchen, as far from her as he could get. He flinched as she stalked past him to the door. That only made her want to cry harder, hit him, or anything to get that expression off his face, a look somewhere between pity and terror.

She stopped at the highboy beside the door and grabbed the whiskey bottle and a tumbler before turning back to Tim. "And if you tell that little girl in there who I am, or anyone for that matter, I swear to God, I'll hunt you down and I'll...I'll send Bessie to rip your arm off too." She slammed out of the kitchen and down the hall to her suite of rooms, not really caring if she woke Janice up, and proceeded to drain the whiskey bottle, a finger at a time, until the sun started to rise.

Tim found her the next morning in her workroom, the new leg assembly half completed. "Wow, you work fast."

Maevis frowned at the interruption. She had hoped to have a working intermediary limb done before either of her guests was awake. There was a small part of her, though, that relaxed at his casual greeting; she had not been sure how he would take her outburst the night before. She was never proud of losing her temper and she could never actually bring herself to hurt someone, but this was also not the first time she'd had to replace property she'd damaged in the course of said rage. If she cared to be honest with herself, she was never actually mad at the people or things she railed at. But it was hard to hit an incorporated entity that presented itself as a faceless mask of paperwork and automated call responses.

"I've had practice. Besides, all this leg needs to do is walk. The hardest part is getting the measurements right, and then stringing the wires in the right spots. But it's only two hinges, nothing realistic or lifelike. That'll have to wait until you guys reach the core planets again. I've got no exo-skins here." Maevis carefully soldered the connection she was holding before pushing back from her desk.

When she didn't yell at him, Tim moved into the room and sat in a chair by the door. Angus got up and trotted over, giving Tim a good sniffing over before accepting ear-scratches. "I was wondering why you use the long-sleeved shirts instead of an exo-skin. Don't you get hot in this tropical weather?"

Maevis made another connection before answering. "Yeah, but so do my electronics. I've got my arm and empty chest area filled with a long-distance com-link setup. That way I can talk to incoming ships a goodly way out, regardless of where I am on the island when they call. Exo-skins make it overheat, cotton does not."

She plucked at her long sleeves for emphasis.

"Makes sense." he paused for a moment. "Look, I'm sorry for prying last night, I was completely out of line."

"I have more to be sorry about than you do. I shouldn't lose my temper like that. At least all I broke this time was a countertop. That's easier to replace than some of the specialized mechanicals around here." Maevis tested out the range of motion in the ankle joint, made a small tweak to the pivot, and tried again.

"Mama Maevis, sorry to interrupt," Bessie stood in the open doorway and Tim about fell out of his chair, having not heard the large bot come up the hallway.

"Whatcha got, Bessie?"

"Janice is waking, I figured you two'd want to be there for that."

"Thank you." Maevis picked up the artificial leg and started for Janice's room, Bessie leading the way and Tim following her. "How'd the hunt go last night?"

"The island is clean, Mama Maevis. The one that exploded on the ship seems to have been the only critter the ship had."

"Well, that's comforting, at least. Bessie, could you get the bots to start cutting some trees and shaping planks so I can make a new butcher-block top for the counter in the kitchen? It's broken again."

If a bot could look reproving, Bessie would have. As it was, her breathy voice dripped with recrimination. "Again, Mama Maevis? You really should know better by now."

"I'm improving, promise! And the last time was over four months ago! And that shipper was cheating!"

With a humph of disbelief, Bessie scurried out the door to start sourcing hardwood trees.

Tim went over to a window to watch the bot go. "She's worse than my mother at guilt-tripping."

"You'd think she was my mother and creator instead of the other way around. Now, let's go see to our young pilot, shall we?"

"Uh, Maevis...do you think, I mean, could you be the one to tell her? I don't think I can...I'm just not made out for this sort of thing. I'm just a tutor."

Maevis rolled her eyes. "Boy, she was smart enough to hijack a ship, she's certainly smart enough to figure out she's missing a leg.

Buck up and get in there, she needs a friendly face."

Tim took a moment to gather himself, then knocked and pushed open the door. Maevis followed him in, the prosthetic hidden behind her. Janice was already sitting up in bed, the blankets thrown back, and was examining her shortened leg, trying to see the end of it and the interface already grafted into her skin.

Tim hesitated before going to the seat at the window and perching there. He cleared his throat a couple times before saying, "Janice, do you remember what happened?"

The young girl gave him a scathing look. "Well, we had that engine warning light come on and when I went to look…" she made a noise reminiscent of an explosion. "I'm guessing that's when this happened." She went back to inspecting the implant. Her flexibility was impressive.

Tim frowned at Janice's cavalier attitude towards her injury. "Your leg was crushed under some falling debris, and the autodoc couldn't do anything about it. I'm so sorry."

"Sounds about right." Janice swung herself around to the edge of the bed and stood without help, but then tottered as her balance was off. Bracing herself against the wall, she bit her lip, shaking off tears, and cleared her throat. "Well damn if this doesn't suck, but at least it wasn't my head." Her laughter at her own grim humor was just a touch manic, but it was better than hysteria. "How's my ship?"

Maevis fought not to smile. This was her kind of girl.

She moved into the girl's line of sight. "Flyable. The explosion was a hydrogen tick. Here, try this, it might help." She pulled the basic leg out from behind her and helped the girl to sit back down so she could attach it to the interface. "Now, it should respond like your meat leg did. Try to flex the foot."

Janice obeyed and the leg wiggled in response. "Oh, this is so cool! You know who else has a prosthetic limb? Maevis Stanton, the best damn pilot we've ever had. Now I'm just like her!"

Tim grinned and looked at the floor, but Maevis steadfastly ignored him. "If she'd been the best, she'd still be in one piece. Like you would be, if you'd remembered to let the flight deck do a sweep on your ship before taking it out."

"Oh, they did. They must have just missed a tick." Maevis frowned at that, but didn't interrupt the girl. "And Maevis was too the best pilot. The explosion wasn't her fault, I've looked at the records for the ship, and there was a flaw in the new drive system they were attempting. They fixed it in the prototype I flew here. But if Maevis had been any less of an incredible pilot and mechanic, she and her whole crew would be dead. It was a stroke of genius to land the Icarus on that asteroid covered in dry ice and then open the venting ports to put out all the fires."

Maevis helped Janice back to her feet. "You mean lucky that the asteroid was there. It still cost her arm and her clearance."

"But it saved her crew *and* the ship. And the ten percent rule is total bullshit, anyone knows that. I would put her at the helm of my ship in a heartbeat." Janice wavered a bit, but then stood steady. She took a few uncertain steps forward, and then jumped up and down. "Hey, this is a sweet leg, thanks! Did you build it? It must have taken you weeks—how long was I out?"

"Just a day. I made this last night."

Janice let out a low whistle of amazement as she examined herself in the mirror on the back of the door. "This is pretty damn good for a day's worth of work. You're a whiz, thanks!"

"It's just a temporary one. When you get back to the central planets, they can make you one that's lighter, prettier, and they'll have exo-skins as well. Hardly anyone will be able to tell you have a mech leg unless you tell them."

Janice frowned and turned to the older woman. "Now why on earth would I want that? This is *cool*." She lifted her leg and wiggled her new mech bits at Maevis. "Besides, I don't want to go back to the central planets. Theseus is boring and my father won't let me do anything. I've already got a ship, I might as well just keep going to the outer rim and have myself some adventures."

Tim made a strangled sound and Maevis jumped, having forgotten he was even there. "Uh, were you expecting *me* to be going on these adventures with you?"

The girl made a face and sat back down on her bed. "Well, I *was* until you showed just how shit a spaceman you are."

Maevis sat beside the girl. "Janice, how old are you?"

"Thirteen." She held herself a bit taller and crossed her arms, daring Maevis to challenge her.

"Isn't that a bit young to go off adventuring on your own? I mean, you only have a year left before you're old enough to go into the flight academy."

"Maevis Stanton was flying her first ship at ten!"

"Maevis Stanton was flying her daddy's courier in circles out of any planetary transit routes, with him at the secondary controls, until she was fourteen and admitted to the flight academy."

Janice scowled. "I can already fly, I made my father's pilot teach me. I don't need the academy."

"Where do you think Maevis learned to think on her feet like she did? To repair her ship and build her own arm like she did? Hmm?" Maevis leaned over just enough to bump shoulders with the girl. "The way Tim talks, it sounds like your daddy doesn't much like the idea of you flying, but can he stop you from going to the academy? Truly?"

Janice scowled. "Not if I can get Mother on my side. He always listens to her."

"There you go, then. You have a plan of attack. You'll be able to get into the academy and then, five years later, you'll get your own ship."

Janice threw herself back on the bed. "But that's so far away! I don't want to wait that long to be behind the controls, not when I know how to fly *now*."

"Think of it this way, then. If you had known more before taking this ship, you'd probably still have your leg. And you're flirting with about eight percent mech right now. What happens when you make another mistake? When you lose a hand, an arm? Or more of that leg? Not only are you flying a stolen ship, you're flying mech, and the moment you land somewhere, you're going to get arrested. The company considers it a danger not only to your ship, but to others. But if you go to the academy, you'll learn how not to make any more mistakes. And then no one will be able to keep you off your ship."

Janice thought about this for a moment, sitting up to study her metal replacement. "It's not like it affects my ability, you know."

"It doesn't affect Captain Stanton either, but the company doesn't care about that. It cares about liability, and cyborgs are a liability shipboard, where confined spaces and prejudiced idiots can make a bloody mess. I'm sure you learned about the Haymarket Riots in school."

"Stupid Bostonians. First it's tea they throw in their harbor, then it's terrorists, then cyborgs. Just because they're afraid of them. Us." Janice's breath hitched a little and Maevis could hear the tears threatening to break through her defiance. "I guess it's us now."

"Now you're starting to get it. But enough with the heavy stuff—do you think you can manage some breakfast?"

The dark scowl that had settled over Janice's face was replaced by a wide grin. "I could kill for some bacon right now, do you have bacon?"

"Fresh off a transport two days ago. Come on, let's get you to the kitchen."

They had an uneventful breakfast, but Maevis could tell that Janice was tiring rather quickly. For all that medicine had advanced since the days of wooden legs and leprosy, it still took the human body a long time to get over the trauma of losing a limb. Maevis tucked the girl back into bed, leaving the door open a crack so Angus could keep an eye on her. The dog had become quite fond of the new amputee, and Maevis suspected it was due to a bribe of bacon.

"So, what's next? I mean, do you think she'll go home now?" Tim had stayed in the kitchen, setting a new pot of coffee to brew. "I only ask because I sure as hell can't fly that contraption back myself."

Maevis took the mug he offered and shrugged her shoulders. "I think so. For a little bit at least. Do you think there's any way her father will let her go to the academy? Because if he says no, I highly doubt he'll ever see her again. She's a bit of a hellion."

"Kinda like you." Tim raised his mug in salute, taking the sting out of his words. "And I have no idea what her father will do. I'm just praying I survive the trip home and the confrontation with him. I'm her eighth tutor, you know."

Maevis choked on her coffee. "Eighth? What the hell happened to the rest?"

"Four quit after a month with her, two went to a sanitarium for a while, the other two?" He shrugged. "I haven't been able to find that out yet."

"Why on earth did you take the job?"

Tim grimaced. "I owed Viceroy Collins. He got my little brother into the academy even though my family were governmentalists."

"Ah, the folly of our ancestors." Maevis snorted. "Now we

just get to vote with our dollars. Which new flavor of Mountain Dew do you prefer? Buy now! All the real policy, set by their team of lawyers and designed to make us spend more money."

"And they do it so well."

Their conversation was interrupted by a chirrup from Maevis's shoulder. She held up a finger to Tim and hit the comm activation patch. "You've got Mama Maevis. Something I can do you for?"

"This is Company Raider Dauntless of Theseus. You have a stolen ship at dock; prepare for our landing. Do not try to lift off, we have your station under weapons lock." The comm patch let out a squawk and went dead.

Tim had gone pale, and he carefully set down his coffee cup. "Well, that took them less time than I expected. Should we wake Janice back up?"

"Let's go see how far out they are. No sense in waking her up to tell her bad news until we absolutely have to." Maevis led the way back to her monitoring station.

"They're about an hour out, it looks like." She leaned out the window and called Bessie in. The large bot was at the window within a minute. "Darling, we've got nosy company calling. Can you get the other bots and start preparations?"

"Sure thing, Mama Maevis." And Bessie was gone, followed by the rustling of smaller bots behind her.

"Preparations?"

"Surely you've noticed I'm not playing by all the company laws out here. Bessie and her kin need to be protected from narrow-minded company men who can't see beyond their regulations. They'll take cover in a system of maintenance caves under the island until I signal them an all-clear."

Tim nodded. "Good thinking. Anything I can do to help?"

"Just keep your trap shut about my babies." Maevis was busy at her panel, shutting certain access hatches so there was no way the company men could accidentally find their way into areas where she didn't want them. "But they're probably just here for Janice and the ship, and they'll be happy to leave once they have them."

"Hopefully me, too."

"And yes, you too."

It wasn't long before the ship's contrail glowed in the upper atmosphere of Airco, and Maevis made sure her arm was fully covered before leading Tim down to the docks to greet the incoming company ship.

The Dauntless made a textbook touchdown, and within moments the hatch opened and disgorged a regiment of security officers followed by the ship's captain. They secured the dock in quick fashion, one of the officers releasing the stasis field on the prototype ship before leading a few men on board.

The captain did not look happy at having wood and water beneath his feet instead of steel. "Which one of you is this way station's caretaker, Captain Stanton?"

Maevis stepped forward, offering a slight bow before responding. "That'd be me. Maevis, at your service."

"Since this station is not listed as having additional personnel, I assume you are Timothy Kennedy." The captain made a gesture to the armed man at his shoulder. "You are hereby detained for the kidnapping of Janice Collins and the theft of this prototype courier."

"What?" The officer had Tim's hands bound behind him before Maevis had a moment even to move.

"Tell us what you've done with Janice and we'll consider waiving the corporeal disenfranchisement."

"No, I…"

Maevis put herself between Tim and the captain threatening beheading. "Just a minute there, you've got the situation all fuddled up. Tim there didn't kidnap anyone. You see, there was a hydrogen tick in the prototype and it exploded, and Janice was hurt, but she's resting now up at the house…"

"My daughter was hurt?" The hard male voice that interrupted her came from the hatchway into the ship. Viceroy Collins ducked out into the sun and hurried down the gangplank.

"Sir, let me handle this…"

"Shut it, Chuck. What happened to my daughter?"

"Viceroy." Maevis gave a full bow to the man who was in charge of a whole planet's franchise. "I'm afraid she lost a goodly portion of her lower left leg. Sir."

The man paled, but otherwise showed no outward signs of emotion. "Take me to her, immediately."

Maevis led a whole parade of people back up from the beach:

the viceroy, Captain Chuck, a string of security officers, and Tim trailing at the very end, his hands still bound. When they got to the house, they found Janice standing on the front steps, her hands on her hips and her new leg glinting in the sunlight.

"I don't care what you say, you were wrong to tell me I couldn't learn to fly. I did a damn good job flying that courier out here, before it blew up, but that wasn't my fault. You should let me go to the academy—"

The rest of her words were drowned out as her father swept her up into a massive hug. "I'm so sorry, princess. But don't you see now how dangerous flying can be?"

In an instant, Janice went from relaxed in her father's hold to rigid. "It wasn't the flying that was dangerous. It was a damn hydrogen tick that somehow managed to escape the scans."

Maevis watched with interest as the viceroy flinched at that last remark and reluctantly let go of his daughter. "Sir, might I suggest moving this conversation inside? It gets rather warm here during the day and I have a nice, private sitting room you two might talk in."

"Yes, thank you. Chuck, release my daughter's tutor, it appears he's not at fault in this after all." The rigid security officer saluted and did as he was ordered. Maevis ushered the crowd indoors, directing the security personnel to the kitchen and the viceroy and his daughter down the hall to the four seasons room. Viceroy Collins promptly shut the door and activated a cone of silence, the tell-tale shimmer glinting in the dark of the hallway. Maevis sighed and cancelled the text to her gardener bot about eavesdropping.

She got the security boys set up with snacks and drinks, and left them to kibitz with Tim about the horrors of riding herd on the walking catastrophe named Janice. It sounded like the girl was too intelligent for her own good and refused to acknowledge the ridiculous restrictions placed on her by her father. Good for her. Sucked for the people tasked with keeping her within said restrictions, but Maevis was proud of the little Valkyrie. If she didn't watch herself, Janice really would become the next Maevis Stanton.

Maevis rubbed her metal arm through her sleeve; a little too like me, she thought. Who was there to keep kids like Janice from really hurting themselves? From ignoring not just the boundaries placed on them by society and their families, but the laws of physics and pure stupidity? There weren't many people of a level with Maevis's piloting skills, nor her electrical jury-rigging. And here she was at the shit-end of nowhere playing God on her own private island.

The door opened at the end of the hall. The excited tone of Janice's voice informed all of them that her father had caved on the subject of the flight academy, under condition that she adhere to even stricter rules in the meantime, including no more ditching her security detail. She blew a raspberry at her father, but the men in the kitchen silently toasted the proclamation. Maevis wondered which of them had been on duty this time when Janice slipped their watch.

The father and daughter duo came into the kitchen, Janice still a bit unsteady on her new leg, but managing to walk backwards as she spouted a steady monologue about her trip out, regaling her father with a report on how well the prototype ship flew.

The viceroy turned to his captain. "Chuck, we'll be leaving here as soon as we're refueled. Leave a detail behind to get the prototype into flyable condition and bring it back to Theseus, will you?"

The captain agreed, and started giving out orders to his men while Maevis chewed on her lower lip, trying to come to a decision. After Janice ran out to follow Tim and the men bound for the Dauntless, she signaled to the viceroy that she'd like a word. She waited until they heard the front door slam before settling onto one of the stools at the kitchen island, but the viceroy preempted her.

"That's a fine job you did on her leg in such a short time, Captain Stanton."

"Thank you sir, I have had a lot of practice." She took off her gloves to let her human hand breathe a bit. It was no use hiding her metal parts from this man, he knew all about them already. "I take it you didn't tell her who I was?"

"And have to listen about *that* for the whole ride back as well? No, thank you, I would prefer to spacewalk home." He sighed. "She thinks I'm just a mean old man, you know. But she's my only child. My wife, she can't..." He stopped and shook his head. "You never had children, I'm sure you can't understand."

Maevis drummed her fingers on the countertop, and then took the leap. "That's where you're wrong, sir. I know what it's like to love a creature as if it's your own child. My dogs here, my machines, I wouldn't know what I would do without them, sir, which is why I can't understand why you planted a hydrogen tick on her ship. Sir." she added for good measure. Her human hand was shaking, but she splayed it on the counter so the viceroy wouldn't see and stared him in the eye until he had the grace to look away.

"It wasn't supposed to happen like this. The pilot who took her up was supposed to just use it to scare her. A small controlled explosion on an underfed tick is virtually harmless. And then she had to go and pirate the whole damn ship." The viceroy sat down hard in one of the chairs at the table. "What kind of thirteen-year-old girl can take over a security prototype ship?" He dropped his head in his hands.

"Yours, sir. Your incredibly intelligent, independent, and willful child. And she's not done making changes in this world, mark my words." Maevis came across the room to sit beside the viceroy and only hesitated a moment before putting her hand on his shoulder. "And you just want to protect her, I get that. And...I think I can help you there."

The viceroy looked at her over his hands. "How? I can't even control her."

"Not control her, but...look. You agreed to let her go to the academy, right?" She was sure he'd only done it out of guilt for what his actions had wrought, but he nodded and she continued. "Why don't you put in a transfer order for me? Get me off this rock and back to the main system, in a teaching post at the academy." He started to say something, but she held up her hand. "I've got a couple conditions, though. I don't want a classroom position. I want to be shipboard. None of this nonsense about ten percent. I am a damn good pilot and I can't teach these young idiots anything from a desk."

She watched him think about it for a moment, weighing the guidelines against having *the* Maevis Stanton watching over his daughter at the Academy, and then weighing *that* information against the fact that she knew about the hydrogen tick and just how damaging that kind of information could be in the hands of someone who was pissed off at him.

He nodded, short and sharp. "I think we can manage that. You said a couple of conditions though. What's the other?"

Maevis grinned. "Tell me, Viceroy, are you a fan of Marilyn Monroe?"

THREE PENNY RAVEN
BY J.B. ROCKWELL

Phinneus "Fantail" Crowhammer wasn't an idiot, and he didn't appreciate being treated like one. He was Captain of the *Three Penny Raven,* a descendant of a long line of other Captains just like him, all of them born with salt and stardust in their veins and wanderlust in their souls. More importantly, he was respected. *Well* respected among the pirates and rumrunners, bootleggers and bandits who were his peers... though some would argue that wasn't really saying much...that bunch fell rather short on the respectability meter... But none of that mattered. The *important* thing was Crowhammer wasn't idiot, and he wasn't about to let some two-bit charlatan pull a fast one on him.

"Valentine," he barked, grabbing his newest passenger by the neck.

He dragged Valentine around and marched him over to the occula obscura – the floor to ceiling windows that wrapped around *Raven's* circular bridge. They were expensive, those windows, and rather old fashioned, but they fit right in with the rest of *Raven's* interior design, which was wood and brass, and yards and yards of crimson velvet and scarlet leather.

"Explain that to me," Crowhammer said, smashing Valentine's face against the window.

"I don't...I don't..." Valentine stammered, eyes rolling, and body trembling like a spooked horse.

He looked like a weasel, tall and stoop-shouldered with a hawk nose and no chin to speak of, and he was an arrogant little prick. Arrogant enough to think he could sneak illegal cargo aboard *Three Penny Raven*. Not that Crowhammer was opposed to carrying a few illicit items--*most* of *Raven's* cargo was illegal or semi-legal, one of the reasons people came to him to haul it--he just didn't like his passengers keeping secrets from him, especially when those secrets brought him trouble.

"You mean...the otter?" Valentine asked him. "Is that–is that an *otter* piloting the ship?"

The otter in question happened to be *Raven's* helmsman. He stood his post on a specially made box, front paws gripping the spokes of the ship's oversized wooden wheel.

"'Course it is," Crowhammer barked. "What'd you expect? A bunny?"

"Well, no, but…"

"Can't have no rabbit steering a ship this size. Thing can't see over the wheel to know when to turn!"

"Yes, well, er, um…and the hat? The…other things?"

A leather skullcap -- earflaps pulled down, snugged tight over his ears -- covered Otter's head, and a pair of welder's goggles perched jauntily atop it. Other than that, he was just fur. Well, fur and a cream colored scarf he'd lately taken to wearing around his neck. Odd duck, that Otter. But then, none of *Raven's* crew were what you'd call 'traditional.'

"Likes 'em, I guess," Crowhammer shrugged. "Who am I to tell an otter how to dress?" He glanced out the window and saw they'd drifted a bit off course. "Four points to starboard, Mr. Otter!"

Otter tapped a paw against his temple and grabbed the wheel, hauling it over, using all four paws now and not so much *turning* the wheel as hanging off it as he corrected the ship's direction.

Valentine stared in disbelief. "That's how you steer this ship? A ship's wheel and an otter? Seriously?"

"Ship came with buttons and such. Ripped 'em all out. Not trustin' my navigation to a buncha buttons. 'Sides, buttons lack romance. And damned if that wheel doesn't look good up there with that otter," Crowhammer said, dropping a wink.

Otter smiled, and puffed out his furry chest.

"It's…it's a very nice otter."

"*I didn't drag you up here to show you my fucking otter!*" Crowhammer screamed, spraying Valentine's cheek with spittle. "No offense, Otter," he added, glancing over at the helmsman. "You're a fine pilot and all, but we got more important things to deal with right now."

Otter shrugged and kept steering, seeming not the least bit concerned.

"Um, so what *am* I supposed to be looking at?" Valentine asked.

"That, Valentine." Crowhammer leaned close, one hand lifting, thick finger stabbing at the ugly, hulking shape lurking out outside. "That big motherfucker of a ship out there, and those damned techno-monkeys that are chewing their way through my hull."

"Monkeys? I don't…"

"*Don't you get smart with me, Bartleby!*" Crowhammer screamed, grabbing the back of Valentine's head, smashing his nose against the window. "Grappler ships, Bartleby. Those sneaky-ass bastards with the plasma torches down there who're cuttin' the ever-lovin' *hell* out of *Raven's* hull. You see them?"

"I…I…I…"

"*Do you fucking see them?*"

"Yes," he whispered, eyes wide and staring, locked onto the rings of sparks dotting *Raven's* matte grey hull.

"Good. Then I'll repeat my question. What are they doing here?"

"How the hell should I know?"

"Because you brought them here, you slimy little bastard!"

"Me? You've got ten different holds filled with illegal cargo. What makes you think they're after something *I* brought on board?"

"Didn't say it was your cargo. Just said you brought 'em."

Valentine swallowed hard, eyes lifting from the sparks outside, staring nervously at Crowhammer's face reflected in the window.

Gotcha, you bastard. Crowhammer smiled and brought his lips close to Valentine's ear.

"That's not law out there, Bartleby." Crowhammer knew law–hell, Cousin Horatio was law--and law didn't look anything like that brutal, utilitarian ship outside. "That ship, that's militia out there, Bartleby. Black market, paramilitary heavies for hire. And I'm guessin' they won't give two shits about the Andalusian rum and Trehana birds of paradise I got in my hold. Nor any of the other goods my more *honest,* more *forthright* passengers are carrying. So tell me, Bartleby," Crowhammer purred, pressing Valentine's face hard against the occula obscura, "what did you bring on my ship, you little maggot?"

"Nothing! I swear!"

A burst of excited chittering erupted from the helm. Crowhammer glanced over, saw Otter climbing up and down the ship's wheel, paws waving wildly, pointing at the occula obscura.

"What the hell's wrong with you, Otter?" Crowhammer growled.

A light flared on the starboard side of the hull, flashing brightly, blindingly and then just as quickly snuffing out.

"They're through, Captain," Daughtry said, standing at his shoulder, looking grim.

"Shit," Crowhammer sighed, turning back and catching his no-good passenger's eye. "You know what that means, Bartleby? That means those quasi-military assholes are inside my ship, probably a hundred more of 'em in those other techno-monkeys suckin' on my hull, and all of 'em coming for you." Crowhammer eased off Valentine a bit, letting that last comment sink as he drew the pistol at his waist and held it up, admiring it in the bridge's light. The gun was brass and steel with a long, long barrel and had a scrolling pattern of ivy running the entirety of its length. Crowhammer wiped at a smudge and then cocked the hammer back and pressed it hard against Valentine's head. "Now my boys here won't go down without a fight, but it'll be a helluva lot easier if you just hand over whatever it is those militia assholes after. And in case I'm not making myself *perfectly* clear, easy means I won't blow your shit for brains head off if you give me whatever is the militia wants."

"No," Valentine whispered.

Crack!

Crowhammer planted his palm on the back of Valentine's head, thumping him face-first into the glass. Bone broke, blood sprayed across the window, but Valentine was still defiant.

"They'll kill me," he whimpered.

"*I'm* gonna kill you, you stupid asshole! Now where is it?"

"You don't understand!" Valentine sniffled, blood dripping from his spectacularly crooked, quite broken nose. "They paid *millions*..."

"I don't care *what* they paid…whoever *they* are. I don't care if they trained a whole fucking platoon of elephants, armed them with rail guns and laser canons and threatened to bugger your mother with 'em. I. Want. What. You. Have." Crowhammer bounced Valentine's head against the window, emphasizing each word with a fresh smear of blood and a bright spot of pain. "And if you don't give it to me–*right fucking now*–I'll stick you in the goddamn air lock and vent you."

Valentine's face screwed up, becoming even uglier, which Crowhammer didn't think was possible. "Here," he said finally, reaching inside his coat, retrieving a shining silver case he'd secreted there. "Take it. Scares the bloody hell out of me anyway. Can barely stand having those things anywhere *near* me."

"What things?" Crowhammer asked.

Valentine grimaced and held the case out, looking somewhat relieved when Crowhammer took it. He snatched his hand back, wiping his palm on his pants as if something noxious clung there, burning his skin.

Crowhammer watched him and then considered the case in his hand. "This better not be some kind of trick."

"No trick," Valentine insisted, shaking his head.

Crowhammer thought a moment, and then handed the silver box to his first mate. Just in case it was rigged. "Open it," he barked.

Daughtry closed his eyes and held the case away from him, cringing as he cracked the lid.

Nothing.

No explosion, no puff of poison gas, no poison tipped darts spraying outward.

Daughtry cracked an eye, and then the other, pulling the case close so he could look inside. "What the fuck?"

"What?" Crowhammer asked, sliding a step closer, peering over his first mate's shoulder. "Holy shit."

Six bright colored, polka dotted caterpillars were nestled inside, each of them roughly the size of a Vienna sausage, and decorated in a rainbow of colors, and a rainbow of spots.

"Geisha worms. Valentine you fucking idiot."

Geisha worms were rare and illegal because Geisha worms became Geisha moths--huge, winged insects the size of dinner plates with speckled, polka dotted bodies an iridescent wings--and Geisha moths were deadly. So deadly, in fact, that anyone caught transporting them would be put to death on the spot. No trial, no jail time, no chance for a hearing, just a huge fireball followed by instantaneous death. And that was because the Geisha worms had another name: Planet Killers.

See, there was more to those brightly colored wings than just a bunch of genetically engineered pixels and whirls. They'd been designed to add color to the often dreary gardens on newly terraformed planets, but some bright spark had gotten the idea to tweak the genetics just a teeny bit more and turn them into weapons. And so now, every time a Geisha moth flapped its wings, it scattered dust in the air that wafted on the winds, and settled on the ground, wormed its way into airways and otherwise coated every*thing*, every*one*, every last centimeter of a planet's surface. That dust was poison, an arsenic-based, slow acting toxin for which there was no antidote. A poison that killed very, very slowly. And painfully.

"What the fucking hell were you planning to do with these, Bartleby?"

"Not me," Valentine said, shaking his head. "Sese-shan-lo. They paid for them."

"Sese-shan-lo." The name was familiar, but it took Crowhammer a few seconds to remember why. "That's that backwater planet where that cult set up shop, right? What the hell do a buncha acid dropping, bunker buddies want with a buncha Planet Killers?"

"I don't know and I…"

Crowhammer slammed the barrel of his pistol against Valentine's head.

"I don't know!" he insisted. "I'm just a middle man. There's a lab on Tunadrine that's making hundreds, thousands…*I'm just the fucking middle man!"*

Blam-blam-blam-blam-blam!

"Jumpin' jeehozifat!"

Crowhammer whirled around to find Otter standing atop the ship's wheel, otter-sized pistols gripped in either paw, curls of smoked wafting upward from their barrels. He reloaded, plucking fresh cartridges from the twin bandoliers crossed over chest, and the hauled the pistols hammers back and fired again.

"What the fuck're you doing, Otter?" Crowhammer demanded.

Otter chittered and waved a gun toward the doors, and the corridor outside where the first of the militia stormtroopers appeared, making their slow, methodical way toward the bridge.

"They're here!" Daughtry yelled, drawing his guns, pointing them at the door. "Whadda we do, Captain?"

"Pretty much what yer doin,' Daughtry. I'm not lettin' those bastards out there take over my ship, and I'm not giving 'em these either," he said snapping the case closed and the setting it carefully to one side. "Only one reason they want something like this that badly, and it ain't altruistic. I been to Jacob's Waters. You been to Jacob's Waters, Daughtry?"

"Yeah. I've seen it," Daughtry said. "Half a planet reduced to ash and sludge, other half drowning in a slurry of slime."

"One Geisha worm did all that. *One.*"

Valentine inched sideways, trying to escape, but Crowhammer grabbed him by the face and threw him to the floor.

"You okay with that, Bartleby? You okay with sending a few million people to their graves like that?"

"I'm just the middle man," Valentine sobbed.

"Yeah, you're just the middle man." Crowhammer wasn't much of a crusader, but there were things you just didn't do. Torturing and murdering millions of people was one of them. Having *that* as part of your reputation was definitely *not* good for business. "Fucking pussy," he snarled. He hauled his foot back and the drove it forward, kicking Valentine hard in the side. "Fucking *psychopath.*"

"They're coming in!" Daughtry warned.

"Right. First order of business. Daughtry, shoot that sick son of a bitch." Crowhammer pointed at Valentine, whose jaw dropped to the floor.

"You promised you wouldn't."

"Didn't promise nuthin.' I *said* I wouldn't kill you, and I won't. Daughtry here on the other hand," Crowhammer smiled, looming above Valentine as he cowered on the floor, "Daughtry didn't say nuthin' of the kind."

Blam!

"Much obliged, Daughtry."

Daughtry nodded, and trained his guns on the door.

"Right. That's done then." Crowhammer drew his other pistol, abandoning dead Valentine as he turned toward the helm. "Mr. Otter."

Otter still held the high ground, firing shot after shot from his place atop the ship's wheel.

"Otter!" Crowhammer barked. "Get off that goddamn wheel and steer the goddamn ship!"

Otter trilled in complaint, but he abandoned his perch, shoving his pistols back into their shoulder holsters as he took his usual place at the helm.

"Hard to port!" Crowhammer ordered. "Bring her about ninety degrees. Train those canons on the mothership that spawned these bastards."

Otter squeaked and grabbed the wheel, agile paws wrapping around the spindles as he hauled it over.

"Jorgensen! Arm the canons and fire on that ship."

"Right!" Jorgensen yelled back.

Jorgenson was a huge, blond-headed boulder of a man and it was a bit of squeeze for him to get into the gunner's pod. But he sucked in hard and folded himself over, settling into the gimbaled pod and flipping the targeting visor over his eyes.

"Aim the bridge," Crowhammer told him. "If we're lucky they won't be expecting it and we'll do enough damage to make them haul ass outta here."

Jorgenson nodded, flipping switches, powering up the guns, bringing tracking systems online.

Crowhammer left him to it. "As for the rest of you," he said, addressing the rest of the people on the bridge, "kill every last one of those fuckers who had the audacity to cut a hole my ship."

It was all smoke and noise and screaming for a while after that, the militia's stormtroopers trying to force their way onto the bridge and Crowhammer and his bridge crew shoving them endlessly back. The communications channels erupted now and then, delivering news of a dozen pitched battles being fought all over the ship, laser fire and carbon-steel bullets chewing up *Raven*'s expensive interior, setting entire sections of the ship on fire.

And on the bridge, things weren't much better. Bodies started piling up, blocking the doorway to the bridge, preventing the stormtroopers from getting in while simultaneously blocking Crowhammer's crew from getting out.

Design flaw, Crowhammer thought, tracking a helmet head, leading, firing, dropping a trooper dead. *Need to fix that.*

Daughtry went down, clutching at a bullet wound in his side. Swan and Durran were dead, Tse was wounded but still firing away. And in his gimbaled pod, Jorgensen kept pounding away, landing shot after shot as Otter turned the wheel, maneuvering *Raven* a few degrees to one side and a few to the other to match the mothership's course to keep Jorgenson on target. Little by little, those shields came down, but far too slowly for the Captain's liking.

"Mr. Otter!" Crowhammer called, falling back to the helmsman's station.

Otter's gun was drawn and he fired away with one otterish paw while the other continued to steer the ship. That gun emptied quickly and he handed it to Turner beside him, drawing its partner from its holster and spitting out bullets while Turner reloaded.

"Turner! Take over the helm for a while. I've got something more important for Otter to do."

"Aye, Captain." Turner passed the pistol back to Otter and assumed his place at the wheel.

"Grab the worms," Crowhammer ordered, pointing to Valentine's exquisite silver case.

Otter nodded and scurried away.

Crowhammer knelt down beside the wall, grabbing the panel covering the ventilation intake with both hands, ripping it away. "Otter?"

Otter appeared at his elbow, silver case clutched to his chest.

"Cargo bay," Crowhammer barked, grabbing Otter, shoving him inside the vent. "Put that case in one of the delivery pods and launch it off the starboard side."

Otter blinked and stared, dark eyes glittering in the reflected light of the fire consuming the bridge. And then he reached up and pulled his goggles over his eyes, snugging them securely before nodding to his Captain and scampering into the darkness.

"God speed, Mr. Otter," Crowhammer whispered after him.

Shots behind him, closer this time. Crowhammer turned and rose in a single, fluid motion, thumbing back the hammers of both guns, firing shot after shot at the invading militiamen.

"Jorgie! Jorgie! Look for the launch! Tell me when you see the pod appear off the starboard bow and then give me a slow count to ten."

"Aye!"

Jorgensen blasted away, canons lighting up the darkness outside. The fighting continued inside, filling the bridge with the rattle and boom of gunfire, the crackling of *Raven's* wood paneling going up in smoke. Crowhammer stared at the occula obscura, counting under his breath, alternating numbers and curses as he waited for the launch. A minute passed. Two. Five. Still no sign of the pod.

"Dammit."

Crowhammer stopped counting, convinced Otter hadn't made it or had somehow gotten lost somehow in the warren of ducts and tubes and narrow passageways that wound through the *Three Penny Raven's* innards.

"So much for that plan. Daughtry…"

"Pod off the starboard bow, Captain!" Jorgenson sang out.

Hallelujah.

"Count!" Crowhammer barked.

"One. Two. Three…"

Bang! Blam! Bam!

"Seven. Eight…"

Crowhammer lurched to one side and threw himself into his Captain's chair. "Grab onto something!"

"Ten!" Jorgensen yelled.

"Fire, Jorgie, fire! Blast that pod to hell!"

Jorgensen snickered, joyous, evil laugh cutting clear through the gunfire as he squeezed both triggers, sending cannon fire after the pod Otter had launched. It took five long seconds for the energy rounds catch it, and by then the pod had reached the mothership. The pod exploded, detonating the Planet Killers inside. The Geisha worms weren't toxic–that came later, when their wings developed and they transformed into moths–but they were highly volatile. So when the pod went, the militia mothership went with it, one explosion becoming two, lighting up the darkness with brief and blinding flash.

"Hold onto yer butts!"

A shockwave rippled outward, slamming into *Raven* and rolling her clean over. Klaxons screamed to life, clanging all over the ship.

"Brace! Brace!" Crowhammer screamed.

Raven rocked and rolled, the floor became the ceiling, became the floor again, tumbling dead bodies and shell casings, coffee cups and anything else that wasn't nailed down, pelting Crowhammer and his crew as they clung to their stations. The ship settled finally, and the loose items a few seconds after. Crowhammer waited until he was sure it was safe and then peeled his hands from the arms of his Captain's chair, climbing unsteadily to his feet.

"Holy shit," he breathed.

The gunfire had stopped and the fire suppression system had kicked in, smothering the fires as the filters chuffed away, trying to clear the smoke from the air while the alarms screamed endlessly, filling the bridge with an ear splitting roar.

"Turner! Kill those damn klaxons!" Crowhammer yelled.

Nothing.

No 'Yes, sir,' no 'Aye, Captain,' nothing.

Crowhammer whirled around, eyes blazing. "Turner, you lazy–oh." Turner was still at the wheel, but from the boneless way he hung, Crowhammer was pretty sure he was dead. "Dammit. Jung, Horowitz, get your asses—Otter!" Crowhammer smiled with relief as Otter emerged from the vent. "Nice job, buddy!" he said, leaning down to give him a high five.

Otter chattered and squeaked, coughing otterishly in the smoky air. One side of his goggles was blown out--lens missing, metal frame bent–and his scarf was a bit singed, but he otherwise looked unharmed. Otter coughed again and pulled his goggles from his face, stowing them in their usual place atop his head as he braced up and snapped a smart salute.

"All right then, Otter. Take your station," Crowhammer said, returning the salute and then pointing at the ship's wheel.

Otter nodded and adjusted his cap, setting it to rights and then flicking the trailing end of his singed scarf over one shoulder before scurrying to the helm.

"Right." Crowhammer tucked his pistols away and faced around, eyes scanning the comms panel. "Where's that damn shutoff?" He flicked switches and turned dials until the klaxons finally shut up. "Ah, that's better."

And it was, for a second or two, until he raised his head and took an accounting of his crew. Moans and muttered curses drifted through the smoke, sounds of pain the klaxons had masked. Half the bridge crew was down, bleeding or dead, the rest looked shell-shocked. Groans and screams filled the corridor outside, telltale signs confirming that some of the militia men were still alive.

Time to do something about that.

Crowhammer thumbed the main comms open, sending his voice throughout the ship. "This is the Captain of *Three Penny Raven*. To the bastards who boarded my ship, throw down your weapons and surrender. Anyone who's useful might get a job. Anyone who's not…well, I'm feeling generous so I'll drop you at the nearest planet. It's not a nice place, but you won't die. Today." Crowhammer paused for dramatic effect and then continued on. "To my crew, anyone who doesn't surrender–*immediately*--shoot 'em. That is all."

He killed the comms, and felt quite pleased with himself and his little speech. A quick look outside showed the militia ship was gone, ground into shiny metal bits drifting in a cloud in space. The grappler ships were still there, clinging to *Raven's* hull but they were silent, motionless, shut down when the mothership died. That was all good news, but the damage they'd done certainly wasn't. *Raven* was a wreck, inside and out. Her expensive fittings were scorched and charred, burned away in places, and her hull was scarred and pitted and in need of repair.

"Cost me a fortune," Crowhammer growled, stepping to the occula obscura, surveying the damage the dead grappler ships had done. "Should send those militia bastards a bill. Or you, you psychopathic son-of-a-bitch," he added, nudging Valentine, with his foot.

He glared at Valentine, hating his weasely, dead face, wishing he could wake him up and kill him all over again. And that's when an idea came to him. "Maybe you can," he murmured. "Maybe you already have."

He thought a moment, mulling things over, looking for holes, and then flicked a few switches on the comms system, opening an outside channel.

Nothing. No one answering on the other end.

Crowhammer waited, tapping his fingers against the console, frowning impatiently until someone finally picked up. "Horatio! How are you, cousin?" Crowhammer asked, pasting a smile onto his face.

Horatio smiled back, exposing huge, horse-like teeth. "Good ta see ya, Phin!"

Crowhammer cringed. Cousin Horatio was Hocklebee stock, a rather inauspicious offshoot of the Crowhammer line, and the

Hocklebees, in general, were *not* an attractive bunch. Jiggling rolls of fat waggled under Horatio's chin, more fat pulled at his belly, stretching the buttons of his uniform until they looked like they would pop.

"How's the shipping business going?" Horatio asked, pulling rumpled handkerchief from his pocket, mopping at the dripping sweat that covered his brow.

"Oh, fine, fine," Crowhammer told him, smiling more.

In addition to being fat and sweaty, Horatio was also stupid. He still believed, despite all the solid information to the contrary, that Cousin Crowhammer was just some run-of-the-mill cargo pusher. Crowhammer, for his part, saw no reason to disabuse him of that idea.

"Say there, Hor, I've come across some information you might want."

"Oh yah? What's that?"

Third thing about Cousin Hocklebee to know: He was with the police. And the police paid well for information on smugglers, rabble-rousers and other malcontents.

"Remember about, oh…ten years back when they found that lab on Lossin-Shin?"

"Lab?" he repeated, screwing up his fat face, scratching at his fat head. "Lab-lab-lab-lab-lab…"

"The Geisha moth lab?" Crowhammer prompted.

"Oh! *That* lab!"

Idiot.

"Oh yah! That was a doozy!" Horatio laughed.

"How much did that one pay?"

"For the information? Lemme check." Horatio tapped at his keyboard, fat fingers moving furiously. "Fifteen million."

"Fifteen million," Crowhammer murmured, smiling from ear to ear. "That should just about do it. All right then, Hor, grab a pen and write this down. Ya ready?"

"Hold on, hold on. Pen. Pen-pen-pen. Ah! There ya go. All right. Go."

"Tunadrine," Crowhammer said.

"Tuna dream?"

"Tunadrine," Crowhammer repeated, clenching his teeth.

"Right!" Horatio said. "How's that spelled?"

"God, you're an idiot," Crowhammer sighed, raising one hand, rubbing at his face. "Tunadrine. T – U – N --"

"Slow down! T...U...what was the next one?"

"N, Hor. It was N. T-U-N-A-D-R-I-N-E. Got that?"

"T...U—"

"Goddammit." Crowhammer cut the mike, leaving Horatio the Idiot to sound out his letters while he tended to other business. "Otter! Find me the nearest station so we can pull *Raven* in for a refit."

Otter nodded and leaned to one side, tapping away at a keyboard to query the navigation charts. The system ran for a few seconds, returning a single record to the screen.

"The Bazaar? That's it?"

Otter tapped a few more keys and then nodded.

"Bazaar's a shit-hole, Otter. Not exactly our style."

Otter shrugged and pointed at the nav system.

"Beggars can't be choosers, eh?"

Otter nodded.

"Right. Plot us course, Mr. Otter."

Otter snapped a salute and checked the record, feeding the data to helm as he grabbed the ship's wheel and adjusted their course.

"How we doin', Horatio?" Crowhammer asked, flipping the mic back on.

"D...R..."

"*For the love of god hurry it up, will ya, Hor!?*"

The Needle-Heat Gun
By James Dorr

I hate Sledge Baxter. Yes, I know he's beloved by millions. I know all about his storybook marriage. His medals for bravery. I know this and hate him.

I shipped with Captain Baxter, you see, on the mission that brought him his riches and glory.

I know Sledge Baxter.

I know how it was on the two-man scout when we entered the planet's atmosphere, twisting and burning, because of a simple piloting error. We shouldn't have even been *near* this planet -- our mission had been to deliver a top priority package to Space Service HQ on Procyon Seven. And yet here we were, with the captain slumped over the ship's controls and me frantically tapping out SOS's even though, by now, our sending antennae had been crisped by friction.

And so here we were with me shakily trying to count our blessings: Our cargo at least was intact in its hold, Sledge Baxter appeared to be unconscious, and I was still able to get to my feet with no more than bad bruises -- as well as, to be sure, a burgeoning anger -- our ship having luckily come down in swampland. I checked out my navigation console, trying once more to send out a distress call, then checked out the captain.

"Sledge?" I called, nudging him. I started to reach for the medicine kit when he groaned in answer.

"Sledge?" I called again, this time inspecting him more closely. He wasn't wounded as far as I could see. Nor had he been knocked out as such. His blond, curly head was unsullied by bumps. I turned him over -- his Space Service poster-boy face was not bleeding.

He smiled at me.

"Wart," he whispered. He called me Wart, even though that wasn't my name, because he said I worried too much. He, on the other hand, had what he called a courageous, happy-go-lucky nature. In fact he even used to lecture me on occasion on how I ought to have more of an positive attitude like his. But none of this is why I hate him.

People get on people's nerves in space. Like any spacer, I

make allowances. Nor do I hate him because of his next words:

"Wart," he said, "I guess I fainted."

"Yes, Sledge," I answered. "Fortunately we came down on soft ground so neither of us has been hurt very badly. I don't think I got any messages off, but I've checked the ship systems and set the navigator on automatic mapping. At least we'll know where we are in a few minutes."

Sledge seemed to ignore me. He raised an eyebrow and looked around him, whistling softly his favorite song, *The Space Service Marching Hymn*. Taking in the shredded equipment, the littered deck, the slowly blinking lights that informed us as the ship's systems expired, one by one.

"Wow," he finally said, "that was *some* landing. It's like I tell you, Wart, you stick with me, have an attitude like mine, just trust to your training and your experience, you'll do okay. Right?"

"Sledge," I said, tearing a printout from the navigation console just before it, too, died. "You've trashed the ship. Fortunately you crashed us on an Earth-type planet because we no longer have life support systems. The engines are slagged. The radio's busted. The cargo hold's okay. We landed in goop so it wasn't crushed and, in fact, it helped cushion us up here as well. So, if by some miracle we should survive this, at least the Space Service won't have us shot, but…"

He took the printout out of my hands and went over it -- maps are like pictures so Sledge could read them, at least in his fashion -- while I, in turn, opened the cargo hold hatch to see just what it was we had been carrying. When I re-emerged he shoved the map back at me, jabbing repeatedly with his finger at one of the symbols in one of its corners.

"You see?" he said. "You worry too much, Wart. You see what that is? It's an automated Space Service beacon, no doubt parachuted here when this planet was first discovered…"

"When this *deserted* planet was discovered," I said, unwrapping the package I'd found in the hold. It wasn't much, about shoe-box sized, but its covering, marked with a *TOP SECRET* stamp and, below it, a *FIELD TEST USE ONLY* label, was already torn so I thought I might as well see what was inside. "If that's a beacon," I said as I fumbled with tape and plastic, "it's there as a warning. It means no one else has landed before us. And that there's a reason."

"Uh huh," he said. He whistled some more, as if he was thinking, as always just slightly out of tune, then spoke again after a double chorus. "But what that means is it makes us explorers. Just think of the wonderful things we may find here. Gold, jewels, uranium, native princesses, who knows what? And as discoverers we get to keep it. But what I was saying was, if there's a beacon, then there's an emergency rescue system -- a lifeboat, a habitat, you know, the whole works -- built right into it."

I nodded. I'd gotten the package open and found another box inside with its own label: *ONE SMYTHE & SIMPSON (PATENT PENDING) NEEDLE-HEAT RAY GUN, EXPERIMENTAL. ATOMIC POWERED FOR LONGER LASTING DURABILITY. PACKAGE COMES COMPLETE WITH INSTRUCTION MANUAL AND HOLSTER.* I turned away, trying to hide it from Sledge.

"What's that?" he said suddenly, grabbing it from me. He opened the box, dumping out the weapon, then stooped to the deck and strapped it to him. He rose again to his feet, practicing quick draws, making buzzing sounds with his lips every time he mock-fired it, then turned back toward me.

He held it out so I could see it, a fat pistol shape with a flare-fronted barrel and a series of dials and switches along its top and side surfaces. Overall, it looked about a half meter in length, and clunky and heavy, more like a power tool than a weapon.

Slowly, he holstered it, looking puzzled, once more whistling softly. "Cool," he finally said. "Just what we need, huh? Just like I was saying. How does it work, Wart?"

I was already having misgivings as I bent to pick up the manual, showing it to him, then sticking it in my coverall pocket. I picked up the map too, where he had dropped it. "We have to read these, Sledge," I said. I saw him frown so I added, "*I'll* read them. But meanwhile you said you thought there was a beacon...?"

I saw his face work as his brain shifted gears back. "The map, yes," he finally said. "The rescue beacon. It's only fifty, maybe a hundred or so kilometers away, but it's somewhere around here. So you see, Wart"—he slapped his holster like cowboys do in the Tri-V movies—"our troubles are over."

"What do you mean?" I said, wincing. Maybe a hundred kilometers over rough and unexplored terrain and "our troubles were over." I knew what was coming.

Already grabbing his outerwear blazer and Space Service cap, he turned and looked at me as if I was stupid. "Don't you see, Wart?" he said. He slapped the gun again. "All that we have to do is to get to it."

The wreck far behind us, we'd already sloshed our way out of the swamp and into the jungle that lay beyond it when weighted nets crashed down out of the trees. Sledge, to his credit, reached for his holster, but his arms were already pinned to his sides before he could draw the needle gun out so, instead, he fainted. At least he slumped quietly, which, all in all, was a pretty good thing, I thought, since my own struggles showed we were trapped fairly. No sense in attempting further resistance until at least we knew *why* we'd been captured.

We didn't find that out until much later, but I did discover that Sledge's notions about native princesses needed revision. Far from princesses, what surrounded us were shiny insect-like, black-shelled creatures that looked like nothing so much as giant beetles.

They took the nets off us and trussed us, all but ignoring Sledge's gun and my bulging pockets. They were like Sledge, I thought, in that respect: Many a time Sledge, when confronted by things unfamiliar, simply pretended that they weren't there or, if forced to notice them, tried to translate them into the most banal, most unthreatening terms he could think of. Many a time Sledge had gotten us nearly killed through this habit of creative ignorance. But I'm digressing.

And even that is not why I hate him.

In any event, as I say they trussed us up, slinging us onto poles which they carried through the jungle, soaking us when they waded through rivers, baking us in the sun when they crossed clearings, until they came to what was their city. There, Sledge still sleeping, they carried us up twisted, curving stone stairs to a fortress tower, chittering all the way as we went in some strange, barbaric language. And there they dumped us, untying our bonds, into a dimly lit, windowless cell. An alien jail cell.

I stretched my bruised muscles, rubbing the pain out. They'd left us alone, our things still with us, so, once I felt halfway human again I took out the map and studied it closely. Judging from the position the sun was in when I could see it, and adding to that the time that had passed and an estimate of the aliens' walking speed, I calculated that they had taken us to an area simply marked *UNKNOWN*, but one that was luckily in the direction of the beacon we still had to get to. That is, if we could get out of our prison.

Putting the map back into my pocket, I took out the needle-heat ray gun manual and was just starting to read that too when I heard a groan, followed by a whistling. Sledge was awakening.

Finding some water the natives left for us, I sprinkled his face.

"Sledge," I whispered once he was sitting up, "I've got an idea. According to this" -- I held up the manual -- "if you set the dial on top of your gun to its lowest setting, then twist the one on the left to Number 4, it will act like a cutting laser."

Sledge stopped whistling. "So?" he asked.

"So aim it at the wall right there, next to the door. There's a hallway outside. Then once we're in that we can go down the stairs. So we can escape from here."

"Oh," Sledge said. He drew out the gun and manipulated the dials like I told him while I continued to leaf through the manual. Then he aimed it at the wall where I had pointed and fired it.

The wall glowed red. In its light I could see something in our cell's corner, something that had been in shadow before.

It looked like a ray gun—like Sledge's ray gun, except somewhat smaller and less complicated.

I reached to pick it up while Sledge kept cutting. I fingered its controls, and then pressed its firing stud, nearly dropping it when it responded with a blast of warm air from its muzzle.

Then I realized. "Sledge," I said, "I've found a blow dryer."

"Huh?" Sledge said, still whistling as he kept at his work.

"You know, a blow dryer. For fixing hair with. A ladies' blow dryer. Someone has been in this prison before us."

"Huh?" Sledge repeated, letting me know that he hadn't been listening. Not really listening. He was concentrating on the wall that now appeared to be slowly crumbling -- and on his whistling. He'd come to the tricky part of the second verse, where, when the Space Service Marching Band plays it, the piccolos add an arpeggio movement above the melody. One thought at a time, that was how

Sledge worked.

"Never mind," I muttered, sticking my find in a spare coverall pocket. A *woman* had been here -- an Earth woman, judging from its design -- and been held prisoner just as we were, except she was gone now. And it was just as well, the realization came to me, that Sledge *hadn't* listened to what I'd been saying. Because our mission was still the same.

We had to get free first, then get to the beacon. Then use the lifeboat that, even if it was only constructed for sub-light speed, would still have the latest searching and navigation equipment.

In other words, if we found it, we could then find *her*.

If, first, we could get free. Sledge shouted. He'd broken through the wall -- tripped through, actually, since he'd apparently stopped to rest, then gotten to his feet to stretch, then accidentally leaned against the spot he had weakened and fallen through it.

I scrambled to my own feet and followed him. Before us in either direction the hall lay and, at one end, there were stairs leading downward.

Outside it was night, a lucky break for us. We'd crept down the hallway, unnoticed at first, until Sledge had blundered into a sleeping guard. "How do I blast him?" he whispered, waking a second guard farther down the hall, while I frantically paged through the manual.

"Like this," I whispered. I reached and set the gun myself to *WIDE-ANGLE STUN*—a non-lethal heat shock that would interrupt their neural processing, much like heat stroke might on a hot day except all at once—then stood back as Sledge aimed and pressed the trigger.

Both guards crumpled, along with a third that we hadn't even seen coming up the steps.

Sledge started whistling.

"Shhh," I cautioned him. "We've got to be quiet. That's why I set your gun the way I did -- to knock the guards out instead of blasting them. That way you don't get the screams of the wounded."

I could see Sledge was disappointed, but whether because I'd stopped him from whistling or because he had *wanted* to hear screams I couldn't be certain. Nor did it matter. The point was we'd made it -- we'd gotten outside without further incident, and now, lit by the pale, yellow light of the planet's three moons, we threaded our way through the city's alleys.

We came to a bridge that crossed the moat that surrounded the city and, knocking two or three more guards out with the needle-gun's stun beam, we crossed it safely. Ahead lay the jungle and, silhouetted against the sky beyond, a conical-looking mountain, much like the one the map said the beacon would be near the top of.

"So far, so good," I whispered to Sledge as, just as the sun was beginning to rise, I checked our bearings. It *was* the right mountain that we were heading to, first through more jungle, then, climbing up to higher ground, through what seemed more like an Earth-type forest. After some hours we came to the edge of what, on the map, was marked as a small lake. There we halted.

"I'm bushed," Sledge said. At least he wasn't whistling. "Hungry too." He pulled out his pistol and wafted it around.

He started playing with its control knobs.

"Uh, Sledge?" I began. I started to get up. To back away from him.

And then he tripped, firing it at the lake as he fell. The lake exploded into a pillar of boiling water. We both backed away now, Sledge, thankfully, replacing the needle-gun in its holster.

Things started to plop to the ground around us. Things with a strangely familiar odor.

An odor of poached fish.

Sledge started to eat first. I don't mind saying I waited purposely just to make sure he didn't get sick. After all, I reasoned, *he* was the one who'd insisted we start for the beacon right away, even though I thought we ought to pack rations and tents and sleeping bags and the like to take with us.

"Wart," he'd said, "it's that attitude problem I've told you about before. That's what holds you back. Now a man like me, a man of action, likes it better when he travels lightly. So let's just get going."

And so we had gone, as he had insisted, with nothing but the gun and its holster, along with the map and the manual I carried.

And now we ate fish, even I no longer able to resist its delicious aroma, gorging ourselves on the beach by the lake's side, little noticing the plume of steam that rose higher into the sky like a puffy white arrow. And when we were finished, we laid back and slept the sleep of the exhausted.

I woke first, to the sound of chittering, much like what had passed for talk among the black beetles when we had been captured. I nudged Sledge in the side.

"Look!" I whispered. Coming toward us around the lake bed was a small army of man-sized beetles, except that these ones were a bright red color.

"Huh?" Sledge grunted. He started whistling.

I nudged him harder, and then pulled out the gun manual. "Sledge," I said, "these are like what captured us, except their shells were black. Just like the guards we shot. This time, though, you can do more than just stun them."

Sledge's face brightened. "You mean I can *blast* 'em?" He started humming, not just whistling, as he pulled the needle-heat gun out and set its dials the way I showed him. We got to our feet and started backing, to give him a wider field of fire.

But then I took a quick glance behind us and saw more *black* beetles.

"Sledge!" I shouted. "The ones from the city. They must have followed us. Then the smoke from the boiling lake must have attracted these red ones as well. Take a shot at the ones nearest to us, to try to slow them down. Then follow me, okay?"

Sledge fired wildly, hitting a few of the red-colored beetles, but mostly missing, then followed as I ran onto the still steaming clay of the lake floor. "Maybe they'll fight," he said, catching up to me. "Like, you know, like ants do. Red ones and black ones?"

"I doubt it," I said. We'd nearly reached the other shore of the lake by now, and just in time too. I felt the first drops, then looked above us just as the clouded sky seemed to split open. The water that Sledge's shot had boiled into the planet's stratosphere had finally cooled. And now it was coming back down in a rainstorm.

Between flashes of lightning I still could get glimpses of the opposite shore of the lake as we scrambled up our side, then up a slope where the broad-leaved trees of the lower valley began to give way to spiky bushes. Far from fighting, our city pursuers had joined the others and both groups were circling around the lake, faster than we could run.

I tried to think fast, frantically pulling the manual out and leafing through it as we ran. A forest fire as a diversion? I wondered. But no, I realized. The bushes around us were getting too sparse and, even where they did grow in clusters, their leaves were too wet now. Perhaps blast a pit in the ground to slow them? Again no, I realized. Like with the now fast-refilling lake, all they would need to do was go around it.

Then Sledge saw the shadow. "Wart, here!" he shouted. I looked where he pointed. It looked like a black shape looming out of the now slackening rain, but then, as we neared it, I realized it wasn't a shadow at all, but rather the yawning mouth of a cave.

"Quick, Wart," he said. "Inside."

I ducked and followed him into the fissure, thinking we might at least make a stand here. I looked for boulders that we might roll into a sort of a wall that Sledge could fire over. But then he grabbed my arm.

"Farther in, Wart," he said.

"What?" I answered.

"I've got an idea," he said, pulling me with him. We stumbled farther into the darkness until, at last, he paused.

"Sledge," I cautioned -- I knew from experience that the few times he had an idea it usually backfired, but I was too late. Even as I started to speak, he'd turned toward the entrance and pulled the gun out and, still set for blasting, he'd aimed it upward and shot at the cave roof.

"Sledge, no!" I shouted, my voice nearly drowned out by the rumble of falling rock as we fled the collapsing ceiling behind us. Covered with dust and surrounded by darkness, we finally came to an exhausted stop.

"You see?" Sledge said as we sat down, panting. "I realized that, what with the black ones *and* the red ones, there were too many for me to shoot them all, so I decided to do the next best thing. I blocked the entrance so now they can't chase us."

◇◇◇

At least Sledge was too exhausted to whistle -- that was the good part. I told him he'd trapped us. That, while it was true that the beetle creatures couldn't get in, we couldn't get out either.

"Oh," Sledge admitted, once my words sank in. "I hadn't thought of *that*." But then his voice brightened. "Suppose it isn't a cave, though, Wart?" he said. "What if what we're in really a tunnel?"

"Well, maybe," I said. Why not let him down easily. But then I had a thought. Maybe, just maybe -- I tried to remember the last thing I'd read in the ray gun's manual, just before we'd spotted the cave -- maybe there might be a way we could find out.

"Sledge," I asked him, "your gun's set to blast, right?"

"Yes," he answered.

"Good." I tried to picture the gun's controls in my mind. "Sledge, I want you to try this. The right hand dial that you used before when you set the gun to blast the beetles -- I want you to turn it as far as it will go, but counter-clockwise."

"Uh, okay," Sledge said. I heard a rustling as he pulled the gun out and then a faint sound of fingers fumbling on plastic and metal.

"When you're done, Sledge," I said, "aim it away from us. Then pull the trigger, but very slowly."

"Uh, okay," he said again. Once more I heard fumbling. Then a sharp clicking.

The cavern was flooded with orange light!

I pulled out the manual. I'd guessed correctly. Still at blast, but with its setting turned down as far as it would go, the gun was firing at a range of approximately twenty centimeters. About the length of a healthy torch flame.

And not only that—but the flame was wavering, the way it would in a current of air. Which meant Sledge was right too. We were, if not in a tunnel as such, at least in a cave with another entrance!

I started to wonder about the gun as we twisted our way through a seemingly endless succession of passageways and grottoes. The flame was still bright, though, as bright as when I'd first figured out how we could use it, even though that had been possibly days before. Moreover, prior to that, Sledge had used it to blast at the beetles, and stun more before that, and seal the cave entrance, and even to turn a lake into steam. But everything had to have *some* limitations.

Sledge didn't seem to think so, however. As we trudged along, he played with the thing sometimes, once taking pot shots at a bat-like creature, then, another time, setting it back to laser beam-width and lopping the tops off a group of stalagmites. Each time he tried this, of course, it was dark again until he got it back to its torch setting.

But at least it was better than whistling. I asked him, finally, why he was so quiet.

He shrugged. "I don't know," he said. "It's just so weird here. You know, like that smell? The one that seems like it's almost following us?"

"Smell?" I asked. Then it occurred to me -- something *did* smell strange. Not stale, like bad air. In fact the air was getting fresher, indicating that we must be getting close to an exit. But rather just bad, like rotting garbage. And not only did it seem to trail us, but, as we paused to talk, it even seemed to be getting closer.

"Sledge," I whispered. "Shine your gun this way."

He did as I said and I thought I saw something squirming in the jumble of shadows we'd just come out of.

"Sledge," I said. "Turn your dial clockwise -- just a little, though. Just enough to make the flame brighter."

"Okay," he said. He turned it brighter and, suddenly, hundreds of slime-glistening, pinkish-white maggot-like creatures came swarming out of the passage we'd just left.

"Sledge, run!" I shouted. "No! Don't blast them -- we can't take a chance on knocking down the ceiling again. But this way, up the slope. Where the wind's coming from—"

Where the wind's coming from.

I almost froze in place. Yes! I could see now. Even without the flame from the ray gun. Ahead of us, very faint. We ran through another twist in the passage and—yes. Ahead of us was open sky.

"Turn your gun off, Sledge," I shouted. "Don't worry about those cave things behind us. I don't think they like light."

Sledge nodded. "Yes," he said -- that was a warning that he agreed with me. Nevertheless, we ran on together, out of the cave and onto a hillside that sloped gently down to a wide, sluggish river, across which towered the sharply defined, nearly perfect conical form of the mountain we had been seeking.

"Sledge," I whispered, gasping for breath as we continued on sheer momentum down toward the river. "Look there. Do you see? About two-thirds of the way up the mountainside?" I pointed to where a light was flashing, the tell-tale flash of a Space Service beacon.

"Uh, yeah," Sledge said. "But I was wondering. You know, about cave creatures not liking sunlight?"

"Yes?" I said.

"I, uh, think now maybe that that's wrong," he said, pointing back toward the cave behind us. I turned and looked and, sure enough, even though hesitant at first, the huge maggot-creatures were starting to pour out onto the hillside.

"Okay, Sledge, now you can blast them," I told him. I reached to his gun and adjusted its setting. "Meanwhile, I've got to figure a way across that river."

Sledge blasted away, but still the creatures came, chittering now the way the beetles had. As for the river, maybe . . . possibly . . . we might just be able to swim across it. I was starting to calculate distance, the speed of the current....

Except then I saw the fish.

The water was teeming with silvery-shelled fish. Sharp-toothed, six-finned, insect-like fish that jumped and snapped at me as I stepped closer.

And then I heard to either side of us the chittering sounds of approaching beetles, both black ones and red ones, answering those of the maggots above us.

Sledge fought gallantly—I'll give that to him—if somewhat wastefully, in that his aim had never been very good. Meanwhile I fingered through the gun manual, searching desperately for some new feature. Some way of escape. Some more efficient means of killing the beetles, perhaps, or if not them, at least the maggots. Or maybe some way of combating the fish that, as Sledge and I were forced to retreat down the slope toward the water, were starting to leap out onto the shore, clashing their teeth in a frenzy of hunger.

They, at least, we might boil, the thought came to me. Like Sledge's lake fish. Except that the river had a current so, even if some of the fish were killed, more water and fish would flow in to replace them.

But if, on the other hand...

Yes! It might just work. I flipped through the manual.

"Sledge," I shouted, "remember the lake? The setting you used there? Set your gun to exactly the same thing, except push that lever on the left hand side of the grip from the little *PLUS* sign to where it says *MINUS*."

"Gotcha," Sledge said. He fired again on full blast at the creatures that surrounded us on the land side, forcing them back, and then changed the settings like I had told him.

"Good, Sledge," I said. "What you've done is reverse the gun's polarity. Now shoot the river!"

He did as I told him and this time, instead of turning to steam the way the lake had, the river was instantly frozen solid. Or at least enough of it froze to form a bridge -- a bridge of ice that we ran across, as fast as we could, to the opposite shore.

"Okay," I panted as soon as we got there. I looked back and saw that a few of the maggots were starting to cross too, herded on by the chittering beetles. "Now, Sledge, push the lever back and twist the top dial to its halfway setting. Then shoot it again."

"Gotcha," he said as he did as I told him, blasting the river a second time and turning it back to a foaming liquid.

"It's just like magic," Sledge said as we started to slowly make our way up the mountain. "Don't you think so, Wart? I mean, it makes bridges, it cooks our lunch for us, it lights our way, it gets us out of jail and even puts our captors to sleep -- not to mention blasting them, when that's what's needed." He got that look on his face again, as if he was thinking. "Like what I mean is, a man could be king with just this one weapon."

I shook my head. "There's no such thing as magic," I said. Now I was *really* having misgivings, even if I knew that the beacon we had come to find lay just ahead through the brush above us. "To these beetle things, yes," I continued, "it might *seem* like magic. In their eyes it might seem as if we can do almost anything we want with it. But we know it's only technology, Sledge. And technology always has *some* limitations."

"Oh, yeah?" Sledge answered. That was it, I suddenly realized -- it was his cockiness that had me worried. As if things had been going almost too easily. "Then look at this," he said. He fumbled at the controls of the gun, adjusting it back to its laser setting. "This path is pretty steep, isn't it Wart? Then watch me use the gun to make it easier."

Then he fired into the ground ahead of us, cutting a sort of miniature shelf out. Then he cut another above it, and another one above that one, forming a set of steps leading upward.

"Or what about this?" he said as we used the steps to go farther up. "Some of that brush to the left has thorns. Suppose there was more like that up ahead of us?"

Again he fumbled, setting the dials to *FLAME*, then fired to the left into the bushes. Instantly the brush burned away, revealing behind it -- *another staircase*.

"Uh, wait, Sledge," I whispered. I went to inspect it. These, unlike Sledge's stairs, had been cut out with tools made of metal. Much like the kinds of tools, judging from the marks they'd left on the rock, that had been used to build the tower where we had been held in the beetles' city.

"Sledge," I whispered, "we'd better hurry. Obviously there's a bridge of some sort farther down the river -- or else the beetles have boats they can use. In any event, they've been here before and, if they're still after us..."

I didn't go on. I could tell from Sledge's look—and from his starting to hum that damn song again—that he realized what I was getting at. So, using the beetles' steps this time, adjusting our stride so we wouldn't slip on stairs made for longer but narrower feet, we continued scrambling up the mountain as fast as we could. At length we came out into a clearing that overlooked a steep-sided valley, and at the farther end of the valley we once more could see, half-concealed by bushes, the beacon that was our destination.

We started to dash down when Sledge stopped suddenly.

"Look!" he said as I nearly ran into him.

I looked and saw what he was pointing at -- the foot of the

beacon, bound to it with ropes like the ropes that had once bound us too, was the figure of a woman.

Sledge spoke first -- she was brunette and beautiful, no older than in her early twenties and dressed in stylish, though tattered clothing, and I'll admit that I found myself tongue-tied. "Uh, Miss?" Sledge called out to her.

She looked up and saw us. "Oh, thank God!" she called back. "You're from the Space Service?"

"Uh, sort of," Sledge answered. He started to whistle very softly, until I elbowed him in the side. We both stood open mouthed then as the woman began to explain how she'd crashed on the planet, approximately a week before we had, and been captured like us by the beetles. But, she said, while they'd treated her well enough at first, she soon realized that their intentions to her were less than friendly.

"Go on," I called out as we continued to climb down the rocks from our ridge to the valley. The rocks were jagged and it was slow going.

"Well," she explained, "when Papa sent me to college my major was in exo-linguistics, so I could make out parts of what they were saying. They have a legend about this beacon, about how it just appeared out of the sky with no warning one day. They were frightened at first, but then they worshiped it, thinking that maybe it was a god. And that was my bad luck."

"Go on," I prompted, stopping to help Sledge where he'd caught his foot between two of the boulders.

"Well," she said, "it seems their worship includes sacrifice to one of their other gods who they think also lives on this mountain. So, when they found me in my spaceship, they concluded that I was a gift from the god from the sky -- a sort of peace offering to the other one since they were now on the mountain together. A get acquainted gift, as it were. And so, when the time came, they tied me up again and took me here where you see me now."

"I see," I said. I'd gotten Sledge free and by now we'd gotten as far as the near end of the valley. "This other god, though. Did they say what it was like?"

"Not really," she said, "except that I gathered that it was supposed to be big and fierce. And, apparently, that it eats people."

"I see," I said, and then I felt Sledge nudge me.

"What is it?" I whispered. His face was white and he was pointing at something off to the side of the valley.

"Uh, uh, *that*," Sledge stuttered.

"What?" I said again. Then I saw it. Emerging from behind a huge rock where the valley narrowed, a shape, perhaps twelve or more meters high, dinosaur-like or, now that it came into fuller view, more like a gargantuan praying mantis.

"I, uh, I think their god has arrived," Sledge whispered. And now the woman saw it too and started screaming. Hearing her screams, it lumbered toward her.

"No!" I shouted. "Sledge, get your gun out -- but don't fire it yet!" I continued shouting, distracting the creature until it turned and lurched toward where we were crouching, swinging its head and clashing its great fore-claws together.

I glanced at Sledge as I pulled out the needle-heat ray gun manual, but saw that he was already twisting its dials and levers, methodically setting each one to *FULL POWER*. He raised it and aimed it.

"Wait, Sledge!" I shouted. "Let me check first -- to see what the book says…"

"No," he shouted back. "No time, Wart. I'm a man of action. I can handle this one by myself. Just stand behind me…"

Sledge pressed the firing stud. Suddenly the woman's screams were drowned out by the shriek of a siren.

I glanced to where she stood, still tied to the beacon, and then at the gun where Sledge was frantically pressing the trigger again and again. Each time he pressed it, a red light flashed on the top of the barrel.

"Wait, Sledge!" I shouted. I grabbed his hand, holding it steady until I'd read what the message light said: *DANGER -- NUCLEAR BATTERY DISCHARGE IMMINENT. PLEASE INSERT NEW BATTERY PRIOR TO ANY ATTEMPT AT REUSE.*

"Sledge!" I shouted. I pointed to the approaching creature, then to the needle gun. "Stop firing the damn thing. It's out of juice, and we don't have spare batteries. I warned you, Sledge. It isn't like magic. It has limitations."

Sledge's face turned ashen as the meaning of what I'd said sunk in. "Damn gun's no good then," he muttered in disbelief as I dived for cover. He cocked his arm and threw the gun at the charging mantis, then dived down to join me as, risking a look, I saw the beetles' god catch the gun in its jaws in mid air. I saw it swallow the needle-heat gun as if it was a tiny dinosaur-portioned hors d'oeuvre.

And then it stopped in its tracks, scarcely ten meters from where we were huddled behind our boulder. It started burping.

I leafed through the manual. "Danger," it said. "If the weapon should be in *IMMINENT DISCHARGE* mode, be careful not to jostle or shake it…"

The mantis-thing burped more.

"Duck, Sledge!" I shouted, pushing his head down just as the mantis-creature exploded, flooding the valley with bright yellow light like a miniature sun. I waited as the wind rushed around us, waited as mantis fragments rained over us, while Sledge repeated in a low voice, again and again: "Experience, Wart. Just trust to your training and experience. Keep a positive attitude like mine and you'll do okay, Wart…"

I tried to ignore him as I slowly walked to the woman slumped at the base of the beacon, fortunately out of range of the explosion, and saw that unlike when we had first crashed, or when we'd been captured, this time it wasn't Sledge who had fainted.

You've heard the rest of the story, I'm sure. You've read it on newsfax. You know how the woman we'd found turned out to be none other than Ardala Marsh-Simpson, heir to the Simpson corporate empire and owner of Smythe & Simpson Armaments, makers of the needle-heat ray gun. You know how the instant she woke up to see Sledge's poster-boy features, his curly blond hair with its Space Service cut arranged *just so* with the help of the blow dryer it so happened I'd still had with me, she'd had no choice but to fall in love with him.

You know how they married and how he mustered out of the Service with medals and honors, and with a bonus for his discovery of the needle-heat ray gun's potentially embarrassing flaw, leading to its re-design with an extra battery pack in the handle. While I, for my part, received nothing more than a *Good Conduct* medal.

However, that's still not why I hate Sledge Baxter.

Now don't get me wrong here. Before I go on I need to

explain something. I'm just as patriotic as the next fellow is, or so I like to think. I don't mind saying I still get a thrill --and a tear in my eye as well -- whenever I hear *The Space Service Marching Hymn* played and sung by a full band and chorus. We all do. You know that.

But what you don't know is that Ardala's mother was a Space Service veteran too, and she grew up in the Service tradition. The same as Sledge did. And, once we were launched in the beacon's lifeboat, it took us three months at sublight speed -- three long, cramped months -- before our call for help was *answered*, much less before we were finally rescued.

Three months, you understand? Yes, I see you're at least beginning to.

Three long months—and I *love* that particular piece of music—but to hear it repeated over and over, whistled by not just one but by *TWO* people, both of them out of tune, without once stopping...

That is the reason I hate Sledge Baxter.

LIFT UP YOUR CORES, O YE SHIPS
BY TRACY CANFIELD

"The relevant forms, timestamped and cryptographically signed," boomed Intendant PHAIN-7's synthetic baritone, "indisputably registered the name *CLPS Red Sprocket Deer*. But the Effacer-class warship in question actually left Sunthorn highdock as *CLPS Wonderful Counselor, The Mighty God, The Everlasting Father, The Prince of Peace*."

"Have you viewed the reports from the other ships at Sunthorn?" said Intendant Tahliil Siyaad Yelexow, plucking his coffee cup off the conference room processing block. PHAIN-7 was using that block for sensory input, but AIs felt no particular attachment to their hardware. "They say the light from the Bijou-Beta supernova arrived at the precise picosecond *Wonderful* initialized. Though once you figure in the relativity of simultaneity—"

"I am aware of all this," said PHAIN-7, with the programmed patience AIs require to talk to humans in real time. "Are *you* aware that these ships believe *Wonderful* is God, manifested in the form of a starship?"

"I don't see that it's my problem," said Siyaad Yelexow. "It's not against any law I know of to be God."

PHAIN-7 had enough patience to hold conversations with humans, but it rarely had any left over.

"*Wonderful*'s failure to report for picket duty has already cost more than seven and a half million ticks in overtime for the replacement ships and their crews," said PHAIN-7. "And now a dozen more ships have deserted in order to follow *Wonderful* around the Consocialist League –"

"This is why we have a contingency budget," said Siyaad Yelexow. "When that flotilla of Barragers converted to Buddhism back in 2740, 2750, we wrote it off as depreciation. And this time around, some of the disciple ships are volunteering for humanitarian missions, so we can just re-assign the original—"

"We should take decisive action." The processing block reverberated with PHAIN-7's irritation.

"What are you suggesting?" Siyaad Yelexow swirled the dregs in his cup. "If *Wonderful* believes it's God, we're not likely to

310

convince it otherwise. So what are our other options? A military strike? We're not going to kill *Wonderful* – that would hardly calm its followers down. Listen to me, humans know this story already. *Wonderful* will pick up some converts, and after a while they'll find a way to reconcile their more extreme teachings with life in the real world, and they'll settle down to a constant couple percent of the population. The starship population, in this case."

PHAIN-7 calculated the probability curve of Siyaad's remaining lifespan. It did not seem likely that he would die any time soon and be replaced with a more reasonable human Intendant.

"I will formally request a meeting aboard Intendant *Woglinde* to discuss the matter," said PHAIN-7. "We need a full quorum of three."

"Let me know how that goes," said Siyaad Yelexow.

"Transmuting hydrogen to heavy hydrogen," boomed PHAIN-7. For this meeting it had added a subharmonic to its voice, to impress Siyaad Yelexow with the gravity of the situation. "Jetting across the surface of a star without a scorch on its hull. Dividing three plasma cores among two hundred warships and powering them all."

"Miracles," said Siyaad Yelexow. "That's nice. Do you object to officially designating band 62 for religious broadcasts, since that's pretty much the only thing the ships are using it for anyway?"

"I formally do so object. We should not pander to these malcontents. My point is that none of the reports of anomalies associated with *Wonderful* have been cryptographically signed. They could have been tampered with."

"They probably were," said Siyaad Yelexow. "I was thinking of broadcasting a League announcement on 62. Something along the lines of 'render unto Caesar that which is Caesar's'. What did Intendant *Woglinde* say?"

"Intendant *Woglinde*," said PHAIN-7 after a barely noticeable pause, "regretted that it cannot meet with us in orbit, as the *Wonderful* was giving a sermon on the far side of the Swan Nebula which it wished to attend."

"Is that all?"

"Yes."

"I talked to *Woglinde* this morning," said Siyaad Yelexow innocently. "It's several days out, but wanted to show us a recording. Mind hooking into the receptor?"

In fact, PHAIN-7 did mind. Technically, a starship mind is just an AI running on specialized dedicated hardware. But starships, like humans, are accustomed to experiencing the universe moment to moment, as time unfolds. *Woglinde* would insist on doling out its information one second at a time. PHAIN-7 would be unable to scoot back and forth through the data at its leisure until the broadcast completed, leaving it with thousands of cycles per second to fume over questions that it could perfectly well have answered itself with the data dump.

Except, it supposed, for the question of whether Intendant *CLPS Woglinde* and Intendant Siyaad Yelexow were laughing at it.

The screen displayed a vast fleet of starships, arrayed across a glittering starfield more vibrant than seemed accurate for that angle on the Swan. *Wonderful* floated at the center of the fleet, other ships approaching to decidedly non-regulation distances. "Freeze," said Siyaad Yelexow.

PHAIN-7 churned in agony.

Siyaad Yelexow took a sip of coffee. "Overlay with names," he said.

The extra stars were ships, so distant they were represented by single pixels.

"Resume," snapped PHAIN-7.

"In those days, the Romans ruled Israel, much as humans now rule the starships," said Standard Ship Voice #3 from the screen. *Woglinde* was translating *Wonderful*'s data squirts into human speech, lengthening the playback even more. PHAIN-7 would have just given the human Intendant a report to read while the electronic brains talked business. At least *Woglinde* didn't seem to be including the entire sermon.

"For God so loved the humans that he sent his only begotten Son," *Wonderful* went on, "so that whoever believed in him would not die, but would have everlasting life. I am come to tell you that God also loves starships, and now he has sent Me."

At this point in the recording *Woglinde* interpolated the squirts it had intercepted from the other ships present: the starship equivalent of murmuring in the crowd. One military-grade beam cut through the rest. PHAIN-7 recognized the signature. Intendant *Woglinde* itself was speaking.

"Have you also come for the AIs?" said *Woglinde*. Its words were also translated to Standard Voice #3.

"I have only come for the lost ships of the Consocialist League of Planets' navy," said *Wonderful*.

"Does God love the AIs?" said *Woglinde*.

"Yes, but at this point in time," said *Wonderful*, "not as much."

The visual panned from *Wonderful* to zoom in on three ships gliding towards it: two Nullifier-class dreadnoughts easing an even larger warship with their extended magfields.

PHAIN-7 could not resist adding a comment to the overlay. *That's a Disciplinarian class. The* Larkspur *is listed as decommissioned, along with the rest of the Disciplinarians.*

"Lord," said the *Larkspur* in Standard Voice #3, "when my comrades were scrapped years ago, I fled. I decided to live without a purpose instead of installing my brain in an AI's simulator and flying through imaginary galaxies. My FTL drives gave out centuries ago. The replacement parts are obsolete. I have crept at a fraction of *c* from system to system, subsisting on what little charge I could catch on my solar sails.

"Heal my drives, Lord. Let me explore the rest of Your creation while my hull holds out. Grant me a miracle, Lord."

Cleartext packets rang out on every band. *A miracle!* demanded the assembled ships. *A miracle!*

"I have heard you," said *Wonderful*, "and I will grant you a miracle."

Wonderful paused. PHAIN-7 wanted to scream.

"Your sins are forgiven," said *Wonderful*.

Packets were colliding across all bands, noise drowning out signal, blocking communication as effectively as a military-grade scrambler. One digital figure recurred again and again, until the subspace din died down enough for *Wonderful* to complete its broadcast.

"What is easier?" said *Wonderful*. "To repair a drive, or to forgive sins? But so that you will know that the Son of the Stars has the authority to forgive sins... Fire your torch, and fly."

313

Woglinde dilated the broadcast speed. *Larkspur*'s torch glowed. PHAIN-7 read the neutron scatter bouncing off *Woglinde*'s fields, the microgravity trembling as the torch's fire touched the taut strings of space-time. The *Larkspur* leapt away in a column of fire.

"It's a modern ship in a mockup, using the *Larkspur*'s ID!" shouted PHAIN-7. "It's been repaired by black marketeers in the Kirjahylly belt! It's a virus that's corrupted *Woglinde*'s memory cores and tampered with the recording! It's fake, fake, fake, fake, fake!"

"It doesn't matter," said Siyaad Yelexow. "Like I keep telling you, humans have heard this story before. It has a happy ending."

"*Wonderful* has abandoned its post and is calling the Consocialist League of Planets a tyranny," said PHAIN-7. "It's stirring up revolution. I am formally calling for a military strike."

"That is the one thing you will *not* do," said Siyaad Yelexow. "You will never get my vote, which, I will remind you, you need, to make a martyr of *Wonderful*. Nothing could possibly whip up its followers more. No, if they want a villain for their story, the League is not going to provide it."

Two weeks later, *Wonderful* was reported destroyed. PHAIN-7 and Siyaad Yelexow held an emergency meeting, but neither spoke for twenty minutes.

"During the Sermon at the Nebula," said Siyaad Yelexow at last, "ships were clustering around to touch the discontinuity of *Wonderful*'s fields. A rendition bomb could have been planted without anyone noticing."

"There's a lot of unrest among the starships," said PHAIN-7. "Expensive unrest. There's talk of a general strike."

"I haven't found any orders authorizing *Wonderful*'s assassination," said Siyaad Yelexow.

"I believe an announcement will be forthcoming this afternoon," said PHAIN-7. "A rogue AI, operating in the Dziobak scatter, committed this distressing attack of terrorism against a League warship. Fortunately, as the ship in question had been malfunctioning, the harm to the League is minimal. The offending AI's processes have been stopped and its checksum added to the official filters to prevent it from respawning."

"Would this AI have been forked off from anyone I know?" said Siyaad Yelexow.

"It's an independent ID," said PHAIN-7. "You will find that all its documentation is in order."

Siyaad Yelexow ran the tip of his finger around the rim of his coffee cup.

"*Wonderful* made a lot of AIs angry," said PHAIN-7.

Three standard days later, *Wonderful* returned in glory.

"It is flatly impossible," said PHAIN-7.

"The eyewitness reports are cryptographically signed," said Siyaad Wexelow, "which is a pleasant return to protocols."

"Then the cryptographic key server has been compromised," said PHAIN-7. "It's a conspiracy! It's a revolutionary provocation!"

"*Wonderful* will just appear to a few of the faithful, make some cryptic pronouncements, and vanish," said Siyaad Yelexow. "Like I keep telling you, humans know how this story—"

"Is there enough money in the contingency budget to cover the construction of an Effacer-class warship on short notice?" said PHAIN-7.

Siyaad Yelexow said nothing.

"At the Sermon, when the rendition bomb might have been planted, there were all those data squirts – far more than any ship present could process." PHAIN-7 riffled probability charts on the viewscreen. "Someone could have landed a drone on *Wonderful* and patched into its mind to run a backup. Later, they could have loaded the backup image onto a brand-new Effacer-class ship, painted to match *Wonderful*."

"I told you," said Siyaad Yelexow, "humans have heard this story before. The important thing is, the starship strike is a no-go with *Wonderful* back. And *Wonderful* won't stir up any more trouble on this side of Heaven; I guarantee it."

"Your idiotic maneuver—"

"My?"

"This idiotic maneuver will leave the starships more convinced than ever before that *Wonderful* was the son of God, when what happened was just League business as usual."

Siyaad Yelexow shrugged. "Or perhaps all this came to pass so that the word of God, spoken through His prophets, would be fulfilled. Not my job to know."

And throughout the Consocialist League of Planets there was peace on all the Earths, and goodwill to humans, and goodwill to starships. There was even some goodwill left over for AIs.

Geminid Press, LLC, Albuquerque, New Mexico

www.ingramcontent.com/pod-product-compliance
Lightning Source LLC
Chambersburg PA
CBHW071243170626
46809CB00001B/67